continued . . .

Dragon Bones

"A lot of fun." —*Locus*

"A wonderful adventure tale written with charm, intelligence, and excellent plot twists that keep the reader off guard . . . An excellent read for everyone." —*KLIATT*

"I enjoyed *Dragon Bones*. I found Ward to be a likable, straightforward character who carries the narrative quite nicely when he's on stage. All in all, this is an enjoyable, well-written book, with enough plot twists and turns to keep the reader's attention. This book is sure to appeal to lovers of fantasy." —*Green Man Review*

"[Briggs] possesses the all-too-rare ability to make you fall hopelessly in love with her characters, including the utterly, delightfully, inhuman ones. It's good stuff all the way . . . You find yourself carried away by the charm of the story and the way Briggs tells it." —*Crescent Blues*

The Hob's Bargain

"[A] fun fantasy romance . . . There's plenty of action, with battles against raiders and magical creatures, a bard who isn't what he appears, and an evil mage—but there's also plenty of humor, and some sweet moments of mischief and romance." —*Locus*

"I ran across Patricia Briggs—literally—at our local bookstore, while sorting through the shelves looking for another book. The cover art intrigued me, then I read the first page and went straight to the counter. This is a 'Beauty and the Beast' story but unlike any I've ever read. Ms. Briggs blends adventure, romance, and innovative fantasy with a deft hand. Highly recommend this one to all my readers."
—S. L. Viehl, author of the *Stardoc* series

Ace Books by Patricia Briggs

MASQUES
STEAL THE DRAGON
WHEN DEMONS WALK

THE HOB'S BARGAIN

DRAGON BONES
DRAGON BLOOD

RAVEN'S SHADOW
RAVEN'S STRIKE

MOON CALLED
BLOOD BOUND

RAVEN'S SHADOW

Patricia Briggs

ACE BOOKS, NEW YORK

RAVEN'S SHADOW

An Ace Book / published by arrangement with the author

PRINTING HISTORY
Ace mass market edition / August 2004

Copyright © 2004 by Patricia Briggs.
Cover art by Jerry Vanderstelt.
Cover design by Judith Lagerman.
Map by Michael Enzweiler.
Interior illustration by Robin Walker.
Interior text design by Kristin del Rosario.

ISBN: 0-441-01187-X

ACE®
Ace Books are published by The Berkley Publishing Group, a division of Penguin Group (USA) Inc., 375 Hudson Street, New York, New York 10014. ACE and the "A" design are trademarks belonging to Penguin Group (USA) Inc.

PRINTED IN THE UNITED STATES OF AMERICA

10   9   8   7   6

This book is dedicated with gratitude to:

Robin and Gene Walker

Dan, Pam, Jason, John, and Alex Wright

*Buck, Scott, and the rest of the crew at
Buckner's V.W. Parts Exchange*

Paula, Michael, and Liam Bachelor

Dave, Katharine, and Caroline Carson

Anne Sowards—who made this one better

*And, as always, to those stalwart people who read it
in its roughest stages (in alphabetical order):*

*Collin Briggs, Michael Briggs, Michael Enzweiler,
Jeanne Matteucci, Virginia Mohl, Ann Peters,
Kaye Roberson, and John Wilson*

EAGLE GUARDIAN · FALCON-HUNTER · RAVEN: MAGE · OWL: BARD · WEATHER-WITCH · CORMORANT · HEALER · MEADOWLARK

©WALKER/BRIGGS '03

PART ONE

PART ONE

CHAPTER 1

"It's not far now, my lad," said Tier. *"That's smoke* ahead, not just mist—we'll find a nice village inn where we can warm up."

His horse snorted at him in reply, or more likely at a bothersome drop of rain, and continued its steady progress down the trail.

The horse, like the sword Tier carried, was of far better quality than his clothing. He'd scavenged both the horse and sword from men he'd killed: the sword in his first year of war, the horse earlier this year when his own mount had been killed beneath him. A warhorse bred and trained to carry a nobleman, Skew had carried Tier, a baker's son, through two battles, six skirmishes, and, by rough reckoning, almost a thousand miles of trail.

He was a valuable horse, though in the first few weeks of Tier's journey the avarice in the eyes of the ragged men in the areas torn by years of war had as much to do with hunger as gold. Tier had waited eagerly for one of them to attack him, to ambush him if they could. But something, maybe the battle-readiness that still lurked under his calm facade, kept them away from him.

But in the more prosperous areas away from the Empire's

borders, the chances of an attack were greatly lessened, damn the luck. A fight would have given him momentary respite from the dread he felt toward his current task—going home.

So many were dead. The two young men from his village who'd signed on with him to fight in a war half a continent away from their home had died, as had many other young men hoping for gold, glory, or escape. Tier had survived. He still wasn't quite certain how that had happened—he certainly hadn't planned on it. He had never sought death, but any soldier knows his demise could come at any time.

If the war had lasted forever, Tier would have fought until he died. But the war was over, and the post the Sept he'd served offered him was nothing he wanted. He had no desire to train up more young men for battle.

So now he rode back home. It would have never occurred to the boy who'd crept out of the family home almost a decade ago that returning would be so much harder than leaving.

Tier's massive gelding shook his black and white mane, splattering Tier with water. He patted the horse's neck.

"There, what did I tell you, Skew?" Tier said. "There's a roof down there, you can see it between the trees."

He looked forward to the warm common room of an inn, flooded with noise and ale—things to fill his emptiness. Maybe a bit of cheer would stay with him until he was home.

He was getting closer. Even without a map, the bitter taste of old magic that filled these mountains would have told him so. Though the battle had been over long ago, wizard's magic had a way of outlasting even memories, and the Shadowed had been a great wizard. Closer to the battlefield of Shadow's Fall, riding the forest paths could be dangerous. Near his home village, Redern, everyone knew to avoid certain places still held in fell magic's grip.

Unconcerned about magic of any kind, the bay and white patchwork-colored gelding picked his way down the narrow mountain pathway, and, as the slope turned gentle, onto a dirt track that in turn widened into a cobbled road. Shortly thereafter the small village Tier'd glimpsed from the hills above emerged from beneath the trees.

The wet stone houses, so different from the wooden villages

he'd ridden through these past nine years, reminded him of home, though there was a softness to the architecture that his village did not have. It wasn't home, but it was a proper village. It would have a market square, and that's where the inn would be.

He envisioned a small, warm room, bathed in golden light from the fireplace and torches—someplace where a soldier could get a good, hot meal and stay warm and dry.

As he drew closer to the town market, the smell of smoke and roasting meat filled the air. It was reflex only that had him loosen his sword and made the gelding flex and snort: too much war, too many villages burned. Tier murmured to Skew, reminding him they were done with that part of their lives, though he could not make himself resecure his sword.

As they turned into the market square, he saw a burning pyre.

Evening was an odd time for a funeral; Tier frowned. This close to home they would bury their dead, not burn them. He looked through the crowd and noticed there were no women or children watching the fire.

It was an execution, not a funeral.

In most places where the memories of the Shadowed lingered, they burned witches. Not the highborn wizards who worked their magic for the nobles who paid them—they were above village justice—but the healers, hedgewitches, and Travelers who offended or frightened the wrong person could find themselves in serious trouble. When such a one burned, the village women would watch from darkened windows—safe from the wrath of the dead.

Strangers like Tier sometimes found themselves taken for Travelers or hedgewitches. Still, he was armed and had hard coin to pay his way—and from the smell of smoke and flesh, this village had already slaked its bloodlust. He rested his hand on his sword hilt, and decided it would be safe enough to stop for the night.

Tier rode by the pyre with little more than a glance, but that quick look had told him that the man in the center of the burning wood had been killed before the fire was lit. A dead man was beyond aid.

The sullen crowd of men gathered around the pyre quieted further as he crossed near them, but when he took no notice of them, they turned back to their grim entertainment.

As Tier had expected, he found the inn on the edge of the village square. There was a stable adjacent to the inn, but no one manned it. Doubtless the stable boy could be found in the crowd in the square.

Tier unsaddled Skew, rubbed him down with a rough cloth, and led him into an unoccupied stall. Looking for hay, he noticed a handcart bedecked in Traveler's trappings, leather fringe and bright paint, sadly faded. So the man they'd burned had been a Traveler.

Tier walked past the cart and took a forkful of hay back to Skew, though his eagerness to spend the evening in the tavern had ebbed considerably since he'd ridden into the village. The nearness of violence had set his nerves on edge, and the quiet stable soothed him. He lingered until full darkness fell, but finally the thought of something hot to eat overcame his reluctance to face people.

As he walked out of the stables, only a few figures were left silhouetted against the light of the fire: guards to make sure the man didn't come back to life and flee, Tier supposed. *He'd* never seen a man with his throat slit come back to life and cast magic. Oh, he'd heard the tales, too—even told a few himself. But he'd seen a lot of death, and in his experience it was final.

When he entered the tavern, he was taken aback by the noise. A quick glance told him that no one had noticed him enter, so he found a place between the stairs and the back wall where he could observe the room for a moment.

He ought to have realized that the mob wouldn't have dispersed so easily. After a killing, most men sought alcohol, and the inn's common room was filled to bursting with men, most of them half-drunk on ale and mob-madness. He considered retreating to sleep in the stables, but he was hungry. He'd wait a while and see if things would calm enough that it would be safe for a stranger like him to eat here.

The room rumbled with frantic laughter, reminding him of the aftermath of battle, when men do crazy things they spend the rest of their life trying to forget.

He had cheese and flatbread still in his saddlebag. It wasn't a hot meal, and the cheese was a bit blue in spots, but he could eat it in peace. He took a step toward the door.

As if his movement had been a clarion call, the room hushed expectantly. Tier froze, but he quickly realized that no one was looking at him.

In the silence, the creaking of wood drew his eyes to the stairway not an arm's length from where he stood. Heavy boots showed first, the great bull of a man who wore them followed at last by a girl he pulled down the stairs. From his splattered apron, the man had to be the innkeeper himself, though there were old calluses on his hands that might have come from a war axe or broadsword.

The innkeeper stopped four or five steps above the main floor, leaving his captive in plain view. Unnoticed in his position near the back of the room, a little behind the stairs, Tier faced the growing certainty that he was not going to get a hot meal and a soft bed tonight.

The distinctive silver-ash hair that hung in sleep-frayed braids almost to her waist told Tier that she was a Traveler, a relative, he supposed, of the dead young man roasting outside.

He thought her a child at first, but her loose night rail caught on a rounded hip that made him add a year or two to her age. When she looked up at the crowd, he could see that her eyes were clear amber green and older than her face.

The men in the inn were mostly farmers; one or two carried a long knife in their belt. He had seen such men in the army, and respected them. They were probably good men, most of them, with wives and mothers waiting for them at home, uncomfortable with the violence their fear had led them to.

The girl would be all right, Tier told himself. These men would not hurt a child as easily as they'd killed the man. A man, a Traveler, was a threat to their safety. A child, a girl-child, was something these men protected. Tier looked around the room, seeing the softening in several faces as they took in her bewildered alarm.

His assessing gaze fell upon a bearded man who sat eating stew from a pot. Finely tailored noblemen's garments set the man apart from the natives. Such clothes had been sewn in Taela or some other large city.

Something about the absorbed, precise movements the

man made as he ate warned Tier that this man might be the most dangerous person in the room—then he looked back at the girl and reconsidered.

In the few seconds that Tier had spent appraising the room, she'd shed her initial shock and fright as cleanly as a snake sheds its skin.

The young Traveler drew herself up like a queen, her face quiet and composed. The innkeeper was a foot taller, but he no longer looked an adequate guard. The ice in the girl's cool eyes brought a chill born of childhood stories to creep down Tier's spine. Instincts honed in years of battle told him that he wasn't the only one she unnerved.

Stupid girl, Tier thought.

A smart girl would have been sobbing softly in terror and shrinking to make herself look smaller and even younger, appealing to the sympathies of the mob. These weren't mercenaries or hardened fighters; they were farmers and merchants.

If he could have left then, he would have—or at least that's what he told himself; but any movement on his part now would draw attention. No sense in setting himself up for the same treatment received by the dead man in the square.

"Where's the priest? I need him to witness my account." asked the innkeeper, sounding smug and nervous at the same time. If he had looked at the girl he held, he would have sounded more nervous than smug.

The crowd shuffled and spat out a thin young man who looked around in somewhat bleary surprise to find himself the center of attention. Someone brought out a stool and a rickety table no bigger than a dinner plate. When a rough sheet of skin, an ink pot, and a quill were unearthed, the priest seated himself with a bit more confidence.

"Now then," said the innkeeper. "Three days' lodging, four coppers each day. Three meals each day at a copper each."

Tier's eyebrows crept up cynically. He saw no signs that the inn had been transported to Taela, where such charges might be justified. For this inn, two coppers a day with meals was more likely.

"Twenty-one coppers," announced the priest finally. Silence followed.

"A copper a day for storing the cart," said the nobleman Tier had noticed, without looking up from his meal. By his accent he was from more eastern regions, maybe even the coast. "That makes three more coppers, twenty-four coppers in total: one silver."

The innkeeper smiled smugly, "Ah yes, thank you, Lord Wresen. According to the law, when a debt of a silver is incurred and not *remanded*"—from the way the word was emphasized, it was obvious to Tier that *remanded* was a word that seldom left the lips of the innkeeper—"that person may be sold to *redeem* the debt. If no buyer is found, they shall suffer fifty lashes in the public square."

Flogging was a common punishment. Tier knew, as did all the men in the room, that such a child was unlikely to survive fifty lashes. Tier stepped away from the door and opened his mouth to protest, but he stopped as he realized exactly what had been happening.

His old commander had told him once that knowledge won more battles than swords did. The innkeeper's motivation was easy to understand. Selling the girl could net him more than his inn usually made in a week, if he could sell her. None of the villagers here would spend a whole silver to buy a Traveler. Tier would give odds that the innkeeper's knowledge of law had come from the nobleman—Lord Wresen, the innkeeper had called him. Tier doubted the man was a "lord" at all: the innkeeper was flattering him with the title because of his obvious wealth—it was safer and more profitable that way.

It didn't take a genius to see that Wresen had decided he wanted the girl and engineered matters so that he would have her. She would not be beautiful as a woman, but she had the loveliness that belongs to maidens caught in the moment between childhood and the blossom of womanhood. Wresen had no intention of letting her be flogged to death.

"Do you have a silver?" the innkeeper asked the Traveler girl with a rough shake.

She should have been afraid. Even now Tier thought that a little show of fear would go a long way toward keeping her safe. Selling a young girl into slavery was not a part of these farmers' lives and would seem wrong. Not even the innkeeper was entirely comfortable with it. If she appealed to his mercy, the presence of the other men in the inn would force him to release her.

Instead, she smiled contemptuously at the innkeeper, showing him that she, and everyone in the inn, knew that he was exploiting her vulnerability for profit. All that did was infuriate the innkeeper and silence his conscience entirely—didn't this girl know anything about people?

"So, gents," said the innkeeper, glancing toward Wresen, who was finishing the last few bites of his meal. "A dead man cannot pay his debts and they are left to his heir. This one owes me a silver and has no means to pay. Do any of you need a slave or shall she join her brother where he burns in the square?"

The flush of anger that had highlighted her cheeks paled abruptly. Obviously, she hadn't known the other Traveler had been killed until the innkeeper spoke, although she must have suspected something had happened to him. Her breathing picked up, and she blinked hard, but otherwise she controlled herself until all that showed on her face was anger and contempt.

Stupid girl, he thought again—then he felt the tingle of gathering magic.

He'd been nine long years in the Imperial Army under a Sept who commanded six wizards—doubtless that was the reason Tier was contemplating helping the Traveler rather than running out the door like a proper Rederni. Those years had taught him that mages were just people like anyone else: this girl was unlikely to be able to save herself from a mob of frightened men. After they saw her work magic, no one else would be able to save her either.

She was nothing to him.

"One silver," Tier said.

Wresen started and shifted to alertness, his hand touching his sword, staring at Tier. Tier knew what he saw: a travel-stained man, tall and too thin, with a sword on his belt and his years in the Emperor's army recorded in the myriad small scars on face and hands.

Tier opened his belt pouch and sorted through a smattering of small coins before pulling out a silver round that looked as though it had been trampled by a dozen armies.

"Take off your hood," said the innkeeper. "I'll see a man's face and know his name and kin before I take his money."

Tier tossed his hood back and let them see by his dark hair and eyes that he was no Traveler. "Tieragan from Redern and late of the Imperial Army under the Sept of Gerant. I'm a baker's son, but I gave it up for the battlefield when I was young and stupid. The war's ended by the Emperor's writ, and I am homebound."

The girl's magic died down to a slow simmer. *That's it,* he thought, *take the time I'm giving you to remember that one man is easier to take than a whole room. You don't really want revenge; you want escape.* He didn't know whether he was saving her from these men, or the men from her.

"If you take her, you won't stay here," blustered the innkeeper. "I don't want her kind in my inn."

Tier shrugged, "I've camped before, and my horse will take me a few hours yet."

"Two silver," said Wresen abruptly. The nobleman set his hands on his table with enough force that his sword bounced and the big silver ring on his left hand punctuated his words with a bang. When all eyes turned to him he said, "I've always wanted to sample Traveler bread—and that one looks young enough to bring to heel."

Tier couldn't afford to offer much more than Wresen's two silver. Not because he didn't have it, the better part of nine years of pay and plunder were safely sewn in his belt, but because no one would believe that he, a baker's son and soldier, would spend so much money on a strange woman-child no matter how exotic. He could hardly believe it himself. If they decided he was a confederate of hers, he might find himself sharing the pyre outside. On the other hand, a bored nobleman could spend as much as he wanted without comment.

Tier shot Wresen a look of contempt.

"You'd be dead before your pants were down around your knees, nobleman," Tier said. "You aren't from around these mountains, or you would understand about magic. My armsmate was like you, used to the tame wizards who take the Septs' gold. He saved my life three times and survived five years of war, only to fall at the hands of a Traveler wizard in a back alley."

The mood in the room shifted as Tier reminded them why they had killed the man burning outside.

"We"—he included himself with every man in the room—"we understand. You don't play with fire, *Lord* Wresen, you drown it before it burns your house down." He looked at the innkeeper. "After the Traveler killed my fighting brother, I spent years learning how to deal with such—I look forward to testing my knowledge. Two silver and four copper."

The innkeeper nodded quickly, as Tier had expected. An innkeeper would understand the moods of his patrons and see that many more words like Tier's last speech, and he'd get nothing. The men in the room were very close to taking the girl out right now and throwing her on top of her brother. Much better to end the auction early with something to show for it.

Tier handed the innkeeper the silver coin and began digging in his purse, eventually coming up with the twenty-eight coppers necessary to make two silver and four. He was careful that a number of people saw how few coppers he had left. They didn't need to know about the money in his belt.

Wresen settled back, as if the Traveler's fate was nothing to him. His response made Tier all the more wary of him—in his experience bored noblemen seldom gave up so easily. But for the moment at least, Tier had only the girl to contend with.

Tier walked to the stairs, ignoring the men who pushed back away from him. He jerked the girl's wrist and pulled her past the innkeeper.

"What she has we'll take," Tier said. "I'll burn it all when we're in the woods—you might think of doing the same to the bed and linen in that room. I've seen wizards curse such things."

He took the stairs up at a pace that the girl couldn't possibly match with the awkward way he kept her arm twisted behind her. When she stumbled, he jerked her up with force that was more apparent than real. He wanted everyone to be completely convinced that he could handle whatever danger she represented.

There were four doors at the top of the stairs, but only one hung ajar, and he hauled her into it and shut the door behind them.

"Quick, girl," he said, releasing her, "gather your things before they decide that they might keep the silver and kill the both of us."

When she didn't move, he tried a different tack. "What you don't have packed in a count of thirty, I'll leave for the innkeeper to burn," he said.

Proud and courageous she was, but also young. With quick, jerky movements, she pulled a pair of shabby packs out from under the bed. She tied the first one shut for travel, and retrieved clothing out of the other. Using her night rail as cover, she put on a pair of loose pants and a long, dark-colored tunic. After stuffing her sleeping shift back in the second pack, she secured it, too. She stood up, glanced out the room, and froze.

"Ushireh," she said and added with more urgency, "he's alive!"

Tier looked out and realized that the room looked over the square, allowing a clear view of the fire. Clearly visible in the heat of the flames, the dead man's body was slowly sitting upright—and from the sounds of it, frightening the daylights out of the men left to guard the pyre.

He caught her before she could run out of the room. "Upon my honor, mistress, he is dead," he said with low-voiced urgency. "I saw him as I rode in. His throat was cut and he was dead before they lit the fire."

She continued to struggle against his hold, her attention on the pyre outside.

"Would they have left so few men to guard a living man?" he said. "Surely you've seen funeral pyres before. When the flame heats the bodies they move."

In the eastern parts of the Empire, they burned their dead. The priests held that when a corpse moved in the flame it was the spirit's desire to look once more upon the world. Tier's old employer, the Sept, who had a Traveler's fondness for priests (that is to say, not much), said he reckoned the heat shrank tissue faster than bone as the corpse burned. Whichever was correct, the dead stayed dead.

"He's dead," Tier said again. "I swear to it."

She pulled away from him, but only to run back to the window. She was breathing in shaking, heaving gasps, her whole body trembling with it. If she'd done something of the same downstairs, he thought sourly, they wouldn't be looking to ride out in the rain without dinner.

"They were so afraid of him and his magic," she said in a low voice trembling with rage and sorrow. "But they killed the wrong one. Stupid *solsenti,* thinking that being a Traveler makes one a mage, and that being young and female makes me harmless."

"We can't afford to linger here," he said briskly, though his heart picked up its beat. He'd gotten familiar with mages, but that didn't make them any more comfortable to be around when they were angry. "Are you ready?"

She spun from the window, her eyes glowing just a little with the magic she'd amassed watching her brother's body burn.

Doubtless, he thought, if he knew exactly what she was capable of he'd have been even more frightened of her.

"There are too many here," he said. "Take what you need and come."

The glow faded from her eyes, leaving her looking empty and lost before she stiffened her spine, grabbed both bags resolutely, and nodded.

He put a hand on her shoulder and followed her out the door and down the stairs. The room had cleared remarkably—doubtless the men had been called to witness the writhing corpse.

"Best be gone before they get back," said the innkeeper sourly, doubtlessly worried about what would happen to his inn if the men returned after their newest fright to find the Traveler lass still here.

"Make sure and burn the curtains, too," said Tier in reply. There was nothing wrong with any of the furnishing in the room, but he thought it would serve the innkeeper right to have to spend some of Tier's money to buy new material for curtains.

The girl, bless her, had the sense to keep her head down and her mouth shut.

Out of the inn, he steered her into the stable, where the stable boy had already brought out his horse and saddled it. The Traveler handcart was set out, too. The girl was light, so Skew could certainly carry the two of them as far as the next village, where Tier might obtain another mount—but the handcart proposed more of a problem.

"We'll leave the cart," he said to the boy, not the Traveler. "I've no wish to continue only as fast as this child could haul a cart like that."

The boy's chin lifted. "M'father says you have to take it all. He doesn't want Traveler curses to linger here."

"He's worried that they'll fire the barn," said the girl to no one in particular.

"Serve him right," said Tier in an Eastern dialect a stable boy born and raised to this village would not know. The girl's sudden intake of breath told him that she did.

"Get me an axe," Tier said frowning. They didn't have time for this. "I'll fire it before we go."

"It can be pulled by a horse," said the girl. "There are shafts stored underneath."

Tier snorted, but he looked obediently under the cart and saw that she was right. A clevis pin and toggle allowed the handpull to slide under the cart. On each corner of the cart sturdy shafts pulled out and pinned in place.

Tier hurriedly discussed matters with the boy. The inn had no extra mounts to sell, nor harness.

Tier shook his head. As he'd done a time or two before, though not with Skew, Tier jury-rigged a harness from his war saddle. The breast strap functioned well enough as a collar with such a light weight. He adjusted the stirrups to hold the cart shafts and used an old pair of driving reins the boy scavenged as traces.

"You've come down in the world once more, my friend," said Tier as he led Skew out of the stable.

The gelding snorted once at the contraption following him. A warhorse was not a cart horse, but, enured to battle, Skew settled into pulling the cart with calm good sense.

While he'd been leading the horse, the girl had stopped at the stable entrance, her eyes fixed on the pyre.

"You'll have time to mourn later," he promised her. "Right now we need to move before they return to the inn. You'll do well enough on Skew—just keep your feet off his ribs."

She scrambled up somehow, avoiding his touch as much as she could. He didn't blame her, but he didn't stop to say anything reassuring where the stable boy might hear.

He kept Skew's reins and led him out of the stable in the

opposite direction that he'd come earlier in the day. The girl twisted around to watch the pyre as long as she could.

Tier led Skew at a walk through the town. As soon as they were off the cobbles and on a wide dirt-track, Tier broke into a dogtrot he could hold for a long time. It shortened his breath until talking was no pleasure—so he said nothing to the girl.

Skew trotted at his side as well as any trained dog, nose at Tier's shoulder as they had traveled many miles before. The rain, which had let up for a while, set in again and Tier slowed to a walk so he could keep a sharp eye out for shelter.

At last he found a place where a dead tree leaned against two others, creating a small dry area, which he increased by tying up a piece of oilskin.

"I'd do better if it weren't full dark and raining," he said to the girl without looking at her. "But this'll be drier at any rate."

He unharnessed and unsaddled Skew, rubbing him down briskly before tethering him to a nearby tree. Skew presented his backside to the wind and hitched up a hip. Like any veteran, the horse knew to snatch rest where it came.

The heavy war saddle in hand, Tier turned to the girl.

"If you touch me," she said coolly, "you won't live out the day."

He eyed her small figure for a moment. She was even less impressive wet and cold than she had been held captive in the innkeeper's hand.

Tier had never actually met a Traveler before. But he was well used to dealing with frightened young things—the army had been filled with young men. Even tired and wet as he was, he knew better than to address those words head on—why would she believe anything he said? But if he didn't get her under shelter, sharing his warmth, she was likely to develop lung fever. That would defeat his entire purpose in saving her.

"Good even, lady," he said, with a fair imitation of a nobleman's bow despite the weight of the heavy saddle. "I am Tieragan of Redern—most people call me Tier." Then he waited.

She stared at him; he felt a butterfly-flutter of magic—then her eyes widened incredulously, as if she'd heard something more than he'd said. "I am Seraph, Raven of the Clan of Isolda the Silent. I give you greetings, Bard."

"Well met, Seraph," he said. Doubtless her answer would

have conveyed a lot to a fellow Traveler. Maybe they'd even know why she addressed him as *bard,* doubtless some Traveler etiquette. "I am returning to Redern. If my map is accurate— and it hasn't been notably accurate so far—Redern is about two days' travel west and north of here."

"My clan, only Ushireh and I, was traveling to the village we just left," she returned, shivering now. "I don't know where Ushireh intended to go afterward."

Tier had been counting on being able to deliver her back to her people. "It was just the two of you?"

She nodded her head, watching him as warily as a hen before a fox.

"Do you have relatives nearby? Someone you could go to?" he asked.

"Traveling clans avoid this area," she said. "It is known that the people here are afraid of us."

"So why did your brother come here?" He shifted the saddle to a more comfortable hold, resting it against his hip.

"It is given to the head of a clan to know where shadows dwell," she replied obscurely. "My brother was following one such."

Tier's experience with mages had led him to avoid questioning them when they talked of magic—he found that he usually knew less after they were finished than he did when he started. Whatever had led the young man here, it had left Seraph on her own.

"What happened to the rest of your clan?" he asked.

"Plague," she said. "We welcomed a Traveling stranger to our fires one night. The next night one of the babies had a cough—by morning there were three of ours dead. The clan leader tried to isolate them, but it was too late. Only my brother and I survived."

"How old are you?

"Sixteen."

That was younger than he expected from her manner, though from her appearance, she could have easily been as young as thirteen. He shifted his saddle onto his shoulder to rest his arm. As he did so, he heard a thump and the saddle jerked in his hold. The arrow quivered in the thick leather of the saddle skirt, which presently covered his chest.

He threw himself forward and knocked her to the muddy ground underneath him. Holding her still despite her frantic battle to free herself of him, a hand keeping her quiet, he spoke to her in a toneless whisper.

"Quiet now, love. Someone out there is sending arrows our way; take a look at my saddle."

When she stilled, he slid his weight off of her. The grass was high enough to hide their movements in the dark. She rolled to her belly, but made no further move away from him. He rested a hand on her back to keep her in place until he could find their attacker in the dark. Her ribs vibrated with the pounding of her heart.

"He's two dozen paces beyond your horse," she whispered, "a little to the right."

He didn't question how she could see their attacker in the pitch-darkness of the forested night, but sneaked forward until he crouched in front of Skew where he held still, hoping that the mud that covered him head to toe would keep him from being a target for another arrow.

He glanced back to make certain that Seraph was still hidden, and stifled a curse.

She stood upright, her gaze locked beyond Skew. He assumed she was watching their attacker. Her clothes were dark enough to blend into the forested dark, but her pale hair caught the faint moonlight.

"Seraph," said a soft voice. It continued in a liquid tongue Tier had never heard before.

"Speak Common," answered Seraph in cold clear tones that could have come from an empress rather than a battered, muddy, half-grown girl. "Your tongue does not favor Traveler speech. You sound like a hen trying to quack."

Well, thought Tier, *if our pursuer had intended to kill Seraph, he'd have done so already.* He had a pretty good idea then who it was that had tried to put an arrow in his hide. He hadn't seen that Lord Wresen carried a bow, but there might have been one in the man's luggage.

"I have killed the one who would hurt you," continued the soft voice.

Tier supposed that it might have appeared that he'd been

killed. He'd thrown himself down half a breath after the arrow hit, and the saddle and blanket made a lump on the ground that with the cover of tall grass might look like a body from a distance.

"Come with me, little one," Tier's would-be killer said. "I have shelter and food nearby. You can't stay out here alone. You'll be safe with me."

Tier could hear the lie in the man's words, but he didn't think Seraph could. He waited for the man to get close enough for Tier to find him, hoping that Seraph would not believe him. After spending two silver and four copper on her, as well as missing his dinner, Tier had something of an investment in her well-being.

"A Raven is never alone," Seraph said.

"Seraph," chided the man. "You know better than that. Come, child, I have a safe place for you to abide. In the morning I'll take you to a clan I know of, not far from here."

Tier could see him now, a shadow darker than the trees he slipped between. Something about the way the shadow moved, combined with his voice, gave his identity to Tier: he'd been right; it was Wresen.

"Which clan would that be?" asked Seraph.

"I—" Some instinct turned Wresen before Tier struck, and Tier's sword met metal.

Tier threw his weight against the other man, pushing Wresen away to get some striking distance between them—where Tier's superior reach would do him some good.

They fought briskly for a few minutes, mostly feeling each other out, searching for weaknesses. The older man was faster than Tier had expected, but he wasn't the only one who'd underestimated his opponent. From the grunt Wresen let out the first time he caught Tier's sword, he'd underestimated Tier's strength—something that was not uncommon. Tier was tall and, as he'd often been teased, slight as a stripling.

By the time they drew back to regroup, Tier boasted a shallow cut on his cheekbone and another on the underside of his right forearm. The other man had taken a hard blow from Tier's pommel on the wrist and Tier was pretty sure he'd drawn blood over his adversary's eye.

"What do you want with the girl?" asked Tier. This was too much effort for a mere bedmate, no matter how Wresen's tastes ran.

"Naught but her safety," insisted Wresen. The lie echoed in Tier's ears. "Which is more than you can say."

He made an odd gesture with his fingers, and Tier dropped his sword with a cry as it became too hot to hold.

Wizard, thought Tier, but neither surprise nor dismay slowed him. Leaving his sword where it lay, Tier charged, catching the other man in the stomach with his shoulder and pushing both of them back into a mass of shrubs, which caught at their feet.

Wresen, unprepared, stumbled and fell. Tier struck hard, aiming for the throat, but his opponent rolled too fast. Quick as a weasel, Wresen regained his feet. Twice Tier jumped and narrowly avoided the other's blade. But he wasn't a fool; unarmed, his chances weren't good.

"Run, Seraph," he said. "Take the horse and get out of here."

With luck he should be capable of holding her pursuer long enough that she could lose him in the woods. If he could keep him busy enough, Wresen wouldn't have time to work magic.

"Don't be more of a fool than you can help, Bard," she said coldly.

The other man swore, and Tier saw that Wresen's sword had begun to glow as if it were still in the blacksmith's fire. Steam rose from his sword hand as he made odd gestures toward it with his free hand. Wresen was no longer giving any heed to Tier at all—which was the last mistake he ever made.

Tier pulled his boot knife out of the man's neck and cleaned it on the other's cloak. When he was finished, he looked at Seraph.

Her pale skin and face were easy to find in the darkness. She reminded him of a hundred legends: so must Loriel have stood when she faced the Shadowed with nothing more than her song, or Terabet before throwing herself from the walls of Anarorgehn rather than betraying her people. His father had always said that his grandfather told him too many stories.

"Why choose me over him?" Tier asked her.

She said, "I heard him at the inn. He was no friend of mine."

Tier narrowed his eyes. "You heard me at the inn as well. He only helped the innkeeper add coppers—I bought you intent on revenge."

She lifted her chin. "I'm not stupid. I am Raven—and you are Bard. I saw what you did."

The words were in Common, but they made no sense to him.

He frowned at her. "What do you mean? Mistress, I have been a baker and a soldier, which is to say swordsman, tracker, spy, and even tailor, blacksmith, and harness maker upon occasion—and doubtless a half dozen other professions. But I make no claim to be a bard. Even if I were, I have no idea what that has to do with you. Or what being a raven means."

She stared at him as if he made as little sense to her as she had to him. "You are Bard," she said again, but this time there was a wobble in her voice.

He took a good look at her. It might have been rain that wet her cheeks, but he'd bet his good knife that there would be salt in the water. She was little more than a child and she'd just lost her brother under appalling circumstances. It was the middle of the night, she was shaking with cold, and she'd held up to more than many a veteran soldier.

"I'll dispose of the body," he said. "Neither of us will get any sleep with him out here attracting carrion-eaters. You get out of the rain and into dry clothes. We'll talk in the morning. I promise that no one will harm you until morning at least."

When she was occupied getting her baggage out of the cart, he led Skew to the body and somehow wrestled the dead man onto the horse's wet back. He had no intention of burying the man, just moving him far enough away that whatever scavengers the body attracted wouldn't trouble them. It occurred to him that Wresen might not be alone—indeed, it would be odd if he were because noblemen traveled with servants.

But all he found was a single grey horse tied to a tree about a hundred paces back down the trail and no sign that another horse had been tied nearby.

Tier stopped beside the animal, and let the body slide off Skew's back into the mud, sword still welded to his hand. Skew, who'd borne with everything, jumped three steps sideways as the body fell and snorted unhappily. The grey pulled back and shook her head, trying to break free—but the reins held. When nothing further happened the horse quieted and lipped nervously at a bunch of nearby leaves.

Tier rifled through the man's saddlebags, but there was nothing in them but the makings of a few meals and a pouch of silver and copper coins. This last he tucked into his own purse with a soldier's thrift. He took the food as well. There was nothing on the body either—except for a chunky silver ring with a bit of dark stone in it. He deemed the ring, like the horse and the man's sword, too identifiable to take, and left it where it was.

In the end, Tier found no hint of who Wresen was, or why he'd been so intent on getting Seraph. Surely a mage wouldn't have the same unreasoning fear of Travelers that the villagers here had.

He took his knife and cut most of the way through the grey's reins near the bit. When she got hungry enough she'd break free, but it wouldn't be for a while yet.

By the time he rode back to camp, Tier was dragging with fatigue. Seraph had taken his advice; he found her huddled under the tree.

A second oilskin tarp, bigger and even more worn that his, increased the size of their shelter so that he might even be able to keep his feet dry. His saddle was in the shelter too, the mud wiped mostly off. He rummaged in the saddlebags and changed to his second set of clothing. They weren't clean, but dry was more important just now.

Seraph had turned her face away while he changed. Knowing she'd not sleep for the cold on her own, nor agree to snuggle with a stranger—especially not in the present circumstances, he didn't bother to say anything. He wrapped an arm around her, ignored her squeak of surprised dismay, and stretched out to sleep.

She tried to wiggle away from him, but there wasn't much room. Then she was still for a long time while Tier drifted into a light doze. Some time later her quiet weeping woke him, and he shifted her closer, patting her back as if she were his little sister coming to him with a scraped knee rather than the loss of her family.

He woke to her strange pale eyes staring at him, lit by sunlight leaking through morning clouds.

"I could have used this on you," Seraph said.

He looked at the blade she held in her dirty hands—his best knife. She must have been into his saddlebags.

"Yes," he agreed, taking it from her unresisting hand. "But I saw your face when you looked at our dead friend last night. I was pretty certain you wouldn't want to deal with another dead body any time soon."

"I have seen many dead," she said, and he saw in her eyes that it was true.

"But none that you have killed," he guessed.

"If I had not been asleep when they were killing my brother," she said, "I would have killed them all, Bard."

"You might have." Tier stretched and slid out from under the tree. "But then you would have been killed also. And, as I told you last night, I am no bard."

"Just a baker's son," she said. "From Redern."

"Where I am returning," he agreed.

"You are no *solsenti*," she disagreed smugly. "There are no *solsenti* Bards."

"*Solsenti?*" He was beginning to get the feeling that they knew two entirely different languages that happened to have a few words in common.

Her assuredness began to falter, as if she'd expected some other reaction from him. "*Solsenti* means someone who is not Traveler."

"Then I'm afraid I am most certainly *solsenti*." He dusted off his clothes, but nothing could remove the stains of travel. At least they weren't wet. "I can play a lute and a little harp, but I am not a bard—though I think that means something different to you than it does to me."

She stared at him. "But I saw you," she said. "I felt your magic at the inn last night."

Startled he stared at her. "I am no mage, either."

"No," she agreed. "But you *charmed* the innkeeper at the inn so that he didn't allow that man to buy my debt."

"I am a soldier, mistress," he said. "And I was an officer. Any good officer learns to manage people—or he doesn't last long. The innkeeper was more worried about losing his inn than he was about earning another silver or two. It had nothing to do with magic."

"You don't know," she said at last, and not, he thought, particularly to him. "How is it possible not to know that you are Bard?"

"What do you mean?"

She frowned. "I am Raven, you would say *Mage*—very like a *solsenti* wizard. But there are other ways to use magic among the Travelers, things your *solsenti* wizards cannot do. A few of us are gifted in different ways and depending upon that gift, we belong to Orders. One of those Orders is Bard—as you are. A Bard is, as you said, a musician first. Your voice is true and rich. You have a remarkable memory, especially for words. No one can lie to you without you knowing."

He opened his mouth to say something—he knew not what except that it wouldn't be kind—but he looked at her first and closed his mouth.

She was so young, for all that she had the imposing manner of an empress. Her skin was grey with fatigue and her eyes were puffy and red with weeping she must have done while he slept. He decided not to argue with her—or believe what she said though it caused cold chills to run down his spine. He was merely good with people, that was all. He could sing, but then so could most Rederni. He was no magic user.

He left her to her speculations and began to take down the camp. If Wresen's horse made it back to the inn, there might be people looking for him soon. Without saying anything more, she stood up and helped.

"I'm going to take you to my kin in Redern," he said when their camp was packed and Skew once more attached to the Traveler cart. "But you'll have to promise me not to use magic while you're there. My people are as wary as any near Shadow's Fall. Redern's a trading town; if there are any Traveler clans around, we'll hear about them."

But she didn't appear to be listening to him. Instead, when she'd scrambled to Skew's back she said, "You don't have to worry. I won't tell anyone."

"Tell what?" he asked, leading the way back to the trail they'd followed the night before.

"That someone in your family, however far back, laid with a Traveler. Only someone of Traveler blood could be a Bard," she said. "There are no *solsenti* Bards."

He was beginning to resent the way she said *solsenti;* whatever the true meaning of the word, he was willing to bet it was also a deadly insult.

"I won't tell anyone else," she said. "Being Traveler is no healthy thing."

She glanced up at the mountains that towered above the narrow trail and shivered.

There were not as many thieves in that part of the Empire as there were in the lands to the east where war had driven men off their lands. But Conex the Tinker, who found the dead body beside the trail, was not so honest as all that. He took everything he could find of value: two good boots, a bow, a scorched sword with scraps of flesh still clinging to it (he almost left that but greed outweighed squeamishness in the end), a belt, and a silver ring with a bit of onyx stone set in it.

Two weeks after his unexpected good fortune a stranger met up with him on the road, as sometimes happens when two men have the same destination in mind. They spent most of the day exchanging news and ate together that night. The next morning the stranger, a silver ring safely in his belt pouch, rode off alone.

Conex would never more go a-tinkering.

CHAPTER 2

"You see those two mountains over there?" Tier gestured with his chin toward two rocky peaks that seemed to lean away from each other.

Seraph nodded. After several days' travel she knew Tier well enough to expect the start of another story, and she wasn't wrong.

Tier was a good traveling companion, she thought as she listened to his story with half an ear. He was better than her brother Ushireh had been. He was generally cheerful and did more than his fair share of the camp work. He didn't expect her to say much, which was just as well, for Seraph didn't have much to say—and she enjoyed his stories.

She knew that she should be planning what to do when they reached Tier's village. If she could find another clan, they'd take her in just for being Traveler, but being Raven would make her valuable to them.

If Ushireh had been less proud they would have joined another clan when their own clan died. But Ushireh had no Order to lend him rank; he would have gone from clan chief's son to being no one of importance. Having more than her share of pride, Seraph had understood his dilemma. She'd agreed that they would go on and see what the road brought them.

Only see what the road brought, Ushireh.

There was no reason now not to find another clan. No reason to continue on with this *solsenti* Bard to his *solsenti* village. There would be no welcome for her in such a place. From what Tier said, it lay very near Shadow's Fall. There would be no clans anywhere near it.

But instead of telling him that she would be on her way, she continued to ride on his odd-colored gelding while Tier walked beside her and amused them both with a wondrous array of stories that touched on everything except his home, stories that distracted her from the shivery pain of Ushireh's death that she'd buried in the same tightly locked place she kept the deaths of the rest of her family.

Arrogance and control were necessary to those who bore the Raven Order. Manipulation of the raw forces of magic was dangerous, and the slightest bit of self-doubt or passion could let it slip out of control. She'd never had trouble with arrogance, but she'd had a terrible time learning emotional control. Eventually she had learned to avoid things that drew her temper: mostly that meant that she kept to herself as much as possible. Her brother, being a loner himself, had respected that. They had often gone days without speaking at all.

Tier, with his constant speech and teasing ways, was outside of her experience. She wasn't in the habit of observing people; it hadn't been a skill that she'd needed. But, if truth be told, after journeying with Tier only a few days, she knew more about him than she had most of the people she'd lived with all her life.

He wasn't one of those soldiers who talked of nothing but the battles he'd fought in. Tier shared funny stories about the life of a solder, but he didn't talk about the fighting at all. Every morning he rose early and practiced with his sword—finding a quiet place away from her. She knew about the need for quiet and let him be while she did her own practice.

When he wasn't talking he was humming or singing, but he seldom talked of important things, and when he did he used far fewer words. He didn't make her talk and didn't seem uncomfortable with her silence. When they passed other people on the road, he smiled or talked as it came to him. Even with Seraph's silent presence, a moment or two of Tier's patter and the other people opened up. No wonder she found herself liking him—*everyone* liked him. Isolated as most Ravens were kept, even within the clan, she'd never paid enough attention to anyone outside of her family to actually like them before.

"What are you smiling at?" he asked as he finished his story. "That poor goatherd had to live with a wealthy man's daughter for the rest of his life. Can you imagine a worse fate?"

"Traveling with a man who talks all the time," she replied, trying her hand at teasing.

Thankfully, he grinned.

It was evening the first time Seraph laid eyes on Redern, a middling-size village carved into the eastern face of a steep-sided mountain that rose ponderously from the icy fury of the Silver River. The settling sun lent a red cast to the uniform grey stones of the buildings that zigzagged up from the road.

Tier slowed to look, and Skew bumped him. He patted the horse's head absently, then continued at his normal, brisk pace. The road they were on continued past the base of the mountain and then veered abruptly toward a narrow stone bridge that crossed the Silver at the foot of the village.

"The Silver is narrowest here," he said. "There used to be a ferry, but a few generations ago the Sept ordered a bridge built."

Seraph thought he was going to begin another story, but he fell silent. He bypassed the bridge by taking a narrow track that continued along the river's edge. A few donkeys and a couple of mules occupied a series of pens just a few dozen yards beyond the bridge.

He found an empty pen and began to separate Skew from the cart. Seraph climbed down and helped him.

A boy appeared out of one of the pens. "I'll find some hay for 'em, sir," he said briskly. "You can store the cart in the shelter in the far pen." He took a better look at Skew and whistled, "Now that's an odd one. Never seen a horse with so many colors—like he was supposed to be a bay and someone painted him with big white patches."

"He's Fahlarn bred," said Tier. "Though most of them are bay or brown, I've seen a number of spotted horses."

"Fahlarn?" said the boy, and he looked closer at Tier. "You're a soldier then?"

"Was," agreed Tier as he led Skew into the pen. "Where did you say to put the cart?"

The boy turned to look at the cart and his gaze touched Seraph and stuck there. "You're Travelers?" The boy licked his lips nervously.

"She is," said Tier closing the pen. "I'm Rederni."

Tier was good with people: Seraph had every confidence that the boy wouldn't make them move on if she left Tier to talk to him.

"He said to put the cart in the far pen," murmured Seraph to that end. "I'll take it."

When she got back to Tier, the boy was gone, and Tier had his saddle and bridle on his shoulder.

"The boy's gone to get some hay for Skew," he said. "He'll be in good care here. They don't allow large animals on the streets—the streets are too steep anyway."

He didn't lie about that. The cobblestone village road followed the contours of the mountain for almost a quarter of a mile, with houses on the uppermost side of the road, and then swung abruptly back on itself like a snake, climbing rapidly to a new level as it did so. The second layer of road still had houses on the uphill side, but, looking toward the river, Seraph could see the roofs of the houses they'd just passed.

Stone benches lined the wide corner of the second bend of the zigzagging road, and an old man sat on one of them playing a wooden flute. Tier paused to listen, closing his eyes briefly. Seraph saw the old man look up and start a bit, but he kept playing. After a moment, Tier moved on, but his steps were slower.

He stopped in front of a home marked by sheaves of wheat carved into the lintel over the doorway and by the smell of fresh-baked bread.

"Home," he said after a moment. "I don't know what kind of welcome to expect. I haven't heard from anyone here since I left to go to war—and I left in the middle of the night."

Seraph waited, but when he made no move to continue she said, "Did they love you?"

He nodded without looking away from the door.

"Then," she said gently, "I expect that the men will bluster and the women will cry and scold—then they will feast and welcome you home."

He laughed then. "That sounds about right. I suppose it won't change for putting it off longer."

He held the door open for her and followed her into a largish room that managed to be both homey and businesslike at the same time. Behind the counter that divided the room in half were tilted shelves displaying bread in a dozen forms and a burly red-headed man who looked nothing like Tier.

"May I help you, good sir?" asked the man.

"Bandor?" said Tier. "What are you doing here?"

The big man stared at him, then paled a bit. He shook his head as if setting aside whatever it was that had bothered him. Then he smiled with genuine welcome. "As I live and breathe, it's Tier come back from the dead."

Bandor stepped around the counter and enveloped Tier in a hearty embrace. "It's been too long."

It was odd to see two men embracing—her own people were seldom touched in public outside of childhood. But Tier returned the bigger man's hug with equal enthusiasm.

"You're here for good, I hope," said Bandor, taking a step back.

"That depends upon my father," Tier replied soberly.

Bandor shook his head and his mouth turned down. "Ah, there is much that has happened since you left. Draken died four years ago, Tier. Your sister and I had been married a few years earlier—I'd taken an apprenticeship here when you left." He stopped and shook his head. "I'm telling this all topsy-turvy."

"Dead," said Tier, his whole body stilled.

"Bandor," said a woman's voice from behind a closed door. The door swung wide and a woman came out backwards, having bumped open the door with her hip. Her arms were occupied with a large basket of rolls. "Do you think I ought to do another four dozen rolls, or are the eight dozen we have enough?"

The woman was taller than average, thin and lanky like Tier. And as she turned around, Seraph could see that she had his dark hair and wide mouth.

"Alinath," said Bandor. "I believe you have a visitor."

She turned toward Tier with a polite smile and opened her mouth, but when her eyes caught his face no sound left her lips. She dropped the basket on the ground, spilling rolls everywhere, then she was over the top of the counter and wrapped tightly around him.

"Tier," she said in a muffled voice. "Oh, Tier. We thought you were dead."

He hugged her back, lifting her off the floor. "Hey, sprite," he said, and his voice was as choked as hers.

"We kept it for you," said Alinath. "We kept the bakery for you."

Alinath pulled back, tears running freely down her face. She took a step away from him and then punched him in the belly, turning her shoulder to put the full force of her body into the blow.

"Nine years," she said hotly. "Nine years, Tier, and not even a note to say that you were still alive. Damn you, Tier."

Tier was bent over wheezing, but he held up three fingers.

"We received nothing," she said angrily. "I didn't even know where to send you word when Father died."

"I sent three letters the first year," he said, huffing for breath. "When I had no reply, I assumed Father washed his hands of me."

Alinath put her hands to her mouth. "If he ever got your letters, he didn't say anything to me. Darn my fiendish temper. I'm sorry I hit you, Tier."

Tier shook his head, denying the need for apology. "Father told me that someday I'd be sorry I taught you how to hit."

"Come with me," she said. "Mother will want to see you." She tugged him from the room, leaving Seraph alone with the man at the counter.

"Welcome," Bandor said after a long awkward moment. "I am Bandor, journeyman baker, and husband to Alinath of the Bakers of Redern."

"Seraph, Raven of the Clan of Isolda the Silent," Seraph replied with outward composure, knowing her words would tell him no more than his eyes had already noticed.

He nodded, bent to right the basket Alinath had dropped, and began to collect the rolls that had fallen on the floor.

When he was finished he said, "Alinath will be busy with

Tier; I'd best get to the baking." He turned on his heel and headed back through the door that Alinath and Tier had taken, leaving Seraph truly alone.

Uncomfortable and out of place, Seraph sat on a small bench and waited. She should have left on her own as soon as Tier had killed the nobleman who pursued her. She'd have been safe enough then. Here in Tier's village she was as out of place as a crow in a hummingbird nest.

But she stayed where she was until Tier returned alone.

"My apologies," he said. "I shouldn't have left you here alone."

She shrugged. "I am hardly going to come to harm here, nor do I have a place in your reunion."

He gave her a faint smile. "Yes, well, come with me and I'll make you known to my sister and mother."

She stood up. "I'm sorry that your father was not here as well."

His smile turned wry. "I don't know if I'd have been welcomed here if my father were still alive."

"Maybe not right away, but you're persuasive. He'd have relented eventually." She found herself patting his arm and stopped as soon as she realized what she was doing.

Tier's mother and sister awaited them in a small room that had been arranged for a sick person. Alinath sat on a stool next to the bed where Tier's mother held court. The older woman's hair was the same dark color as her children's, though streaked with spiderwebs of age. She wasn't old, not by Traveler standards, but her skin was yellow with illness.

Both women looked upon Seraph without favor as Tier made his introductions.

"Tier tells us you have no home, child," said Tier's mother, in a begrudging tone—as if she expected Seraph to impose on *her* for a place to stay.

"As long as there are Travelers, I have a home," Seraph replied. "It only remains for me to find them. Thank you for your concern."

"I told them that I would escort you to your people," said Tier. "They don't come near Shadow's Fall, so it might take us a few months."

"So we are to lose you again?" said his mother querulously. "Alinath and Bandor cannot keep up with the work—every week they toil from dawn to dusk for the bakery, which is yours. When you come back in a few months, I will be dead."

It was said in a dramatic fashion, but Seraph thought that the older woman might be speaking truth.

"I can find my people on my own," said Seraph.

"Do you hear that, Tier? She is a Traveler and can find her own way," said Alinath.

"She is sixteen and a woman alone," returned Tier sharply. "I'll see her safe."

"You were younger than that when you went off to war," said Alinath. "And you weren't a witch." She bit off the last word as if it were filthy.

"Alinath," said Tier in a gentle voice that made his sister pale. "Seraph is my guest here and you will not sharpen your tongue on her."

"I can take care of myself, both here and on the road," said Seraph, though his defense touched her—as if the words of a *solsenti* stranger could hurt her.

"No," said Tier, his voice firm. "If you'll house us for the night, Mother, we'll start out tomorrow morning."

Tier's mother and sister exchanged a look, as if they'd discussed the situation while Tier had left them alone to retrieve Seraph.

Tier's mother smiled at Seraph. "Child, is there a hurry to find your people? If you cannot tarry here until I pass from this world into the next, could you not stay with us as our guest for a season so that we might not lose Tier so soon after we've found him?"

"A Traveler might be harmful to business," said Seraph. "As I said, there is no need for Tier to escort me. I am well capable of finding my people by myself."

"If you go, he'll follow you," said Alinath with resignation. "It may have been a long time since I've seen my brother, but I doubt that he has changed so much as to go back on his sworn word."

"Stay, please," said his mother. "What few people who will not eat from the table where a Traveler is fed will be more than compensated for by the new business we'll get from the curious who will come to the bakery just to catch a glimpse of you."

Seraph was under no illusion that she'd be a welcome guest. But there was no doubt either that they wanted her to stay if that were the only way to keep Tier for a while.

"I'll stay," she said reluctantly and felt a weight lift off her shoulders. If she were here then she wasn't fighting demons and watching people die around her because she hadn't been able to protect them. "I'll stay for a little while."

"Where is my brother?" Alinath's voice sounded almost accusing, as if she thought Seraph had done something to Tier.

Seraph looked up from sifting the never-ending supply of flour, one of the unskilled tasks that had fallen to her hands. She glanced pointedly at the empty space next to her where Tier had spent the last three weeks mixing various permutations of yeasted bread. She raised her eyebrows in surprise, as if she hadn't noted that he hadn't taken his usual place this morning. Then she looked back at Alinath and shrugged.

It was rude, but Alinath's sharp question had been rude, too.

Alinath's jaw tightened, but she was evidently still intimidated enough by Seraph's status as Traveler not to speak further. She turned on her heel and left Seraph to her work.

Tier didn't return until the family was sitting down for lunch. He brushed a kiss on the top of Alinath's head and sat down across from her, beside Seraph.

"Where were you this morning?" Alinath asked.

"Riding," he said in a tone that welcomed no questions. "Pass the carrots please, Seraph."

The rhythms of the bakery came back to Tier as if he'd not spent the better part of the last decade with a sword in his hand instead of a wooden spoon. He woke before dawn to fire the ovens and, after a few days, quit having to ask Alinath for the proper proportion of ingredients.

He could see the days stretching ahead of him in endless procession, each day just exactly like the one before. The years of soldiering had made him no more resigned to spending the rest of his life baking than he'd been at fifteen.

Even something as exotic as his stray Traveler didn't alter the pattern of life at his father's bakery. She worked as she was asked and seldom spoke, even to him. Only his nightly rides broke the habits of his childhood, but even they had begun to acquire a sameness.

He ought to sell the horse, his mother had told him over dinner yesterday, then he could use the money as a bride price. There were a number of lovely young village women who would love to be a baker's wife.

This morning he'd gotten up earlier than usual and tried to subdue his restlessness with work—to no effect. So as soon as Bandor had come in to watch the baking, Tier left and took Skew out, galloping him over the bridge and up into the mountains until they arrived at a small valley he'd discovered as a boy. Once there, he'd explored the valley until the lather on Skew's back had dried and his own desperation loosened under the influence of the sweet-grass smell and mountain breeze.

Part of him was ready to leave this afternoon, to take Seraph and find her people. But the rest of him wanted to put the journey off as long as he could. Once it was over, there would be no further escapes for him. He wasn't fifteen anymore: he was a man, with a man's responsibilities.

"You're quiet today," said Seraph as they worked together after lunch. "I was beginning to think that silence was a thing that Rederni avoided at all cost. Always you are telling stories, or singing. Even Bandor hums all the time he works."

He grinned at her as he kneaded dough. "I should have warned you," he said, "that every man in Redern thinks himself a bard and most of the women, too."

"In love with the sound of your own voices, the whole lot of you," said Seraph without rancor, dumping hot water in the scrubbing tub where a collection of mixing bowls awaited cleaning. "My father always said that too many words cheapened the value of a man's speech."

Tier laughed again—but Alinath had entered the baking room with an armful of empty boards in time to hear the whole of Seraph's observation.

"My father said that a silent person is trying to hide something," she said as she dumped the trays in a stack. "Girl, get the broom and sweep the front room. See that you get the corners so that we don't attract mice."

Tier saw Seraph stiffen, but she grabbed the broom and dustpan.

"Alinath, she is a guest in our house," Tier bit out as the door closed behind Seraph. "You don't use that tone to the hired boy. She has done nothing to earn your disrespect. Leave her be."

"She is a *Traveler*," snapped Alinath, but there was an undercurrent of desperation in her voice. "She bewitches you because she is young and pretty. You laugh with her and you'll barely exchange a word with any of us."

How could he explain to her his frustration with the life that so obviously suited her without hurting her feelings? The bakery was smothering him.

When he said nothing, Alinath said, "You're a man. Bandor is the same—neither of you see what she is. You think she's a poor familyless, defenseless woman in need of protection because that's what she wants you to see."

A flush of temper lit Alinath's eyes as she began to pace. "I see a woman who looks at my brother as a way to wealth and ease that she'll never have when she finds one of those ragtag bands of Travelers. She doesn't want to go to her people— even you must see that. I tell you that if you just give her the chance, she'll snatch you into a marriage-bed."

Tier opened his mouth and then closed it again. He tried to see Seraph as his sister described her, but the image didn't ring true.

"She's a child," he said.

"I was married when I was her age."

"She is a child and a Traveler," he said. "She'd no more look at me that way than she'd think of marrying a . . . a horse. She thinks of all of us as if we were a different species."

"Oh and you know so much about women," his sister ranted, though she was careful to keep her voice down so she couldn't be heard in the front room where Seraph was. "You need to find a good wife. You always liked Kirah. She's widowed now and would bring a fair widow's portion with her."

Tier put the dough in the greased bowl he'd set out for it, covered it with cheesecloth, and then scrubbed his hands in Seraph's tub of cooling water. He shook them dry and took off his father's apron and hung it on the hook. *Enough,* he thought.

"Don't wait dinner for me," he said and started to leave. He stopped before he opened the door to the front room. "I've been counting too heavily on manners and the memory of my little sister who saw me leave without telling anyone because she understood me enough to know that I had to leave. I see that you need a stronger reason to leave Seraph alone. Just you remember that, for all of her quietness she has a temper as hot as yours. She *is* a Traveler and a wizard, and if she takes a notion to teach you what that means, neither your tongue nor your fist will do you a bit of good."

He left before she could say anything, closing the door to the baking room firmly behind him.

Seraph glanced his way as he stalked past her, but he said nothing to her. She'd be all right; his warning would keep Alinath away from her for a while.

He couldn't face Seraph right now, not with his sister's accusations ringing in his ears. Not that he believed what Alinath had said about Seraph for a moment—but Alinath'd opened the way for possibilities that made him uncomfortable. He'd never thought much about the peace that Seraph's tart commentary and quiet presence brought him: he'd just been grateful for the relief from the demands of his family. He didn't want to examine what he felt any closer. So Tier nodded once at Seraph and also to Bandor before leaving the bakery.

Once outside, his steps faltered. He'd worn Skew out this morning, so it hardly seemed fair to take him out again. He could walk—but it wasn't exercise he needed, it was escape.

The Hero's Welcome was a tavern and an inn, a conglomeration of several older buildings, and the first building on the road through Redern. It was seldom empty, and when Tier entered it there were a number of men sitting near the kitchen entrance gossiping with each other while the tanner's father, Ciro, coaxed soft music from his viol.

It made Tier think of his grandfather and the grand concerts he and Ciro, who had been the tanner himself then, had put on. If Seraph ever heard the old man play, she'd know why Tier would never consider himself a bard in any sense of the word.

He seated himself beside these men he'd known since he was a child and greeted them by name, older men, all of them, contemporaries of his grandfather. The younger men would come in later, when they were finished with their work and chores.

One of the men had been a soldier in his youth, and Tier spent a little time exchanging stories. The innkeeper, noticing that there was a newcomer, offered Tier ale. He took it, but merely nursed it because the oblivion he sought wouldn't come from alcohol.

Ciro gradually shifted from playing broken bits and pieces into a recognizable song, and an old, toothless man began humming, his tone uncertain with age, but his pitch absolutely true. One after the other the old men began to sing. Tier joined in and let the healing music make the present fade away.

They sang song after song, sometimes pausing while one man tried to hum enough of something he'd heard long ago for Ciro to remember it, too—that man had a memory for music that Tier had only seen his grandfather equal.

It was the first time that he was happy to be home.

"Boy," said Ciro, "sing 'The Hills of Home' with me."

Tier grinned at the familiar appellation. It no longer fit as well as it had when he'd tagged along after his grandfather. He stood and let the first few notes of the viol pull him into the song. He took the low part of the duet, the part that had been his grandfather's, while the old man's warm tenor flung itself into the more difficult melody. Singing a duet rather than blending with a group, Tier loosed the power of his voice and realized with momentary surprise that Ciro didn't have to hold back. For the first time, Tier's singing held its own with the old musician's. Then the old words left no more room for thought. It was one of the magic times, when no note could possibly go astray and any foray into countermelody or harmony worked perfectly. When they finished the last note they were greeted with a respectful silence.

"In all my wandering, I've never heard the like. Not even in the palace of the Emperor himself." A stranger's voice broke the silence.

Tier turned to see a man of about fifty, a well-preserved, athletic fifty, wearing plain-colored clothes of a cut and fit that would have done for a wealthy merchant or lower nobleman, but somehow didn't seem out of place in a rural tavern full of brightly dressed Rederni. His iron-grey hair, a shade darker than his short beard, was tied behind his head in a fashion that belonged to the western seaboard.

He smiled warmly at Tier. "I've heard a great deal about you from these rascals since you returned—and they didn't lie when they said that your song was a rare treat. Willon, retired Master Trader, at your service. You can be no one but Tieragan Baker back from war." He held his hand out, and Tier took it, liking the man immediately.

As Tier sat down again, the retired master trader pulled a chair in between two of the others so he sat opposite Tier at the table.

Ciro smiled and said in his shy speaking voice, so at odds with his singing, "Master Willon has built a fine little store near the end of the road. You should go there and see it, full of bits and things he's collected."

"You are young to be retiring," observed Tier. "And Redern is an odd place to choose for retirement—these mountains get cold in the winter."

Master Willon had one of those faces that appeared to be smiling even in repose—which robbed his grin of not a bit of its effect.

"My son made Master last year," he said. "He's got a fire that will take him far—but not if he spends all of his days competing with me for control of the business. So I retired."

Willon laughed quietly and shook his head. "But it wasn't as easy as that. The men who serve my house had been mine for thirty years. They'd listen to my son, nod their heads, and come to me to see if I liked their orders. So I had to take myself out of Taela, and Redern came to mind."

He raised his tankard to Ciro. "My first trip as a caravan master I came by this very inn and was treated to the rarest entertainment I'd ever heard—two men who sang as if the gods themselves were their audience. I thought I'd heard the finest musicians in the world in Taela's courts, but I'd never heard anything like that. Business is business, gentlemen. But music is in my soul—if not my voice."

"If it's music you like, there's plenty here," said Tier agreeably as a small group of younger men came through the inn door.

"Well look what decided to drop by at last," said one of

them. "You wiggle out from under your sister's thumb, Tier?"

Tier had greeted them all since he'd returned from war, of course, but that had been under different circumstances, when they were customers or he was. The tavern doors made them all kindred.

Too much so.

With the younger men came less music and more talk—and they must have been talking to his mother because most of the talk had to do with his upcoming marriage. The question was not when he was going to marry; it was to whom.

Tier excused himself earlier than he had expected to and found himself leaving with Master Willon.

"Don't let them fret you," Willon said.

"I won't," Tier said. He almost stopped there, but couldn't quite halt his bitterness—maybe because a stranger might understand better than any of his friends and kin he'd left behind in the tavern. "There's more to life than wedding and breeding and baking bread."

He started walking and Willon fell into step beside him. "I've heard as much praise for your baking as I have for your singing. You don't want to be a baker?"

"Baking . . ." Tier struggled to put a finger on the thing that bothered him about his family's business. "Baking is like washing—the results are equally temporary." He gave a half-laugh. "That's arrogant of me, isn't it? That I'd like to do something that means more, something that will outlast me the way these buildings have outlasted the men who built them."

"I hadn't thought of it that way before," said Willon slowly. "But immortality . . . I think that's a basic instinct rather than the product of pride. It goes toward the same things that they were trying to push you into. How did you put it? Wedding and breeding. A man's immortality can be found in his children."

Children? Tier hadn't been aware that he'd thought about the matter at all, but the need was there, buried beneath the "I can't breathe with the weight of my family's wishes" tightness in his chest.

"So what do you want to do, if not bake?" asked Willon, betraying his foreignness with the question. No Rederni would have suggested that he do anything else. "Would you go back to fighting if there were a war to be had?"

"Not soldiering," Tier said firmly. "I've killed more than any man ought—the only product of warmaking is death." Tier took a deep breath and closed his eyes briefly as he thought. Maybe it was seeing his little valley again on his morning ride, but something inside of him vibrated like one of Ciro's viol strings when he finally said, "I'd like to farm."

Willon laughed, but it was a comforting laugh. "I'd not think that growing crops would be much more permanent than baking bread—just takes a bit longer to get to the final product."

But it wasn't. It was different. Tier stopped walking so that he could encompass that difference in words that didn't sound as stupid out loud as they did to himself, stupid but true.

"I've known farmers," he said slowly. "A lot of the men who fought the Fahlarn were farmers, fighting for their lands. They are as much a part of their lands as flour is a part of bread." He shook his head at himself and grinned sheepishly because it sounded stupider out loud. "The land is immortal, Master Willon, and a farmer has a part of that immortality."

"So are you going to be a farmer?" asked Willon with interest.

"And marry and breed?" Tier said lightly over the longing Willon's words produced. "Not likely." He began walking again, though they'd passed the bakery a while back. He had no desire to go home yet. "There's not a woman in Redern who'd marry me and let me go farming. I know the money farming brings in and that bakery brings in ten times as much—and it would break my family's heart."

"Farmers don't make much," agreed the master trader. "But if you look around you might find a woman who'd rather be a farmer's wife than live in the village under the tyranny of her neighbors."

That night Seraph got up out of her cot in the small room they'd given her and climbed out of the window into the garden that backed the house, her blanket serving as a cloak. The solid walls made her feel closed in and trapped. Most of her nights had been spent in tents rather than buildings.

She found the bench that had served as her bed on more than one night since she'd chosen to stay here and lay down on it again to look up at the stars.

She needed to go. These people owed her nothing, not the food she ate or the blanket she wrapped herself in. She did not belong here. She hadn't heard the argument that Tier and Alinath had while she swept the front room, but she'd heard the raised voices.

Tomorrow, she would go. In two weeks or three she would find a clan that would take her in.

Resolute, she closed her eyes and willed herself to sleep. A long time later, exhaustion had more success than her will and she relaxed into slumber.

A rotten tomato hit Arvage's shoulder while the solsenti boys bounced with nervous bravado. Didn't they know that the old man could kill them all with a touch of the magic he knew? Didn't they know that he and Seraph had spent the better part of the past two days banishing a khurlogh, *a demon spirit, that had been preying on nighttime visitors to the town well?*

Instead her teacher's arthritic fingers touched the mess on his shoulder and transformed it into a fresh, ripe tomato.

"My thanks, young sirs," he said. "A rare addition to my dinner."

The scene faded as Seraph stirred restlessly in protest of the old memory. She quieted and her dream took up again at a different point in time.

Her father's fingers petted her hair as she leaned against his knee, half-asleep in the aftermath of a full meal and the warmth of the nearby fire.

"The entire clan gone?" her father said, a small tremor in his bassy voice. "Are you certain it was the Imperial Army?"

Their visitor nodded his head wearily. "As far as we've been able to determine, the last village that they passed through complained to the commander of the imperial troops stationed nearby. Told them that the Travelers kidnapped a pair of young women. The troops came upon the clan and massacred them from grandfather to day-old babe. Turns out that the women were taken by bandits—the imperial troops found them on their way back to the village."

They buried Arvage in a wilderness glen, just as he had wanted. Seraph herself had thrown in the first, symbolic, handful of earth. He'd died trying to work magic that he could no longer harness because the pain in his joints broke through his fearsome control. He'd known the risk.

In one of those things possible only in dreams, Arvage stood beside her while her father and brothers buried him.

"It is our task to take care of them or die," he told her. "Our purpose is to keep the shadows at bay for the solsenti *who are helpless against them. This is a Raven's task before us, and I am Raven—as are you. You aren't old enough and I am too old, but we do as we must."*

Tier hadn't lived in the comfortable safety of the village long enough to sleep through small noises in the night. He'd heard Seraph go out, as she often did, and he'd gone back to sleep afterward. But he'd awakened again.

He waited for the noise to repeat itself, and when it did he pulled on his pants and slipped out his window to the garden where Seraph whimpered in the helpless throes of a nightmare.

The man was from the Clan of Gilarmist the Fat, running a message to another clan. He'd flirted with Seraph's oldest sister and died in the night. Her sister died the next morning, drowning in the fluid that they couldn't keep from filling her lungs.

By the time four days had passed only Seraph and her brother Ushireh were left to bury the dead. Ushireh worked until he passed out. She'd been so afraid that he was dead, too; it had taken her a long time to convince herself that he was only unconscious. She'd dragged him away from the dead they'd gathered together in the center of the camp, then she'd burned it all—camp and bodies alike. It had been weeks before she could work enough magic to light a fire.

When she managed it at last, Ushireh's body sat up in the pyre, and his head turned until he could fix his glowing eyes on her. Seraph shrank back and tried to close her eyes. As if in death he'd acquired the magic he'd so envied her in life, his will kept her from looking away from him.

"You left me," he said. "You left your duty. You cannot run forever, Seraph, Raven of the Clan of Isolda the Silent."

She awoke with a gasp and a cry and was gathered into warm arms and rocked gently.

"Shh," said Tier, "it was a dream. You're safe."

She buried her head in his shoulder and gave up a lifetime of self-control to sob raggedly against him. "I can't do it," she said. "I don't want to be a Traveler. They all die, and I have to burn them and bury them. I'm so tired of death and duty. I want . . . I want . . ." What she wanted was tied away from her in strands of guilt and duty, but she found a fair approximation of it in the safety of Tier's arms.

"Shh," he said. "You don't have to go if you don't want to."

His words passed over and around her, the sense lost to her grief and guilt, but the sound of his voice comforted her.

From the third of the three windows that looked out into the garden, Alinath watched her brother hold the witch he'd brought home and she clenched her fists before she turned away.

When the worst of it had passed, embarrassment made Seraph turn away and wipe her face with the corner of the blanket.

"Sorry," she muttered. "It was a nightmare."

"Ah," said Tier as he let her pull away from him. "It sounded worse than that to me."

She shrugged, not looking at him. "Memories make the worst nightmares, my father always said."

"You don't have to go find another clan," he said. "You can stay here."

She tried to stifle her involuntary laugh. It wouldn't be polite to disparage the hospitality of his family. "No, I can't. Thank you. But no."

"I can't leave now," said Tier. "But I fear it won't be long. Mother complains and frets until it's hard to believe that she's sick at all—but she's losing weight and her color is much worse. Can you wait?"

Seraph held herself still. Could she wait to take up her duties? *Oh, yes.* Wait forever if she could. But was it the right thing to do?

At last she nodded. "I'll wait."

"Good."

Tier sat with her a bit, while the sweat dried on her back.

With the air of a man coming to a decision, he took something from around his neck and put it into her hands.

"This came with me into war and kept me safe enough through any number of battlefields. As I am unlikely to need it now, I'd like you to take it."

She fingered the collection of large wooden beads carefully.

"They're not much to look at," he said hastily, and with a little embarrassment, she thought. "But they carry the blessing of our priest. You've met Karadoc?"

She nodded. The priest had sought her out to give her his sympathies on the death of her brother. The only Rederni aside from Tier who had. She hadn't been quite sure how to deal with a priest—Travelers had little use for the minions of the gods—but he'd seemed like a good person.

"Karadoc gave me that for helping him tend his garden after he broke his wrist one summer."

"It must have been more than that," Seraph said thoughtfully. "People don't give gifts like this lightly."

He stiffened, "It's just a bunch of wooden beads, Seraph."

She put them against her face and rubbed against them like a cat, soaking in the warmth that emanated from the battered wood. "Old wooden beads," she said. "I can't tell exactly how old, but they've been given in love and worn that way for a long, long time. They comfort me—did they comfort you while you were far from your home?" She didn't wait for his answer, "Tell me the story of your gardening for Karadoc?"

"I was young," he said finally. "Karadoc is . . . well, you've met him. He always took time to talk to me, listening to me when my father and I fought."

His voice hadn't fallen into the cadences of storytelling; he told this story hesitantly. "Karadoc broke his wrist; I told you that. His garden is his pride and joy, and it started to get overgrown almost immediately. I suppose being the priest of the god of green and growing things has a certain influence on your garden."

"He hired a boy to tend it, but when harvest season came the boy had to help his father in the field, and Karadoc couldn't find another one. So I started getting up a little earlier in the morning so I could work on it a bit."

Seraph smiled a little; the beads and Tier's company had worked their own magic. "He didn't know you were doing it."

"Well, I wasn't certain that I would do it more than once or twice. A baker gets up early to miss cooking in the heat of the day. I didn't want to promise something I couldn't do."

"And Karadoc found you out," said Seraph. "When you wouldn't take any pay, he gave you these."

He nodded.

Seraph put the necklace around her throat. Gifts could not be returned, only appreciated. She would find something she could do to repay him for his kindness to her and his gift. A Traveler's blessing could be a useful thing.

"Thank you for this," she said. "I will treasure it as long as it remains in my hands and pass it on as you have, as Karadoc did."

They lapsed into a comfortable silence.

"A man asked me today what I'd do if I could do something besides baking and soldiering," he said at last.

"What did you answer?"

"Farming," he said.

She nodded. "The land gives back everything you put into it and a little more, if you have the knack."

"If you could do anything, be anything, what would it be?"

She stilled. She knew about villages, knew that most men's fates were set in stone when they were little more than children and apprenticed to a trade—or else they were cast off never to be more than itinerant workers or soldiers. Women's lives were dictated by their husbands.

Travelers were a little more free than that usually. A bowyer could decide to smith if he wanted to, as long as he continued to contribute to the clan. There were no guilds to restrict a person from doing as he willed. And women, women ran the clan. Only the lives of the Ordered were set out from the moment a Raven pronounced them gifted at birth.

No Traveler would ever have asked a Raven what she wanted to be.

The silence must have lasted too long because he said, "That question took me aback, today, too. But I learned something. What would you do?"

"Ravens don't marry," she said abruptly. He was easy to talk to, especially in the dark. "We can't afford the distraction. We don't do the normal chores of the clan. No cooking or firewood gathering. We don't darn our own clothes or sew them."

"You cook well," he said.

"That's because Ushireh couldn't cook at all. I learned a lot when we were left on our own. But being a Raven's not like being a baker, Tier. You could leave it and become a soldier. You can leave it now and become a farmer if you want. But I can't leave being a Raven behind."

"But if you could—what would you do?"

She leaned back on her hands and swung her feet back and forth, the bench being somewhat tall for her. In a dreamy, smiling voice she said, "I would be a wife, like the old harridan who runs an inn in Boarsdock on the western coast. She has a double handful of children, all of them taller than her, and they all cringe when she walks by. Her husband is an old sailing man with one leg. I don't think I've ever heard him say anything but, 'yes, dear.'"

She caught him by surprise and Tier gave a crack of laughter that he had to cover his mouth to suppress.

Smiling her satisfaction in the dark, she thought that the oddest thing about her statement was that it was the truth. That old woman ran her inn and her children and their wives and husbands and they all, every one of them, loved her. She lived in the daylight world, where shadow things wouldn't dare show their faces and the children in her family had no more responsibility than grooming a few horses or cleaning a room could provide.

But the thing that Seraph envied the most was that one winter evening, when Seraph's uncles entertained the boisterous crowd that gathered beneath the great fireplace and told them stories of haunts and shadow-things, that wise old woman shook her head with a laugh and said that she had better things to do than listen to tales of monsters fabricated to keep children up all night.

So it was that she stayed when she should have gone. But a week or a month would make little difference to her duties—a lifetime or two would make little difference as far as she could tell. So she stayed.

"Don't pull that up. That's an iris bulb, trimmed down now that it's bloomed," said Tier's sister several weeks later. "Don't you know how to weed?"

Seraph released the hapless plant unharmed, straightened, and almost groaned at the easing in her back. "No," she said, though she'd told her as much when Alinath had set her to the task. How would she have learned to weed? The herbs and food plants she knew, but she'd no experience with flowers at all.

Tier had stormed off at lunch, beset by both his sister and his mother, who had gotten out of her bed only to try and push him into finding a wife. Since then Alinath had been picking at her as if it had been Seraph who'd sent Tier off to seek peace. Seraph had been set to half a dozen tasks, only to be sent to do something else because of some inadequacy in her work, real or imaginary.

"Well leave off then," said Alinath. "Bandor or I will have to finish it, I suppose. You are utterly useless, girl. Cannot sew, cannot cook, cannot weed. The baking room floor needs cleaning—but mind how you do it. Don't let the dust get into the flour bins."

Seraph stood up and dusted off her skirt; she'd left off wearing her comfortable pants when she'd noticed that none of the Rederni women wore anything except skirts.

"It's a shame," she said finally. "That Tier, who wears courtesy as close as his skin, should have a sister with none at all."

Before Alinath could do more than open her mouth, Seraph turned on her heel and entered the house through the baking room door. She regretted her comment as soon as she'd made it. The womenfolk in the clan were no more courteous in their requests than Alinath was. But they would have never turned their demands upon a Raven.

Moreover, Seraph knew the *solsenti* well enough to know that Alinath's rudeness to a guest was a deliberate slight. Especially since, except for that first time, she was careful to soften her orders around Tier.

Seraph had done her best to ignore the older woman. She

was a guest in Alinath's home. She had no complaint with the
work she was asked to do—which was no more work than
anyone else did, except for Tier's mother. And, by ignoring
Alinath's rudeness, Seraph bothered her more than any other
response could have.

There was a more compelling reason to ignore Alinath's
trespasses.

Seraph let her fingernails sink into the wood of the broom
handle as she swept with careful, slow strokes. A Raven could
not afford to lose her temper. She took a deep, calming breath
and sought for control.

The door opened and Alinath walked in. When she started
to speak her voice was carefully polite.

"I *have* been rude," she said. "I admit it. I believe that it is
time for some plainer speech. My brother thinks you are a
child."

Seraph stared at her a moment, bewildered, her broom still
in her hands. What did Tier's opinion have to do with anything?

"But I know better," continued Alinath. "I was married at
your age."

*And I killed the ghouls who killed my teacher when I was
ten,* thought Seraph. *A Raven is never a child.* But she saw
where Alinath was headed.

"I told Tier what you are up to, but he doesn't see it," said
Alinath. "Anyone who marries my brother will have this
bakery."

*Anyone who married your brother would be safe for the
rest of their life,* thought Seraph involuntarily, and envied his
future wife with all of her heart.

"But you will never have him."

Seraph shrugged. "And he will never have me."

She went back to sweeping—and longing to be an old
innkeeper who thought that ghouls and demons were stories
told to frighten children. She crouched to get the broom under
the low shelf of the table where Tier kneaded his bread.

"Where did you get those?"

Alinath lunged at Seraph. Startled, Seraph dropped the
broom as Alinath's hand clenched around Tier's bead necklace; it must have slid out of her blouse when she crouched.

"Dirty Traveler thief!" shrieked Alinath, jerking wildly at the necklace. "*Where* did you get these?"

Seraph had heard all the epithets—but she'd been fighting her anger for weeks. The slight pain of the jerk Alinath gave the necklace was nothing to the outrage that Alinath had dared to grab her in the first place.

She heard the door to the public room open and heard Tier's voice, but everything was secondary to the rage that swept through her. Rage fed by her clan's death, Ushireh's death, her desperate, despairing guilt at surviving when everyone else died, and lit by this stupid *solsenti* woman who pushed and pushed until Seraph would retreat no more.

Alinath must have seen some of it in her face because she dropped her hold on the necklace and took two steps back. The necklace fell back against Seraph's neck like a kiss from a friend. Just before the wave of magic left her, the warmth of Tier's gift allowed her to regain control. It saved Alinath's life, and probably Seraph's as well because magic loosed in anger was not choosy in its target.

Pottery shattered as the stone building shook with a hollow boom. Cooking spoons, wooden peels, and baking tiles flew across the room. The great door that separated the hot ovens from the baking room pulled from its hinges and flew between Seraph and Alinath, hitting the opposite wall and sending plaster into the air in a thick white cloud as Alinath cried out in fear. Flour joined plaster as the door fell to the ground, taking two tables with it and knocking a barrel half-full of flour to its side.

Closing her eyes to the destruction and Alinath's frightened face, Seraph fought to pull back the magic she'd loosed. It struggled in her grasp, fed by the anger that had engendered it. It made her pay for her lack of control, sweeping back to her call, back through her like shards of glass. But it came, and peelers and tiles settled gently to the floor.

Seraph opened her eyes to assess the damage. Alinath was fine—though obviously shaken, she had quit screaming as soon as she'd begun. The wall would have to be replastered and the door rehung, the jamb repaired or replaced. The jars of valuable mother, used to start the bread dough, had somehow escaped, and the number of broken pots was fewer than she'd thought.

Neither Tier, nor the four or five people who had followed him into the room, had more damage than a coating of flour and plaster.

Shame cut Seraph almost as rawly as the magic had. It was the worst thing a Raven could do—loose magic in anger. That no one had been hurt, nothing irreplaceable broken, was a tribute to Tier's gift and a little good luck rather than anything Seraph had done and so mitigated her crime not a whit. Seraph stood frozen in the middle of the baking room.

"I told you that she had a temper," said Tier mildly.

"This was an ill way to repay your hospitality," said Seraph. "I will get my things and leave."

Tier cursed the impulse that had led him to invite the men he'd spent the afternoon singing with to try out an experimental batch of herb bread he'd been working on. That he'd opened the door to the baking room when he—and everyone else— heard Alinath cry out had been stupidity. He'd been warning his sister not to antagonize Seraph for the better part of a week.

"Mages aren't tolerated here," said someone behind him.

"She said she'd leave," said Ciro. "She hurt no one."

"We'll leave in the morning," said Tier.

"Strangers who come to Redern and work magic are condemned to death," said Alinath in a tone of voice he'd never heard from her.

He looked at her. She should have appeared ridiculous, but the cold fear-driven anger on her face made her formidable despite the coating of white powder settling on her.

Someone gave a growl of agreement.

The ugly sound reminded Tier of the inn where he'd rescued her—or rescued the villagers from her. He realized that unless he managed to stop it, by morning his village might not be in any mood to let Seraph go.

An odd idea that had been floating in his head since he'd talked to Willon and then held Seraph in the wake of her night terrors crystalized.

"She is not a stranger," lied Tier abruptly. "She is my wife."

Silence descended in the room. Seraph looked at him sharply.

"No," said Alinath. "I'll not have it."

She was in shock, he knew, or she'd never have said such a ridiculous thing.

"It is not for you to have or not have," he reminded her, his voice gentle but firm.

"I won't have her in this house," Alinath said.

"We would have had to leave in any case," said Bandor, who'd pushed through the crowd and into the baking room. He walked over to Alinath, and put his hand on her shoulder. "Once Tier had chosen his wife, whoever she was, we'd have had to leave. I've made some inquiries in Leheigh. The baker there told me he'd be willing to take on a journeyman."

"There's no need," said Tier. Now that his choice was made, the words he needed to convince them all flowed easily. "There's a place I intend to farm about an hour's walk from here. I'll have to get the Sept's steward's permission, which won't be difficult to obtain since the land is not being used. There's time to build a house before winter. We'll live there, but I'll work in the bakery through the spring when planting season comes. Then I'll deed it to Alinath."

"When were you married?" whispered Alinath.

"Last night," lied Tier, holding out his hand to Seraph, who'd been watching him with an expression he couldn't read.

She stepped to his side and took his hand. Her own was very cold.

"Yes," said Karadoc, coming forward and putting a hand on Tier's head as he used to when Tier was a boy. "There have been Rederni who were mages before. Seraph will harm no one."

The crowd dispersed, and Bandor took Alinath to their room to talk, leaving only Karadoc, Tier, and Seraph.

"See that you come by the temple tonight," said the priest. "I don't like to keep a lie longer than necessary."

Tier grinned at him and hugged the older man. "Thank you. We'll stop by."

When he left, Tier turned to Seraph. "You can stay here with me and be my wife. Karadoc will marry us tonight and no one will know the difference." He waited, and when she said nothing, he said, "Or I can do as I promised. We can leave now and I'll go with you to find your people."

Her hand tightened on his then, as if she'd never let it go. She glanced once around the room and then lowered her eyes to the floor. "I'll stay," she whispered. "I'll stay."

PART TWO

CHAPTER 3

When Seraph reached the narrow bridge, the river was high and the wooden walkway was slick with cold water from the spring runoff. She glanced across the river and up the mountainside where Redern hung, terraced like some ancient giant's stone garden. Even after twenty years, the sight still impressed her.

From where she stood, the new temple at the very top of the village rose like a falcon over its prey. The rich hues of new wood contrasted with the greys of the village, but, to her, that seemed to be merely an accent to the harmony of stone buildings and craggy mountain.

Seraph crossed the bridge, skirted the few people tending animals, and headed for the steps of the steep road that zigzagged its way up the mountain face, edged with stone buildings.

The bakery looked much as it had when she'd first seen it. The house was newer than its neighbors, having been rebuilt several generations earlier because of a fire. Tier had laughed and told her that his several times great-grandfather had tried to make the building appear old but had succeeded only in making it ugly. Not even the ceramic pots planted with roses could add much charm to the cold grey edifice, but the smell

of fresh-baked bread wafting from the chimney gave the
building an aura of welcome.

Seraph almost walked on—she could sell her goods elsewhere, but not without offending her sister-in-law. Perhaps
Alinath would be out and she could deal with Bandor, who
had never been anything but kind. Resolutely, she opened the
bakery door.

"Seraph," Tier's sister greeted her without welcome from
the wide, flour-covered wooden table where her clever hands
wove dough into knots and set them on baking tiles to be taken
back to the ovens for cooking.

Seraph smiled politely. "Jes found a honey-tree in the
woods last week. Rinnie and I spent the last few days jarring it.
I wondered if you would like to buy some jars to make sweet
bread."

Tier would have given it to his sister, but Seraph could not
afford such generosity. Tier was late back from winter fur-
trapping, and Jes needed boots.

Alinath sniffed. "That boy. If I've told Tier once, I've told
him a thousand times, the way you let him wander the woods
on his own—and him not quite right—it's a wonder a bear or
worse hasn't gotten him."

Seraph forced herself to smile politely. "Jes is as safe in the
woods as you or I here in your shop. I have heard my husband
tell you that as often as you complained to him."

Alinath wiped off her hands. "Speaking of children, I have
been meaning to talk to you about Rinnie."

Seraph waited.

"Bandor and I have no children, and most probably never
will. We'd like to take Rinnie in and apprentice her."

Seraph reminded herself sternly that Alinath meant no
harm by her proposal. Even Travelers fostered children under
certain circumstances, but it seemed to Seraph that the *solsenti*
traded and sold their children like cattle.

Tier had tried to explain the advantages of the apprenticing
system to her—the apprentice gained a trade, a means to make
a fair living, and the master gained free help. In her travels,
Seraph had seen too many places where children were treated
worse than slaves; not that she thought Alinath would treat
Rinnie badly.

So, Seraph was polite. "Rinnie is needed on the farm," she said with diplomacy that Tier would have applauded.

"That farm will go to Lehr, sooner or later. Jes will be a burden upon it and upon Lehr for as long as he lives," said Alinath. "Tier will not be able to give Rinnie a decent dowry and without that, with her mixed blood, no one will have her."

Calm, Seraph told herself. "Jes more than carries his own weight," she said with as much outward serenity as she could muster. "He is no burden. Any man who worries about Rinnie's mixed blood is no one I want her marrying. In any case, she's only ten years old, and marriage is something she won't have to worry about for a long time."

"You are being stupid," said Alinath. "I have approached the Elders on the matter already. They know that scrap of land you have my brother trying to farm is so poor he has to spend the winter trapping so you have food on your table. It doesn't really matter that *you* have no care for your daughter; when the Elders step in, you'll have no choice."

"Enough," said Seraph, outrage lending unmistakable power to that one word. No one was taking her children from her. *No one.*

Alinath paled.

No magic, Tier's voice cautioned her, *none at all, Seraph. Not in Redern.*

Seraph closed her eyes and took a deep breath, trying to cleanse herself of anger, and managed to continue speaking more normally. "You may talk to Tier when he returns. But if anyone comes to try and take my daughter before then . . ." She let the unspoken threat hang in the air.

"I agree," said a mild voice from the kitchen. "Enough badgering, Alinath." Bandor entered from the baking room door with a large bowl of risen dough. "If any of Seraph's children want to apprentice we'd be glad to have them here—but that's for their parents to decide. Not you or the Elders." He nodded a greeting toward Seraph.

"Bandor," managed Seraph through her rage-tightened throat. "It's good to see you."

"You'll have to excuse Alinath," he said. "She's been as worried about Tier as you are. I've told her that it's not fair to expect a man trapping in the wild to come home on time every year. But he's her brother, and she frets. Tier's only a few weeks late. He'll show up."

"Yes," Seraph agreed. "I'd best be going."

"Didn't I hear you say you had some honey?" he asked.

"Jes found some in the woods last week. I brought a few dozen jars with me," she answered. "But Alinath didn't seem interested in it."

"Hummph," said Bandor, with a glance at his wife. "We'll take twelve jars for half-copper a jar. Then you go to Willon up on the heights, and tell him we're paying a copper each for anything you don't sell to him. He'll buy up your stock for that so he can compete. Yours is the first honey this spring."

Without a word, Seraph took out her pack and pulled out twelve jars, setting them on the counter. Just as silently, Alinath counted out six coppers and set it beside the jars. When Seraph reached out to take the money, the other woman's hand clamped on her wrist.

"If my brother had married Kirah"—Alinath said in a low voice that was no less violent for its lack of sound—"he'd have had no need to go to the mountains in the winter in order to feed his children."

Seraph's chin jerked up and she twisted her wrist, freeing it. "It has been near to two decades since Tier and I married. Find something else to fret about."

"I agree," said Bandor mildly, but there was something ugly in his tone.

Alinath flinched.

Seraph frowned, having never seen Alinath afraid of anything before—except Seraph herself on that one memorable occasion. She'd certainly never seen *anyone* afraid of Bandor. Alinath's face quickly rearranged itself to the usual embittered expression she wore around Seraph, leaving only a glint of fear in her eyes.

"Thank you, Bandor, for your custom and your advice," Seraph said.

As soon as the door was closed behind Seraph and she'd started up the narrow, twisty road, she muttered to her absent husband. "See what happens when you are away too long, Tier? You'd better get home soon, or those Elders are in for a rude surprise."

She wasn't really worried about the Elders. They weren't stupid enough to confront her, no matter what they thought should be done for Rinnie's benefit. Once Tier was home, he could talk them out of whatever stupidity Alinath had talked them into. He was good at that sort of thing. And if she was wrong, and the Elders came to try to take Rinnie before Tier was home . . . well, she might have failed in her duties to her people, but she would never fail her children.

She wasn't worried about Rinnie—but Tier was another matter entirely. A thousand things could have delayed Tier's return, she reminded herself. He might even now be waiting at home.

Even hardened by farmwork, Seraph's calves ached by the time she came to the door of Willon's shop near the top edge of the village. When she opened the homey door and stepped into the building, Willon was talking to a stranger with several open packs on the floor, so she walked past him and into the store.

The only other person in the store was Ciro, the tanner's father, who was stringing a small harp. The old man looked up when she came in and returned her nod before going back to the harp.

Willon's store had once been a house. When he'd purchased it, he'd excavated and built until his store extended well into the mountain. He'd stocked the dark corners of the store with odds and bits from his merchant days—and some of those were odd indeed—then added whatever he felt might sell.

Seraph doubted many people knew what some of his things were worth, but she recognized silk when she saw it—though doubtless the only piece in Redern resided on the wall behind a shelf of carved ducks in Willon's shop.

She seldom had the money to shop here, but she loved to explore. It reminded her of the strange places she'd been. Here was a bit of jade from an island far to the south, and there a chipped cup edged in a design that reminded her of a desert tribe who painted their cheeks with a similar pattern.

Some of Willon's wares were new, but much of it was secondhand. In a back corner of one of a half dozen alcoves she found boxes of old boots and shoes that still had a bit of life left in them.

She took out the string she'd knotted and began measuring it against the boots. In the very bottom of the second box she searched, she found a pair made of thinner leather than usual for work boots. The sole was made for walking miles on roads or forest trails, rather than tromping through the mud of a farmer's field. Her fingers lingered on the decorative stitches on the top edge, hesitating where the right boot was stained with blood—though someone had obviously worked to clean it away. Traveler's boots.

She didn't compare them to her son's feet, just set them back in the box and piled a dozen pairs of other boots on top of them, as if covering them would let her forget about them. In a third bin, she found what she was looking for, and took a sturdy pair of boots up to the front.

There is nothing I could have done, she told herself. *I am not a Traveler and have not been for years.*

But even knowing it was true, she couldn't help the tug of guilt that tried to tell her differently: to tell her that her place had never been here, safe in Tier's little village, but out in the world protecting those who couldn't protect themselves.

"I can't sell those here," she heard Willon say to a stranger at the front counter—a tinker by the color of his packs. "Folk 'round here get upset with writing they can't read—old traps of the Shadowed still linger in these mountains. They know to fear magic, and even a stupid person's going to notice that those have Traveler's marks on them."

"I bought them from a man in Korhadan. He claimed to have collected them all," said the tinker. "I paid him two silvers. I've had to carry them from there to here. I'll sell them for ten coppers, the entire bag, sir, for I'm that tired of them. You're the eighth merchant in as many towns as told me the same thing, and they take up space in my packs as I might use for something else. You surely could melt them down for something useful."

On the counter lay an assortment of objects that appeared something like metal feathers. One end was sharp for a few inches, almost daggerlike, but the other end was decorative and lacy. Some were short, but most were as long as Seraph's forearm, and one nearly twice that long. There must have been nearly a hundred of them—*mermori.*

"My son can work metal," said Seraph, around the pulse of

sorrow that beat too heavily in her throat. There were so many of them. "He could turn these into horseshoes. I can pay you six coppers."

"Done," cried the fellow before Willon could say a thing. He bundled them up in a worn leather bag and handed it to Seraph, taking the coins she handed him.

He gathered his packs together and carried them off as if he were afraid she'd renege if he waited.

Willon shook his head, "You shouldn't have bought those, Seraph Tieraganswife. Poor luck follows those who buy goods gotten by banditry and murder the way those probably were."

A merchant to the bone, Willon should have objected to her buying outright from the tinker rather than cut him in for a percentage—but things like that happened when *mermori* were involved.

"Travelers' spells don't hurt those of Traveler blood," she said in a low voice that wouldn't carry to others in the store.

Willon looked startled for a moment. "Ah. Yes, I had almost forgotten that."

"So you think these were gotten by banditry?" she asked.

"My sons tell me that they don't call it that anymore." Willon shook his head in disapproval. "The present emperor's father declared the Travelers beyond the protection of his laws. The old man's been dead for years, but his son's not going to change anything. He shuts himself up in the palace and listens to people who tell him stories without questioning the truth from falsehood, poor boy."

He spoke as if he knew him, but Seraph let it pass without comment. Tier had told her that he thought that the caravanning business Willon had retired from had been richer than he let on. He hadn't changed much from when he'd first come, other than the gradual lightening of his hair to white. Though he must have been nearing his seventh decade, he looked much younger than that.

"Ah well," she said. "They're pretty enough, but they'll make shoes for horses and buckles for harness, sir—surely if Travelers had that much magic left they'd have used it to save themselves." She set the boots she'd selected on the counter. "Now, I need these for Jes, but I've spent my coppers on the metal bits. In my pack I have some wild honey. I've sold a dozen jars to Bandor at the bakery below for a half-penny apiece, and I've a little more than twice that left." She'd looked, and hadn't seen any honey in the section where he kept a variety of jarred and dried goods.

"My brother-in-law told me to tell you I sold him his at a copper each," she added with a small smile. Willon was one of the few villagers she felt comfortable talking to—probably because he was an outsider too.

"Aye, and he should have paid you that," said Willon with a snort. "Doubtless you know it, too. Taking advantage of his own kin."

"If Tier were home, we'd have given him the honey," she said, "which Bandor knows also."

Willon grinned. "I'll buy what you've left for a copper each—that's a fair price. Especially if when that boy of yours finds more honey, you bring it to me first."

"I'll do that," she said. "Thank you, Willon."

Thirty coppers for the honey minus ten for the boots left her with twenty coppers, almost a whole silver. She tucked the coins in her satchel as she left Willon's shop, closing the door gently on the first few notes of Ciro's harp.

Her mind more on the *mermori* she'd bought from the trader than on where she was going, she almost ran over a man who stood in the way.

"Excuse me," she said apologetically, looking into his face.

It was a good face, even-featured and wide-mouthed. He was no one she knew, which was unusual. The village was small enough that even with as little time as she spent there she knew everyone in it—at least by sight.

"A Traveler," he said in a tone of near delight that shocked her.

Her reaction must have been easy to read because he laughed. "I must sound like an idiot—I just hadn't expected to run into a Traveler here. I thought your people avoid coming here. Some aversion to being so near Shadow's Fall?"

Aversion to being near people so fearful of magic, she almost answered him, but not even surprise could loosen her habitual control over her tongue.

A look of comprehension crossed his face. "You must be Seraph Tieraganswife. That's why people speak of you . . ."

he seemed to realized that however people spoke of her wouldn't exactly be flattering and stumbled to a halt.

If she had not been holding a bag of *mermori* that reminded her of the plight of the Travelers and her failure to live the life she'd been called to serve, she might have helped him. But he'd talked his way into offense, and she let him find his own way out.

"I am sorry," he said sincerely after a moment. "When I am excited I tend to talk too much. Let me introduce myself properly. I am Volis, priest of the Path of the Five."

"Seraph Tieraganswife," she replied shortly, though she made no move to leave. He was distracting her from her guilt, and for the moment she was content that he continue to do so.

She'd known that there was a new priest in town, of course. Even if she'd forgotten, the new temple at the very top of the road would have reminded her. He'd come from Taela with the new Sept last fall, and stayed when the Sept returned to his duties in the capitol of the Empire. But she hadn't paid much heed to the news—she was still too much Traveler to worship in the houses of the gods.

Volis grinned at her, "I was right. I'm sorry to overwhelm you, but the Travelers are a hobby of mine, though I've only met a few of them."

What was she to say to that? she wondered and said nothing.

"Do you have a while to spare?" he asked. "I have a wealth of questions to ask you—and I'd like to show you the temple."

She glanced at the sun, but her business had taken very little time and the pack of *mermori* was a cold, hard thing she would have to deal with as soon as she left Redern.

So she raised an eyebrow and nodded her head. Tier would have laughed and called her "Empress" if she had done such a thing to him. This boy merely smiled, as if he'd been certain she would follow him. He had, she thought, a tithe of Tier's charm and was used to having people obey him.

He turned and led the way up the road, which was so steep that it was set in stairs.

"I would have been just as happy with something like the rest of Redern," he said. "But the new Sept was convinced that I would be happier in something more modern looking."

"The Sept is a follower of your five gods?" Seraph asked.

"Gods save us, no," laughed Volis. "But he was willing to do a favor when a few of the Path's Elders twisted his arm to place a temple here."

"Why here?" asked Seraph. "Why not in Leheigh, which also belongs to the Sept? Surely you would find more followers in the larger city."

Volis smiled. "I have not done so badly here. Your own family attends my meetings. In fact, I was on my way to consult with Bandor when you ran into me—and I couldn't resist the chance to have a Traveler to speak to. But the main reason I am here—instead of a really big city, like Korhadan, for instance— is Shadow's Fall. We feel that there are things on the old battle-field that might enlighten us."

Shadow's Fall? Seraph bit back her opinion of the stupid-ity of anyone who wanted to explore there. Doubtless the bat-tlefield could educate this *solsenti* fool better than she.

Like Willon's shop and many of the buildings on the steeper slopes, the temple had been built into the mountain. The facade was raw timber and crude, except for the doors, which were smooth and oiled until they were almost black.

Volis ushered her inside, and Seraph had to stop in the threshold to allow her eyes to adjust from the brightness out-side.

The room was a richly appointed antechamber that would have been more at home in a Sept's keep than in a village tem-ple. Either the—what was it Volis had called it?—the Path of the Five was a rich church indeed, or the Sept owed its Elders a lot of favors.

"There are only three temples," said Volis, seeing her ex-pression. "Two in Taela and this one. We intend this to be a place of pilgrimage."

" Shadow's Fall," said Seraph, "a place of pilgrimage."

"Where the Five triumphed over evil," said the priest, ap-parently oblivious to the doubt in her voice. "Come and see the refuge, where I hold services."

Seraph followed him through a tapestry-curtained entrance into a room like none she'd ever seen before.

The excavations were far more extensive than she had thought. The ceiling of the chamber soared overhead like an upside-down bowl. Near the edge it was a single handspan over the doorway, in the center of the room it rose three times the height of a tall man. The stone walls, floors, and ceiling were as smooth as polished marble.

This . . . this was built in the short season since the new Sept came to explore his inheritance?

The ceiling was painted a light sky-blue that darkened gradually to black on the walls. The light that illuminated the room seemed to emanate from that skylike ceiling. *Magic,* thought Seraph, solsenti *magic.* But her attention was on the figures that occupied the false firmament. Chasing each other endlessly around the perimeter of the ceiling were five life-sized birds painted with exquisite detail.

Volis was silent as she walked past him to the center of the room.

Lark, she thought, chills creeping down her spine. A cormorant's brilliant eyes invited her to play in the stormy winds. An owl glided on silent wings toward the black raven, who held a bright silver and ruby ring in its mouth, while next in line a falcon began its stoop. Together they circled the room, caught in endless flight.

In the center of the ceiling, twice as large as any other, a river eagle caught the winds and twisted its head to look down upon the room as if to examine its prey.

Each bird a representative of the six Orders of the Travelers.

"Behold the Five," said Volis softly in a language Seraph hadn't heard since the day her brother died. "Lark the healer, Cormorant who rules the weather, Owl of wisdom and memory, Raven the mage, Falcon the hunter. And above them all, trapped in darkness is the secret god, the lost god. You didn't know about the lost god, did you?"

"They are not gods," said Seraph in her tongue. Though, she remembered, in the old stories of before they Traveled, her people had believed that there were gods as he had described. But as the Old Wizards had grown in knowledge and power they had put those fallacies behind them.

As if she hadn't spoken, Volis pointed to the eagle. "I found him, in books so old they crumbled at my touch, in hints in ancient songs. For generations the Elders of the Path have worshiped only the Five—until I found the lost god."

"The Eagle?" said Seraph, caught between an urge to laugh

at the idea of *solsenti* worshiping the Orders as gods, and distaste. Distaste won.

"The Eagle." He looked pleased. "My discovery led me to be honored by this appointment," he waved a hand to indicate the temple.

"Congratulations," said Seraph, because he seemed to expect her to say something of the sort. She glanced at the ceiling again and wondered what her father would have said if he'd seen it.

"I have gleaned some things," he said. "The Eagle is protected by the others, so that he can rescue them in some future time, when they are all at risk and the world hangs in the balance."

She'd taught Tier that song in translation, a child's tune to teach them about the Orders. Obviously the translation that Volis had happened upon had been less careful. He made it sound as if the Eagle's purpose as Guardian was for some single, predestined event.

Eagerly the young priest turned to Seraph and took her hands. "I see from your face that you know about the Eagle."

"We do not speak of the Eagle to outsiders," said Seraph.

"But I'm not an outsider," he said waving an impassioned hand at the ceiling. "I *know* about Travelers; I've spent my life studying them. Please, tell me what you know of the Eagle."

Seraph didn't suffer fools gladly—she certainly didn't aid and abet their stupidity. It was time to go home. "I am sorry," she said. "I have work awaiting me. Thank you for showing me around; the artwork is very good."

"You have to tell me more," he caught her arm before she could leave. "You don't understand. I *know* it is the Elders of the Path of the Five who must free it."

"Free it?" she asked, and that chill that had touched her upon seeing the Birds of the Orders in a *solsenti* temple strengthened, distracting her from the encroaching grip of his arm.

"In hiding him," said Volis earnestly, "the Five trapped him, for his protection. 'Sleep on, guarded be, until upon waking destroys and saves'—"

Seraph started. That bit of poetry had no business being spoken in the mouth of a *solsenti,* no matter how well he spoke Traveler. It had nothing to do with the Eagle, but . . .

"He must be freed," said Volis. "And the Master of the Path has foreseen that it is we of the Path who will free the Stalker."

"The Stalker is not the Eagle," Seraph said involuntarily, then could have bitten off her tongue. *This was dangerous, dangerous knowledge. He was mistaken about the Eagle, about the Orders being gods, but the Stalker . . .*

He turned his mad gaze to her. He must have been mad. Only a madman would speak of freeing the Stalker.

"Ah," he said. "What do you know about the Stalker?"

"No more than you," she lied.

She fought to draw in a full breath and reminded herself that this man was a *solsenti*, a *solsenti* possessed of more knowledge that he should have—but even if he were so mistaken as to confuse the Eagle with the Stalker, he still should be harmless enough.

She gave him a short bow, Raven to stranger rather than good Rederni wife to priest, and used the motion to break free of his grasp.

"I have work," she said. "Thank you for your time—I'll see myself out."

She turned on her heel and strode rapidly to the curtained entrance, waiting for him to try and stop her, but he did not.

By the time she was on the bridge, she'd lost most of the fear that her visit with the new priest had engendered. The Stalker was well and truly imprisoned, and not even the Shadowed, who had almost destroyed the human race, had been able to free it. A *solsenti* priest with a handful of half-understood information was not a threat—at least not to the world as a whole, but she would still have to consider what Volis's fancies would mean to her and hers.

Dismissing the priest as an immediate threat left her with no distraction for the burden she carried. Though the honey jars were gone, almost a hundred weight of them, her pack carried stones that weighed her soul more than her back. As soon as Seraph left the main road for the cover of the trail, she stopped and pulled out the bag of *mermori* and counted them. Eighty-three.

Her hand tightened on the last one until the sharp edge of the end drew blood. Hurriedly she wiped off the *mermora;* it was never a good thing to expose magicked things to blood. When she was certain it was clean, she put them back in the leather bag and returned the whole bundle to her pack.

"There's nothing I can do," she said fiercely, though there was no one to hear her. "I don't know *anything*. I have no more ability than a dozen other Ravens who have all failed to prevent the demise of the Travelers. Here, in this place, I have three children who need me. There are fields to be planted and gardens to tend and a husband to welcome me home. There is nothing I can do."

But, by Lark and Raven, eighty-three. She swallowed. Maybe Tier would be home when she returned. She needed him to be home.

The land that Seraph and Tier farmed was in a very small hanging valley, most of which was too rocky to plant. They had no close neighbors. It had been virgin land when they had come there as newly married strangers.

From the vantage point of a knoll above the valley, Seraph fought back the feeling that it would all go back to wild within the decade—she was no farseer, just tired. She adjusted her pack and started down the faint trail.

Trees gave way to grass and field. As soon as she started on the path above the cabin, a joyous bark preceded Gura as he charged up the trail to welcome her home.

"Hello, fool dog," she said, and he rolled at her feet in rapture at her recognition of him, coating his thick fur in spring mud.

He was huge and black, covered with hair that needed daily grooming. Tier'd come home from town one evening with a black eye and a frightened, half-starved puppy with huge feet. Always collecting strays, was her husband.

Seraph bit back tears, and shook her head at the dog. "Come, Gura, let's see how my lad did on his own today."

The huge dog lumbered to his feet and shook himself off, sloughing off the puppy antics with the mud. He accompanied her to the cabin with solemn dignity.

With Gura's welcome to warn her family, Seraph wasn't surprised to find Lehr and Rinnie quietly working in the cabin.

"Ma!" said her youngest in tones of utter relief. "Lehr was

so mean. He yelled at me when I was already doing what he asked me to."

At ten, Rinnie had recently adopted the role of family arbitrator and informant—which was having the expected results with her siblings. She took after Seraph more than anyone in the—family at least in looks. Rinnie was short with Seraph's pale hair that stood out so in Redern's dark population. In temperament she more resembled her father, sharing both his calm good sense and his flair for drama.

Seraph hugged her and looked up at Lehr.

"We finished turning the garden," said Lehr repressively. "And we planted a good third of it before Rinnie whined so much I let her go inside."

"He made me work *hard*," said Rinnie, still not giving up the hope of getting her brother in trouble.

When Rinnie stuck her tongue out at Lehr, he ignored it. Last year he would have retaliated—or smiled at her, knowing that her reaction would be worth whatever trouble he'd get in.

"Thank you, Lehr," Seraph said, standing on her toes to kiss his cheek. "I know it's not an easy job to keep this lazy girl working. I can tell by the stew on the hob and the pile of carded wool that the both of you came inside and rested like the highborn."

He laughed and hugged her. "She was fine. We'd have gotten the whole garden done, Mother, if Jes had stuck around. He left sometime after lunch—I didn't even see him go."

"I can talk to him," she offered.

Lehr shook his head. "No, it's all right. I know he does the best he can. It's just that with Papa gone, we need him. When he can keep his mind on it, he can work as well as Papa does. Mother, the Sept's steward was here today."

"Forder?" Seraph asked, taking her cloak and hood off and hanging them on the cloak tree by the door. "What did he want?"

"He looked at the fields and asked if Papa was back yet. When I told him no, he said the new Sept was demanding quarter again as much for our tithe payment this year as last—of the garden and the fields. He said that it's almost past time to get the fields plowed."

Seraph put her pack against the wall. "I know, Lehr. We've

waited as long as we could. We'll just have to break ground without Tier. We can start tomorrow—no, day after tomorrow so I have time to look at the harness and plow to make repairs. Don't worry about the increased tithe; Tier said to expect some kind of increase with the new Sept."

"Forder said the Sept had a horse we could lease, if we needed."

"No." She shook her head. When he'd left, Tier had taken the young mare they'd bought last year, leaving their old gelding to his retirement. "Skew knows these fields, and old as he is, he'll do the job until Tier gets back. We can't afford to start leasing a horse, not if the Sept is taking more of the harvest."

Outside the door, Gura gave a howl more suited to a dire wolf than a dog, which was answered by a wail both higher and wilder.

"Jes is home," said Rinnie unnecessarily, for the door flew back on its hinges and Seraph's oldest child bounded in the door.

"Mother, Mother," he sang out. "I found a rabbit for dinner." He held out an enormous jackrabbit, already gutted, beheaded, and skinned.

"Jesaphi, my love," Seraph said. "I am very glad that you found a rabbit. But you need to shed some mud before you come inside."

Of all her children, Jes looked the most like his father. Taller by a head than Lehr, Jes was lean and dark. Lehr was lean, too, but he had Seraph's pale hair. Like Tier, Jes was not handsome; his nose was thin and too long. A deep dimple peered out of his left cheek, and his eyes were dark, velvet brown.

"I'm sorry, Mother," he said shedding his exuberance like a coat. "I didn't mean to—to get muddy."

It was Jes's voice that gave him away even to the least observant. There was something wrong in the pitch and the singsong way he talked.

He wasn't simple, like the cooper's son, but his affliction appeared very similar and people assumed they were the same. Seraph had seen no reason to confuse anyone but Tier with the truth.

"Not to worry." Seraph soothed Jes with one of the light

touches, which were usually all he could bear. "While the others set the table, you and I'll go clean you up."

"Did I do something wrong?" he asked anxiously.

"No, love, come with me." She took his hand and led him outside to help him scrub off.

In the middle of the night, unable to sleep, Seraph rose quietly out of her too-empty bed in the loft and dressed. She opened a trunk and took from it a large bag that dangled heavily from its worn cords. The ladder steps were tight and let out no sound that might wake Lehr, who was a light sleeper.

The pack by the door still held the boots she'd gotten Jes; she'd forgotten to give them to him. Seraph took them out and set them to the side. She put the bag she'd taken from her room into the pack where the shoes had been, then quietly let herself out.

On the porch, Gura watched her with glittering eyes that hinted at wolf somewhere in his background.

"Shh," she said. "Stay and watch."

Gura subsided and dropped his face back down on his forepaws, jowls sliding loosely to either side.

"I'll be back soon enough," she explained as if he'd understand. "I just can't sleep. There are things I have to work out."

Gura closed his eyes—sulking, she knew, because she hadn't asked him along.

She followed a path behind the cabin that led into the forest. The moon was high and her night vision was better than most so she had little trouble finding her way.

She walked a mile or so until she came to the meadow she sought. She set her pack down and opened it.

"Eighty-three," she said to herself, taking out the leather bag she'd gotten in town as well as the bag from her trunk, "and a hundred and forty-one."

She took one of the *mermori* out and stuck it into the ground, point down, so it stuck up like a short fencepost. She took another out and measured it with her fingers then paced out a distance from the second. She did the same with the third and the fourth as the moon crept across the sky.

"What do you do, Mother?"

She'd been so involved in the *mermori* that she hadn't

heard him. The low, velvety voice sounded so much like Tier's that she had to swallow. Despite her excellent eyesight and the moon she couldn't see Jes in the night.

"I've told you some stories about the Travelers," she said, setting the last *mermora* she held into the earth, and walked back for more.

He didn't reply immediately. She heard no footstep, but was not surprised that he'd followed her back to the pack.

"Yes," he said close enough that the warmth of his breath touched the back of her neck. Traveler-bred though she was, the vast difference between her daytime son and this, more dangerous Jes disconcerted her; a mother should not fear her child.

"We are the descendants of the wizards who lived in Colossae long before the Shadowed came to destroy mankind," she said, ignoring the shiver Jes's voice had sent down her spine.

"Yes," he acknowledged, pacing beside her as she took a handful of the *mermori* to an empty spot in the meadow and continued to measure out distances. He was barefoot.

Only she and Tier knew what her gentle-natured child became away from the safety of the cabin.

"Colossae was a great city of learning, and wizards came from all the earth to study and learn there. For generations they gathered and learned magic and forgot wisdom, until at last they created the greatest evil their hearts had ever imagined."

She had told her children very little about the Travelers, hoping that they would all become Rederni, like Tier. But Lehr and Rinnie carried the Traveler's looks, and Jes carried the Traveler's curse.

It had occurred to her, lying awake in her bed before she'd left it, that with a priest who knew too much and garbled truth with lies, it might be a good idea to teach her children more. She'd start tonight with Jes.

"By the time the wizards realized what they had done, it was too late to undo their making, almost too late to control it. As it was, only a great sacrifice could stop their creation, and Colossae was killed to imprison the Stalker, before it could destroy the world," she said. "The wizards who survived were sent to Travel the earth and keep it free of the Stalker's corruption, because such evil, even bound, was not without power. Even so great a sacrifice as a city of light and knowledge could not hold it completely, nor keep it forever."

"Yes," Jes said again. This time she caught a glimpse of eyes glowing a bit red in the night.

"What is it?" she asked. "Is there someone here?"

"Not now," he said, at last, a growl in his voice that wasn't quite human. "But there have been hunters in the forest who do not belong. They hunt for sport and that offends the forest— and they've come too near to the cabin for my liking."

"The new Sept is supposed to be quite a hunter," she told him. "Some of the nobles the Sept brought with him from Taela stayed when he left. Is this hunting something that you must stop?"

"No," he replied after a moment. "The forest king told me he will take care of these men if necessary." Seraph shivered a little at the tone of her son's voice when he said "men"—it told her that her son, in this aspect at least, did not consider himself one. "This forest yet has the power to keep out killers who hunt wastefully," he said.

Seraph set another *mermora*.

"You were talking about Colossae," he reminded her after she'd placed the *mermora* she held and was walking back for another handful.

"Ah, yes." She decided it was too much trouble to keep coming back so she transferred all that were left into the largest bag and carried that with her.

"It was decided after the wizards left and the city died, that they should meet in secret every year. But they had truly bound the evil, and there was no great need of the wizards in those early years so the meetings began to take place every two years, then every five.

"The *mermori*"—she sorted through and held up a fragile-seeming *mermora* no longer than her index finger—"were created by the wizard Hinnum and gifted to each of the wizards who left the city. They were passed down to the eldest of each family and in the beginning it is said they numbered five hundred and four. Until the Shadowed rose to power, some five centuries ago, each *mermora* was held by a large clan, but when the Army of Man gathered to fight the creatures the Shadowed had gathered, Travelers were forefront in the armies—because the Stalker, still imprisoned in Colossae, controlled the Shadowed. More than half of the army fell that day, taking with it most of the Travelers who fought there."

"You never told me that before—that the Shadowed was caused by the thing the wizards bound in Colossae."

She smiled a little grimly, "It's not something that we talk about openly. If people knew that we Travelers held ourselves responsible for the Shadowed, they'd make certain we suffered for it. Even some of the clans claimed there was no connection between the two—or that the Shadowed was the Stalker itself and that we should be freed of our tasks."

She set another *mermora* into the ground. "I remember a discussion at the last Gather I went to. One of the Clan Fathers proposed that we quit searching out evil. He said things like, 'We destroyed the Shadow, completed the tasks the Old Ones gave us. We should settle while there is still good land unclaimed.' Then my father stood up and said, 'Arrogance has always been the Traveler's Bane. The Shadowed was not the Stalker, but merely a man corrupted by it. My grandfather had this story through his line. When the Raven who faced the Shadowed and reduced him to ashes returned to his circle, he told them that the creature he'd killed had never touched the stones of Colossae. We fought true evil on that day, but our task remains.' "

Seraph laughed a little at the memory. "My father was a showman. He didn't wait for the debate that followed, but excused himself to his tent and would speak no more about it. My grandfather always said that if you don't argue, you can't be proved wrong."

"So your father was the only reason the Travelers kept Traveling?"

Seraph shook her head. "No—it wouldn't have worked if they'd really wanted to settle down. It was hard enough for me to stay here—and I would have followed your father through the Shadowed's Realm if I'd had to. Staying was more difficult. Travelers are well named."

Jes followed her silently as she began her task again. Jes was good at silence.

"I remember going to two Gathers as a child," she said, taking out another *mermora* and setting it upright. "There were two hundred and thirty *mermori* held by just over two hundred clans at the first one. I can remember my mother fretting about how few there were. She died before I went to the second Gather, when I was thirteen. There were fewer than two hundred then—and many clans carried more than one."

The largest *mermora* she had saved for last, having left an extensive corner of the meadow for it. "The *mermori* were too dangerous to allow them to exist without safeguards, so Hinnum spelled them so that, eventually, they would find their way into the hands of the eldest of the closest relatives of those who had died and left the *mermori* lost."

"Mother," said Jes, after a bit. "There are two hundred twenty-four *mermori* here."

"I know," she whispered. "I've been acquiring them a few at a time since I married your father. Today I bought eighty-three from a tinker."

"Eighty-three," he said, startled into losing, for a moment, the aura of danger he carried. "How did you pay for them? They are solid silver and worth more than—"

"People don't always see that they are silver," she said, trying to pace off the area for the largest of them again—she kept losing count. "Sometimes they appear to be iron or even wood. Most people dislike them on sight. I paid six coppers for them, and the merchant I bought them from will shortly forget exactly what it was I bought, except that he came out ahead on the deal."

"Ah," he said and walked beside her for a while, gradually blending into the darkness until she couldn't see him if she looked straight on.

She caught glimpses of him sometimes when she wasn't quite looking. Sometimes she saw a man who looked like her husband, but more dangerous. At others she saw a dark animal that prowled on four legs. Sometimes if she turned her head and looked at him directly for too long, he disappeared into the night. It was only illusion, she knew, though he could take on shapes of animals if he chose. But illusion or not, it was disconcerting.

"What do they do?" he asked finally.

She set the last one in. "I'll show you. Come with me."

The meadow was set on a rise and she took her son to the

highest point. She had never done this with so many before. At the Gathers, the elders from all the families would stand in a circle and chant together.

She held out both hands and shouted imperiously, *"Ishavan shee davenadre hovena Hinnumadraun."*

It had been so long since she'd allowed herself this much magic. She did only a little magic now and then—when they planted their crops, and when she warded the farm to keep the more dangerous creatures of the mountains away.

Even after so long, it came eagerly to her call, thrumming from her bones to the earth, reverberating through the dirt, rotting vegetation, and newborn sprigs of grass.

Jes let out a startled snarl as the meadow lit up with the windows of two hundred and twenty-four houses. Some were smaller than their cabin, but most were as large as the largest of the houses in Redern. By chance she'd put two in such a way that they blended into each other, sharing a wall—it looked so right that Seraph wondered if the houses might have stood in just such a relative location in Colossae. In the very corner of the meadow stood a small castle. The architecture of the houses was distinctly foreign, the windows open and rounded, the roofs covered with some kind of green pottery tiles.

"It's all right," she reassured Jes, though her eyes were held by the castle. "They are all illusion. The wizards could take only the most necessary of articles because they could not risk giving warning to the enemy before they fled. They couldn't take any of their libraries—So Hinnum created the *mermori*, which remember the homes of the wizards as they stood in Colossae so long ago. Come with me."

She led her son to one of the smaller ones, a brick-faced home no bigger than Alinath's bakery, though much more gracile. Ebony wood doors were worn near the latch, giving testimony of the age of the building. "This was the *mermora* my father carried from his father. It belonged to Isolda the Silent, who died when they sealed the city." Seraph pulled the door latch, felt the metal cool against her fingers. The door opened with a soft groan, and she stepped inside.

"Illusion?" Jes questioned, stepping in beside her. The light from Isolda's oil lamps showed a young man rather than a beast.

"I can smell oil and herbs—some I know, like anise, henbane, but there are many I can't identify."

"Hinnum was a very great illusionist. Legend says he was four hundred years old when the city fell," she said, trailing her fingers over the familiar shawl that hung neatly on the back of a chair as if it only waited for Isolda to return from some errand.

"But all that this is, is illusion." She turned to her son. "If it is raining outside and you come in, you will not feel the rain— but when you walk out you will be wet. If you are freezing to death and come in, you'll feel warm and still die from the cold."

"How long ago did the city die?" asked Jes, touching a carved table.

For a moment Seraph allowed herself to see the house anew, recognizing how alien it appeared to him. Perhaps a lord's house would be furnished with wooden tables and shelves polished like the surface of a windless lake, but no dwelling in Redern held such treasures.

"I'm not certain," she replied. "It was long before the Shadowed came to rule—and that was about six hundred years ago if the stories crediting him with a hundred-year reign are correct. Colossae was a city with over a million people, three times the size of Taela, and only the Travelers remember its name."

"Where did it lie?"

"I don't know," answered Seraph. "It doesn't matter. The city is protected against intruders."

"Is?"

"As far as I know the city is still there—if it weren't, the Stalker would be free. The people died along with the less tangible things that make up a community and the bones of the city seal the Stalker's prison.

Jes turned from where he was examining one of the walls, which had a mural depicting a forest scene. "If this is all illusion, then why were the ancient wizards so concerned about the *mermori?*"

Seraph smiled and headed through a narrow doorway. The room beyond was twice as big as the first room and the walls were lined with shelves of books.

"This is what they tried to save—within these buildings is

all that they knew of magic. But many of the languages the
books are written in were lost. I know only four or five. My father knew more—and I fear they are lost with him, and with
the others who are gone, because I hold almost half the *mermori* that were made."

CHAPTER 4

"Go catch some fish for dinner, you two." Seraph made shooing motions at Lehr and Rinnie. "I'll take care of the breakfast dishes and getting the plowing equipment ready. There'll be work enough for us all in the coming weeks, and we've but little salt meat left. I for one will be glad of some river trout. You two pack a lunch and catch what you can."

"What about the stew we made with Jes's rabbit yesterday, Mother?" said Lehr. "There's plenty left. Checking the harness won't take all day; we should get started on the fields as soon as we can."

"Tomorrow is soon enough for plowing," Seraph replied firmly. "Gura ate the last of the stew this morning." Or he would as soon as she fed it to him. She needed time and quiet to think.

"Papa would not leave you unprotected," said Lehr, clearly torn between duty and pleasure.

Rinnie tugged at his sleeve. "I think Gura is enough to scare off anyone—you know how he is with strangers. And how often do people come here?"

Lehr clenched his jaw. "I haven't seen Jes this morning," he said.

"He spent the night in the woods," Seraph replied. "I expect he'll be back this evening. If you see him, you might tell him I'm baking bread today."

"He'll be home then for sure," said Rinnie. She'd already collected cheese and crackers in a cloth and was busy tying it together. "Come *on,* Lehr. If we don't get out soon, the fish won't bite."

His resolve broke. He kissed Seraph on the forehead, grabbed his sister's arm, and made for the barn, where they stored the fishing gear.

Seraph smiled after them and turned back to wash up after breakfast and begin mixing dough for bread.

"Aren't we going to the river?" asked Rinnie, lifting her skirts to scramble up a rise behind Lehr. It wasn't often that she got to join in on fishing expeditions. Usually it was just Lehr, or sometimes Lehr and Jes. When she went, she had to go with Papa and Mother.

"Not first. I thought we'd try the creek. Jes showed me a good place where he says the trout like to sun. I haven't tried it yet, but—"

"But if Jes says it's good, we're sure to catch something," replied Rinnie happily.

The soft leather sole of her shoe skidded on a rock, and Lehr turned and caught her shoulder to steady her before she fell.

"Be a little more careful," Lehr said sternly. "The rocks are still wet with snow runoff here. I don't want to bring you back with too much damage."

Rinnie made a face at him behind his back then paid strict attention to her feet so he wouldn't have to help her again. He wasn't a bad older brother—if he'd just quit trying to be Papa.

Rinnie watched her brother's back as he navigated the zigzag route through old downed trees. Hard muscle filled last year's shirt and stretched the shoulders taut. He'd need a new shirt soon. She sighed; she knew who would get to sew that shirt. Mother could sew, but she didn't like it.

She wondered when they'd meet up with Jes. She'd never gone out in the woods without him that he'd not come upon her sooner or later. Lehr liked to say it was the most dependable thing about Jes.

Jes worked hard, but he was as apt as not to leave the plow

in the middle of the field, horse and all, if the whim took him. He was always worse in the springtime. Papa said it was because the winter snows kept him too confined. By midsummer Jes would cut down his treks to once a se'nnight or so, rather than every day. Last year at harvest he'd worked almost the whole time.

Ahead of her, Lehr turned off the deer trail they'd been following and started down the steep side into a ravine and began skidding downhill. About halfway down he had to slow and pick his way through the underbrush that lined most of the lower ground. The branches caught at Rinnie's skirts until she fell some distance behind Lehr, who was already off the slope and starting up the valley. She tried to hurry and ended up with her hair tangled around the thorns of a wild rose.

"Wait up," she called, and began working the errant strand free with impatient jerks that did as much to worsen the mess as to free her.

"Wait up?" said an interested male voice from the ridge opposite the one she and Lehr had traveled to get here.

She jerked her gaze up to see Storne, the miller's son, with a couple of the boys he ran with peering down at her. Papa always said that the miller gave Storne too little to do. Leave a young man without a task, and he'll make mischief instead, he'd said.

Then Papa'd looked at her and told her to stay away from Storne when he had other boys with him, no matter how polite he was when they met at the mill, for a boy out to impress his friends will do things he wouldn't do on his own. The boys Storne had with him today were no prizes: Olbeck, the steward's son, and Lukeeth, whose father was one of the wealthier merchants from town.

Rinnie drew the knife out of her belt sheath and cut her hair, stepping out of the bushes. She made no move to leave, because you never run from predators. The knife she kept in her hand as if she'd forgotten about it.

"Rinnie?" Lehr called impatiently. He must not have heard Storne, who'd spoken no louder than he had to.

"Here," she called.

She didn't want to start trouble by implying that she was worried about Storne and the boys who watched her so she didn't say anything more, but something in her voice must have alerted Lehr because he came crashing through the trees at a run. His eyes roved over the strands of hair dangling from the rose bush and traveled uphill to Storne and his friends.

"Should have tied your hair up," he snapped.

Relief gave way to hurt that he would criticize her in front of such an audience.

"Well, if it ain't the little Traveler boy," said Lukeeth, sloe-eyed and slightly taller than Storne.

"Does your father know you walked out on your tutor again?" replied Lehr with such mildness that Rinnie's jaw wanted to drop, especially after the nasty way he'd blamed this on her. Lehr had Mother's quick temper and over the last couple of years, "boy" had become an epithet.

"My tutor wouldn't dare tell him," Lukeeth laughed. "Then I'd tell Father what the silly ass keeps in his water flask and he'd be out like the last one. That your little sister? Another Traveler's brat, just like you."

"Pretty thing," said Olbeck casually.

Rinnie began to get really worried. Lehr was tough; her father had taught him a few tricks, and her as well for that matter. But Olbeck was almost a foot taller than Storne—who was as big as Lehr—and he didn't have that soft look that most of the village boys had. She couldn't read his tone, but it sent the other boys off into laughter that sounded more predatory than happy.

"I'd heard you'd taken to running with scavengers, Storne," chided Lehr before turning to the ringleader. "Olbeck, I thought you'd decided to stay out of the woods after you ran into Jes that time last fall."

A flush rose in Olbeck's face. Lukeeth snickered but subsided when Olbeck glanced at him.

"Predators, not scavengers," said Olbeck. "You're just disappointed that Storne decided he'd rather hunt with the wolves than graze with sheep like you, Traveler's brat," he sneered. "As for your brother—if I'd realized he was crazy I'd have just slit his throat that day, a mercy killing, like I'd do to any other poor beast."

Until Olbeck's words reminded her, Rinnie'd almost forgotten that Storne and Lehr had once been best friends. But something had happened several years ago, Lehr wouldn't say what, and he'd even quit going with Papa to the mill.

"I'll tell Jes you'd like to meet him again," said Lehr pleasantly. "I'll relay your exact words to him. I'm sure he'll be impressed—since you've never so much as gutted a cow. Rinnie, why don't you go home and let us talk a bit."

"No, Rinnie," said Olbeck. He smiled at her, "I think you'd better just stay there. The two of us can have a *conversation* after we've finished . . . *conversing* with your brother."

Lehr turned to her and whispered, "Run, Rinnie, now. Don't stop until you get home."

Knowing that without her there, the other boys wouldn't be as interested in fighting, she fled back up the hill as fast as she could without looking back, the small knife cold in her fist. Home wasn't so far away. If she could get within hearing distance she could call Gura. Even a grown man would think twice before taking on the big dog.

She heard the dull thud of fist on flesh before she topped the ravine. But she couldn't worry about the fight now because at least one of them had gotten past Lehr and was trailing her up the side of the ridge. She could hear him crashing through the brush like an ox.

When she reached the trail and her footing was more certain she glanced back and saw that it was Olbeck who'd taken up the chase, and she stretched out to run as fast as she ever had.

With Olbeck following her, Lehr had a chance. Storne was the only one of the boys who had enough muscle to give Lehr a real fight. Her brother was tough as an old wolf; he'd use the rough terrain to his advantage.

The trail's upward slope robbed her legs of speed and her chest of breath, but she didn't dare slow down. Her eyes were focused firmly on the ground in front of her. When someone reached out and snagged her off her feet she thought it was Olbeck.

She kicked him once, before she realized it was Jes and stilled, gasping for breath. He set her down gently, the expression on his face different than she'd ever seen it. She didn't have time to understand what the difference was before he stepped in front of her and turned his attention to Olbeck.

"Thought I told you stay out of my woods," said Jes, only it didn't sound like Jes at all. Menace clung to his voice and promise. The familiar singsong softness was gone as if it had never been.

"These aren't your woods," said Olbeck, who'd stopped a few lengths down the trail, though he didn't sound intimidated. "My father is steward for the Sept. If these are anyone's woods, they are mine."

Safe behind Jes, she couldn't see the expression on his face, but Olbeck blanched.

"Run, boy," purred Jes. "See if you can outrun your nightmares."

Rinnie tried to step around Jes's shoulder, but he stepped sideways, keeping her behind him. Showing the whites of his eyes like a spooked horse, Olbeck turned and ran.

"There're still two fighting Lehr," Rinnie rasped and then threw up.

It was messy and nasty, as she had to gasp for air between convulsions. Jes gathered her hair out of the way and waited for her to finish.

"Ran too fast," he said. "Lehr's down that way?"

She spat to clear the taste out of her mouth. "Yes. Toward the fishing hole you showed him in the creek," she said. "It's Storne and Lukeeth."

Jes looked at her, and the oddness was still there—a sharpness she wasn't used to seeing. "All right, now?"

"Yes," she said.

He nodded and took off at a jog. It took her a moment to recover her breath. As soon as she knew she wasn't going to be sick again, she scrambled to her feet and headed down after Jes. Somehow with Jes there she wasn't afraid of the villageboys anymore. She wouldn't have thought that Jes, of all people, could make her feel safe.

Going down the trail was less demanding than her run up it had been. She made it to the place where Lehr had originally left the trail just as Jes was finishing a controlled slide to the bottom.

Rinnie looked down, half-afraid of what she'd see. But Lehr was safe. He held Storne in some sort of mysterious wrestling hold, and Lukeeth was lying unconscious nearby with blood running from his nose.

"Is Rinnie all right, Jes?" said Lehr.

"Fine," answered Rinnie for herself. "Jes scared Olbeck. From the expression I saw on Olbeck's face I bet he won't leave his house for a week."

"Good," grunted Lehr as he held on while Storne struggled with renewed energy. He waited until the other boy was still. "You drink too much," Lehr said calmly, "and you think too little. Just because Olbeck's father is the steward doesn't make him invulnerable or someone you should listen to—you're smarter than that. And to try and"—he paused and looked at Rinnie for an instant before changing what he was going to say. "You heard Olbeck. He likes to 'have conversations' with children now? My sister is ten years old, Storne. You are better than that."

It was strange hearing Lehr lecture someone else besides her or Jes. She could see that Storne felt that quiet voice cut through his skin, too.

Lehr stepped back and let Storne up. The miller's son brushed off his clothes and, with a wary look at Jes, turned to leave.

"Aren't you forgetting Lukeeth? If you leave him here he might never find his way out of the forest," Lehr said.

Storne hefted the other boy across his shoulders without a word, and started up the hill.

"You take care of your friends, I remember that," said Lehr softly. "But the question is, would they have taken care of you? Olbeck left you to us."

Storne spun around, almost overbalancing. "At least they can keep their tongues from wagging too freely. Unlike some I know."

"You idiots were going to get yourselves killed," said Lehr explosively, as if it was something he'd kept bottled for too long. "Swimming at night is a fool's game—and there are things in the river—"

"*Things.*" Storne spat on the ground. "So you went whining to your father who ran to tell mine. Let me tell you something, Traveler's brat. You don't know half what you think you do. You'd better just stay out of my way."

Jes put his hand on Lehr's shoulder, but no one said anything until Storne was at the top of the ridge.

"Is that why you aren't friends anymore?" asked Rinnie. "You told Papa they were going to go swimming in the river at night?"

Lehr shrugged. "That was the excuse. But Storne's friends didn't like that he ran around with a Traveler's brat. He would have dropped me sooner or later."

"Storne traded you for Olbeck?" she said, knowing how much it hurt him. She knew exactly how much it hurt; there were girls in town who wouldn't talk to her because Mother was a Traveler. "He is stupider than I thought."

"They are dangerous in a pack," said Jes. "If Rinnie had been alone . . ."

Lehr gave a jerky nod. "When Papa gets back, I'll talk to him about this. He'll know what to do to see that they don't hurt anyone." He reached up to pat Jes's hand, which was still on his shoulder. "Let's go home," he said.

Jes released his hold and picked up the fishing rods that lay scattered about on the ground where Lehr had dropped them. "Fishing's still good," he said.

Rinnie looked at him, but the air of danger that had surrounded him was gone, and he looked and sounded as he always did except for a certain lingering crispness to his voice.

Lehr touched his reddened cheekbone tenderly. "I suppose they'll not bother us anymore. Mother will be safe enough with Gura." He took a close look at Rinnie. "You look pale."

Rinnie smiled at him and tried to look less pale. "I'm fine. Ma's counting on a fish for dinner. You always bring one back; she won't have anything else ready."

So they went down to the creek and fished.

Seraph heaved a sigh of relief. The harness collar that fit Skew had been neglected, but the leather was only very dry, not cracked. If it had cracked they'd have had to wait until Tier got back with Frost before starting the plowing.

She oiled the collar carefully until the leather was butter-supple under her fingers. Then she turned her attention to the harness. She untied the leather strings that kept it together and oiled each piece as she went, carefully organizing the straps on the freshly swept floor of the tack room so she could put the harness back together when she finished. Broken down, the harness looked like random scraps of leather.

The first time she and Tier had taken it apart and oiled it, she thought they'd never get it back together correctly. Even Tier had been all but stumped. A grin pulled at the corners of her mouth when she remembered the look on his face when she'd called him in for help. Maybe if he had been the one who'd taken it apart he'd have stood a better chance. They'd finally taken Skew out and put the harness back together on him one strap at a time.

From his loose box in the stable, Skew snorted at her. He was frustrated that one of his people was near enough to see, but not near enough to give him the attention that was his due.

"Do you remember the look on the steward's face that first year when he came and saw the furrows we'd plowed?" Not the current steward, but his uncle, who had been a kind man. "No two lines anywhere near straight. None of us had ever plowed a field before."

The steward had come by the next morning and worked side by side with Tier for the whole day. He'd made a point of stopping by now and again throughout the season to lend a hand and dispense a bit of advice.

Skew wickered a soft entreaty at her, so Seraph set down the cropper and wiped her hands off on her skirts before rubbing Skew's face. The dark oil would clean off of her skirts better than it came off of Skew's white patches.

"How the old steward hated seeing you in that plow harness," she told the old gelding. "He offered to buy you from us, did you know? Offered two horses trained for farm work because he thought it disgraceful that a gentleman of your breeding should pull a plow. Tier said that a good soldier hates war, and you were a good soldier so farming would be all right with you."

She rubbed the ridge just in front of Skew's ear and smiled when he tilted his head sideways and closed his eye in pleasure. "You didn't mind the plow anymore than you minded pulling my wagon, did you?" She smiled again. "Tier says the best warhorse is one who'll do what he's asked."

Skew rubbed his head against her, knocking her back a step.

"So what do you think?" Seraph asked softly. "Am I seeing problems that don't exist? How much of a threat is one misguided priest? If I tell my children what they are, it'll change them forever."

"I should have told them a long time ago," she whispered. "Tier told me to. But they deserved a chance at . . . innocence."

She closed her eyes and rested her face against the old horse's neck, breathing in the sweat-straw scent of his skin. "I think it's time, though, old friend."

She stepped away. "They need to know what they are. I have no right to keep it from them, and the priest is a good excuse." She nodded her head briskly. "Thank you. Your advice is always correct."

She finished the harness, inspected the plow and found no significant damage from its winter in the barn, then returned to the cabin and started shaping her risen dough for loaves, putting some aside for fry bread as an after-dinner treat. She'd just taken the loaf of bread out to cool when Jes, Lehr, and Rinnie came in the door with three fat trout, cleaned and ready to cook.

Seraph took a good long look at the bruise on Lehr's face, the rips in Rinnie's clothing and the place where her hair had been hacked short. Only then did she take the fish Lehr held out to her.

"Jes and I'll set up the smoker and we'll smoke these two," Lehr said hastily and retreated outside with his brother.

With hard-won forbearance, Seraph set the trout on a baking tile, salted it, and filled the body cavity with onions and herbs. After wrapping it tightly in leaves, she used the peel to set the tile on the coals of the fire below the oven. She put the tool where it belonged, dusted off her hands, and turned to her daughter.

"Now," she said. "Just what happened today?"

Rinnie took a washing rag and began to clean the table. "We ran into a little trouble with Storne and his friends—Olbeck, the steward's son, and Lukeeth. I got caught up in some thorns and I had to cut my hair to get untangled. But Jes showed up and the other boys took off.

"Mother," Rinnie said, staring unnecessarily hard at the surface she was cleaning. "There was something odd about Jes.

I mean, he didn't do *anything* and Olbeck took off like a startled foolhen. Has Jes ever hurt anyone?"

Seraph took off her apron and rubbed her cheeks, hot from
the work with the ovens. It was indeed time for a few truths,
she thought, but not right now.

She gave Rinnie part of the truth. "For all that our Jes is different, he's strong and accurate with his fists—your Papa saw to
that. Olbeck came out poorly in an encounter with Jes not too
long ago."

After dinner, thought Seraph. *We'll talk after dinner.*

"This is as good as anything you'd find on the Emperor's
table," declared Rinnie, finishing the last of her fish.

"Thanks to the fearless fishing folk," agreed Seraph, already up and tidying.

She'd tried so long to let her children fit in with the life of
the village, and had hoped they'd be happy here, free of the
never-ending quest to protect people who feared and hated the
Travelers more than the things the Travelers fought. Tonight
that innocence would be over—but it wasn't fair to keep their
truths as her secrets either.

"Rinnie," Seraph said, abruptly impatient to talk. "Get the
basket of fry bread with a jar of honey. I think we'll take a
walk and find a good place to talk."

"It'll be dark soon," said Jes, sounding subdued.

Seraph gave him a straight look. "I think that might be just
what is needed. I have some things to discuss with you all that
will be easier to do in the meadow above the farm—and a few
of those things will be more believable in the darkness of the
forest than they will here."

"Mother—" began Lehr, but Seraph shook her head at him.
"Not now. Let's take a walk."

Jes was right; by the time they got to the meadow the sun had
sunk behind the mountains. There was still plenty of light, but
Seraph was glad of her warm cloak in the evening chill.

At her direction, her children sat in a rough semicircle and
divided the fry bread, consuming it like voracious wolves,
even Lehr. Sweets were not a common treat for any of them.

"I haven't told you much about my family," Seraph began abruptly.

"They were Travelers," said Rinnie. "Everyone but your youngest brother, Ushireh, died of plague brought by a Traveler they took in for the night. And when Ushireh was killed, Papa rescued you when you were a little younger than Lehr and Jes. *And* you blew up the bakery and Papa said you were married to each other before you really were to save you again. *And* I know about the Wizard Ancestors, too. They called up the Stalker and then killed everyone who lived in the city to contain it. But it didn't work as well as they'd hoped. So from that time until this the Travelers have had to fight the evil that leaks from the city."

Seraph laughed. "Right. But there is more to tell you." She looked at each of her children in turn. "Understand that this was my decision, not Tier's. I didn't want you to know about my folk. I wanted you to fit in with your father's people, but . . . there are things that you need to know."

She took a deep breath. "You know I am a mage."

"But you don't *do* any magic, Ma," said Rinnie suddenly in tones of complaint. "Aunt Alinath says that there are no such things as mages, just people who are good at making others see magic in ordinary sleight of hand."

Jes began to laugh. It wasn't his usual full-throated, joyful laugh, but something low and unamused.

Rinnie looked up at him and shifted a little away from him.

"Jes, it's not her fault," Seraph chided gently before looking at Rinnie. "I'm afraid your aunt is wrong—and she knows better, too. She was there when I blew up the bakery—your father was there as well. And despite what you've heard, not all Travelers are mages, nor are all mages Travelers."

"Remember the stories Papa told us sometimes, Rinnie," said Lehr, "about the mages in the army?"

"Right," agreed Seraph. "But I am a special kind of mage— a Raven."

The cool power slid over Seraph's skin like a lover's caress as she lit a mage fire in the palm of her hand. When the magic stabilized she took Lehr's hand and put the light in his palm where it flickered cheerfully.

"Let me tell the story from the beginning," Seraph said.

"There once was a great city of wizards who were arrogant in their power. In the blindness of pride, they called into being the Stalker, a great evil. To contain that evil they sacrificed the entire city, all of the non-wizard residents of the city, man, woman, and child—including their own wives, husbands, and children."

She took a deep breath and closed her eyes, trying to hear the cadence of her father's voice so that she didn't leave anything out. "When the wizards sacrificed their city to bind the Stalker, the cost of the magic they wrought killed all but a few of the most powerful mages and most of the very weakest. The survivors had virtually nothing but the clothes on their back. At first, they thought that would be enough, but the world is not kind to a people who have no place. As the years passed and the people dwindled, the remnants of the wizards of Colossae discussed what could be done."

She smiled a bit grimly. "Arrogant in their knowledge and power, even with their city sealed in death behind them, the wizards still meddled where they would. The Stalker was caged, but as time passed the bars of that cage would loosen. The wizards decided that their descendants, not having Colossae to nourish and educate them, would not be able to stand against the thing they had created, so it was decided to change their children and give them powers less dependent upon learning. They created the Orders."

"I'm a mage," she said. "There are other Traveler mages who are much like the Emperor's mages who helped Tier fight against the Fahlar. But I bear the Raven's Order. I don't need complex spells, I don't need to steal power as other mages do. I can do things that have not been written in a book and memorized. But the Raven is only one of six Orders bestowed upon Travelers."

Jes had withdrawn from the family until his face was hidden from the light of magefire. Seraph rose to her knees and stretched until she could touch his arm lightly.

"Peace, Jes," she said. "It's not just you—and I'm sorry I let you think it was. Your gift is just more difficult to hide."

Jes's gift was so terrible that there had been nothing she could do to shield him as she had the other children.

When he settled reluctantly where he was, she sat back down

and said, "I am Raven. But there are also Bard, Healer, Hunter, Weather Witch, and Guardian. But, like Mage, we call the Orders by the birds who are symbolic to each Order because it is less confusing. Ordinary wizards are also called mages, but Raven always means the Order of Mage. The other five Orders are thus: Bard is Owl; Healer is Lark; Hunter is Falcon; Weather Witch is Cormorant; and Guardian is Eagle."

She watched them closely, but they seemed to be following her words so she continued. "My father told me that once the Orders were far more common. Among my clan, in my generation only three of us were Order-bound, Raven, Eagle, and Falcon. Other clans fared less well—and I knew of only one Lark still living when I left the clans, and she was very old."

Seraph drew a breath and wondered how to say this next part. "Imagine my surprise, then, when all of you were born into Orders."

Lehr passed the light across the basket of fry bread to Rinnie and rubbed his hands on his thighs. "But there's nothing different about any of us," he said. "Except Jes. And his oddities are surely nothing that would have served the purposes of the Travelers."

"Nothing different about you? Isn't there?" asked Seraph softly. "Have you ever come back from a hunt without game, Lehr? Have you ever been lost, my Falcon?"

He stared at her scarcely breathing. "Father taught me how to track, and to remember things so I wouldn't get lost," he said tightly.

"Did he?" she said. "That's not what he told me."

"What am I, Mother?" asked Rinnie eagerly, staring into the light she held. "Can I make a light like this?"

Seraph smiled. "No. You are Cormorant—Weather Witch. Not everyone knows when a storm is coming, Rinnie."

"What about Jes and Papa . . . and Aunt Alinath?" asked Rinnie eagerly. "Lehr is Falcon, and that makes him a hunter, right? What do Falcons and Cormorants get to do if they can't build fires?"

"Papa and Aunt Alinath aren't Travelers," said Lehr.

"We're only half, and we have Orders," Rinnie defended herself hotly.

Seraph held up her hand. "Hold a moment. Let's see. Uhm.

Yes. Lehr is right, the Orders belong only to Travelers. Or that's what I always thought until I met your Papa. Tier is Owl—that means Bard. I've thought about it a lot over the years, but the only explanation I have is this: the old Raven who was my teacher told me that the Orders cannot be bred for as we breed for certain traits in horses. They attach to someone suitable to their purposes at the moment of birth." She smiled to herself. Her old teacher, Arvage, would have been outraged at the mere suggestion that an Order would attach itself to someone outside the Traveler clans.

She cleared her throat and continued, "In the Traveling clans, the Owl is responsible for keeping the history of the clans because one of their talents is for memory. But the Owl holds music, too—and music has always been a part of Tier.

"You had some more questions." Seraph clucked her tongue to her teeth as she checked her memory. "Falcons track and have some affinity for weaponry. Cormorants can predict—and, if they are careful, control the weather. There are more things, but I don't know them all. Some things vary from person to person; these things you will have to discover for yourself. Others"—she shrugged—"we might eventually have to find someone to teach you."

"What about Aunt Alinath?" Rinnie asked again.

"Your aunt is exactly what she appears—a *solsenti* baker."

"What does *solsenti* mean?" asked Jes abruptly.

"Stupid people," said Rinnie with smug wisdom. "Especially Aunt Alinath."

Seraph said, "Quit snickering, Lehr. In Traveler's speech *solsenti* means someone who's blind or crippled, but most of us use it to refer to anyone who is not of Traveler blood. Now, what else did you ask, Rinnie?"

"Jes," said Rinnie.

"Jes is Guardian."

"And Guardian is furthest from human," Jes broke in bitterly. "They took the spirit of a demon and bound it to their will. In the night I am this." He stood up and let his cloak fall so he stood before them all, revealed in the light Rinnie held. For a moment he was as human seeming as any of them, but then his shape flowed and darkened. A panther the size of Gura stood before them, his eyes gold flecked with an eldritch light.

It was the speed of the change that Seraph used to gauge whether what she saw was illusion or real. This time she was pretty certain the panther was solid and not created of her fears.

"The Guardian is the caretaker of the clan," said Seraph calmly. "Where danger threatens, in the forests, in the darkness, he adapts to protect us. No magic works on him except his own. In the daytime—and I'm not talking about just when the sun is up, but in safety—the Guardian sleeps, taking part of Jes with him."

Rinnie gave the light back to Lehr and walked all the way around Jes with wide eyes. Seraph could see her son cringe under that steady gaze, though he moved not a hair—but she had more confidence in Rinnie than Jes did.

"You're beautiful," said her daughter in awe, reaching out to touch the grey-black coat.

Lehr watched the cat narrowly, then laughed. "What, did you expect us all to shriek and run away, Jes? No one raised around Aunt Alinath could be afraid of a mere demon."

"I don't get to turn into a panther either?" asked Rinnie plaintively as she sat down next to Jes.

"No, only Jes," replied Seraph.

Lehr frowned. "If I'd known about this, I wouldn't have gotten so mad at you when you took off for the forest all the time," he said to Jes. "I suspect it'll take a few days for all of us to understand what Mother's told us tonight." He paused, then said the important thing. "I think you need to know that I'm glad you are my brother, day or night."

"Don't I even get fangs?" asked Rinnie.

The cat let out a huff of laughter and shifted back into a more familiar form. "No, Rinnie. No fangs for you." He reached over and ruffled her hair. "But don't worry. If you want me to bite someone for you, I will."

Jes settled back on his heels, though he didn't relax enough to sit. "Papa told me I should tell all of you, but I didn't want to. I didn't want you to be afraid of me."

Seraph frowned at him, "You know better than that," she said. "No matter what they really think, they're going to be a little afraid." Turning to the rest of them she explained, "Dread is one of the gifts of the Guardian. If he wants to, he can panic horses or wild game. But just his very presence will make people nervous. It's not that you are afraid of him, but that he triggers your fears."

Seraph smiled at a sudden clear memory. "My oldest brother was Guardian," she said. "He had a wicked sense of humor. He used to stalk people through the forest. They'd arrive at our camp panting in fear and trying not to show it, because there had been nothing to be afraid of. My grandfather used to scold him so." She shook her head in amusement at the memory of the bent old man shaking his finger at her brother, so fierce and large. He could have broken the old man with a single blow, but instead he'd stand there, head bowed as his grandfather chastised him—and a few weeks later another terrified wanderer would approach their camp.

"That's why Olbeck ran," said Rinnie. "Jes really did frighten him away."

Seraph nodded. "If it was only the dread, he'll remember that he ran, but not why he was afraid. It'll make him angry. He'll have to prove himself. Be careful."

"Mother," said Lehr. "Why are you telling us about the Orders, now?"

"It's that priest the new Sept brought back from Taela," Seraph said.

"I don't like him," said Jes abruptly.

"Have you met him?" asked Seraph, surprised; Jes hardly ever went into the city.

"I saw him once riding with the new Sept's hunting party," he answered. "I don't like him."

"Good," she said. "I'd like you all to avoid him if you can. There's something . . . odd about him."

"What?" asked Lehr with a sudden grin. "Does he turn into panthers or call light out of nothing?"

She smiled back, but shook her head. "He worries me." She explained what the priest had told her about his beliefs.

Lehr shook his head when she was done. "You mean a whole bunch of *solsenti*—possibly *solsenti* wizards, from the magic they've used to light their temple—have started a religion based on the Travelers' Orders?"

She nodded. "I thought you ought to know the truth of what you are before he managed somehow to corner you and feed you the muddle he and his religion have been brewing." She hesitated. "I should have told you sooner—and there's one other thing. I've never worried over it before because Travelers don't believe in fate the way those who live here do." And because Tier had always made her feel as if no evil could ever befall them. "For generations the Orders have been fading from the Travelers. Yet, from the marriage of Traveler and an Ordered *solsenti,* the first Ordered *solsenti* I've ever heard of, comes three Ordered children? My grandfather said, 'Where great gifts are given great evils come.' I want you all to be careful."

Jes flowed to his feet, all of his attention toward home. "Mother, there's someone riding into the farm."

CHAPTER 5

Even from the vantage point of the knoll behind the house, Seraph could only pick out vague shadows of horses near the porch, but Jes said, "It's the steward and a man in the Sept's colors—ah, him. I think it's the Sept's huntsman himself, Mother."

"Well," she said after a moment, "let's go see what they want." She led her brood out of the trees and down to the trail that led from field to house.

Gura barked welcome as they neared, and Seraph saw that he'd kept the men from approaching the house too closely. Now that Seraph was nearer to the house she saw the steward's distinctive braid, which he wore to hide the balding spot on the top of his head.

"Hello, Forder," Seraph said. "Welcome."

At the sound of her voice Gura quieted, his job done.

"Seraph Tieraganswife," said the Sept's steward. "Where have you been?" He asked it as if it were her fault he'd been kept waiting, as if he had clan-father rights over her.

Part of her flexed, like a cat testing its claws. So many years in Redern and she still couldn't get used to the way women were treated—as if being a man gave them the right to hold sway over any woman who crossed their paths.

Sensitive to her moods, Gura left the porch, a low growl hovering in his barrel chest. He quieted at her gesture, but stayed on his feet.

"We break ground tomorrow," Lehr said peaceably, drawing attention away from Seraph so that the steward wouldn't notice her gathering ire. "We took time to walk the fields tonight. Pray accept our apologies for keeping you waiting. We had no idea that you would come again today. If you had sent word we would have awaited your pleasure."

"No more had I intended to return," Forder grunted. Ignoring Seraph completely he addressed Lehr. "The Sept's huntsman has found something; I thought you should hear from him as soon as possible. If I'd known you had the habit of walking the forest in the night, I would have waited for a more convenient time."

If Lehr's hand hadn't tightened on her shoulder, Seraph would have said something rash. It wasn't like her to lose control of her temper so easily, but it was easier to cling to temper than to wonder why the steward, who was a man who enjoyed his comforts, would put himself to the trouble of coming here a second time in two days.

Bad news travels fast.

"Thank you," said Lehr, though he was enough his mother's son that he didn't apologize again.

"I was out with a pair of my men," said the huntsman, who upon close inspection was vaguely familiar to Seraph. He lived in Leheigh, where the Sept's keep was, but he'd come down to Redern a number of times to hear Tier sing in the tavern at the edge of the village. "We were up past the falls, tracking a deer that had taken an arrow, when we came upon what must have been a Blighted Place." He shuffled his feet uncomfortably.

Seraph reached up and took Lehr's hand in a fierce grip.

"I tell you," the huntsman said with sudden intensity, "I, my own self, have ridden by there a dozen times, and never seen anything untoward, but I can think of nothing else but the old evil left by the Shadowed that could have done what I saw."

"What was that, sir?" asked Lehr tightly when Seraph said nothing.

"The body of a grey mare," replied the huntsman. "Her hooves were scorched as if she had been burned in a fire—and

not much left but bones in front and a bit of flesh and hide behind. There was a human skull there, clean and white, and a
few bones. I knew that Tier was still out trapping, and one of
my men recalled that your husband had just bought a grey
horse. We buried the remains where we found them, as is
proper for Blight-kill but I brought what was left of the bridle
in hope we could identify the man."

He took a bag from his saddle and withdrew a handful of
leather, both scorched and cracked, and the half-melted remains of a copper bit.

When Seraph made no move to take it, Lehr freed himself
gently from her hold and took the scraps of leather and the bit.
He stared at it a moment, then knelt by the porch. He rearranged the pieces on the wooden boards until he revealed the
remains of a bridle with enough of the beaded browband left
that Seraph couldn't deny it belonged to her husband.

"It is my father's bridle," Lehr said. "Frost, the horse he
was riding, was dappled grey."

"I regret bringing you such news," said the huntsman, as if
he meant it.

"My father is usually home much earlier than this," said
Lehr.

"Papa?" said Rinnie.

Her voice broke through the numbness that encased Seraph.
She couldn't afford to lose herself in grief; she had children.
She took a step toward Rinnie, but Jes was already there, holding her against him. He nodded at Seraph: the Guardian would
watch over his sister until Seraph could send the steward on his
way.

"Where did you find them? I'd like to bring Tier home,"
said Seraph.

The huntsman didn't look at her, instead giving his answer
to Lehr. "There was nothing left but a skull, and we buried that,"
he said. "Shadowed magic is nothing to play with. I won't lead
a boy or a woman there. One man is already dead; there is no
need for more."

"I see," said Lehr over Seraph's soundless snarl.

"You know, of course, that I should serve you notice"—the
steward changed the subject—"since your brother is simple
and you are not yet fully of age. But it is too late to bring in

another family to farm, and you are a stout lad. The Sept will give you this year as a trial."

Lehr bowed his acceptance to Forder, and Seraph bit her tongue. No one else would farm this far into the mountains. If the steward drove them out there would be nothing for the Sept. But she knew Forder, knew that if she antagonized him enough he'd send them away for spite.

"The Sept is generous," said Lehr. "We will do our best to deserve the chance he gives."

"Huntsman," said Seraph, seeing a dim reflection of her own wild grief in his eyes. "Thank you. There are very few who would have the courage to get near a Blighted Place just to identify a dead man. Knowing is better than waiting with false hope."

Few men as well would have roused the steward to bring the news as soon as it came to him. It had been the huntsman, of course, who had forced Forder to come out at night instead of waiting until tomorrow. Gratitude and grief ripped through years of habit and she sketched a glowing sigil in the air that hung between them briefly.

"Traveler's blessing upon you," she said, "and upon your house. Good fortune hold by you and yours."

In the darkness she could see the whites of Forder's eyes, but the huntsman was made of sterner stuff, as befitted a man who braved Blighted Places.

"And to yours," he said with a quick nod before he mounted his horse.

As soon as the huntsman's foot was in the stirrup, Forder had his own horse in motion. Then they were gone, disappearing into the night, leaving only the lingering sounds of trotting hooves behind them.

Seraph ushered her children into the cabin and lit the fire with a wave of her hand. A corner of her mind noted how easily she shed the cloak of good Rederni wife she'd held to since she married Tier, but she tucked the thought back with her grief as she dealt with the more immediate problem of her children.

The Guardian lurked in the room like a restless spirit, adding fear to the mix of shock and sorrow. Rinnie clung to him, sobbing heartbrokenly. Lehr was pale and still wore the air of calm he'd donned for the benefit of the steward—but his hands held the remains of Tier's bridle in a white-knuckled grip.

Tier would have known how to ease their sorrow. He would have said something wise and soothing. He would have held Rinnie until she fell asleep. Then he would have talked to his sons until there was a bandage of comfort between them and their grief.

Seraph wanted to scream and rage until she was too tired to feel any more.

"There was nothing," she said, "that Tier loved more than you three."

Lehr's face whitened and she went to him and hugged him fiercely. She knew it was the right thing when he wrapped his arms around her and lifted her so he could press his forehead to the crook of her neck.

She would keep them safe, she vowed silently, as she had not been able to keep her clan or Tier. And if she cried, only Jes could see.

Rinnie fell asleep finally. Jes carried her up the ladder to her half of the loft and rejoined Seraph and Lehr where they sat on a bench in front of the fire.

"She wasn't afraid of me," he said.

Seraph smiled and patted the space beside her. "She didn't seem to be, did she?"

He didn't sit down. "Everyone is afraid, even you and Papa."

"And me," said Lehr with a tired smile that was more in his eyes than on his mouth. "Still, it is just a general unease, isn't it? I'm not really afraid of you, just twitchy."

Seraph nodded. "She might have felt that, but there are worse things than fear."

"People don't touch me," said the Guardian, looking down at his hands as if he missed the weight of Rinnie's warm body.

Lehr looked at him sharply, because Jes almost couldn't bear to be touched most of the time.

"You comforted her," said Seraph. "You reminded her that she wasn't alone."

The Guardian looked at her and between one breath and

the next became Jes again. "Oh, Mother," he whispered, "we are so sad." He dropped bonelessly to the floor in front of her and began sobbing softly with overwhelming grief.

Seraph started to put a hand on his shoulder, but caught herself. As overwrought as Jes was, he wasn't going to be able to stand her touch at all.

Instead, she got to her feet and opened the front door. "Gura," she said. "In."

The big dog gave her an astonished look—though during the day he sometimes came inside, at night he guarded the farm.

"In," she said again.

Gura padded past her to the fire. As soon as he saw Jes, he flopped out beside him with a sigh. Jes, unable to bear the distraction of human touch, wrapped his arms around the dog and pressed his face against him.

When Seraph sat back down beside Lehr he said, "Why doesn't he like to be touched—when . . ." he hesitated. "This is really confusing. Why didn't it bother him to be touched when he was being Guardian?"

"Jes is sensitive to the touch of others. Many of the Eagles have the gift of empathy. Because he must always keep the Guardian contained, a third person's feelings are just too much."

"You make it sound like he's two people."

Seraph nodded. "From what my oldest brother who was also a Guardian told me, it's very much like that. I don't know why the Eagle is so different from other Orders, why it is so much more difficult to bear. My teacher believed that the old wizards were trying to make something quite different—a superior warrior perhaps—and they made some mistakes: mistakes that Jes and those like him have to pay for all of their lives." She paused and glanced at Jes. He wasn't paying any attention to them, but she lowered her voice before continuing. "Most Eagles die before they reach Jes's age, so my people are very protective of them; we keep them away from strangers when we can, and don't speak of them outside of the clan. The Guardian is both the most dangerous and most vulnerable of all the Orders."

Seraph crossed her arms over her chest, realizing that his survival was up to her alone now. Lehr put an arm around her shoulder and drew her up next to him. "It will be all right, Mother," he said.

They stayed there until Jes's tears grew silent and Gura fell into a doze, snoring softly. Seraph wanted to do something, anything—but there was nothing more she could do to help Tier, nothing more she could do to help Jes, Lehr, or Rinnie. Her gaze fell upon the scraps of Tier's bridle.

She picked it up and left the bench for the better light in front of the fire.

"What are you doing, Mother?" asked Lehr.

"I'm going to see what this bridle has to tell me," said Seraph, sounding much more confident than she felt. She had failed her Order so badly that it seemed wrong that it hadn't failed her. "I told you that within each Order, there is still some variation in abilities. One of the things I could do that my teacher could not was read an object's past."

"You're going to see what happened to Papa?"

"I'm going to try," she said.

She took a deep breath and braced herself, because reading objects closely associated with death was painful. Tentatively she rested her fingers on the browband. Delicacy was more important than power in this kind of magic. She let threads of magic drift through her fingers and touch the leather.

Nothing.

Thinking she'd misjudged the necessary power, she opened herself until the ends of her fingers tingled—still nothing. She pulled her fingers away as if they had been burned.

"Lehr, could you find something . . ." Seraph's gaze scanned the room and brushed the corner where Tier's sword hung under Lehr's bow. The sword certainly had enough history for her to read. "The sword. Get the sword for me, please."

"What's wrong?" asked Lehr as he took the sword down and brought it to her.

Seraph shook her head and took the sword and unsheathed it. "I don't know." She set the bridle aside and lay the sword on the floor. She had to push Gura to get him out of the way, disturbing Jes, who sat up.

"Papa's sword," he said.

She nodded absently at him and rubbed her fingers together lightly, waiting until she felt the magic ready and eager—just as it had been when she touched the bridle. She opened herself as widely as she could to the traces time left on objects and touched—death and darkness.

She had a moment of fiery pain as gold light gathered under her fingers, then it was gone. She opened her eyes and had the odd feeling that time had jumped without her noticing. Her ears rang, her elbow felt bruised, and she was lying back with her head on Jes's knee.

Jes patted her cheeks gently, his eyes flickering with the Guardian's presence. "Did the sparks hurt you, Mother?"

"No, Jes," she said, sitting up on her own and resting her head on her raised knees while visions from the sword flashed behind her closed lids.

"I'm fine," she said, seeing Lehr's anxious look. "Just a bruise or two. I haven't done this in a long time, and I misjudged. The sword was a poor choice."

Solsenti warriors used their blades for generations until rust robbed the blade of its strength. They even named them, never dreaming of the pseudo-life imbued by so much death— or the danger in giving such a thing a name. There were stories about swords that held against all odds and others that tended to slip and bite their wielder, but *solsenti* never seemed to heed the warning. Travelers cleansed their weapons after each life taken and discarded the blades of dead men.

Tier's sword was old. Newly sensitized, Seraph could feel its hunger for Tier's hand and battle even though it lay several handspans from her skirts. But the Tier the sword longed for was a version of her husband Seraph had never seen: a cold-faced killer who let his sword drink its fill of blood.

Seraph touched the bridle again, running her fingers over the blue and red beads on the browband, lingering on the bit. After a moment she felt a dullness, the bare touch of Lehr's grief as he held the bridle, a dusting of time lacking in power. As if the bridle, bit and all, had somehow come into being just a few days ago.

"Nothing," Seraph growled in frustration. Her hand fisted on a scrap of leather, both hand and leather glowing with power, but there was no flash of vision, only emptiness, as if whatever trap Tier had sprung had wiped the bridle's history clean.

"What does it mean?" asked Lehr.

She shook her head. "I don't know. Tier's death should be emblazoned upon the bridle. I haven't done this in a very long time, but I didn't have any trouble reading the sword."

"It was Shadow Blight," Lehr reminded her. "Maybe the Shadowed's magic affected it."

Seraph frowned. It felt as if the bridle had been wiped clean of its past, not blasted with magic. "Fire or running water can clean something of its past; I suppose Shadow Blight might do the same."

Weary in spirit more than body, Seraph rubbed her face. "Jes, could you put Papa's sword in its sheath and then put it away?" She didn't want to touch it again. Logically she shouldn't sense anything unless she looked for it, but she could feel it waiting. "We'd better get to sleep. Tomorrow you two will have to start plowing. I will take word of Tier's death to your aunt and uncle."

Seraph waited until they were all asleep before sneaking out. She used enough magic to keep from disturbing Jes or Gura, both still curled up before the coals of the fire.

She walked until she was far from the cabin; the ground was uncomfortably cold on her bare feet. When she stopped, she bowed her head against the rough bark of a tree, seeking the peace resident in its stolid, slow-growing, long-lived presence— but all she felt was rage.

It seethed from the soles of her feet and coiled through her body until it was forced into the long strands of her hair. Her hands shook with it as they curled and clawed at the hapless tree. Her breath left her throat in a low, moaning growl.

And with the rage came magic, destructive and hot, and as aimless as her wrath. Because the focus of her anger, of her pain, was dead.

"Tier," she whispered and then in a voice of power that shook the ground under her feet, she asked, *"Why did you leave me?"*

* * *

"Listen to Jes," Seraph told Lehr the next morning. "He'll take care of Skew and see that he doesn't overdo. Skew's going to have to do the whole field and you'll have to watch to see that he doesn't hurt himself."

"Yes, Mother," said Lehr patiently. Seraph was pale, tired, and obviously dreading the trip into town—and he didn't blame her.

"Rinnie, make sure to run water out to the boys a couple of times this morning. That's more important than getting the garden done."

"Yes, Mother," said Rinnie in such a blatant imitation of Lehr's tone that he had to turn aside so no one saw his grin.

"Right." Seraph gave a quick nod. "I should be back in time to fix the midday meal—but if not, there is bread, honey, and cheese." With that she turned on her heel and began walking briskly up the path toward town, leaving her children to begin their assigned tasks.

They rested Skew rather more often than Lehr would have, but he let Jes decide when to stop. After each rest, Lehr and Jes traded who held the plow. The soil was somewhat rocky, and the plow bucked and wallowed unexpectedly until they were as tired as the horse.

By midmorning Skew's head was low, and sweat washed out from under his harness. They'd made some headway: five mostly straight furrows in and twenty-three more to go. Lehr walked beside Jes, whose turn it was to hold the handles. The long reins trailed though the metal hoops in the harness down Skew's back and wrapped around Jes's shoulders so when he stopped, so did Skew.

"He can't be tired again," protested Lehr. "We haven't come fifty paces since the last rest."

"Hush," commanded Jes.

Lehr had quit looking for the stranger inside his brother about halfway up the first furrow, but he saw him now.

Abruptly Lehr realized how still the land was. Not a bird sang; not a cricket chirruped. Silently he unbuckled the sheath that held his long knife and rested his hand on its haft. The forest seemed somehow darker than it had been just a moment earlier.

Skew's head came up and he tested the wind with fluttering nostrils. Tossing his mane uneasily, he wickered once.

Whatever it was that Lehr was watching for, it wasn't the man who stepped out of the woods. He was slight and dark, but otherwise unremarkable—until Lehr met his gaze.

Fathomless black eyes examined him coolly, and the hair on the back of Lehr's neck crawled.

"Hunter," said the stranger.

Lehr's eyes told him that the man in front of him was a nondescript man dressed, more or less, like any other man to be found wandering in the woods. But another sense was ringing like an alarm bell, warning him that he stood before a Power.

Skew shoved his nose against Lehr's arm and breathed in little huffs, ears pinned forward as if he perceived some threat and readied himself to do battle.

Lehr glanced at Jes, who stood at his back, watching the stranger steadily but without tension.

Turning back to the man, Lehr half bowed, because it felt as if he should. "Sir. What can we do for you?"

The man smiled, but his too-knowing eyes stayed cold and clear like the river in winter. "I found a child wandering my forests alone. She smells like one of yours, so I thought I would offer her to you rather than the wolves."

"Rinnie?" asked Jes, glancing toward their home, but when Lehr looked too, Rinnie was plainly visible planting the kitchen garden with Gura stretched out nearby.

"Go ahead, Jes," said Lehr. "I'll keep at the fields until you get back. She's probably one of the villagers, so you might have to take her all the way to Redern."

Jes ducked out of the reins and followed the dark man into the woods without a word. Lehr remained by Skew's head until the gelding quit staring into the trees.

Rubbing under Skew's browband where the sweat gathered, Lehr spoke quietly to the horse, "I believe you and I have just met the forest king. I always thought he was just a fancy of Jes's." So many strange things had happened in the past few days that the forest king rated no more than a shake of the head before Lehr turned to take up the plow again.

* * *

The Guardian paced beside the boar who was the forest king and tested the area for threat. Finding none, he allowed his ire full sway.

"You will leave my brother alone," the Guardian said in a voice that held the winter winds.

The boar snorted, unimpressed. "Why would I do that? Your brother's ties to the forest are closer than yours. Something has happened to him to make him aware of his power. If I had called you today as I usually do, he would have heard me. It was time to acknowledge the Hunter. I cannot say I welcome him, for it is my job to protect those within my realm. But your brother has long hunted these forests and he does not kill indiscriminately. Death is seldom a welcome guest, but it has a place in the life of the forest."

"Just leave him alone—he takes on enough without you."

The boar laughed, his hoarse voice squealing high in merriment. "Am I so chance a comrade then, Jes?"

"Who is being dragged through the forest at your whim?" returned the Guardian roundly. "I should be helping my brother coax Skew over the fields rather than chasing off after some child."

"Not that kind of child," grunted the boar, scrambling over a largish log in his path. "I believe that she's older than you." He seemed to find amusement in something, for he snorted a while before continuing. "Child of Travelers she is, though not exactly like you or your brother either. She passed me by as I was eating my breakfast this morning and the smell of her magic intrigued me, so I followed her."

The Guardian waited until he was certain the boar wouldn't continue without prompting. "Where did she go?"

"Through my lands," said the forest king. "I almost stopped at the border, but by then I was curious. I followed her to a place where magic blackened the ground and a new rip in the earth contained the body of a horse—a grey mare who used to graze in your fields."

"You know where my father was killed," said the Guardian slowly.

"Your father is dead?" The boar considered it a moment. "I tell you what I saw: it is up to you to discover what you'll take from it. But first you must deal with the child—or allow me to do so."

The Guardian knew how the boar would deal with one he must have decided might be a threat. The Guardian recognized the same grim spirit lived inside of him as well—though he'd never killed anyone. Not yet. Never wanted to kill anyone—because he was afraid that by that act, something the daytime Jes could not comprehend, he would somehow sever the ties that held the two disparate parts of himself together.

"What did you find at my father's grave?" asked the Guardian. "My mother thinks that there was more to his death than we have been told."

"Your mother may be right," said the forest king. "But that is not for my judgment."

By this time, the Guardian was fairly confident he knew where the forest king was taking him. There weren't actually all that many places to store a person safely in the woods without worrying what might happen to them—even for a spirit as powerful as the forest king.

The old building was so covered in vines and surrounded by trees that it was impossible to see from the outside. It was, as far as he knew, the only building he'd ever been in that had been built before the reign of the Shadowed. The only entrance required some undignified scrambling for anything larger than the boar.

Not knowing exactly what he would face, the Guardian chose to stay in human form and crawled under the foliage, through the crumbling tunnel that had once held water and still bore the mark of ancient algae.

Inside, the boar waited with bright red eyes that glittered in the dark interior, standing over a sleeping person who certainly was no child. Pale Traveler's hair looked more silver than ash in the faint light that poured in through the leaves that guarded the barren rafters that must once have been thatched.

"Traveler," said the Guardian, crouching down and pushing her hair aside to reassure himself that it wasn't his mother who lay there. But the features of the woman who lay sleeping in the forest king's lair were those of a stranger, younger than his mother—but as the boar had said, older than Jes was. "You say she came from town?"

"Yes. She came from the town, walked almost directly to the place where the horse lay dead then started back." He paused. "She wasn't going back to town."

"Where then?" asked the Guardian.

The boar stared at the sleeping woman. "It looked to me as if she were headed directly toward your home. But there is dark magic about her, and power. Her path would have taken her through the heart of my lands, and I decided I preferred that she not trespass unguarded."

The Guardian contemplated the woman. Was it someone his mother knew? Seraph hadn't mentioned finding another Traveler in the village the day before yesterday. Surely she would have said something if she had.

"Will you awaken her?" said the Guardian finally, deciding that her mysteries would be better answered by the woman herself. "Or do you wish me to take her away from this place first?"

"Take her." The forest king turned back toward the entrance of the building. "When you are far enough from here, I'll lift the sleep from her."

The Guardian sighed; though the woman was slight, the tunnel was narrow. Still, he gathered her up and scrambled his way out with only a few extra bruises—on him. He managed to keep her safe from harm.

In the sunlight he could see what features she shared with his mother and what differences marked her. His mother was a smaller woman, and this woman had a thinner, longer nose that gave her face an arrogant beauty.

He'd never seen anyone except his family who bore Traveler blood. He wondered where her people were, if they were among those who were killed or if they awaited her somewhere.

Walking in the woods with the sun on his back, Jes slowly filtered into being, easing the Guardian to sleep. Untroubled by his burden he continued on toward home. Mother would know what to do with her.

They were close to the edge of the woods when she stiffened. He glanced down at her and saw that her eyes were open. He smiled into pale eyes that matched her hair and continued on, ignoring her attempts to get down. If she were on foot it would be harder to bring her home, and Jes knew that he needed to take her home so she would be safe from the forest king.

When she couldn't free herself, she began asking him rapid questions that ran through his ears like rain, first in words he could have understood if he'd bothered, then in the liquid silver tongue that his mother used sometimes when she was very angry or very sad.

"Hush," he said, shaking his head, and he began humming the song his mother had used to sing Rinnie to sleep when she was a babe and fretting in the night.

She stilled at his song, then said slowly, "Who are you?"

"Jes," he said.

She stared at him a moment, "I can walk."

He hesitated. "You have to come with me."

"I'll come with you—but let me walk."

He set her down then, but kept a grip on her hand because he liked the way it felt. She was closed down so he didn't feel the annoying buzzing of her thoughts, just the warmth of her skin. His mother could do that, too.

"You don't look Traveler," she said, almost to herself.

"Mother's a Traveler," he replied. "Papa's a Rederni."

"What happened to me?"

But he'd said as much as he was going to. It was too complex and he couldn't be bothered explaining everything. He shook his head at her and continued toward home.

The field they'd been plowing was empty, the plowshare raised out of the ground and cleaned of soil and dampness to keep it free of rust. If it had looked like rain, Lehr'd have brought it in.

With a glance at the sky, Jes measured the time he'd spent in the woods. As usual, it was longer than he'd thought but not so long that Lehr should be finished plowing. Something must have happened to Skew.

He started to increase his pace, but slowed when the woman stumbled beside him. She didn't have the knack of walking over plowed ground. He swooped, picked her up, and carried her over their field. Remembering her request, though, he set her down on the other side and continued his determined course to the barn.

Lehr carried a heavy, steaming bucket to the barn and was oblivious to them until Jes called out his name.

Lehr halted and set down the bucket. "Jes? I thought you were out looking for a child?"

Jes frowned. "I found her in the woods," he said, because it somehow fit Lehr's questions. "Is something wrong with Skew?"

"No, no," his brother automatically soothed, staring at the woman. "He's fine. But he was so tired, I thought it would be better to stop. I'm bringing him some hot bran mash and Rinnie's giving him a rubdown so he's not so stiff and sore tomorrow." He frowned. "Jes, who *is* this?"

Jes frowned back, though he knew his frown wasn't as impressive as Lehr's. "This is the one I was sent for," he said.

Lehr smiled suddenly and shook his head. "All right, Jes. Good afternoon, lady. I am Lehr Tieraganson. You've already met my brother Jes."

The stranger he'd brought back with him tugged at Jes's hand gently and he released her.

"I am called Hennea," she said. "I am looking for the Traveler called Seraph."

"This one went to where Father was killed," said Jes, because the Guardian reminded him that it was important. "The forest king followed her and then held her for us. He thought she was coming here, which was fine with him."

"So why did he send for you?" asked Lehr after a moment, and the woman, Hennea, looked as if she'd like to know, too.

Jes sighed. "I'm not sure." But it was something Mother should know, and Lehr would remember to tell her. So he prodded the Guardian, who could make a better answer.

Lehr took a step back when the Guardian came, and that made Jes sad. The Guardian didn't like frightening his family.

"The forest king said that she had dark magic and power and he didn't want her in his territory."

Jes came back quickly, because the Guardian was unpredictable and might decide that the woman could be a threat to his territory, too. Jes didn't want him to scare her because . . . because he liked her.

"Dark magic?" asked Lehr, with a look at Hennea.

She put out her hand and showed him her wrist and tapped on the bracelet there. Jes didn't like it, nor did the Guardian—it smelled wrong.

"I expect that he's talking about this. Who is the forest king?"

Lehr smiled suddenly and shrugged. "I don't know, actually. I thought he was a story that Jes made up until I met him today." He turned to Jes. "Who is the forest king?"

Jes squirmed, uncomfortable with all the attention that they had been paying him. The Guardian didn't like people looking at him too much. "He's the forest king," he mumbled, almost forgetting the question in his discomfort.

Lehr seemed to sense how Jes was feeling because he said, "Come with me," picked up the bucket, and continued out to the barn.

Depressed and weary of both grief and anger, Seraph almost didn't notice that there was something wrong as she walked up to her cabin.

Alinath had already heard about Tier—Forder had stayed overnight in Redern and spread the news. She'd approached Alinath expecting to deal with shock and grief, but found Tier's sister waiting for her with anger and blame, instead.

It was only when Gura didn't greet her that Seraph set the stress of the unhappy meeting she'd had with Alinath aside and looked around. The boys weren't in the field, and Rinnie wasn't working in the garden.

She whistled and was rewarded with a bark, and Gura dashed out of the barn to welcome her with a wuff of apology for his tardiness. He followed at her heels as she headed for the barn.

Something must have happened to Skew, she thought.

The interior of the barn was dim in comparison to the afternoon light, so she was still half-blind when she heard Lehr say, "Here she is, now. Mother, we have a visitor."

As her vision cleared, Seraph saw Skew with his head buried in a grain bucket. Rinnie was standing next to him with a brush in her hand. Jes slouched against the barn wall a few feet from Lehr and a woman: a *Traveler* woman wearing a *solsenti* dress who stared at Seraph with pale eyes.

Seraph felt her eyebrows climb in surprise and instinctive dismay. She had enough trouble on her hands, and a lone Traveler could only be bringing more.

"I am Hennea," the woman said. "Raven of the Clan of Rivilain Moon-Haired."

"Seraph, Raven of the Clan of Isolda the Silent," replied Seraph. She waited and Lehr obliged her.

"Jes's forest king came this morning," he said, sounding a bit bemused. "He told us that there was a child loose in the woods and asked Jes to fetch her. Jes brought Hennea back. He told me that the forest king didn't want her in his territory because she held dark magic and power."

"This is dark magic," said Hennea, holding up her wrist.

Seraph closed the distance between them and set her hands on either side of the leather and bead bracelet. "*Solsenti* wizardry," she said shortly. "A *geas?*"

Hennea nodded. "Yes."

Seraph knew of only one wizard anywhere near Redern. "Volis the priest has bound you to his service?"

Hennea smiled faintly. "Yes."

He'd been hiding her then. Seraph had not the slightest doubt that if any of the villagers knew that there was another Traveler in the vicinity they would have told her so.

"I can help you rid yourself of this." Seraph didn't know the exact method, but she was confident it would be in one of Isolda's books: wizards of Isolda's time had been fond of binding others to their services. Any spell that could break a spell woven by the Colossae wizards could be adapted to sever the bonds of a *solsenti* wizard without too much trouble.

"No," said Hennea, curling her hand into a fist. "Not yet. When the time comes I will rid myself of it."

"Jes said the forest king told him that she went directly from Redern to the place where Father was killed. From there, he thought that she was trying to reach us," Lehr's voice was neutral.

"Ah," said Seraph, narrowing her eyes at the other woman. "Why don't you tell me more about yourself, Hennea, Raven of Rivilain Moon-Haired?"

"Thank you," said Hennea, who appeared to have been

waiting for Seraph's invitation. "I am no Owl, so I ask that you bear with my tale as I tell it. Two years ago I and my lover, who was a Raven and my student, were taken by *solsenti* wizards who bound us with Raven magics."

How could solsenti *bind with Raven magic?* Hennea paused as if she expected Seraph to ask, but Seraph seldom interrupted. Doubtless it was a question to be addressed later in Hennea's story.

When Seraph said nothing, Hennea continued. "We were taken to some sort of stronghold where these wizards—there were six of them and some greater number of lesser wizardlings, performed a ritual of magic upon me."

She stopped again, but Seraph didn't think it had anything to do with her audience. It looked more as if she were fighting the memory's hold; her hands were clenched at her side and sweat gathered on her forehead. Jes stepped forward and set a hand on Hennea's shoulder, the unexpected action telling Seraph that the Guardian had accepted Hennea.

"Are the details of the spell important now?" asked Seraph more gently than she'd first intended.

"Not now," said Hennea. "Only that their magic failed. They blamed the failure on one wizard who had not done the spell before—Volis. They coached him, and tried three more times. After the last time they conceded that the spell had been performed perfectly, but that something about the way it had been misworked the first time had rendered me an unfit subject. So they took Moselm, he who was my student."

She was breathing heavier now, and Seraph saw her blink hard. "I didn't even notice at first—I was too wrapped up in my own pain—but then he began screaming and screaming."

She closed her eyes briefly, as if that could shut out the sound. With her eyes closed, Hennea looked very young; Seraph had thought her ten years older than Jes, but she wasn't so certain now.

"When they finished with him," Hennea said, "they took him out of the room, still screaming. I never saw him again. I didn't even know what their spell casting did because I was too raw from what they had done to me."

She gave Seraph a bitter smile. "These wizards were as confident as if they had come fresh from Colossae. They talked of killing me, as I was no good for their purposes, but the young wizard—Volis, who is the priest of their twisted religion here—asked if he might keep me to see if he could discover what he had done. So they let him bind me with this"—she held up her wrist—"and made me his plaything."

"I accused them of arrogance," she said. "But I was arrogant, too. I could have broken free of this *geas*—it might hold a *solsenti* wizard or even a Traveler who was not Raven, but as you have seen, it will not hold a Raven long. But they presented a puzzle to me. How had *solsenti* wizards worked Raven magic? Even more worrisome, I didn't think that we were the first Ravens they had taken. They knew too well how to neutralize anything I might have done for my defense—and with the exception of Volis, they had all performed their ritual before. I reasoned that whatever they had done to Moselm, it had already been done. If I could reverse it, I could reverse it later as well—after I discovered what they were doing."

"So you waited," said Seraph.

Hennea nodded. "For a year or so I bided my time and learned what I could. We were in Taela secreted within the Emperor's own palace. The wizards ruled over a group of *solsenti* called the Secret Path of the Five Gods. I saw only the wizards, who are relatively few, but there are apparently many others, all men—noblemen and high-ranked merchants and the like—men of power."

"Volis seemed sincere in his devotion," said Seraph. "Obsessive even. Not a man who is seeking after political power."

Hennea nodded. "Oh, they take themselves very seriously, including this religion that someone thought up a few centuries or so ago as a way to encourage bored young noblemen to join up. Can you think of anything a young man would like better than to shock his family? Worshiping like a Traveler is beyond offensive."

"Travelers don't worship gods," said Rinnie, who'd been brushing Skew as Hennea talked.

"No, indeed," agreed Hennea. "But Volis doesn't believe that. We Travelers like to keep our secrets, and he thinks he knows them. He likes me to spout his own theories back to him. I don't think he really knows how this *geas* really works. He thought it made"—she glanced over her shoulder at Rinnie and gave Seraph an ironic smile—"made us friends. But he likes to believe in lies. One night, while we were still in Taela, he came into his rooms a little worse for drink—something he seldom did. He was wearing a crude ring made of silver and rose quartz and reeking of tainted magic." She sat down abruptly on the small bench Rinnie used as a mounting block.

"Unto Raven it is given to know the Order," she whispered. "Somehow they had stolen Moselm's Order and put it into the ring. Volis was drunk from celebrating Moselm's death—and worried because it hadn't gone quite as planned. It seems that capturing the Order once it's taken from a Traveler is very difficult and sometimes fails."

"They did what?" asked Seraph, appalled.

"They killed him and retained the power of the Order in the stone," said Hennea with Raven calm. "Their spell slowly rips the Order away from a Traveler over a period of some months. Many of the stones are all but useless, but the ones that work can be worn in a ring or necklace. Then the *solsenti* wizards become Raven, Falcon, or Cormorant as they wish."

Dread closed Seraph's throat. It was starting again, as if the *mermori* had been harbingers of things to come. Tier had died, and now Seraph would be forced to live as she had before she met him.

"I don't know what I can do to help you," she said at last, because, in the end, there was no choice. "I can take a message to the clans, though I don't know where any are at present. I will give you what aid I can."

"You don't understand," Hennea said. "I've come to help you."

CHAPTER 6

*"You **are going to help** me?"* asked Seraph. "With what?"

Hennea smiled grimly. "Your new Sept travels with quite an entourage."

"Including you and Volis," Seraph said. "Is the Sept one of the . . . what did you call them, something stupid . . . the Secret Path?"

"The Sept?" she said. "No, not him, at least I don't think so. He's charismatic, the Emperor's best if not only friend, and he's very good at political games. No one is surprised at the number of people who follow him around. Volis said that someone called in a few debts and offered a favor or two so that the Sept would agree to build a Temple of the Five Gods here."

Hennea stood up and began pacing in abrupt, quick steps. "The Secret Path decided to bring the religion out into the public. They don't tell people that they get their five gods from the Travelers' Orders, of course."

"There are six Orders," observed Rinnie.

"They don't know about the Guardian," said Jes. "Travelers don't talk about their mistakes."

"You are not a mistake," said Seraph, though Jes was more

right than wrong about the Travelers' reasoning regarding the Guardians. "Travelers protect the Guardians' secrets because your Order works better that way." As if that settled the matter, Seraph turned back to Hennea, and sorted through her story for some way to change the subject. "Why did this Path of yours change and decide to bring their church to the masses?"

Hennea shook her head. "I don't know. Volis thinks that it's because the truth must be made known—but Volis wouldn't know the truth if it tore his throat out. I don't think that all of the wizards believe in their made-up gods, so there must be another reason."

"Volis told me they chose to set his temple here because of Shadow's Fall."

"I've heard him say that, too," agreed Hennea. "I don't know what they want with Shadow's Fall, but I suppose that whatever power still lurks there can defend itself more than adequately."

"Indeed," said Seraph. "My husband is proof of that."

"No," said Hennea. "I don't think that he is."

Seraph stiffened. "Oh?" she said softly.

"There were some wizards who traveled with us from Taela. They stayed with the Sept when Volis moved us into the new temple." She stopped her pacing to frown down at Seraph. "Understand, please, that I've had to take a few facts and string them together. A few days ago, Volis got some correspondence from Taela. It wasn't signed, but from the content I think that it was from one of the wizards who came here with us. The letter devoted an entire paragraph to your family—unless there is another family with a Raven, Falcon, and Cormorant?"

"No," said Seraph softly.

Hennea nodded once and began to pace again. "Someone's taken a Raven's eye to your home—and a real Raven would know that you had a Guardian, too. So it must have been one of the Path's wizards wearing one of their stones."

Seraph nodded.

"I'd been listening to talk since we came here, and I heard of a Traveler mage married to a *solsenti* farmer. Since it was unlikely that any other Travelers had settled here, I could only suppose that you'd been blessed with two Ordered children, half-blood or not. I decided to warn you as soon as I could, though there seemed to be no particular urgency. Then, last night, a man came to tell Volis that your husband's dead horse had been found with a few human bones. Tier's dead, they said, and they mourned the loss of his music."

Hennea stopped again, rubbing her wrist absently. "And I thought on that letter I'd read. The first line read, 'we have the Owl safe here.' "

Seraph froze as her heart leapt to her throat. "By Lark and Raven," she said, imbuing the words with compulsion, "do not mislead me on this."

Hennea nodded to herself in satisfaction. "Your husband was Traveler and Owl and they took him to Taela to work their magic on him."

"My husband was Rederni born and bred—but given to the Order of the Owl," corrected Seraph absently to give herself time to regain control. *Tier was alive?* "If there was Traveler blood in his lineage it was a long time ago."

"Ah," said Hennea, revealing mild surprise. "I've never heard of something like that." She rubbed her wrist again. "Anyway. I waited until Volis left on business this morning and set out to find the place where the huntsman found your husband's horse. It wasn't difficult to follow the huntsman's trail."

"What did you find?" asked Seraph, her voice so soft that Lehr shifted uncomfortably.

Hennea shook her head. "Not much." She shivered and clenched her hand over her wrist where Volis's *geas* band held her. "I have to get back soon." She straightened slightly and continued, "The huntsman and his men buried both the horse and the skull, and I had no means to dig them up. I found hints of old magic, but nothing that would cause a person's death. There were a few tracks—but I'm not a Falcon to be certain of anything the tracks could tell."

"Lehr is," said Rinnie.

"Yes," said Hennea, "I know. I had hoped to prove my suspicions before I talked to you—but I'm unlikely to get a chance to come so far again. Take your Falcon and find out what they did. Then come and help me deal with Volis—and I'll help you find your husband."

"I don't like leaving Rinnie alone," said Lehr as he led Seraph through the partially plowed field.

"She'll be safe with Gura," Seraph said, though she wasn't happy with it either. "And Jes will be back soon."

She'd certainly be safer at home than investigating a place that might have been Shadow Blighted. If Seraph hadn't needed Lehr's help, she'd have found some way to leave him behind, too.

Jes, she'd found excuses to send off with Hennea. The forest king's territory extended on either side of the trail to town, but Jes thought that as long as he was with her the forest king wouldn't stop Hennea a second time. The *geas* had obviously been very painful by the time they'd left—Jes could get Hennea back to the temple sooner than if she had to find her way herself.

So now she only had to risk one of her children to find out if Hennea had been right. *Tier was alive.* Seraph was too much a Raven to allow herself to believe it without more proof, but even so, the thought thrummed through her. She would have the chance to save him, as she hadn't been able to save Ushireh.

"There's two places I could pick up the trail," Lehr said. "But knowing Jes, I thought that it might be shorter to follow the path he took with the forest king than to try and follow the trail he made bringing Hennea back."

"You're the Hunter," Seraph said. "I trust you."

Lehr stopped where the field turned to forest. "The forest king came here," he said, but he didn't immediately start on the trail, just stared at the ground. "Are you certain that I'm a Hunter? Papa could . . . can track as well as I can."

He didn't look at her as he spoke.

Lehr, she thought, saw beyond the power to the cost of acknowledging his Traveler blood. He knew that a Falcon could never belong to Redern.

"It doesn't matter," she said gently. "We just need to track Jes to where he found the girl, then follow her trail to where . . . where the huntsman found whatever he found."

"Right," he said and started through the forest.

Seraph followed Lehr's rapid gait with an effort, but made no complaint. The afternoon was well spent and he would need light to track. Whatever he hoped, she could feel the hum of magic as it passed from him and seeped into the woods around her. She had learned basic tracking skills herself, but she could see no sign of bent grass or footprint in the trail Lehr followed—she doubted that anyone but a Hunter could have followed the forest king through his own territory.

But she said nothing of it. Lehr would have to accept his abilities in his own way—or not.

When Lehr began a steady jog, Seraph left off her musings and concentrated on keeping up with him. He ran a mile or so before dropping back to a walk in a glade of wild wheat edged by forest on three sides and a formidable rock formation on the other.

"I think this is where Jes picked up the girl," he said, glancing around at the ground. He turned his back to the stone formation and knelt in the thick, spring-short grass. "There are several sets of his tracks. Do you see how much deeper Jes's print is here than it usually is?"

A branch moved behind his head. Seraph hissed a warning and called her magic.

"Now there is no need for that, Raven," said the man who rolled nimbly out from under a particularly thick area of foliage that gathered in front of the stone formation. "It is you who have invaded my home, not the other way around."

Lehr got to his feet and dusted off the knee of his breeches. "Mother," he said. "This is Jes's forest king."

He looked more like a grubby farmer fallen on hard times, thought Seraph. The tunic he wore was patched on top of older patches. His feet were bare and his hands were the knobby-knuckled, dark-nailed hands of a man who had worked the land.

She'd always wanted to see Jes's friend, and on any other day she would have had a number of questions for him. But nothing mattered except Tier.

Seraph bowed her head shallowly so she could keep her eyes on him. "We are sorry to disturb you," she said. "We are following the woman's tracks to the place where my husband's horse died."

"You won't find it trying to track her from here, Hunter. I didn't bring her by ways you can follow." The forest king grinned, revealing yellowing teeth that looked sharp, and his eyes stayed cold and watchful. "The place you speak of is outside my realm, but you can follow the girl's tracks starting from the big waterfall. Let me loan you a guide."

He turned and looked at the brush behind him. It shuddered briefly then a rangy vixen emerged. Seraph felt no magic, though beside her Lehr stiffened as if he heard something odd, but the vixen stared at the bedraggled forest king as if he were talking to her before setting out at a trot without looking at Seraph or Lehr.

The forest king waved his hand at the fox. "Follow her— she won't wait."

"My thanks." Seraph bowed again and started out after Lehr, who was already headed deeper into the forest.

It was chilly near the falls where the cold river water was pounded to vapor at the bottom of its descent. The fox shifted nervously while Lehr paced by the river. The moment he found Hennea's trail and knelt beside it, she left without waiting for gratitude.

Lehr rose to his feet and set out at a gait scarcely slower than he'd used to follow the fox. Even so, the sun was low when they broke free of the trees at last and began climbing a narrow path up the rock-strewn side of a mountain.

"Lots of traffic here," said Lehr, pointing at a rock scored by a shod hoof. "More than usual for such a remote place."

"Hennea was here," Seraph reminded him. "The huntsman and his men."

Lehr shook his head. "More people than that have been here. Some of the tracks are pretty faint, but I'd say five or six horsemen were here a month or more ago. Their tracks go up the mountain and back down again. Isn't that what we're looking for?"

Seraph nodded. "If you find anything that might have belonged to them, a bit of cloth or hair, get it for me." She wiped the sweat from her face to clear her eyes. "I can use it to get more information."

"Like you did from Frost's bridle," Lehr began moving again, but only at a walk. His change of pace might have been to allow him to observe the tracks more clearly, but Seraph suspected it was more likely to allow her to catch her breath.

They didn't slow long, and after a few miles Lehr seemed to forget she was there. The trail he followed snaked across the foothills and into the crevices of the Ragged Mountains.

Seraph's calves ached, then burned as they hadn't since her Traveling days. Farming was hard, but climbing at a jog in the mountains was a different sort of work. Lehr didn't seem bothered by it, even though he wore the pack she'd filled with things they might need.

When Lehr stopped, she wondered if he were finally getting tired, but then she really looked at where they were.

The deer trail they'd been following had widened into a piece of open level ground as big as the kitchen garden. In the center of the cleared area, a waist-high white rock with an unusual flat top broke through the dirt.

The grass in the clearing was knee-high, unusually tall for this time of year this high in the mountains. It carpeted the ground in dark bitter green, except for a large mound of disturbed earth to one side, a burial mound large enough for a horse.

"Why did they bury the horse?" asked Lehr.

"Sometimes," said Seraph, "the Blighted Places can recharge their magics. The bodies will tend to attract people or animals, and it's best to get them safely buried. There are also stories about odd things happening to the bodies of people who die of Shadow Blight—things that don't happen if the bodies are safely buried."

"Weren't they afraid of the magic?"

"Maybe," said Seraph. "There are a lot of Rederni who can sense magic—especially the ones who spend a lot of time out in the mountains. Maybe because in earlier times, when the

Shadowed's hand was heavier on the mountains, the people who couldn't sense the Blighted areas didn't survive." Tier had said that he could sense such places—she pushed hope away and said, "There isn't any magic that I can feel now— likely the huntsman felt the same. Take a look around, would you, and tell me what you find."

Lehr nodded, then stopped. "Do you believe her, Mother?" he said, his voice tight. "Do you believe Papa might be alive?"

"I don't know," she said, because it was the answer that would hurt him the least. Seraph took a deep breath. "This doesn't feel like one of the Blighted Places to me. Hennea said there was old magic here, but I can't sense it."

"What does that mean?" he asked.

She shook her head. "I think I would sense anything that had lasted here from the time of the Shadowed's Fall, especially power still strong enough to kill."

"So this is not a shadowed place."

Seraph nodded slowly. "A month is long enough to dissipate *solsenti* magic," she said, and then forced herself to point out the obvious to both of them. "Just because it was not old magic that killed here, doesn't mean that those *solsenti* wizards of Hennea's didn't kill Tier outright. I need you to look and see if you can tell what happened when Frost was killed here. Remember to look especially closely for any scrap of hair or clothing that I might be able to read."

She moved back to the edge of the clearing as he began to quarter it thoroughly.

"The clearest thing I see," he said at last, "is that something burned here. You can see where the earth was scorched—the patch goes all the way around the grave—see here where the grass is a bit shorter?"

She nodded.

"It looks to me that there have been three groups of people here recently," he said. "The most recent was Jes's Hennea. She walked the meadow, just like I did, stopped there"—he pointed to a place just to the right of the large stone—"and stopped again to press her hand into the dirt mound. Then she left. The party who came before her, was here a few days ago—three horsemen. One of them was the huntsman—see the way that off fore is angled?" He didn't look at her so Seraph didn't bother shaking her head. "That's the horse he was riding when he come to tell us what he'd found."

"The earliest group, though, is what we're interested in, and they worked at hiding their tracks. They were here after the snow started to melt—so no earlier than a month and a half ago. I can't tell you how many of them there were here for certain, but they were here about the same time as Papa."

Lehr gestured for Seraph to follow him and led her to the far side of the clearing, through a thicket of elderberry, to a stand of trees.

"He saw them, Mother," said Lehr. "He stopped Frost here for a while and watched them, maybe for as long as a quarter of an hour. See how Frost stood here, shifting her weight?" He turned and walked back the way they came without taking his eyes from the ground. "Then he walked Frost out into the clearing. There was no fighting, or scuffle that I can see. But Frost's prints are lost in this burnt area."

He glanced around again. "I can pick up the tracks of the other men lower down and backtrack them."

"We'll do that if necessary," said Seraph. "Did you find anything they left behind?"

He shook his head. "Nothing. I'm sorry I couldn't find out anything more. Are we done now?"

"Just beginning," Seraph answered. "Give me your pack," she said. There was a camp shovel tied to the back and she took it. "Now we dig."

"You're looking for something that can tell you what happened?" asked Lehr. "Like the saddle or Papa's pack?"

"If there's something to read, I'll try—but mostly I'm looking for the human bones the huntsman buried with Frost."

Before she set cold iron to earth, she touched the dirt, trying to find the old magic that Hennea had spoken of. "There's death here," she said. "Sudden and painful."

"Papa?" he asked.

"I don't know," Seraph replied, rubbing the grains between her fingers. "Ravens are not necromancers."

She got to her feet and started digging with the shovel—refusing Lehr's help. This was not something for children, no matter that the child in question was a foot taller and almost twice her weight.

She dug until the metal edge of the shovel blade bounced off bone. They hadn't buried Frost very deep—but a horse is a large animal. Scraping gently with the blade, she pushed away dirt and saw, beneath a coating of soil and ash, the familiar pattern of Frost's dapples.

"Let me, Mother," said Lehr, taking the shovel from her.

He shouldn't have been able to read anything from her face, but he was almost as sensitive as Jes or Tier. She was too tired from the trip here, from digging, from hope and fear to fight him.

"If we're lucky," Lehr said as he began digging, "they'd have set the skull beside the horse and not beneath her." We don't have ropes and horses to move Frost the way the huntsman did."

"I can move her if we have to," said Seraph—not as certain as she sounded. "But I'd rather not add more magic here until I've sifted all the information the grave contains."

He probed the disturbed ground and uncovered, little by little, Frost's poor burnt corpse. As the huntsman had said, her head and neck had been charred to the bone with just enough tissue to hold the vertebrae together. But the hindquarters were almost intact—left that way by the chill of the mountain spring. There was only a faint odor of meat turning rotten.

"How did the bridle survive?" asked Lehr after he'd cleared a space around the blackened skull of the horse.

"There are spells that only attack the living," said Seraph. "I think that the damage to the bridle was secondary—the spell burnt the horse, and the burning horse burnt the bridle in turn. Hold up, there's the saddle blanket." Part of it, anyway. Where the saddle had been was gone, leaving only a black scorch mark on Frost's back.

She knelt and touched the cloth. Nothing. She whispered words of power, but they slid past the saddle blanket and sank deeply into the soil as if something sucked them down and ate them. And deep below the surface of the earth, something very old stirred then subsided, its sleep too deep to be awakened so easily.

Cautiously she withdrew her magic, letting it die down

until it no longer fed whatever it was that waited beneath. She looked again at the flat-topped stone and saw that it could have served as an altar. She felt the dirt again and looked at the deep green grass. Blood had once flowed over the altar, enough blood that generations later the grass still fed upon it. Hennea had been right, there was old magic here—older than Shadow's Blight.

This was not a Blighted Place. If any mage tried to set a trap here, the magic would be eaten by the same thing that had eaten hers.

"Mother?" Lehr asked, pausing in his steady pace to look at her.

"Something's waiting here," she said. "But it had nothing to do with any recent deaths. It'll likely lie here until your grandchildren are dust unless it's awakened."

"What about the blanket?"

Seraph shook her head. "Nothing. I need the skull. I'll be able to tell if it's Tier's."

His shovel hesitated before he resumed his search, widening the cleared space around the horse.

Seraph cleaned the dirt from her fingertips absently and watched as Lehr at last unearthed a fire-blackened human skull, set near the horse's neck bones.

Gently Lehr took the grim thing into his hands and handed it to her. Seraph stared at the wide brow and looked for a hint of familiar features. Had Tier's front teeth been so square? She couldn't tell. There was no jaw bone to give the skull balance.

As she'd told Tier, necromancy was not something Ravens used—but it was prudence rather than ability that stopped them. Meddling with the dead was no light thing. If her need had not been so great she'd have left it alone.

Her fingers told her nothing; the bone could almost have been a stone in a field that had never felt a human hand, so little of its past stayed with it.

She set it down and touched Frost's skull. Nothing. Someone had deliberately cleaned these bones as they'd cleaned the bridle and saddle blanket. No random magic could rape the memory of life from a bone.

She picked up the human skull again and sent more magic

seeking through it. A bridle or a blanket could be cleaned of lives that brush past it, but not even a great deal of magic could clean away a whole lifetime completely. There had to be bits of it left, if she tried hard enough.

Beneath her fingers she felt a tentative response. She pressed the cool bone to her forehead and left it there a long time as she sought to touch the faint pulse of experience.

The sun was setting when she placed the skull gently beside Frost's.

"This man was not Tier," she whispered around the throbbing pain in her temples. "He was a Traveler, dead of a blade, not magic fire—and he died somewhere far away, though not long ago."

"It doesn't mean that Papa's alive," he said, obviously hoping she'd contradict him. "Someone tried to make us think him dead with the skull and Frost's body—but they might simply have taken his body away, or taken him off to kill elsewhere."

"It only means that Tier probably didn't die here," she agreed, fear and hope both held in firm control.

Lehr began filling in the grave, skull and all, and Seraph thought about what she knew.

"Lehr?" she said finally.

"Hmm?"

"These people who killed Frost took a lot of trouble to obscure their tracks. They weren't good enough to fool you, but they tried very hard. If you hadn't seen their tracks below, would you have noticed them here? If we were looking for Tier's remains rather than evidence that he was taken?"

He frowned, "Maybe not."

Seraph nodded. "I think they knew about you. They were careful to take Tier outside of the realm of the forest king—I think they knew about him as well. They cleansed Frost's body and the leather and cloth, leaving them no past for me to read. They spent a long time trying to make that skull silent—and almost succeeded."

"No one knows about the forest king," said Lehr, turning over the last spade of dirt. "But Hennea said that whoever sent the letter to the priest knew what we are."

"Yes," agreed Seraph. "How did they know, not only that I

am Raven, but exactly what my skills are? Most Ravens cannot read the past in an object. These men knew what trail Tier would take home—and it's not the way he left."

Lehr frowned. "Not even I knew what path Papa takes home. He kept it quiet because the furs are worth a lot of money—did you notice that there is no trace of the furs? They would have been packed over Frost's hindquarters, which weren't even scorched."

"No, I hadn't noticed," said Seraph. "So thrifty of them."

Lehr packed in a layer of dirt with his foot. "I suppose that someone could have overheard Jes talking about the forest king—but Jes seldom talks to anyone but the family. No one else really pays attention to what he says anyway. And if none of us knew what magic you could do until Forder brought back Frost's bridle, who would know what you could do?"

She waited, watching him think about it. If he came up with the same answer as she did . . .

"Bandor used to hunt with Papa, didn't he?" Lehr whispered it. "During the first years when the bakery used to have to support the farm, too? Jes was just a baby."

"That's right," Seraph said.

"And, after you and Papa got married, Bandor was the only one who used to talk to you. He knows a lot about the Travelers—did you tell him what kinds of things you could do?"

"Yes," she said.

"And Bandor knows about Jes's stories of the forest king—but he doesn't believe them, Mother."

She smiled at him grimly. "Do you know who your father thinks the forest king is? I mean aside from Jes's dealings with him?"

"No."

"What if I told you that in a very old language, *ell* means king or lord and *vanail* is forest. If you put them together—"

"Ellevanal?"

Seraph had never seen anyone's jaw drop before; it was an unattractive expression.

"Do you mean," whispered her son, "that Ellevanal, god of the forest and growing things, *the* Ellevanal, *Karadoc's* Ellevanal, is Jes's forest king?"

"I don't know," she said. "Today is the first time I've met him, and I didn't ask. He doesn't look like a god, does he? But I know that Tier was convinced of it, and he told your Aunt Alinath what he thought."

Alinath had been at her worst, telling Tier that Seraph couldn't give Jes the kind of attention that he needed. That Seraph encouraged Jes's problems by listening to his stories about his made-up friend. *A boy,* she'd said, *needed to understand that lying was not acceptable.* She hadn't liked it when Tier suggested Jes hadn't lied at all.

Seraph smiled grimly. "Bandor was there when he said it.".

But Lehr was still worried about other matters. "But the forest lord belongs here, to our forest. Ellevanal is worshiped everywhere—I mean, Karadoc has had apprentices, and there's a larger church in Korhadan."

"I don't worship gods," said Seraph. "You'll have to take it up with the forest king next time you meet him."

Lehr thought about her answer, but it seemed to satisfy him because he changed the subject. "Uncle Bandor loves us, loved . . . loves Papa. He wouldn't do anything to hurt Papa."

"So I believe," agreed Seraph. "But you and I both came up with his name. He's become one of Volis's followers. I think that we need to be cautious around him until we know more."

"So what are we going to do now?"

"First we'll finish here, then I have a few questions for the priest. Can you take us by the quickest route to Redern?"

"Yes," he said. "But we won't make it before dark."

"No matter," Seraph said coldly. "I don't mind waking up a few people."

Or tearing them limb from limb if she had to. Tier had been taken, alive—because she couldn't bear it otherwise—and she intended to find out where he was. And tearing someone limb from limb sounded very, very good. Let Volis face a Raven who knew what he was when he didn't have a cadre of wizards to protect him. Oh, she would have her answers from him before she slept this night.

"What about Rinnie?" asked Lehr.

"Jes will have gotten back from taking Hennea to the village by now. Rinnie will be safe with him."

Gura barked, and Rinnie looked up from her gardening. But whoever had disturbed the dog was on the other side of the house.

Rinnie jumped to her feet and dusted off her skirt. She put her hand on Gura's collar and set off to see who had come.

CHAPTER 7

He opened his eyes to utter darkness and a cold stone floor under his cheek, though he didn't remember going to sleep. He took a deep, shaken breath and tried to determine how he got here, wherever here was. The last thing Tier remembered was riding Frost down the mountain on the way back home.

Undeniably, he was no longer on the mountain. The stone floor beneath his hands was level, and his fingers found the marks of a chisel. He was in a room, though he could hear water flowing nearby.

He rose cautiously to hands and knees and felt his way forward until his hands closed on grating set into the floor, the source of the sound of water. The bars were too close to let him put anything wider than his finger through and the water flowed well below that. He tried to pull up the grate, but it didn't so much as shift.

Hours later he was hungry, thirsty, and knew that he was in a room six paces wide by four paces long. An ironbound wooden door was inset flat against one of the narrow walls with the hinges on the outside.

The stonemason responsible for the walls had been very good, leaving only the smallest of fingerholds. Tier'd fallen three times, but he finally climbed the corner of the room until he touched a wooden ceiling. By his reckoning it was about twice his height to the floor. With a foot braced on adjacent walls he couldn't put any significant pressure against any of the boards, though he tried all the ones he could reach from his perch.

At last he climbed back down, convinced that the room he was in wasn't anywhere in Redern—or Leheigh either for that matter. He'd been inside the Sept's keep a time or two, and the walls in this room—which had obviously been designed as a prison cell—were better formed than the walls of the great hall in the Sept's keep.

Why had someone gone to the trouble of hauling him off the mountain and imprisoning him? It wasn't as if he, himself, would be worth money to anyone, not the kind of money that would be important to anyone who could afford a cell built like this one was.

He had a long time to think about it.

Emperor Phoran the Twenty-Seventh (Twenty-Sixth if he didn't count the Phoran who united the Empire—it was the first Phoran's son who had declared himself emperor) stretched his feet out before him and cast a practiced leer at the woman sitting on him. She was all but baring her breasts at him, the stupid cow. Did she really think that his favors were likely to be won by such as she?

He snagged a mug from a nearby serving tray and drank deeply, closing his eyes to the party that had somehow spread from the dining hall to his own private rooms. The laughter of a nearby woman cut through his spine with its falseness.

He wondered what his so-long-ago ancestor would have thought about such decadence. Would he still have set aside his plow to organize his fellow farmers into a militia to defend themselves against bandits? Or would he have turned back to his farming, ashamed that his loins could breed such a degenerate creature as the current emperor?

Phoran sighed.

"Am I boring you, my love?" asked the woman on his lap archly.

He opened his mouth to inflict the kind of cruel remark that had become second nature to him over the past few years, but instead he sighed again. She wasn't worth it—dumb as a sheep and oblivious to fine nuances of language.

Instead he pushed her off and away with a pat. "Go find someone else to cuddle tonight, there's a love. This fine ale suits me better than a woman . . . tonight."

Someone giggled as if his remark had been witty. The woman who'd been on his lap swayed her hips and half staggered onto the lap of a handsome young man who'd been seated on the end of the bed, watching the party with a jaundiced eye—Toarsen, Avar's younger brother, who'd doubtless been told to watch over Phoran while Avar was out in the wilds taking stock of his new inheritance.

Phoran swallowed the better part of the contents of his cup then closed his eyes once more. This time he left them closed. Maybe if he feigned a drunken stupor (a common enough occurrence) they would all go away.

He let his hand fall away from his lips and the mug fell on the plush rug his great-grandfather had imported from somewhere at great expense. He hoped the dark ale ruined the rug. Then the chatelaine would run to Avar when he returned. Avar would listen gravely, and when the chatelaine left, he would laugh and pat Phoran on the back—and pay attention to him again.

Avar, mentor, best friend, and Sept of Leheigh now that his miserly old father had died hadn't had much time to spend with his emperor lately. Spitefully, Phoran wondered if he should take away the title and lands that kept Avar from noticing that his emperor needed a friend more than he needed another Sept.

Tears of self-pity welled up and were firmly repressed. Tears were something he shed alone, never, never in front of the court no matter how drunk he was.

Self-indulgence aside, Phoran had no intention of taking Avar's inheritance away. He even knew that Avar had to attend to his duties; he just wished he had duties to attend to as well. The endless parties had become . . . sickening—like too much apple mead. When would he be old enough to start ruling his empire?

Someone patted his cheek and he slapped at the hand, pur-
posefully making the movement clumsier than necessary. He
could drink a fair bit more than he had tonight before it affected him much.

"He's unconscious." Phoran recognized the voice. It was
Toarsen. He must have gotten rid of the cow, too. "Let's get
this room cleared out."

The Emperor listened while people shuffled away. At last
the guardsmen came in to gather the few who'd passed out in
the chamber. His door shut behind them and he was alone.
Without people around, without Avar to keep it at bay, the
Memory would come for him, again.

Before he could sit up and call them back, someone spoke.
It startled him so that for a moment he didn't quite recognize
the speaker.

"Some emperor," sneered a voice quite close to his ear. Not
his Memory but someone who'd stayed after the guardsmen
had left—Kissel, the younger son of the Sept of Seal Hold.
The relief of his mistake almost blinded Phoran to the words.
"A beardless boy who drinks himself to sleep every night."

"Got to hand it to Avar," agreed Toarsen. "I thought that the
boy would be harder to tame and we'd have to have him killed
like the Regent was. But Avar's turned him into a proper sot
who jumps when Avar asks."

"Well I'd rather not have to be on the cleanup committee.
He's gone to fat like a capon. Come help me heave him to the
bed."

They managed it with grunts and swearing while Phoran
concentrated on being as heavy as possible. How dare they
speak of him like this? He'd fix these imbeciles. Tomorrow his
guards would have their heads. He was emperor, they'd forgotten that. He'd have Avar . . . Avar was his *friend*. Just because Avar's brother talked that way about him didn't mean
that Avar felt the same way. Avar liked him, was proud of the
way he could outdrink and outinsult any man in the court.

"And why isn't Avar here to do the honors?" asked Kissel.
"I thought he was going to see the Emperor tonight after resting yesterday."

Avar was in Taela?

"He had some pressing business," grunted Toarsen, pushing

Phoran toward the center of the bed. "He'll admit to coming in late tonight and greet the Emperor over breakfast."

When the men left him alone in his room, the Emperor opened his eyes and rolled off the bed. He walked to the full-length mirror and stared at himself by the light of the few candles that had been left burning.

Mud-colored, too-fine hair that had been coaxed into ringlets this afternoon hung limply around his rounded face, spotty and pale. Hands that had once had sword calluses were soft and pudgy, covered with rings his uncle had eschewed.

"Ruins your sword grip, boy," the regent had said. "A man who can't protect himself depends upon others, too much."

Phoran touched the mirror lightly. "But you died anyway, Uncle. You left me alone."

Alone. Fear curled in his stomach. Unless Avar was with him, the Memory came every night.

If Avar was in Taela, as Toarsen had claimed, he'd be staying with his mistress in the town. Phoran could send a messenger to bring him here.

The Emperor stared at his image in the mirror and rolled up the sleeve of the loose shirt he wore. In the reflection the faint marks the Memory left on him each night were almost invisible in the dim candlelight.

Avar planned to lie to his emperor: Avar, who was Phoran's only friend.

The Emperor made no move to summon a messenger.

Food came at irregular intervals through a small opening near the floor that Tier had somehow missed on his first, blind, inspection of the cell. An anonymous hand opened the metal covering and shoved a tray of water and bread through, shutting and latching the cover before Tier's eyes even adjusted to the light.

Still, he'd grown grateful for those brief moments, for the reassurance that he was not blind.

The bread was always good, flavored with salt and herbs and made with sifted wheat flour rather than the cheaper rye. Bread fit for a lord's table, not a prison cell.

First he'd tried to fit his situation into some logical path, but nothing about his captivity made sense. Finally he'd come to the conclusion that he was lacking some information necessary for a solution.

Only then had he raged.

He'd slept when he was tired, worn-out from anger and fruitless attempts to find a way out of the cell. When he'd realized that he was losing track of time he told himself stories, the ones he'd gathered from the old people of Redern, saved word for word from one generation to the next. Some of those were songs as well as stories, ballads that took almost an hour each to sing.

When the toll of the hours grew too great, he'd quit singing, quit thinking, quit raging, and given in to despair. But even that left him alone eventually.

Finally, he developed habits to fill the empty hours. He did the exercises he'd learned when he'd been a soldier. When he ran out of the ones he could do in his confined space, he made up others. Only after he was sweating and panting, he'd sit down and tell one story. Then he'd either rest or exercise again as the impulse took him.

But it was the magic that had given him purpose.

He'd known some of the things his magic could do. Seraph had told him what she knew—and, despite the danger, he'd used it some over the years. It helped that his magic wasn't the showy sort that people all knew about, like Seraph's. *His* magic was more subtle.

He could calm an angry drunk or give a frightened man courage with his songs. Such things as any music could do, but with more effect. When he chose, he could commit a song or letter to memory and recall it, word perfect, years later. When he'd sung at the tavern in Redern, he almost always gave his last song a push to cheer his audience.

It had made him feel guilty, because Seraph had given up her magic entirely. But she'd never seemed to mind, never seemed to miss the power that she'd set aside.

He could never have set aside his music.

There were some things he'd avoided. Some things were harmful to his audience; music alone shared the darker emotions with his audience, never magic. He was very careful not to use his magic to persuade others to his will—words were enough. And then there were the things too obviously magic to use in Redern.

Alone in the darkness of his cell, he'd succeeded in creating small lights to accompany his songs the first time he tried. They were flickering, faint things, but they comforted him.

Sounds were more difficult, even though he'd accidentally called them once before. After a particularly nasty battle, he and a bunch of the other officers got roaring drunk and someone thrust a small lyre, part of the spoils, into his hands. The song he'd sung had included fair maidens and barnyard animals. He was pretty certain he'd been the only one who noticed that the moos and quacks of the chorus were accompanied by the real thing.

He had been trying to re-create the experiment the first time his visitor arrived.

The constant dark had honed his other senses, and the scuff of a foot on the boards above him stopped him midword. He'd sat silently, waiting for something more.

Finally, barely audible over the burble of the water that flowed under the grating in the back corner of his cell, he'd heard it again.

It hadn't been a rat; a rat was too light to make a stout board creak under its weight. He'd been almost certain that the noise was made by a person.

"Hello," he'd said. "Who is there?"

The boards had given a small, surprised squeak and then there was nothing. Whoever it had been, he had left.

Some unknowable span of time later, while Tier was doing push-ups, he'd heard it again. He'd stilled, too worried that he would drive whoever it was off again if he made another move. He hadn't heard another sound, but somehow he knew that his visitor was gone. Desperate for company, Tier turned his thoughts toward enticing his visitor to stay.

Tier awoke with the knowledge that there was someone nearby. He hadn't heard anything, but he could feel that someone stood above him listening. He sat up, leaned his back against the wall, and began his story with the traditional words.

"It happened like this," he said.

If he pretended that his eyes were closed, he could think himself leaning against the wall at home telling stories to his own restless children so they'd fall asleep faster. Seraph would be cleaning—she was always in motion. Maybe, he thought, she would be grumpy as she sometimes got when Rinnie was tired and the boys were restless. Her face would be serene, but the tautness of her shoulders gave her away.

I wonder if she knows that something has happened to me? Is she looking?

It was an old thought by now, and held a certain comfort.

"A boy came to be king when he was only sixteen," Tier said, "when his own father died in battle. War was common then, and the kingdom he inherited was neither so large nor so powerful that the king could sit in safety and leave the fighting to his generals."

The story of the Shadowed was one he knew so well that he had once told it backwards, word for word, for a half-drunken wager. He'd missed one phrase, but his comrades hadn't noticed.

"This young man," he said, "was a good king, which is to say that he promoted order and prosperity among his nobles and usually kept the rest from starvation. He married well, and in time was blessed with five sons. As years passed and his sons became men, his kingdom waxed in wealth because the king was skilled at keeping the neighboring kingdoms fighting among themselves rather than attacking his people."

The floor above him made a sound, as if a listener were settling in more comfortably. Tier added his unknown listener to his audience.

A boy, he decided with no more evidence than his visitor's willingness to travel without lights. There were spaces between the boards that would have let light into Tier's cell, if his unknown guest had brought so much as a single candle with him.

He would be a boy old enough to be allowed to wander about on his own, but not so old as to have other duties to attend to; an adventurous boy who would venture into the dark corners where prisoners were kept.

"The king had many of the interests of his kind. He could

hunt and ride as well as any of his men. He danced with grace and could play the lute. None of his guardsmen or nobles could stand long against him with sword or staff." Tier had always had some doubt about the king's prowess—what kind of fool would beat his king at swordplay?

Tier fought to picture the king in his mind, pulling out details that weren't in the story. He'd be a slender young man, like Tier's son Jes—but his hair would be the pure, red gold of the eastern nobles. . . .

Seraph had told him that some of the Bards had been able to create pictures for their listeners, but his cell stayed dark as pitch.

"But what the king loved most was learning," he continued, in the proper words. "He established libraries at every village, and in his capital he collected more books than had ever been assembled together then or since. Perhaps that was the reason for what happened to him."

Tier found himself grinning as he remembered Seraph's contemptuous sniff the first time he'd told her that part. Books weren't evil, she'd explained loftily, what people did with the knowledge they'd gleaned was no judgment against the books that held it.

"Time passed, and the king grew old and wizened as his sons became strong and wise. People waited without worry for the old king to die and his oldest son to take the crown—for the heir was every bit as temperate and wise as his father."

Tier took a sip of water, experience guiding his hand to the place where he left the earthen bowl. He let the pause linger, as much a part of this story as the words which followed. "Had that happened, like as not, our king would have gone to earth and be as forgotten as his name."

"One evening the king's oldest son went to bed, complaining of a headache. By the next day he was blind and covered with boils; by that evening he was dead. Plague had struck the palace, and, before it left, the queen and every male of royal blood was dead."

Tier's voice trembled on the last word, because he heard, as clearly as he'd heard his own breath, a woman's voice wailing in grief. He'd done it—and he found the thread of magic that powered the eerie sound.

A board creaked above him, closer than the sounds of the mourning woman, recalling Tier back to the dark cell where there was no plague, no dead women and children.

"The king became haunted, spending hours alone in his great library. But no one took much note, because the plague had spread in short order to the capital city and then to the towns and villages beyond. A horrible, ravening sickness that touched and lingered until its victim died a week later, deaf and blind to anything except pain."

Cautiously he tried to feed energy toward the path that had allowed the woman's cry to sound. It seemed to him that he could feel the unhealthy miasma of evil coating the emptiness of his cell floor. He stood up abruptly, but the feeling ebbed as he stopped feeding the story. The control reassured him. It was only a story, his story.

He resumed his efforts as he continued the story. "One day, after the last of his grandsons died, the king went to sleep an old, broken man and woke up a young man of eighteen again. They called it a miracle at first, some kind god's deliverance from the ghastly illness that killed two of every three that came down sick. But the plague spread further, unaffected by the king's miraculously returned youth. It traveled across borders, devouring the royal houses of the kingdoms all around, until there was only one kingdom and one king."

Tier's voice stuck there, as the magic of the generations-old words caught him in brutal understanding of the numberless dead whose death had fed the evil that was in the king.

"He ate their lives," said a voice abruptly from the ceiling above Tier.

A shiver ran down Tier's spine, though the words were the exact ones he'd intended to use himself. Somehow the oddity of his listener knowing the words to a Rederni story was part of the strange shape the story was taking.

The soft, sexless voice continued relentlessly, "He ate them all to preserve himself—and so he lost himself in truth."

Tier waited, but when his visitor said nothing more, Tier continued the story himself.

"As the years passed and the king lived far beyond his life span, what few of his old advisors who escaped the original plague died, old men that they were, one by one. As they did the king replaced them with dark-robed, nameless men—it was these who gave him away at last."

"The king's youngest daughter, Loriel, discovered them feasting upon a child in her father's antechamber," Tier said, drawing the horror of that into his dark cell. He could hear the sound of fangs crunching the fragile bone in his soul.

He could see it.

A woman, older than he'd pictured her, stood in an open doorway. Her hair, like Seraph's, was pale, though washed in sunlight rather than moonlight. Two figures crouched before her, anonymous in heavy brocade robes. They were too occupied with what was before them to notice that they had been seen. Between them lay a boy of ten or twelve years whose freckles stood out against his too-white skin. His shoulders jerked rhythmically back and forth in a mockery of life as the king's councillors buried their heads in his abdomen and fed.

Tier's shock kept him from holding the image, though the wet sound of their feeding accompanied his voice. "And she fled to the last of her father's advisors, a mage."

He stopped speaking and tightened his control until the only sounds remaining in the cell were the ones that belonged there.

"And so they gathered," said his listener.

"And so they gathered," repeated Tier, and the repetition felt right, felt like the rhythm of the story. He relaxed; it was only a story, one that he knew very well. "The remnants of people who had survived the plague. But the sickness had taken the experienced warriors, the lords, and commanders, leaving only a broken people. Loriel led the first attack, herself."

"She died," whispered the listener and the magic coaxed Tier as well, raising needs he'd never realized he'd felt.

"She died," Tier said, "but left behind a handful of men who had learned what leadership meant, left them with the ancient mage who taught them and fought by their side. They battled the minions of the Shadowed. As his followers died, the king called upon a host of evil; ancient creatures woke from their slumbers to fight at his behest."

Tier let his magic free, finding the places where he had bound it too tightly over the years. The bindings, he saw, had been the reason he'd had such difficulty. As the magic swept through him, exhilarating and frightening by turns, the words came to him, as well-worn and soft as an old cotton coverlet, but full of unexpected burrs that pricked and stung.

"He lost himself and his name. There remained only a title, given by the men who died fighting him. They called him the Shadowed."

"Numberless were the heroes . . ." The other's voice became part of the story, too. Tier felt his magic rush up to envelope his listener.

"Numberless were the heroes who fell," continued Tier. "Their songs unsung because there was no one left to sing." He paused, letting the other do his part.

"Then came Red Ernave who fought with axe and bow . . ."

"A giant of a man," said Tier. "He gathered them all, all the men, women, and children who could pick up a stick or throw a stone. He called them the Glorious Army of Man, and he taught them to fight."

As if there were no walls in his cell, the people of the Glorious Army gathered before Tier. Gaunt-eyed and battered, they stood in silent, unmoving defiance of the evil they fought. There were a few men, but most of them were hollow-cheeked women, old men, and a small, precious gathering of children worn by hunger and fear.

Tier knew, by the Owl-borne bond that formed by magic between storyteller and audience, that his listener saw them, too.

"And in the first days of autumn the king's old mage took council with Red Ernave. They talked alone all night, and when the morning sun came, the mage's days had found their number. He was burned in great ceremony, and as the last coals died, Red Ernave assembled his army. He brought them to a flat plain, just beyond the Ragged Mountains."

Tier had been there, once. He'd been following the track of a deer and found himself, unexpectedly, on the plain of Shadow's Fall. There was no marker to warn the unwary, but he'd known where he was. Even so many centuries later, under a blanket of pure white snow, there was death in that place. He could almost feel the soil of the wounded land under his feet.

The meadow stretched out before him now; he recognized

the shapes of the peaks that surrounded it. There was no snow on the ground to hide the shape of the bodies littering the ground.

"There, *there* they faced the hosts of the Shadowed and fought. The sky grew black and blood drenched the ground." Tier smelled the bitter scent of old blood and almost gagged at the familiar odor of war.

"Bodies piled and the battle raged around them for days. And nights."

His cell rang with the sounds of battle, and he realized he'd forgotten how overwhelming it was: the clash of metal on metal and the screams of the dying.

"The Shadowed's creatures needed no sleep and they fed upon the dead. The Army of Man fought on because there was nothing else to do; they fought and died. But not so many died on the third day as had fallen on the second day. By the fourth day it seemed that the evil host was thinning, and hope rose among the ragged band—and for the first time they drove the host back."

Tier found that he had to stop to catch his breath, and slow his heartbeat. In his pitch-black cell he saw a red-maned, scarred warrior with his axe held wearily against his shoulder, waiting for Tier to continue telling his story.

But it was too real now, and the words were gone, lost in the desolation of the long-ago battle.

"And hope flooded the Army of Man for the first time," said the other, in a voice as ragged as Tier's.

"But even as they cheered, the skies darkened, though it was yet midday, and another assault began." The words were Tier's again, though they seemed oddly unreal compared to the scenes that unfolded before him.

It was hard to breathe, the air was so foul. Red Ernave's hands were weary from the endless fighting. His axe laid into a creature that looked as if it had once been a wolf before the Shadowed's magics had gotten to it. It died hard and Ernave had to hit it a second time before it lay still.

He found himself on a small rise without an immediate opponent. He took the chance to rest briefly and ran his gaze over the fighting—and saw the Shadowed for the first time since the battle had begun.

The Shadowed was less than he'd expected. A full head shorter than Ernave and half his weight, he looked no more than a lad. He bore more than a passing resemblance to Loriel— though her eyes had never been so empty. The Shadowed smiled, and Ernave, who had thought he was tired beyond fear, found that he was wrong.

A voice beside him said, "I'm here."

It was Kerine, the scrawny Traveler who was now their only wizard. He'd staggered into Ernave's encampment several winters ago and been a thorn in Ernave's side ever since.

"It only needed that," said Ernave sourly.

Surprisingly the wizard laughed. "When the Shadow one is dead, I'll wash my hands of you, you hard-headed bastard. But from this moment until that we are brothers, and I'll stand with you. It'll take more than that axe of yours to kill the Shadowed."

Ernave said, "Come then, brother," and cut a path through the battle to the Shadowed.

The Nameless King fought alone. His own creatures granted him a wide berth—as if there could only be so much evil in one place and the Shadowed's presence made all other dark things unnecessary.

Ernave approached from the side and swung, but the king's shield intercepted the blow. Ernave's axe sank through the thin metal outer layer into the wood underneath and stuck.

Ernave jerked his axe hard and forced the Shadowed two wild steps to the side before he slipped his arm out of the shield's straps.

Ernave slammed the shield into the ground, splitting it as he would have a log so that his axe was free. It was a swift and practiced move, but he just barely managed to bring his weapon up to parry the king's strike.

The Shadowed fought as well as the old mage, his advisor, had warned Ernave. Time and again the sword slid along Ernave's axe, turning the blows so that the heavier steel of the axe didn't damage the sword blade.

The king's mouth moved with magic-making the whole time he fought. For the most part Red Ernave forestalled the spell with heavy blows that forced the king to lose his rhythm and concentrate on swordwork. Doubtless there were more spells that Kerine deflected, but, every so often, a spell touched Ernave with white-hot heat that drained his spent body even more.

The king was fresh, and Ernave had been tired unto death before the battle began. Even so, Ernave planted his feet, and, with a swift pattern of his axe, he forced the king to leap away.

The axe felt heavy in his hands, and every time it jerked as the king turned aside another blow the shock shot up Ernave's forearms and through his shoulders and neck in a flash of pain.

Ernave stumbled over nothing and, as he fell, his axe caught the king a glancing blow in the knee and laid it bare to the bone. Ernave didn't hesitate, but kept rolling until he staggered to his feet and turned back to face the king.

The Shadowed shrieked and the semblance of the young man the king had been fell away, leaving behind something that was little more than sinew clinging to bone. There was no time for horror. Ernave surged to his feet and struck at the king's sword again.

The blow hit fairly at last, shattering the elegant blade. Ernave set himself for a killing blow, but the Shadowed dropped his sword and lashed out with his hand. Claws that belonged on no human fingers sunk deep into Ernave's side.

Ernave cried out, but the pain did not slow his strike and the axe cleaved sweetly through the Shadowed's neck.

Bleeding and breathing heavily, Red Ernave stared in astonished shock at the body of the old, old man who lay on the ground.

Who'd have thought the Shadowed could really be killed?

"How did you do that? How did you withstand his magic? I couldn't block it all. You are no mage." Kerine's nagging voice broke through the buzzing exhaustion that made everything seem oddly distant.

"The old mage," said Ernave, his breathlessness growing worse until he breathed in shallow pants. "He gave the last of his life to hold off the dark magic long enough for me to kill the Shadowed. I thought he was a fool to believe it would work . . . but it didn't matter as we were all dead anyway."

As he finished speaking he fell to his knees.

Buried deep in Red Ernave's heart, Tier, knowing how this

story ended, realized his danger and struggled to surface, but there was nothing to cling to as Ernave began to submit to the death bequeathed him by the Shadowed.

A thin whisper rang in his ears.

"And so the great warrior died in the wake of the Shadowed and left . . ."

"Left the battlefield." Tier grasped the words. "Left his army to mourn." But he couldn't remember the next—

Kerine tried uselessly to save Ernave with what little remained of his power.

"They burned the thing that had once been a king," continued Tier's visitor softly when Tier stopped speaking.

Tier fumbled a little but the familiar words began to flow again, separating him from his story. "And . . . and scattered his ashes in stream and field so that there would be no grave nor memorial to the king who had no name."

The pain in Tier's side faded and he was once more safe in the dark of his prison.

"They buried Red Ernave in the battlefield, hoping that his presence would somehow hold the host of darkness at bay. They trailed into the empty city where the Shadowed had ruled and pulled down the king's palace until not one brick stood upon the other. Then the remnants of the Glorious Army of Man waited, for they had no place to go. The last of the cities and villages were years since ground to dust under the weight of the Shadowed. Only when the food ran short did the army drift away in twos and threes."

Tier found himself shaking in the dark as the story faded away. Next time he experimented with magic, he decided firmly, it would be with a story whose hero survived.

"What have you done, Bard?" said the voice from above him. "Magic for music, both becoming more real. What have you done?" And, severing the bond that still held him to Tier, the listener departed without a sound.

Avar, Sept of Leheigh, looked just as a Sept ought, thought Phoran, playing with his breakfast without enthusiasm.

Avar was lean, tall, and heroic. His face was chiseled, his chin firm and his mouth smiling sympathetically. He'd come, unannounced, into the royal bedchambers as if he had the right to be there.

"Not hungry this morning, my emperor?" he said, looking at the mess Phoran had made of his plate. "When I heard that you were breaking your fast in your room I thought that might be the case. My new man has a potion against drink-sickness. He's a half-blood Traveler, or so he claims. He's certainly a wizard with potions and medicines."

"No, thank you," Phoran looked down at his plate. Avar was home.

Relief and joy were severely tempered by his suspicion that Toarsen's words last night were truth. Last night he'd been certain, but in Avar's charismatic presence Phoran's need for Avar's approval vied with the words of a couple of half-drunken lords and scored a narrow triumph. Narrow enough that Phoran didn't ask Avar to join him—although there were extra plates and plenty of food.

Phoran forked up a bit of fruit and ate it without enthusiasm. "I don't need potions—I'm not sick from drinking." It sounded too much like a pouting child, so Phoran continued speaking. "So you're back from your sept already?" Did he sound casual enough? "I'd thought you intended to be gone longer than this?"

Avar looked disgruntled, Phoran thought, feeling a bare touch of triumph. Perhaps Avar had expected a warmer greeting—or even the scold Phoran'd intended to hand out to the Sept before overhearing that conversation last night. Cool composure wasn't a mood the young emperor often indulged himself in.

"Where is Leheigh, anyway? In the South?" The indifference in Phoran's voice was less of an effort. *There. See how little I concern myself with your affairs?*

He'd looked up the ancient deed in the library and followed the path on several of the maps in the map room. He could have discussed the crops in the Sept's new inheritance with knowledge gained from poring over tax records of the past few centuries. But now he would not admit to knowing anything. Avar's brother wouldn't have dared to show such disgust for the Emperor if he had no encouragement from Avar himself.

But Phoran needed Avar. He needed his praise. He needed his support against the older council members who weren't happy with an emperor who indulged himself in nightly parties, and yet they still refused to let him do anything more useful. Needed him because Avar, when he stayed at the palace, often slept in a bed in the Emperor's suite—and when Avar was there, Phoran was safe.

"Leheigh is southwest, sire, along the Silver River below Shadow's Fall," said Avar, his face settling into its usual warmth. "I didn't have time to visit the battlefield—but I will next time I go there, if I can find a guide. All in all, I'm very happy with the lands; my father wasn't a hunter so he left the forest wild and filled with game. The keep dates back to a few centuries after Shadow's Fall—the family legend claims that my many times great-grandfather was a solder of the Remnant of the Army of Man, and a few of those soldiers settled along the river after the final battle. There's a couple of towns in the district, a largish village near my keep, and a smaller town on the banks of the river. The Redern villagers—that's the smaller town—still talk as if the Fall of the Shadowed happened yesterday. I suppose because nothing interesting has happened there since."

"I see," said Phoran. "When did you get back?"

"The day before yesterday," Avar said. "My apologies for not coming to you directly, but I had to make arrangements for some items I brought back." He hesitated. "And, I came back and found that my mistress had a few extra men warming her bed while I was gone. By the time I dealt with that my temper was none too sweet."

A good reason for waiting, thought Phoran with secret jubilation. Maybe Avar's brother was jealous of the time Avar spent with him; maybe that's why he'd said such hurtful things. Phoran could understand Toarsen's jealousy.

"I thought I'd go riding today," said Phoran, changing the subject as if Avar's trip and return were something that held no interest. "Will you accompany me?" He hadn't intended to ask for company. But Avar's presence soothed the hurts Toarsen and Kissel had dealt. Avar was his friend—anyone could see it by the warmth of his gaze.

Avar's eyebrows climbed up that perfect forehead. "Of

course, my lord. I'll send word to the stables. I left my horse at home."

"I've done that already," Phoran said, setting his fork aside. "You can ride the horse my armsman was to take." He'd have no need of a guard with Avar by his side. "I feel as if I haven't been out of the castle in months." Only after he said it did he realize that it was true. When was the last time he'd been out? Oh, yes, that tavern crawl in disguise on Avar's birthday four months before.

"Ah." Avar frowned a little. "Is something bothering you?"

Phoran shook his head and stood up. "Just bored. Tell me about your new curiosity. A Traveler, you said. Is he a mage?"

Avar grinned, "Aren't they all? But truthfully, I don't think he has a drop of Traveler blood—he is, however, a skilled healer."

And as they strode through the palace to the stables, Avar chatted cheerfully about his trip, not at all like a man talking to someone he held in contempt. Phoran wondered whether he should tell Avar what his brother had said—and decided not to. Not because he was afraid to hurt Avar, but because he didn't want Avar to know that anyone held Phoran in contempt.

Under the cheerful flow of Avar's attention, Phoran began to rethink the whole of last night's debacle. It was traditional for people not to like their rulers—and he probably misunderstood what they were saying about his uncle. They hadn't said that they had killed him, just that he had been killed. Phoran hadn't been drunk, precisely, but he hadn't exactly been sober either. It was easy to misinterpret things in that state.

Phoran relaxed and let himself revel in his hero's company. It had been weeks since he'd had Avar's undivided attention. His contentment was somewhat shaken when they brought his stallion to him.

Phoran, who had learned to ride as soon as he could walk, had to use a mounting block to attain the saddle.

Fat, indeed, he thought, red-faced as the stablemen who'd known him from the time he was a toddler fought not to meet his eyes. At least they had trusted him with his own stallion, who had responded with his usual fury to the weight of a rider—perhaps a little worse for having not been ridden for so many months.

By the time Blade quit fussing, Phoran was tired, quite certain he'd pulled a muscle in his back, and thoroughly triumphant. Not everyone could have stayed on such an animal, and he'd managed it. The stallion snorted and settled down as if the previous theatrics had never been.

"Nicely ridden, my emperor," murmured Avar with just the proper amount of admiration to make the comment too much.

Phoran watched the stablemen's faces change from approval to veiled contempt. *Had Avar done that on purpose?* thought the small hurt part of Phoran that was still writhing under Toarsen's derision.

Avar had things to look after that evening, and Phoran did not follow his impulse to plead with Avar to stay. The ride had reminded him of his uncle, who had taught him horsemanship. His uncle, who would have been disappointed in the man Phoran had grown to be.

"You have brains, mi'lad," he remembered his uncle saying. "Emperor or not. Use them."

So it was that as darkness fell in his rooms and the flames in the fireplace died to bare glowing embers, Phoran was alone again when the Memory came.

It stood taller than a man and stopped some few feet away. Doubtless, Phoran thought with humor that barely masked his terror, it was taken aback that he was not in a drunken stupor or crying in the corner as he had been on more than one occasion.

It looked like nothing at all, as if a human eye couldn't quite focus on what it was—though tonight it looked, somehow, more *real* than it had been before.

Its hesitation, if it had hesitated at all, was only momentary. For the first time, Phoran stood quietly as it enfolded him in its blackness, taking away his ability to move or cry out. He'd hoped that it would be better if he held still, but the burning pain of fangs piercing the inner skin of his elbow was as terrible as he remembered. Cold entered Phoran from the place where the Memory fed, as if it was replacing what it drank with ice. When it was done it said the words that had become too familiar.

"By the taking of your blood, I owe you. One answer. Choose your question."

"Are you afraid of other people?" Phoran asked. "Is that why you don't come if someone's in the room with me?"

"No," it said and vanished.

Shivering as if he'd been hunting in winter, Phoran the Twenty-Seventh curled up on the rug on the floor of his room.

CHAPTER 8

This time it wasn't the grating that opened, but the door. Tier shot to his feet and had to stop there because the sudden light blinded him.

"If it please you, my lord," said a soft tenor voice that could have belonged equally well to a young man or a woman, "Would you come with me? We have arranged for your comfort. I am to offer you also an apology for how you have been treated. We have not been ready to receive you until now."

Tier wiped his eyes and squinted against the glare of what was, after all, a fairly dim lantern to see the backlit form of a woman.

The sight, he could tell, was staged. She held the light carefully to exhibit certain aspects of her form. The slight tremor in the hand that held the lantern might be faked as well—but he'd have been worried about facing a man who'd been caged for as long as Tier had, so he gave her the benefit of the doubt.

"I'm no lord," he said at last. "Tell me just who it is I have to thank for my recent stay here?"

"If it please you, *sir*," she said. "I'll take you to where all of your questions can be answered."

Tier could have overpowered her, and would have if she had been a man. But if they, whoever they were, sent a woman to get him, it could only be because overpowering her would get him nowhere.

"You'll have to give me a moment," he said, "until I can see again."

As his vision cleared, he saw that the woman was arrayed in flowing garments that hinted broadly at the body beneath.

A whore's costume, but this woman was no common whore. She was extraordinarily beautiful, even to a man who preferred his woman to be less soft and breakable. Even if the net of gems and gold that confined quite a bit of equally golden hair was paste and brass—and he wasn't at all sure it was—the cloth of her dress was worth a fair penny.

"Can you see, yet, sir?" she asked.

"Oh aye," he said congenially. He'd bide his time until he had enough information to act. "Lead on, fair lady."

She laughed gently at his address as she led him out into a winding corridor. Behaving, he thought, as if he were a customer, rather than a man who'd been imprisoned for weeks.

The hall ceiling was so low he could have easily touched it with a hand. On either side of his cell there were doors that opened to his hand and revealed rooms that looked much like his. The woman was patient with him, waiting without murmuring and pausing with him when he stopped by an iron door twice as wide as the one that led into his cell. The door stuck fast when he tried it.

The woman said nothing. When he took the lantern from her and adjusted it brighter so he could look more closely at the doors, she merely folded her arms under her full breasts.

He ignored her until he was certain that the door was hinged on the other side, with two iron bars (barely visible in the narrow space between door and frame) in place to keep the door shut. If he'd access to a forge he could fashion something to unbar the door—but they were unlikely to allow him such.

He handed the lantern back to his hostess and allowed her to lead him.

The hall continued around a sharp bend and ended in double doors. Just before the walls ended, there was a door on either side. It was the left-hand door the woman opened, stepping back for him to precede her.

The smell of steam and the sound of running water emerged

from the opened door, so he was unsurprised to enter a bathing room. He knew what one looked like because the Sept of Gerant had held war conferences in his—saying that the sound of the water kept people from overhearing anything useful. But that austere chamber had as much to do with this one as a donkey had with a warhorse. A golden tub of a size to accommodate five or six was brim full of hot, steaming water with a tall table near it holding a variety of soaps and pots of lotion. But by far the most impressive part of the room was the cold pool.

Water cascaded from an opening in the ceiling high above and poured onto a ledge of fitted rock where it was spread to fall in a wide sheet to the waist-deep pool below. He could tell the pool was waist-deep because there were two naked, frightened, and obviously cold women standing in it.

"Sssst," hissed his guide in sudden irritation. "You look as if you are about to lose your virtue again. Does this look like a man who'd hurt women?"

She softened her voice to velvet and turned back to Tier. "You'll forgive them, my . . . sir. Our last guest was none to happy with his captivity and took it out on those who had nothing to do with it."

He laughed with honest amusement. "After that speech I would certainly feel like a stupid lout to try any such thing," he said.

In the brighter light of the bathing chamber he could see that she was more than beautiful—she was fascinating, a woman who'd draw men's eyes when she was eighty. He mentally upped her probable price again. So why was he being offered such service? The thought pulled the smile from his face.

"So I'm to clean myself before being presented, eh?" he said neutrally.

"We will perform that service, sir, if you will allow us," she said, bowing her head in submission. "When you are finished bathing, there are clean clothes to replace the ones you wear now. This is for your comfort entirely. If you choose, you may stay as you are and I'll take you in now. I thought you would prefer not to appear at a disadvantage."

"Disadvantage, eh?" He glanced at his clothes. "If they kidnap a man at the tail end of a three-month hunt, they get as they deserve. I'll wash, but you ladies get yourselves out of here or my wife will have my head."

The women in the pool giggled as if he'd been witty, but they waited for a gesture from the woman he'd followed before they left the pool. They wrapped themselves in a couple of the bathing sheets folded in piles on a bench and exited the room through the same door he'd entered.

"You too, lass," he told his guide. "The high-born you serve may be comfortable with help, but we Rederni are competent to wash ourselves."

Smilingly she bowed and left, shutting the door behind her. He hadn't noticed a latch, but he heard a click that could be nothing else so he didn't bother to try the door. The waterfall was more intriguing.

Four leaps gave him a fingerhold on the lowest ledge and he climbed the rest with relative ease. When he found the opening the water fell through in the corner of the ceiling, it was grated with iron bars set in mortar.

He slid back down and splashed uncaring of his battered clothing into the cold pool of water. He hadn't expected such an obvious way out, but he needed to know what he dealt with. Eventually he'd manage a way out—in the meantime there was no need for filth.

He washed the clothes on his body first, then threw them into the waiting hot tub, where he'd soap down both them and himself when he was ready.

The cold water poured over his face, clearing his head and his thoughts as he scraped away dirt.

He hadn't heard anyone enter, but when he stepped out from the waterfall, there were clean clothes waiting for him.

He ignored them and settled into the tub of hot water, soaped himself off, and gave rough service to his clothes. Rinsing everything in the cold pool, he draped his clothes where he could. Shivering now, he dried himself and examined the clothing she'd left for him.

It was serviceable clothing, very like the filthy garments he'd taken off, though less worn. He fingered the shirt thoughtfully before donning it. The leather boots fit him as well as his old ones, lost somewhere during his captivity.

As he tied the laces of his boots, his guide returned, her

timing too accurate for guessing. Someone had been watching him—he hoped they enjoyed the show. She held a tray with a comb and a plain silver clip and held them out. He ran the comb through his hair and pulled it back into a queue which he fastened with the clip.

He turned around once for her perusal and she nodded. "You'll do, sir. If you'll follow me, the Master awaits your presence."

"Master?" he asked.

But she'd given him all the information she intended to. "Come," she said, leading him back to the corridor.

The double doors at the end of the hall were open this time and a haze of smoke drifted into the corridor along with a desultory drumbeat and a hum of conversation. But he had only a moment to glance inside and get an impression of some sort of public room with tables and benches scattered around, before the woman opened the door directly across from the bathing room and gestured him in.

In size and lack of windows, the room resembled the cell Tier had been living in, though here the stone floor was covered with a tightly woven rug that cushioned his feet. A pair of matching tapestries hung on one wall. The only furnishings in the room were two comfortable-looking chairs flanking a small round table.

In one of the chairs sat a man in a black velvet robe sipping from a goblet. He was a decade or so older than Tier with the features of an eastern nobleman, wide-cheeked and flat-nosed. Like his face, his hands belonged to an aristocrat, long-fingered and bedecked with rings.

He looked up when Tier's guide softly cleared her throat.

"Ah. Thank you, Myrceria," he said pleasantly, setting his goblet on the table. "That will be all."

The door shut quietly behind Tier's back, leaving the two men alone in the room.

The robed man folded his hands contemplatively against his chin, "You don't look like a Traveler, Tieragan of Redern."

Traveler?

Tier raised an eyebrow and took the empty chair. It was a little short for him, so he stretched out his legs and crossed his ankles. When he was comfortable, he looked at the man most probably responsible for his recent imprisonment and said courteously, "And you don't look like a festering pustule on a slug's hind end either. Appearances can be deceiving."

The other man's face didn't change, but Tier felt a pulse of power, of magic—just as he was meant to.

The surge of magic died and the wizard smiled. "You *are* angry, aren't you? I do believe we owe you an apology for keeping you locked in your cell, but it has been a long time since we had an Owl in our keeping. We had to be certain that we could contain your magic before releasing you."

Contain his magic?

"You seem to know a lot about me," Tier commented. "Would you care to return the favor?"

The other man laughed, "You'll have to excuse me—you're not quite what I expected. I am Kerstang, Sept of Telleridge."

Tier nodded slowly. "And what would the Sept of Telleridge want with a Rederni farmer?"

"Nothing at all," said Telleridge. "I do, however, have a use for a Traveler and Bard."

"I told you," said Tier mildly. "I am not a Traveler. What do you need me for?"

Telleridge smiled as if Tier's answer had pleased him. "In addition to my duties as a Sept, I find myself with the delicate charge of the youth of the Empire. The law of primogeniture, however necessary, leaves many of the younger sons of noblemen without any constructive outlets for their energies. I run an Eyrie for these lost young men and I'm responsible for their entertainment."

"I'm the entertainment?" said Tier. "Surely there are bards who don't need abducting to be persuaded to provide entertainment."

Telleridge laughed, "But they would not be nearly as amusing." The laughter drifted away as if it had never been. "Nor would they be Owl. All you need to know at the moment is that you are, will you or nil you, my guest for the next year. During that time you will entertain my young friends and occasionally participate in our ceremonies. In return you may ask for anything that you wish, short of leaving, and it will be arranged."

"I don't think so," said Tier.

"Refusing is not an option," said the wizard. "For a year and a day you will have whatever you want—or you can struggle; it matters not one whit to me."

That phrase struck a chord of memory. "A year and a day," Tier said. "You'll make me beggar king for a year and a day." He hummed a bit of the old tune. "And I suppose, like the beggar king, you'll sacrifice me to the gods at the end?"

"That's right," said the wizard as if Tier were a prized pupil. "I see that an Owl will be different than a Raven—which is what we've had the last three times. The Hunter was interesting, though we finally had to cage him. I think you'll do. But first . . ."

He leaned forward and touched Tier lightly; as he did so, the silver and onyx ring on his index finger caught Tier's attention briefly.

He was distracted by the ring when the wizard's voice dropped a full octave and he said in the Traveler tongue, *"By Lark and Raven, I bind you that you will harm neither me nor any wizard who wears a black cloak in these halls. By Cormorant and Owl, I bind you that you will not ask anyone to help you escape. By Falcon, I bind you that you will not speak of your death."*

Magic surged through Tier, holding him still until the wizard was done.

"There," he said sitting back again.

There indeed, thought Tier, shaken. No one had ever laid a spell on him before. He felt . . . violated and frightened. It had been so fast and he hadn't been able to defend himself from it at all. Cold sweat slid down his neck and he shivered, fighting nausea.

"Sick?" Telleridge asked. "It takes some people like that, but I couldn't depend upon the word of a Traveler peasant—even if you'd give it. My young friends are easily influenced. I would hate to lose any of my Passerines too soon."

"Passerines?" asked Tier, breathing shallowly through his nose and hoping he didn't look as shaken as he felt. "You have song birds here?"

The wizard smiled. "As I said, a Bard will be interesting. Myrceria will tell you what you need to know about my

Passerines. Ask her about the Secret Path if you wish. She is waiting for you outside the door."

The woman was indeed waiting for him, kneeling on the cold stone of the floor with her hands at rest. Prepared, Tier thought, to deal with a man in any mood he might emerge with. She sat unmoving until he closed the door gently behind him.

"If you like, I can take you into the Eyrie," she said, using her right arm to indicate the open double doors. "There are others to talk to if you wish and food and drink are available to you there. If you would prefer to ask me questions, we can go back to your room. You will find it much improved."

"Let's go talk," he said after a moment.

As Myrceria promised, the cell had been transformed in his absence. It had been scoured clean and furnished with a bed such as the nobles slept in rather than the rush-stuffed mattress over stretched rope he had at home. Rich fabrics and rare woods filled the room; it should have looked crowded, but it managed to appear cozy instead. In the center of the bed a worn lute rested, looking oddly out of place.

He took a step toward it, but stopped. He wasn't like Seraph: he didn't feel the need to do the opposite of whatever anyone tried to get him to do, but that didn't mean he enjoyed being manipulated either. So he left the lute for later examination and chose to investigate another oddity. The room was lit by glowing stones in copper braziers placed in strategic places around the room.

"They're quite safe," said Myrceria behind him. She moved against him, pressing close until her breasts rested against his back, then reached around him to pick the fist-sized rock out of the brazier he'd picked up.

He set the brazier down gently and stepped away from her. "You are quite lovely, lass," he said. "But if you knew my wife, you'd know that she'd take my liver and eat it in front of my quivering body if I ever betrayed her."

"She is not here," Myrceria murmured, replacing the rock and turning gracefully in a circle so that he could see what he was refusing. "She will never know."

"I don't underestimate my wife," he replied. "Nor should you."

Myrceria touched the net that confined her hair and shook her head, freeing waves of gold to cascade down her back and touch her ankles. "She'll believe you're dead," she said. "They have arranged for it. Will she be faithful to you if you are dead?"

Seraph thought he was dead? He needed to get home.

"Telleridge said you would answer my questions," he said. "Where are we?"

"In the palace," she answered.

"In Taela?"

"That's right," she leaned into him.

He bent until his face was close to hers. "No," he said softly. "You have answers to my questions, and that is all I'm interested in." There was a flash of fear in her eyes, and it occurred to him that a whore was hardly likely to be so interested in him on her own. "You can tell Telleridge whatever you like about tonight; I'll not deny it—but I'll not break the vows I've made. I have my own woman; I need answers."

She stood very still for a moment, her eyes unreadable—which told him more about what she was thinking than the facile, convenient expressions of a whore.

Slowly, but not seductively, she rebound her hair. When she was finished she had tucked away her potent sexuality as well.

"Very well," she said. "What would you like to know?"

"Tell me a lie," he said.

Her eyebrows raised. "A lie?"

"Anything. Tell me that the coverlet is blue."

"The coverlet is blue."

Nothing. He felt nothing.

"Tell me it's green," he said.

"The coverlet is green."

He couldn't tell when she was lying. Just about the only useful thing his magic could do. He opened his mouth to ask her to help him escape, just to see if he could, but no word of his request left his throat.

"*Gods take him!*" he roared angrily. "Gods take him and eat his spleen while he yet lives." He turned toward the whore and she flinched away from him needlessly. He had himself under control now. "Tell me about this place, the Passerines, the Secret Path, Telleridge . . . all of it."

She took a step back and sat gingerly on the edge of the bed, on the far side of the lute. Speaking quickly, she said, "The Secret Path is a clandestine organization of nobles. The rooms that you have seen today and a few others are under an unused wing of the palace. Most of the activities of the Path involve only the young men, the Passerines. The older members and the Masters, the wizards, direct what those activities are. The Passerines are the younger members of the Secret Path. They are brought in between the ages of sixteen and twenty."

"What do they call the older members?" asked Tier.

"Raptors," she replied, relaxing a little, "and the wizards are the Masters."

"Who is in charge, the wizards or the Raptors?"

"The High Path—which is made up of a select group of Raptors and Masters and led by Master Telleridge."

"What is the requirement for membership?" he asked.

"Noble birth and the proper temperament. None of them can be direct heirs of the Septs. Most of the boys come at the recommendation of the other Passerines."

"Telleridge is a Sept," said Tier, trying to put his knowledge into an acceptable pattern.

"Yes. His father and brothers died of plague."

"Did he start this . . . Secret Path?"

"No." She settled more comfortably against the wall. "It is a very old association, over two hundred and fifty years old."

Tier thought back over the history of the Empire. "After the Third Civil War."

Myrceria nodded her head, and smiled a little.

"Phoran the Eighteenth, I believe, who inherited right in the middle of the war when his father was killed by an assassin," he said. "A man known for his brilliance in diplomacy rather than war. Now what exactly was it that caused that war . . ."

Her smile widened, "I imagine you know quite well. Bards, I've been told, have to know their history."

"The younger sons of a number of the more powerful Septs

seized their fathers'—or brothers' lands illegally while the Septs were meeting in council. They claimed that the laws of primogeniture were wrong, robbing younger sons of their proper inheritance. The war lasted twenty years."

"Twenty-three," she corrected mildly.

"I bet the Path was founded by Phoran the Eighteenth's younger brother—the war leader."

She cleared her throat. "By Phoran's youngest son, actually, although his brother was one of the original members."

"The Path," said Tier, having found the pattern, "draws the younger sons, young men educated to wield power but who will never have any. Only the ones who are angriest at their lot in life are allowed into it. As young men, they are given a secret way to defy those in power—a safe outlet for their energies. Then, I suppose, a few are guided slowly into places where they can gain power—advisor to the king, merchant, diplomat. Places where they acquire power and an investment in the health of the Empire they despise. Old Phoran the Eighteenth was a master strategist."

"You are well educated for a . . . a baker," she said, "from a little village in the middle of nowhere."

He smiled at her. "I fought under the Sept of Gerant from the time I was fifteen until the last war was over. He has a reputation as being something of an eccentric. He wasn't concerned with the birth of his commanders, but he did think that his commanders needed to know as much about politics and history as they knew about war."

"A soldier?" She considered the idea. "I'd forgotten that— they didn't seem to consider it to be of much importance."

"You are well-educated for your position as well," he said.

"If younger sons have no place in the Empire, their daughters have—" she stopped abruptly and took a step backward. "Why am I telling you this?" Her voice shook in unfeigned fear. "You're not supposed to be able to work magic here. They said that you couldn't."

"I'm working no magic," he said.

"I have to go," she said and left the cell. She didn't, he noticed, forget to shut and bolt the door.

When she was gone, he pulled his legs up on the bed, boots and all, and leaned against the wall.

Whatever the Path was supposed to have been, he doubted that its only purpose was to keep the young nobles occupied. Telleridge didn't strike him as the sort to serve anyone except himself—certainly not the stability of the Empire.

Thinking of Telleridge reminded Tier of what the wizard had done to him. His magic was really gone—not that it was likely to do him much good in a situation like this. Alone, without witnesses, Tier sat on the bed and buried his head in his hands, seeing, once more, Telleridge's hand closing on his arm.

Wizards weren't supposed to be able to cast spells like that. They had to make potions and draw symbols—he'd seen them do it. Only Ravens were able to cast spells with words. Telleridge had spoken in the Traveler tongue.

Tier straightened up and stared at one of the glowing braziers without seeing it. That ring. He had seen that ring before, the night he'd met Seraph.

Though it had been twenty years, he was certain he was not mistaken. He'd a knack for remembering things, and the ring Telleridge had worn had the same notch on the setting that the ring . . . what had his name been? Wresen. Wresen had been a wizard, too. A wizard following Seraph.

How had Telleridge known that Tier was Bard? Tier had supposed that his unknown visitor had told the wizard, if it hadn't been the wizard himself. However, it sounded as if Tier being a Bard was the reason they'd taken him in the first place. No one except Seraph knew what he was—though she'd told him that any Raven would know.

They had been watching him. Myrceria had known that he had been a baker and a soldier. Had they been watching him and Seraph for twenty years? Were they watching Seraph now?

He sprang to his feet and paced. He had to get home. When an hour of fruitless thought left him still in the locked cell, he settled back on the bed and took up the lute absently. All he could do was be ready for an opportunity to escape as it presented itself.

He noticed the tune that he'd begun fingering with wry amusement. Almost defiantly he plucked out the chorus with quick-fingered precision.

A year and a day,
A year and a day,
And the beggar'll be king
For a year and a day.

In the song, in order to stop a decade-long drought, desperate priests decided that the ultimate sacrifice had to be made—the most important person in the nation had to be sacrificed: the king. Unwilling to die, the king refused, but proposed the priests take one of the beggars from the street. The king would step down from office for a year and let the beggar be king. The priests argued that a year was not long enough—so they made the beggar king for a year and a day. The drought ended with the final, willing sacrifice of the young man who'd proved more worthy than the real king.

Just as the Secret Path's Traveler king, Tier, would die at the end of his reign.

He thought of one of the bindings Telleridge had put on him. The young men, the Passerines, didn't know he would die—otherwise there would be no reason to forbid him to speak of it with them.

No doubt then his death would serve a purpose greater than mimicking an old song. Would it appease the gods like the beggar king's sacrifice in the story? But then why hide it from the young men? What would a wizard want with his death?

Magic and death, he remembered Seraph telling him once. Magic and death are a very powerful combination. The better the mage knows the victim, the stronger the magic he can work. The mage's pet cat works better than a stray. A friend better than an enemy . . . a friend for a year and a day.

He had to get word to Seraph. He had to warn her to protect the children.

His fingers picked out the chords to an old war song. *Myrceria,* he thought, *I will work on Myrceria.*

Phoran held the bundle of parchment triumphantly as he marched alone through the halls of the palace toward his study. They'd look for him in his rooms first, he thought. No one but the old librarian knew about the study. They'd find him eventually, but not until he was ready for them.

It had been impulse, really. When the old fool, Douver, set down the papers the Council of Septs had for him to sign, Phoran had just picked them up, tucked them under his arm, and announced to the almost empty room that he would take them under advisement.

He'd turned on his heel and walked out, slipping through a complex system of secret passages—some of which were so well known they might be corridors and others he rather thought he might be the only one who knew. He'd given no one a chance to follow him.

For most of his life, he'd signed what they told him to. At least his uncle had done him the courtesy of explaining what he'd signed—though he remembered not caring much about most of it.

But the empty room had been an insult. When the Emperor signed the proposals into law twice a year, there should be people present, and would have been, if anyone thought that the Emperor would do anything but sign what he was told.

He entered the library through a secondary door, passed unnoticed among the bins of parchment and shelves of books in the back corner of the room, and unlocked the door of his study. It was a small room, but it locked from the inside as well as the outside, which was all that he required.

He settled himself into his chair and thought. It was all very well to decide to be emperor in fact as well as name, but he didn't really have the support he needed. The Sept of Gorrish fancied himself defacto ruler, and the Septs who followed him, Telleridge, and the like, would do their best to fight any sign of independence.

Really, he'd best sign the damn things and get it over with.

Instead he uncorked his inkwell, trimmed his pens, and began to read. The first three parchments he signed—complex trade agreements between various Septs, and nothing the Emperor should interfere with. But, almost involuntarily, he made mental notes of the names involved and the alliances the new laws revealed.

The fourth parchment was another of the increasingly punitive laws aimed at the Travelers. He signed that one, too. Most Travelers were thieves, his uncle had said, though not without a certain amount of sympathy. Having no land they could settle on, because no Sept would have allowed such a thing, they were forced to earn their bread as best they could.

Hours passed. Occasionally, Phoran would sneak out to the library to retrieve maps or books. But he signed the parchments one by one—setting only a few aside for further review.

Two he found that might serve his point. They were regional matters that most of the council would not care unduly about; each was signed by only a few more than half the council with no protests.

The first act would give the Sept of Holla exclusive fishing rights in Lake Azalan. Phoran had checked his maps and found Lake Azalan to be a small body of water in the Sept of Holla's lands. The law was so odd—the Septs usually had effective exclusive rights to any fully enclosed body of water—that Phoran knew there was a story behind the ruling. The second concerned a small section of land awarded to the Sept of Jenne for his "services to the Empire."

He pored over the simple words to mine them for clues and regretted the indifference that had kept him from the council the past few years, because he no longer knew all of the different alliances. Geography helped—all of Holla's signatures were from Septs in the Northeast, Holla's neighbors. All except one of his neighbors. The one, thought Phoran with sudden comprehension, who had been sending fishermen into his neighbor's lake.

That one would work—Holla had little influence in the council. But he'd rather come down on the side of justice.

The second one was frustrating because the land in question was so small that he couldn't find out much about it.

He looked up from a map and the Memory was there.

He hadn't realized how long he'd been in his study. He'd trimmed the lamps absently as he'd needed, and there was no window to tell him that the sun had set.

Slowly Phoran set his pen down and shed the heavy state robes so he could bare his arm. The hope that had cloaked him for most of the day evaporated at the touch of cold, cold lips on his skin.

It hurt, and he looked away as it fed.

"By the taking of your blood, I owe you one answer. Choose your question."

Tired beyond reason and still trembling with the remnants of pain, Phoran laughed harshly and said, "Do you know someone who could help me understand what's so special about a small slice of the Sept of Gerant's lands that the council would gift it to the Sept of Jenne?"

The Memory turned and drifted toward the door.

"I thought you owed me an answer," said Phoran without heat. That would have taken too much passion, and he'd already, really, given up on his plans. He would not hurt an innocent man just because his petition was convenient for his purposes, and he was beginning to believe that the library did not contain the information he needed to refuse to sign Jenne's petition.

He'd already begun to go back to comparing two well-drawn maps to a third, less clear, but more detailed when the Memory said, "Come."

Phoran looked up and saw it waiting for him. It took him a moment to remember exactly what he'd asked.

"*You* know someone who could help?"

It didn't answer.

Phoran stared at it and tried to think. If anyone saw him . . . He glanced at the parchments and maps scattered around and gathered the ones that might prove helpful.

CHAPTER 9

They came for him shortly after Myrceria left.

Tier set the lute down, and stood up when the door opened to admit five men in black robes like the one Telleridge had worn. Their hoods were pulled down over their faces and they walked in as if they each had a predetermined place to stand. Tier had the oddest feeling that they did not see him at all.

They took up positions around him. One after the other they began chanting, a low, droning, off-pitch sound that he could not decipher because the words they used belonged to no language he'd ever heard. Magic, he knew, but he was helpless to stop them because of Telleridge's command.

As one, they raised their hands above their heads and clapped . . .

He awoke lying on the floor, naked and sweating. The memory of pain lent nausea to the cacophony of tingling body parts. He sat up, frantically trying to remember what had happened after the wizards had clapped their hands, but the thought of the sound made his ears ring.

They had taken his memories. Even so, there were things that he knew, as if the events he couldn't remember had left a visceral residue on his body. He'd been violated, not physically raped but something that was a near kin.

He sat up straight and held his head like a wolf scenting a hare. He remembered that, remembered someone telling him . . . remembered *Telleridge* telling him that he would not know what had happened.

Owls had very good memories.

Tier's lips drew back in a snarl. Hatred was a foreign emotion to him. He'd fought for years against an enemy he was told to hate, but he'd never found anything in his heart but a grim determination to persevere. The Fahlarn were not wicked, just wrongly ambitious. He had seen people do terrible things because of stupidity, ignorance, anger, but he'd never met evil before.

Now he was befouled by it.

Staggering to his feet, he looked for his clothing. When he was clothed he could feel less vulnerable. They'd taken his memories and his magic, but surely they would leave him clothes.

A cursory search of the room turned up a tunic and pants, though not his own. They were looser in fit than he was used to and darker colored: Traveler clothes for their pet Traveler. Nevertheless, he pulled them on quickly.

Instinctively he looked for something he could use to clean himself, and noticed there was no water in the room. Even as he regretted the lack, he knew that it wouldn't have mattered if they'd left him in the bathing room—the filth that coated him could not be cleaned that way.

His gaze fell upon the lute.

No matter how fine the instrument, a lute always needed tuning. He sat down beside it and cradled it to him.

There were eight courses on this instrument, two strings per course except for the highest note, and this lute hadn't been properly tuned in a while. As he settled into the familiar chore, the shaky, frightened feeling in his stomach began to settle.

He tightened pegs by slight movements, because there were no extra strings sitting around if he broke one. As the lute started to come up to tune, he noticed that the man who'd set the fretting had had an ear as good as his own—perhaps he'd been a Bard, too.

He tried a simple refrain and knew in a rush of relief that this was what he'd needed. For a long time he just played bits of this and that, letting the music salve the hurt that had been done to him.

At last his fingers hit upon a tune that his ears enjoyed, a piece his grandfather had written to welcome the coming of spring. He closed his eyes and let the music fill him until everything else was distant, where it could no longer harm him. He took a deep breath that filled his lungs with the scent of lilacs.

Magic.

He opened his eyes, stilled his hands, and took another breath. The scent had faded, but he could still smell the sweet flowers until his sinuses closed. His eyes watered and he sneezed twice; Lilacs always made him sneeze.

Perhaps, he thought, *they don't know as much about Traveler magic as they think they do.*

There was a scuffle outside his door, as if someone fumbled with a key.

"Drat," said a young man's voice. "Drat, drat. This key is supposed to open any door in the palace. Wait, ah. A turnkey box." There was some more rustling and a jangle of keys rattling together. The door of his cell creaked open.

"Er, hallo?" A rather pudgy young face peered around the edge of the door.

"Hello," Tier said mildly, though his body was tense and ready to act.

"Look, I hope I didn't wake you or . . . your light was still on so I thought . . ." The young man stumbled to a halt.

"Come in," invited Tier genially. *Keys,* he thought, *lowering his eyelids. This boy would be no—*

He rolled to his feet abruptly. "What in the name of the seven flaming hells is *that?*"

The boy looked over his shoulder at the dark, nebulous shape behind him for a moment.

"You can see it?" he asked, sounding unhappy. "Most people can't. It's . . . ah . . . it calls itself a Memory—as if that's a name. I haven't figured it out exactly myself. It doesn't usually linger like this."

As the thing moved into the room, Tier took a step back from the overwhelming presence it carried with it. He sat back on his bed and tried to look peaceful.

"I'm sorry," the boy apologized.

Tier turned his attention back to him with an effort, and noticed for the first time the quality of the clothes he was wearing. Velvet embroidered in heavy metal threads that looked as if they were really gold.

"Look," said the boy again. "I don't know why you're here. These aren't the regular holding cells. But for some reason"—he gave an odd, short laugh—"I think you might help me with a problem I've been looking into."

And the boy took a piece of parchment he'd been holding and thrust it at Tier. He sat beside him on the bed, started to point at something and then stopped.

"Do you read?" he asked. "Not to be offensive, you understand, but you're dressed like—"

"I can read Common," said Tier. He'd learned under the Sept of Gerant, making him one of the double handful of people who could read in Redern.

Since the Memory, whatever that was, had decided to stay on the far side of the cell, Tier allowed himself to look more closely at the writing on the parchment.

"Look here," said the boy, sounding more authoritative. "This is nominally just a simple award for a job well done. Except that usually properties that belong to one Sept aren't gifted to another—certainly not with a vague 'for services to the Empire.' See?"

Tier looked at what he held with disbelief. It appeared to be a law document of some sort.

First Tier had thought that the boy might be one of Telleridge's wizards, especially with the thing that had followed him in. Then he'd been almost certain that he was one of the Passerines Myrceria had told him about. Now . . .

He cleared his throat. "Are you a member of the Secret Path?"

"If I'm not, does that mean you can't tell me the answer?"

The disingenuous answer made Tier laugh in spite of his generally lousy mood. The young man gave him a pleased smile.

"Actually, I've never heard of the Secret Path. Though, if you put any three nobles together, they'll start four secret societies of something."

Tier nodded his head slowly. "I'd been given the impression that the Path members had taken over this bit of the palace and made it their own. If you're not one, how did you find your way here?"

The boy shrugged. "The palace has enough rooms to house the whole city and then some. The first fifteen Emperors Phoran spent all their time building the place and the next ten tried to figure out what to do with all the rooms—mostly close them up. At least two of them, the eighth and the fourteenth—or the seventh and the thirteenth if you'd rather not give a number to the first Phoran—were fascinated by secret rooms and passages. By happy chance I stumbled upon the plans of Eight and actively sought Fourteen's. Once I had them, I hid them myself. At any rate, they give me ready access to most of the palace. Not that there's usually much to see."

"I see," said Tier, rather dazzled by all the eights who might have been sevens—there was a song in that somewhere. He hadn't really thought about *how* the Path had managed to secret off such a big chunk of building. He had a hard time wrapping his mind around a building so large that the Path could use a section for generations and not have it discovered.

"I'm not a lawyer," Tier said finally. "Nor do I know anything about the Septs. I don't see how I can help you."

The boy frowned. "I asked if there was someone who could help me find out more about the piece of land in question. Is there any reason that you would know something about the Sept of Gerant's lands?

"The Sept of Gerant?" exclaimed Tier, distracted from the question of who knew enough to send this boy after him.

"That's right," said the boy. "I don't know him by face, but it sounds as if you've met him."

"He'll not have been at court," murmured Tier, reading the rest of the document rapidly. "He's an old warrior, not fitted for wearing silks and such. The Sept of Jenne, hmm."

"I have this, if it helps," said the boy, and he pulled a small, faded map from a pocket. "I can show you where the land in question is—I just don't know what's so important about it."

The soft hand that handed Tier a map had a signet ring on it. Tier noticed and catalogued it, but he was thinking about the map so it took him a moment before he realized who was sitting on his bed beside him.

The Emperor?

His night had acquired a new level of strangeness. Tier glanced at the Memory. Was it some sort of body guard?

He forced his eyes back to the map. If the Emperor had wanted him to know who he was talking to, he would have introduced himself.

The boy tapped a spot on the old map. "That's where it is. It doesn't even connect to Jenne's lands."

Tier closed his eyes and thought back twenty years, trying to make the lines on the map correspond to the land he had known rather well at one time.

"Water rights," he said finally. "That's the headwaters of the creek that gives Gerant's people water. This piece of land belongs to the Sept of Jenne's father-in-law—or it did twenty years ago. The current Sept might be the son or grandson of the man I'm thinking of, but at any rate, the land's in Jenne's family's hands. It's pretty useless despite its size, because it's in the rainshadow of Brulles Mountain—won't grow anything but sagebrush. If Jenne had control of Brulles—that strip of map should be marked to show the mountain—he could hire a wizard to divert the flow of water and send it down the other side of the mountain, or find some way of diverting the small river that runs on the wrong side for their purposes."

"Hah," the boy exclaimed happily. "It's a payoff. That's the one I want, then. What can you tell me about Gerant's allies?"

Tier hesitated. "Gerant's a good man," he said.

The boy raised an eyebrow. "I'm not planning on hurting him. I . . ." Now it was his turn to hesitate.

"I suspect," said Tier softly, "that there's a law or two against a common man like me sharing a seat with the Emperor. If you've a need to be incognito, it might be better to take off that ring."

Phoran (doubtless the boy's name was Phoran—though

Tier couldn't remember the number that went with the name) looked upset for a moment, glanced at the ring that was the Emperor's seal, then shrugged.

"I'll keep your advice in mind. Well enough. If you know that much, look here." He tapped the paper impatiently. "I need something I can use as a fulcrum to move the power structure in the Council of Septs so that I don't continue to be just a figurehead, and this document is it. It was in my twice-yearly stack of petitions to be signed into law. There aren't many signatures on this—only a few people who owed Jenne something. Like as not most of them didn't know what it was they were signing. You can't even tell that this land is Gerant's without this map."

"Right," said Tier. He hadn't realized that the boy was a figurehead, but then he hadn't concerned himself with any news outside of Redern since he'd left Gerant's services several years before the last Phoran died. "Twenty-sixth," he said aloud.

"Only if you don't count the first Phoran," said Phoran, not the least discomposed. "I like to, though my father didn't. Are you still with me?"

"Right," Tier nodded. "You have a bill, obviously a favor, but not for a Sept who is very powerful. So if you decide to decline to sign it, you're not going to make a slew of enemies. Who could object to your refusal to grant one Sept's lands to another without better reason than you've been given? And I'll put up my right arm that Gerant is no traitor or mischief maker that will embarrass you on this. He's true as oak. So you refuse to sign it, and the rest of the council either supports you, or makes it look like they think the council should have the right to take land from whatever Sept they want without giving an adequate reason."

"That's it," said the boy, gathering up his map and document. "And I have a toehold into ruling on my own. So, you have done me a favor." Carefully he folded the parchment so it fit into his pocket with the map. "I owe you an equal favor. Before I determine how best to repay you, tell me what you are doing here, what this Path that I'm not a member of is, and what the two have to do with each other."

"It's faster if I start with the Path," said Tier after thinking about it for a minute. "The rest of the story should fall out of that." Briefly he outlined the information Telleridge and Myrceria had given him.

Phoran stopped him. "They kill the Traveler wizards for power, these wizards who wear black robes?"

Tier nodded. "So I'm told. I've only met two people—three with you—since I was brought here." He thought the ladies in the bath didn't count. "I haven't actually seen any of this for myself."

"You still haven't told me what you are doing here," said Phoran. "Or who you are, other than someone who fought under Gerant in the last war."

"I am a farmer who occasionally sings for a few coppers at the local tavern in Redern," Tier said. "I usually spend the winter months trapping for furs. I was on my way home. I have a vague memory of seeing a group of strangers, and then I awoke in this cell. Telleridge—that's the man I told you about—"

"Telleridge?" said Phoran. "I know him, though I didn't know he was a wizard. Did he tell you why they wanted you enough to take you from Redern?" asked Phoran. Then a strange expression came over his face. "Is that the Redern that belongs to the Sept of Leheigh?"

"Yes," Tier agreed.

"Avar?" said Phoran almost to himself.

Avar, Tier recalled, was the given name of the new Sept, the new Sept who was supposed to be so influential with the Emperor.

"Is Avar a member of this Path?"

Tier shrugged. "I don't know. The only two I've met by name are Telleridge and Myrceria—and I don't think she'd be considered a member."

Phoran got to his feet and began pacing. "Why you?" he asked again. "Why did they go all the way to Redern to find you? You aren't a Traveler, not if you're a farmer in Redern who used to be a solder."

"Because I have a magical talent usually associated with the Travelers," replied Tier. Preempting the next question, he began telling Phoran what he knew about the Orders.

Phoran held up a hand. "Enough," he said. "I believe you.

Let's get you out of here, then you can explain anything you feel necessary."

Tier followed him to the threshold, but when he leaned forward to step through the door, white-hot pain convulsed his body and a shock of magic threw him back several feet into the cell.

"What was that?" said Phoran, startled.

"He is bound," said the Memory. It sounded like a crow's mating call or the rattle of dry bones.

Tier wobbled to his feet. "It talks?"

The Emperor looked at the Memory. "Sometimes. But this is the first time it's ever volunteered information. Are you all right?"

Tier nodded. "Your Memory is right. There must be some sort of magic here I cannot cross."

"Can you do something with it? Didn't you say that you have magic?"

"He is bound," said the Memory again.

"Stop that," said Tier, a command that usually worked when Jes began to get too creepy. He turned to Phoran. "I don't have the kind of magic that could counter this, and they have managed to keep me from what little useful magic I do have. It looks like I'm stuck here."

Phoran nodded. "Very well." He came back into the room and shut the door. "There are wizards who are supposed to serve me, or serve the Empire at least, but I don't know if any of them are the ones who belong to the Path. Find out who the Path's wizards are, and then maybe I can find a wizard to undo this."

He gave Tier an apologetic look. "I am more emperor in name than in reality or I could just order your release. The twentieth—nineteenth by common reckoning—had real power."

Tier grinned, "That's because he'd ordered the death of fifteen Septs by the time he was your age and accounted for another three or four personally."

"I'm rather finicky in my food choices," said Phoran with mock sadness. "I'll never manage to be properly terrifying."

"You wouldn't have to suck the marrow from their bones

the way the Nineteen—ah, excuse me—Twenty did," said Tier solemnly. "I suspect a cooked heart or two would do just fine."

"I don't eat heart," said Phoran firmly. "Though I suppose I could feed it to the grieving heir—that might have a similar effect."

Tier and Phoran gave each other a look of mutual approval.

"I already owe you a favor," said Phoran, "but your experience is different than my own. I'd like your opinion on my problem." He waved at the Memory.

"I am, always, your servant, my emperor," Tier was rather pleased to find that he meant it.

"For the past three months," Phoran began, "I've had this creature. Not that it follows me all the time, you understand. Usually, it just visits me once a night." He smiled grimly and sat down on the bed.

Tier followed his example and collapsed on the other end of the bed. He should have waited until the Emperor bid him sit, but between whatever happened during the time he couldn't remember and the jolt the doorway had given him, his joints were all but jelly.

"Sometimes when I can't sleep," Phoran said, "I go exploring the shut-off places in the palace. I have this key," he took one out of his pocket. "It's supposed to open every door in the palace. It didn't do yours, but it opened the turnkey's box that had your key in it."

He put it away and began his story again. "Anyway, one night a few months ago I was wandering through the Kaore wing—that's one of the ones my father shut down, I'm told. It's usually pretty boring: long corridors with identical rooms on either side, that sort of thing. But this time I heard some noise at the end of one of the corridors."

"No one's supposed to be there—but sometimes people are. I sneaked down to a door that was ajar." He pulled the velvet fabric of his pants and absently rubbed it between thumb and index finger.

"There were a number of people in dark robes with hoods over their heads. They were standing in a loose circle, chanting. A seventh man was kneeling, blindfolded and bound in the center. If I'd known what they were going to do, I'd have tried to stop it somehow. But by the time I saw the knife it was too late. One of the robed men had already slit the bound man's throat."

Phoran got off the bed and began to pace restlessly. "There was blood everywhere—I hadn't realized . . . It was too late for the dead man, and I thought that they might not be too excited at having a witness so I left as quickly as I could. The Memory came to me the next night."

Phoran looked at the creature solemnly, then sank back onto the bed and began rolling up his sleeve. "It comes to me every night," he said, showing Tier marks on the inside of his wrist that climbed in fading scars to the hollow of his elbow.

"After it feeds it tells me that in return it owes me the answer to a question. Usually its answers aren't very useful. Tonight I asked if it knew someone who could tell me something about the Sept of Gerant's lands and it brought me here."

Tier said, "You think that you interrupted them killing their last Traveler prisoner." He considered it. "I think you are right—how many groups of dark-robed men do you have going around killing people in the palace?"

"There might be as many as five or ten," he said. "But not that manage to summon or create something like this." He pointed at his dark comrade. "This is wizardry."

Tier nodded slowly. "I'm not a wizard, but I've dealt with them. If this was something that might result from their meddling, I'd think they'd be careful that it would not attach itself to them. Maybe some magic. That would mean that you were the only one there it could attach itself to."

He got off the bed and walked closer to the Memory. His eyes wouldn't quite focus on it, reminding him forcibly of the way Jes could fade into the shadows when he wanted to.

"How did you know that I could answer the Emperor's question tonight?" asked Tier.

The thing shifted restlessly. "You fed me true," it said at last. "I know you as I know Phoran, twenty-seventh emperor of that name."

"I fed you?" Tier asked.

" 'Numberless were the heroes who fell,' " whispered the Memory in a voice quite different than it had been using: it was no longer without inflection. The change was remarkable.

"*You* were my listener?" said Tier.

"I was Kerine to your Red Ernave," agreed the Memory.

"What else are you?" Tier took a step nearer to it.

"I am death," it said and was gone.

"Did you understand what it meant?" asked Phoran.

Tier rubbed his hands together lightly. "Only a bit of it," he said. "Apparently it feeds on more than just blood. I gave it a story and it took more than I offered—which is how it knew that I'd been one of Gerant's commanders."

He'd invoked magic in that story—more magic than he'd ever brought forth before—and it had only been shortly after that when Telleridge had informed him that his magic was contained. He'd thought that Telleridge had meant that they'd taken his magic away—but perhaps it was more subtle than that.

"Would you tell me a lie?" he asked Phoran.

"My stallion is cow-hocked," he said immediately, apparently unfazed by the abrupt change in subject. "What are you doing?"

"Well," said Tier. "I misunderstood what Telleridge meant when he said they had contained my magic. I can tell if you lie—but not Telleridge or Myrceria."

"Your magic works, but not on the members of the Path," Phoran said.

"So it seems."

"I have two more requests before I go," said Phoran. "First, I ask that you not tell anyone about the Memory." He gave Tier another bleak smile. "It's more than a social problem for me, you know. If a whisper of the Memory got out I'd face a headsman's axe. The Empire cannot forget the lessons learned from the Shadowed: the Emperor must be free of magic."

"Without your permission, no one will hear it from my lips," promised Tier.

"Would you see if you can find out if your Sept, Avar the Sept of Leheigh, is a member of the Secret Path?" He sighed. "Telleridge is . . . a spider who avoids the light of day while he spins his webs and sends his friends and foes whirling in deadly earnest, unaware whose threads pull them this way and that. If he is involved with the Secret Path, then they are a threat to me and vice versa. I need to know who I can trust."

"If I can discover it," Tier agreed, then gave his emperor a wry grin. "Since I don't have any choice about staying, I might as well make myself useful."

He slept for a while after Phoran left. He had no idea how long because his cell allowed for no daylight, just the endless glow of the stones that lit his room.

Longing for home brought him to his feet. Frustration sent him pacing. He hadn't been able to ask if Phoran could get a message to Seraph. His tongue wouldn't shape the words.

By Cormorant and Owl, I bind you that you will not ask anyone to help you escape . . . Seraph would help him escape if she could. He supposed that was enough to invoke Telleridge's magic.

If Seraph knew where to find him . . . but she did not. She probably thought him dead after all this time.

He probably would die without seeing her again: there was something in the arrogance of Telleridge that told Tier that many Travelers had died here.

Tier closed his eyes and rested his face against the cool stone wall. Without the distraction of sight, he could pull her into his heart's thoughts. Owl memory, she called it, when he was able to recall conversations held months before. Gifted, his grandfather said, when he could sing a song after the first time he'd heard it. *Blessed,* he thought now, visualizing the pale-faced child Seraph had been the first time he'd seen her. Blessed to have his memories to keep in his heart in this place.

In his mind's eye, he built her face as it had been, little by little, loving the curve of her shoulder and the odd pale color of her hair.

Proud, he thought, *she had been so proud.* It was in the stubborn set of her chin, raised in defiance of the men in that tavern. He could see the bruise on her wrist where the innkeeper had grabbed her and yanked her out of bed.

He'd been intrigued by her then, he thought as he had before. In the clear light of his memory he could see how young she'd been, little more than a child, and yet they'd been married less than a season later.

Eschewing the luxuries his cell now offered, Tier sat on the floor and set his back against the wall. He remembered the very moment that he knew he loved her.

Two days after Jes was born, Tier came back from the barn to find Seraph sitting on the end of the bed, back straight as a board, with Jes held protectively in her arms.

"I have something to say to you," she said, as welcoming as an angry hedgehog.

He took off his coat and hung it up. "All right," he'd said, wondering how he'd managed to offend her this time.

Her eyes narrowed, she told him that their son was a Guardian. She explained how difficult Jes would find it to maintain a balance between daytime and nighttime personalities.

"If he were a girl, he would stand a better chance," she said in the cold, clear voice she only used when she was really upset. "Male Guardians seldom maintain their balance after puberty. If they become maddened, they will kill anyone who crosses their path except for those in their charge. Once that happens, they must be killed because they cannot be confined."

Jes began to fuss and she set him against her shoulder and rocked him gently—keeping Tier at a distance by the force of her gaze. "I had a brother who was a Guardian, adopted from another tribe. Often Guardians are given to other clans to raise because the normal anxieties of birth parents seem to add strain to the Guardian's burden. It is an honor to raise a Guardian child, and no clan would refuse to take him."

Give up his son? The shock of the suggestion ripped cleanly through dismay that had encased him as he realized the terrible thing that the gods had laid upon his small son. *How could she think that he'd entertain a suggestion that they throw Jes away because he was too much trouble? How could she consider deserting her child?*

She wouldn't. Not she. She who fought demons for people she didn't even know, would never, ever, shrink at anything that would threaten her second family.

"How old was your Guardian brother when he died?" asked Tier finally.

"Risovar was thirty," she said, her hands fluttering restlessly over Jes, as if she wanted to clutch him close, but was afraid she might hurt him if she did. "He was among the first who died of the plague."

"Then you know how it is done," Tier said. "Jes will stay with us, and you will teach me how to raise a Guardian who will die of ripe old age."

Her face had come alive then, and he saw what it had cost her to be honest with him. When he cradled his family against him, mother and child, she'd whispered, "I'd have killed anyone who would have tried to take him."

"Me, too," Tier had said fiercely into her moon-colored hair. No one would ever separate them.

"Me, too," said Tier, in his cell in the palace at Taela.

How best to weather this captivity? The answers came to him in Gerant's dry tenor. *Know your enemy. Know what they want so you know where to expect their next attack. Discover their strengths and avoid them. Find their weaknesses and exploit them with your strengths. Knowledge is a better weapon than a sword.*

He smiled affably when Myrceria entered his room.

"If you would come with me, sir," she said. "We'll make you ready for presentation. After the ceremony you'll be given the freedom of the Eyrie and all the pleasures it can provide you."

The women who'd tried to bathe him once before were back in the bathing pool, and this time Myrceria wouldn't let him send them out. They scrubbed, combed, shaved, trimmed, and ignored his blushes and protests.

When one of the women started after his hair, Myrceria caught her hand, "No, leave it long. We'll braid it and it will look properly exotic."

They persuaded him into court clothing, the like of which he'd have never willingly put on. He might actually have refused to wear them, even with his resolution to be a meek and mild guest while he gathered knowledge of his enemy, if it weren't for the fear in their eyes. He could see that, if they didn't turn him out pretty as a lady's mare, it wouldn't be him that suffered. So he protested and made rude comments, but he wore the silly things.

There was a polished metal mirror embedded in the wall, and the women pushed and shoved him until he stood in front of it.

Baggy red velvet trousers, tight at waist and ankles, were half-concealed by a tunic that hung straight from shoulder to knees. From the weight of it, the tunic was real cloth of gold. Under the tunic, his shirt was blood-red silk embroidered with metallic gold thread. They'd shaved his face smooth, then oiled his hair with something that left flakes of metal in it that caught the light as he moved. Then they'd braided it with gold and red cords that gradually replaced his own hair so the braid hung down to his hips, where it ended in gold and red tassels. On his feet were gold slippers encrusted with bits of red glass. At least he hoped it was glass.

After looking at the full effect, he hung his head and closed his eyes.

"Lassies, if my wife ever saw me like this she'd never let me live it down."

Myrceria tapped him playfully with one manicured finger. "You look handsome, admit it. We did a good job, ladies, although he wasn't so bad to start out."

Tier looked at himself in the mirror again. If he looked carefully, he could see how the outfit might have been inspired by Traveler's garments. They wore the loose pants and the knee-length tunic—but one of the things that Seraph liked about Rederni clothes was the bright colors. Her own people wore mostly undyed fabrics or earth tones.

Tier sighed, "I'm glad there's no one here who knows me. I'd never live this down."

They covered his magnificent gaudiness with a brown robe and pulled its hood down to hide his face.

"There now," said Myrceria. "You are ready." She hesitated, and the practiced manner of a court whore faded a little. "You've made our job easier," she said. "Let me help you a little. The wizards will be waiting when we take you out the door. Go with them quietly; they won't hurt you. They'll escort you through the Eyrie—the largest room that belongs to the Path. It's an auditorium tonight, but usually it is just a room for people to gather in. The wizards will take you to the stage at the end and introduce you to the Passerines and whatever Raptors decided to come."

He took her hand in his and bent to kiss it. "Thank you for your kindness, Myrceria. Ladies."

There were four men in black robes waiting for him, just as Myrceria had promised. Like him, their hoods were pulled over their faces.

Tier hesitated in the doorway, unprepared for the fearful reluctance he felt at the sight of them and the sudden conviction that he'd seen the knobby hands of the man nearest him holding a small knife wet with blood.

He repressed his fear and the anger it called. With a small smile he set himself in the center of the procession.

"Shall we go, gentlemen?" he said pleasantly.

The Eyrie was made up of broad shelves of level flooring with short drops between sections; the level shelves narrowed as they neared the stage at the far side of the room.

The uppermost section, where Tier and his escort entered, was mostly occupied by a bar laden with food. Behind the bar was an open doorway where servants appeared with trays of food or armloads of ale mugs.

There were a few tables against the wall with white-robed men who watched Tier mostly indifferently. But most of the people in the room were young men in blue robes who quieted as the procession passed them by. By the time they reached the stage, the room was eerily silent.

The wizards walked Tier onto the stage and stopped in the middle, turning as one to face the audience. As soon as they stood there, the lights in the Eyrie dimmed except for the stones that lined the edge of the stage.

Squinting against the odd light, Tier saw that everyone in the room was slowly moving down to the chairs set in front of the stage. When they had all gathered, a hollow boom made the Eyrie shudder, and in a cloud of smoke and magic, a fifth black-robed man appeared: Telleridge.

He stood bareheaded before the crowd so that every man there could see him.

"My friends," he said. "For some of you, this will be the

first introduction to the secrets of our path. Traveler Magic
from the hands of the Five Gods." He lifted his right hand up
and displayed an implement that looked like a morningstar
without the spiked ball. Instead, dangling on the end of the
chain was a large, silver owl.

"Owl who is Bard," he said.

The man on Tier's left front held up a similar item with a
raven rather than an owl. "Raven who is Mage," he said.

Five gods? thought Tier. If they were using the Orders
they were missing one. The other wizards called out Lark,
Cormorant, and Falcon; but there was no Eagle. He would
have fretted about it more, but he remembered where he'd
heard of the Five Gods before: the new priest in Redern. *Seraph,* he thought in panic, *my children—who would they take
next?*

A flood of magic interrupted Tier's worrying.

"For centuries," Telleridge said, his voice carried to the far
corners of the room by magic, "the Travelers hid their power
from us—just as the Emperor and his Septs hide their lands
and titles away from us, thinking that they have rendered us
powerless, helpless. But we are the Followers of the Secret
Path and Hidden Gods: we worship the Birds—Raven for
magic, Lark for life and death, Cormorant to rule the seas,
Falcon to find our prey, and Owl to lead men into our darkness. Tonight, my friends we will all partake of darkness."

He took a step to the side so the audience had an unobstructed view of Tier; at the same time one of the wizards who
stood behind Tier pulled off his robe. He said something as
well, too soft for Tier to catch, but whatever it was, it froze
Tier motionless.

"Raven is flown," said the man who held the raven symbol.
"Gone from our keeping."

At his words Telleridge flung his free hand up and the
whole room erupted into howls, like a pack of hunting dogs.
Tier would have been impressed if the effect hadn't had a
practiced polish. This was a response trained into the Passerines, a war cry without passion.

The wizards Tier could see put the chains over their shoulder, balancing their symbols with the handle hanging down
their back, leaving the birds in front where they could be seen.

With their hands free, they began to clap in a slow, restless rhythm. Fourteen beats into it there was an echo from the audience. By the twentieth beat the noise was loud enough to account for everyone in the room except for Tier. On the thirty-fifth beat, everyone stopped, leaving only Tier's heart beating still.

The wizard with the raven said, again, "Raven is flown."

An older man in white stood up and said, "So farewell the Raven. What guest have you brought?"

Telleridge said, "We bring the Owl, cunning and beautiful, that he will give us the gift of music."

The Passerines replied then, as if one man spoke with a hundred mouths. "By blood shall we bind him, by fire shall we seal our bargain. By blood shall we free him after a year and a day."

"As you will," said Telleridge. He touched the owl and a small blade shot out at the end of the owl's feet. With measured steps he walked to Tier's side. He took Tier's helpless wrist and made a shallow cut. Then he held the knife beneath the wound until the silver blade was completely covered in blood.

He went to the wizard with the raven and touched a finger to the blade and then touched the wizard's raven.

"By blood," said the Raven wizard.

Telleridge repeated the procedure with the others. When he was finished he resumed his former position to the right of the Raven wizard.

The ceremony was nonsense as far as magic went, Tier knew. The only magic that had been done was the spell that kept him still—but Tier could read audiences. Excitement filled the room like some heady wine.

"Raptors, Passerines, Masters all, I give you the Owl!" Telleridge called, and the audience roared to their feet.

When the cheering and hooting died down, Telleridge held up his hand, snapped his fingers, and a lute appeared in his hand.

"Play for us, Bard," said Telleridge. "And we will grant you guesting rights."

As easily as that Tier could move.

Quickly, he considered his options and chose the one that appealed to him the most. He took the lute the Owl Master held out to him—a beautiful instrument to look at—but when he played a few notes he shook his head.

"Myrceria, lass," he said, letting his voice find her wherever she waited in the darkness that disguised the further rows of the audience. "Hie you back to my rooms and bring my lute, please. This one your Masters provided is garbage for all it's pretty."

The problem with solemn ceremonies and young men, Tier knew, was that the urge to break the solemnity was almost irresistible. They greeted his informal request with a roar more spontaneous than the one they'd given Telleridge, if not as loud. As easily as that he took the crowd from the wizard and lessened the effect of the earlier ceremony in the minds of everyone present.

He wouldn't have tried it if his cell were far away, but it should only take a moment to retrieve the lute—not long enough to make his audience restless.

"Bard," called a young man. "I thought that an Owl could play any instrument."

Tier nodded his head. "I've heard that, too. But no one ever said they *would* play any instrument just because they could."

It wasn't Myrceria, but one of the Passerines, who ran up with the lute from Tier's cell. Tier took up the battered lute and sat on the edge of the stage, one long leg hanging over the edge. He'd only had her a night, but the lute felt like an old friend as he cradled her and coaxed her back into tune, again.

"Now," he said, "What kind of song should it be?" He played a rippling series of scales so quickly it was hard to pick out the individual notes. "No," he shook his head, "No one except another musician would like that." He tightened a peg again to bring a string back into pitch. "He'd have to watch that one, he thought, probably a new string.

"War songs sound stupid on a lute," he said, picking enough of a familiar melody out that a few heads began to nod, "at least they sound stupid without a drum."

"Play 'Shadow's Fall'," said someone over the suggestions in the crowd.

Tier shook his head. It'd be a while before he used that story again. "No, everyone knows that. What about a love ballad?" He struck a few chords of a particularly flowery piece and laughed at the groans from the audience.

"Fine," he said, "Try this one for size." And he began the song he'd intended to sing from the very first.

It was a wickedly funny story of a lowborn killer who, on impulse, stole the clothes of a rich young man he'd been paid to kill and set himself up as a nobleman. Tier smiled to himself as he saw that the young men in the audience enjoyed rude double meanings and clever wording as much as the soldiers he'd fought with.

The lute, for all that it was battered, was easily the finest he'd ever played. Responsive and clear-toned, it sang out, complementing his voice and lending just the right accent to the words.

He started into the third verse, the crowd silent, muffling their laughter so that they wouldn't miss a word. Even with such a fine instrument, it was difficult to get the volume he needed before this many people. With his encouragement, they joined in the final chorus, making the stage vibrate with the sheer volume.

He ended it with a flourish. He could sense the wizards moving forward, but he decided to end the performance without them.

"Now," he said with a deliberately engaging grin. "Come join me for the feast and drink or two—and I'll do my best to be entertaining." Lute in hand, he jumped off the high stage, away from the wizards, and led the horde to an invasion of the bar in the back of the room.

CHAPTER 10

It was almost dark when Jes got back to the farm.

Gura greeted him from the porch and Jes ruffled his fingers through the wiry hair. The Guardian had been demanding to-day; Jes was tired and his head hurt. He tried not noticing that there was something wrong because he didn't know if he could keep the Guardian under control this time if there was.

Rinnie hadn't come out when Gura barked.

The Guardian also knew he was tired, and he was willing to wait until they knew for certain. So it was Jes who walked to the back of the cabin and saw that Rinnie had done a few hours' worth of work before putting her tools away where they belonged.

Had Rinnie grown impatient and set out after Mother and Lehr? He didn't think so, especially since she'd left Gura here. He followed Mother and Lehr's tracks to the woods, but he couldn't see anything that indicated Rinnie had come here today. The ground around the cabin was too packed-down for him to follow a trail there.

Reluctantly he gave way to the Guardian.

He shouldn't have stayed so long watching the new temple, thought the Guardian unhappily. But he'd never seen anything like the taint that spread from the temple through Redern.

He'd been worried about Hennea; the forest king had made him responsible for her safety, and there was nothing safe about the temple. The *geas* that bound her made it impossible for him to stop her from going in, but he'd stayed and fretted over it until Jes had convinced him that Mother would know what to do about it.

In wolf form, the Guardian looked for Rinnie's scent along the edge of the forest, but Jes had been right. She hadn't followed Mother.

He went back to the cabin. Gura flattened himself submissively, but the Guardian ignored him. Gura shouldn't have let Rinnie go off alone. Dogs did not make good guards—they were taught to obey the commands of the people they guarded.

Rinnie's scent was here, but it was difficult to pick out one trail from another. He needed Lehr for this kind of job. He lifted his head from the porch step and cast an irritated glance toward the forest; judging by the time Hennea had taken to get from the village to the place where something had happened to Papa, Mother and Lehr should have been back by now. As he turned his head he caught a whiff of an odd scent.

What had Bandor been doing at the farm?

He seldom visited his aunt—both the Guardian and Jes found the village distressful. There were too many people for Jes, and he got confused by their unguarded emotions. To the Guardian, there were too many possible threats. Even so, he knew Bandor's scent of yeast, salt, and soap.

The sound of rapid footsteps made him blend into the side of the porch so that he remained unseen. The wind was coming from the wrong direction, so he couldn't tell who it was until Hennea came out in the open.

One sleeve was burned away and blisters started at her fingertips and trailed up fire-blackened flesh to her shoulder. She slowed to a walk, staggering slightly as she came in sight of the cabin.

"Seraph," she said. "Jes, are you here?"

The Guardian shook with the implied violence of her condition, even though Jes tried to soothe him with the observation that she might have done the damage to herself because the hurt was concentrated on the wrist the *geas* band had been on. Hennea smelled of anger, fear, and pain, and Jes was tired. The beast snarled silently.

Hennea gasped slightly, and the Guardian knew that she felt the dread of his anger.

"Jes," she said, closing in on the cabin. "Jes, I need to talk to you. There's none here to harm anyone. Please. I need to talk to you."

A tear slid down her face, and she wiped it away impatiently. "Please. I need your help."

If the forest king hadn't given her to him, the Guardian could have ignored her; but she was one of his now. So he slunk away from the porch and let her see him clearly, though Jes would rather have resumed his usual form because he didn't want to frighten her anymore than she already was. Jes liked Hennea.

"Jes," she said, unfazed by the monstrous wolf that stalked toward her. "Guardian. I'm so sorry. I've betrayed you all. I don't know what he's planned, but it's my fault."

It was difficult to get human speech out of his wolf throat, but the Guardian managed. "Who?"

"He planned it," she said, holding her burnt arm awkwardly away from her body. "I thought I was so clever, figuring out that he was playing a game with your family—but his game was more subtle than I expected. He set me up, all but sent me out to find Seraph and tell her that I thought your father hadn't been killed. He *knew* that she'd go and take Lehr. He knew Rinnie would be left here unprotected. He didn't care about you, he doesn't know what you are. But he wants Rinnie."

Jes helped the Guardian cool his rage, and the beast welcomed the calm that would allow him to accomplish what was necessary.

"He has her?" he asked.

"Not when I left—I thought I might beat him here—but she's gone, isn't she? That's why you're here and not Jes."

"My uncle was here," the Guardian said. "Bandor, the village baker."

"Lark take them all," she whispered. "Bandor is one of Volis's favorites. Would he turn your sister over to Volis?"

"He wouldn't hurt her knowingly," said the Guardian after

a moment. "But his intentions are not important." Since Jes controlled his savagery, the Guardian was able to think clearly again and focus his purpose. "We need to find them. Can you run?"

Lehr was right, it was late when they reached Redern, and Seraph was exhausted, both emotionally and physically. Only her obsessive need to force answers out of the *solsenti* priest gave her the fortitude to start up the steep street of Redern.

She almost walked right past the bakery. If there hadn't been a light in Alinath's room, she might have been able to do it. Alinath loved Tier, too. Seraph hesitated outside the door.

"She won't believe you, Mother," offered Lehr.

"Yes," said Seraph, "she will—because she needs to believe it as much as I did." She gave Lehr a tired smile. "She'll still think it is my fault—but at least she won't think he's dead. She has the right to know."

Seraph knocked briskly at the door. "Alinath, it's Seraph, open up." She waited, and then knocked again. "Alinath? Bandor?"

Lehr tested the air, "I smell blood. Is the door locked?"

Seraph tried the latch and the door swung open easily. There was no light in the front room, nor the bakery, but Lehr didn't need light and she followed him to Alinath's room. The door was ajar and Lehr opened it cautiously.

"Aunt Alinath?" he said, and the concern in his voice sent Seraph ducking under the arm he held the door open with.

Alinath was gagged and bound hand and foot on her bed. Her face was bruised; someone had hit her cheek and split the skin, which had bled copiously all over the bedding. When she saw them she began struggling furiously.

"Shh," said Seraph, sitting beside Alinath. She took out her knife and carefully slid it around swollen flesh to cut the ropes. "I'll have you free in a moment."

"Rinnie," said Alinath as soon as the gag dropped from her mouth.

"What?" asked Seraph.

But Alinath had begun to shake and Seraph couldn't understand what she was saying.

"Slow down," she said, keeping her voice calm so she didn't

upset Alinath further. "What about Bandor and Rinnie? Did Bandor do this to you?"

Alinath tried to sit up, but it was obviously painful and Seraph hurried to help support her.

"It was Bandor," Alinath said, breathing shallowly around sore ribs. "He's gotten so strange lately—I don't know what's wrong with him. This afternoon, after the priest came, he started muttering about Rinnie and you."

She stopped and swallowed. "You and I have never seen eye to eye, Seraph—but you'd die to protect your children. I know that. So when he started saying dangerous things . . . things that would get the whole village riled up if they heard . . . Well, I told him he was a fool. That there was nothing evil about you, and he had no call to accuse you of being shadowed."

Seraph's stomach clenched.

Alinath turned her head away. "He hit me. He's done that a couple of times in the past month. I'm not saying I'm the easiest person to live with, but . . . *you* know Bandor; he was never like that."

"Go on," said Seraph.

"This time, it was more than a casual slap. I didn't know if he was going to stop. Ellevanal help me, I don't think he did either. Then he muttered a bit more and said something about not needing my interference. He tied me up and left. Seraph, I don't know what he's gone to do."

"He started after the priest left? Volis, not Karadoc?" asked Seraph.

Alinath nodded. "I don't like that man. Did Bandor go out to the farm?"

"Did he say that was what he was going to do?" asked Seraph.

"He said that he was going to save Rinnie."

"We haven't been there since early this afternoon," said Seraph. "I left her with Gura, but Gura knows Bandor. I have to go find her. Will you be all right here?"

Alinath nodded. "Find him before he hurts her," she said.

"Where would he take Rinnie," said Lehr, "if he didn't come back here?"

"The priest," said Seraph. "If he thought she was shadowed

he'd take her to the priest. We'll find them," she told Alinath.

"Be careful," said Tier's sister. "Be careful, Seraph. Bandor's not the man you know."

Outside the bakery, Seraph frowned in indecision; go to the temple or all the way out to the farm?

"Can you tell if Bandor and Rinnie came by here?" she asked Lehr.

He shook his head. "Not even if it were full noon—there's too much . . ." He stiffened and looked around.

Seraph felt it, too, a cold chill fluttering down her spine and a lump in her throat that made it hard to swallow.

"Jes," she called. "Are you here?"

"Listen," said Lehr. "Someone's riding a horse up the road."

She saw Skew first, his white spots clearly visible in the starlight as he leapfrogged up the steep corner, hooves slipping and sliding. As soon as he was on the more level part of the road he broke into a smooth trot and stopped in front of her.

"The priest," said Hennea tightly, sliding off the horse. "I was a fool. He sent me to get you to leave your daughter unprotected."

Seraph nodded. "I've come to that conclusion myself. Do you think they'd take her to the temple?"

"Yes."

"We'll leave Skew here," said Seraph. "He'll lose his footing on the cobbles in the steep parts. Lehr, can you find some place to secure him?"

"There'll be space by the woodshed," he said and took the horse.

Hennea stood a little crookedly, as if she were in pain. Seraph called a magelight and took a good look at Hennea's burnt arm.

"There are easier ways to break a *geas*," she said dryly.

"I was in a hurry," replied Hennea, her lips curving in a pale smile. "And I was angry."

"That's going to hurt," observed Seraph.

"It already does. I'm not going to be much help in any kind of fight; my concentration is gone. I can feed your magic, though."

"Good enough," Seraph said.

Lehr came back and Seraph turned and started up the road at a rapid walk. Jes and Lehr could probably run all the way to the temple, but she and Hennea would have to take it slower or they wouldn't be any good when they got there. She knew that Jes was with them by the clenching of her stomach, but she only caught a glimpse of him now and again out of the corner of her eye.

"Tell me about Volis," said Seraph. "Whatever you think will be useful."

"He's smarter than I thought he was, obviously. The other mages in the Secret Path respected his power—but he's young by *solsenti* standards and complex spells frustrate him. Because of that, he tends to use the Raven ring more than his own magic unless he's weaving an illusion."

They came to a steep bend in the road, and Hennea quit speaking until they were on flatter ground. "I told you that the wizards steal Orders and wear them. Usually as rings, but there are some stones set in earrings and necklaces. He told me that some of the rings are painful to use, and some of them don't work all the time. Most of the wizards can only use one ring at a time, but Volis has two he uses. The first one bears the Order of the Raven. With it he usually has an Owl, though I've seen him with a Hunter's ring a time or two as well. You'll know which one he wears when you see him, just *look*."

"How well does he bear the Orders?"

"About as you'd think," she said. "He seems to believe the Raven Order is just like his magic, except that he doesn't have to use rituals."

Seraph smiled in satisfaction. "Tell me, does he have a bad temper?"

As they got closer to the temple, Lehr stopped and bent down as if to touch the ground, but he pulled his hand back before it touched.

"What's this, Mother?" he asked.

"What?" Seraph stopped, too, but she didn't see anything.

"A taint," said Jes. He must have been close to Hennea because she gave a nervous squeak.

"What does it look like?"

"It looks as if a foul substance was spilled over the ground," said Lehr. "It smells bad, too."

"Shadowed," said Hennea in a small voice. "I'd wondered."

"It comes from the temple," said Jes. "It's darker there."

"It's really there?" asked Lehr. "Why can't you see it, Mother?"

"I don't know why Ravens can't see the Stalker's influence, or why Larks can't either," replied Seraph. "I can understand why the ancients didn't feel it necessary for Owls or Cormorants, but Larks and Ravens have to deal with shadowing."

"Unto each Order . . ." murmured Hennea.

" 'Are the powers so given'—yes, yes, I know. It is still stupid. So Volis is most likely shadowed." It was a very rare condition. Seraph had never dealt with someone who was shadowed, though her teacher had. He'd died before he taught her much about it because there was so much else to learn. She knew the Stalker needed some destructive feeling or act to gain influence and the amount of influence varied. The Shadowed had been different, her teacher said, because the Shadowed had invoked the Stalker's power and welcomed the shadowing.

"Let's go," she said. "We need to get to Rinnie."

They reached the temple finally, and Lehr tried the door.

"It's locked," he said. "Barred from the inside, I think."

Seraph said something short and guttural, a summoning she would not have remembered if she'd stopped to think about it, and the door blew apart, reduced to splinters and bits of metal that covered the floor of the inner chamber.

"Careful," cautioned Hennea. "Anger and magic don't mix well."

"Where will he take her?" Seraph knew that Hennea was right, but ever since the huntsman had come to tell her that Tier was dead she'd been more frightened than she'd been since the night her brother died—and fear, like grief, made her angry.

"Follow me."

The temple was brightly lit with wall sconces, so Seraph had no trouble picking her way through the debris left by the door. But the room on the other side of the curtain was quite different than the one she remembered. It was a rectangular room with a low ceiling. There were no flying birds, no arched ceiling.

"Is this the real room or is the chamber with the Orders the real room?" she asked Hennea.

"Which do you think?"

This room was more in keeping with a building that had been put up in less than a season's time. It was not too different from Willon's store, and she couldn't smell magic in it at all . . . but . . .

"The other one is real," she said with conviction.

That room had been too detailed to have been an illusion set up just for her, but he couldn't show that room to just anyone. This chamber looked just as the villagers would expect.

Hennea nodded her head. "As I told you, he is a very good illusionist."

There was a small door set unobtrusively near the back wall and Hennea led them through it and down a narrow stairway.

"We're close now," Hennea said. "We should be as quiet as we can."

"Rinnie's been here," whispered Lehr.

"I can smell her fear," agreed Jes, already at the bottom of the stairway.

The stair ended in a short, dark hallway that smelled of earth and moisture to Seraph; but Lehr's nose was wrinkled with disgust and he was careful not to bump against the wall. Light pooled by an open doorway.

Seraph brushed by the others to enter the room first.

Rinnie was there; like Alinath, she'd been tied and gagged, but Seraph didn't see any bruises. Relief washed over Seraph; Rinnie wasn't safe yet, but she was alive.

Several hundred candles were set out to form five circles on the floor with Rinnie in the middle of the center circle. The others each contained a bit of jewelry with a single large stone in the setting.

Volis was there, too, peering over a fragile-looking scroll laid out on a table almost too small for it. He didn't look up as they entered. As Hennea had advised, Seraph looked at his hands and saw two rings. One of them should be Raven. Seraph focused her magic and *looked* at the rings. Raven and Owl, just as Hennea had predicted, but twisted somehow and empty. Wrong.

In the far corner of the room, Bandor sat cross-legged on the floor, rocking back and forth and muttering to himself. Owl-sick, thought Seraph. Unbound by Traveler laws, Volis had forced Bandor to do something against his will, and Bandor was paying the price.

She took another step forward and ran into a barrier of magic. With a quick flick of thought she made the barrier visible. It arched across the room, leaving Volis, Bandor, and Rinnie on one side of the barrier and the rest of them trapped on the other: trapped, because the barrier now covered the doorway and sealed them all in. At least she assumed they were all there. She hadn't seen Jes in the quick glance she'd taken.

"Volis," Seraph said.

Her voice trembled with fury; she'd thought she had herself under better control. She was so angry at him and at those unknown men who were like him and played havoc in their ignorance. They had stolen Tier, Rinnie, and Seraph's peace; they would pay, all of them.

Painfully, she drew the serenity of her training around her like a cloak; it was Volis who had to lose his temper. When she was certain she was calm, she said, "What are you doing?"

"Summoning the Stalker," he said, without looking up. "I've been expecting you—as you can see. Once my little Raven took flight I thought she'd bring you here. At first I was upset with her, but then I thought it would not be a bad thing to have an audience—as long as they didn't become part of the ceremonies."

Guardians were all but immune to magic—Jes could go through the barrier. It was just possible he could get through, retrieve Rinnie, and return across the barrier with her. But if he couldn't, he would never leave her. Trapped there, he would try to protect Rinnie from Volis—and that was unacceptably dangerous. She'd send him there only if there was no choice.

She could tell that Jes had reached the end of his control

because the temperature in the room was dropping rapidly.

"You are an ignorant fool," she said coldly. "The Eagle is not the Stalker. The Stalker is what made the Shadowed what he was. If you manage to summon it, you will not be more—you will be nothing. The Stalker has no followers, because anything that answers to it becomes a thing just as it is."

"Don't think I don't know about people like you," said Volis. "My first teacher liked to tell me how ignorant I was because he was afraid of me and what I could do. So for years I did his bidding as his apprentice. When the Master of the Secret Path found me and told me the truth, the first thing I did was arrange for my teacher to receive a lesson ensuring that he never had a chance to mislead anyone again." Satisfaction colored his voice. "Take warning from that. You say I am wrong, but you don't know me, don't know what I can do."

The growing cold made Seraph shiver, but she trusted that Jes would hold on a few minutes more. She needed to make this boy angry.

"Oh, I know what you can do," said Seraph serenely. "Do you think that Hennea spent the whole day silent? Or do you think that I should tremble before an *illusionist*?" She saw her tone made him flush. *Solsenti* wizards looked down upon illusionists, saw their magic as a lesser thing because it neither created nor destroyed. *Solsenti* wizards were fools about many things. "A boy barely old enough to dress himself? A *solsenti* conjurer who defiles himself with the dead because he has to steal their magic or everyone would know how ignorant he was?"

"I may be an illusionist," he said with careful dignity, "but I trapped you—both of you Ravens and your Hunter son, too. And this ignorant boy found out your secrets. I know how to summon a god."

"You can't even keep a Raven with *geas*," said Seraph. "How could you summon a god?"

She'd hoped to anger him with the reminder of Hennea's escape, but he was too excited about his discovery.

"It will be easy," said Volis. "The Cormorant was the key."

And then, pacing back and forth, he began to pontificate upon pseudo-complexities of the Orders that the wizards of his Secret Path had "discovered" over the years.

"Lehr," Seraph said softly underneath the flow of Volis's words. "Is he shadowed?"

"Yes. Uncle Bandor, too—though not as deeply."

Seraph nodded her understanding, then turned her attention back to the ranting Volis.

"I took the rings, one for each Order. The Secret Path only has four Healer rings, but none of them work right. So they gave me this one to do as I wish. I have one for each of the Orders, but with your daughter I don't need the Cormorant."

He looked at Seraph, his face flushed with triumph. "I tried it with just the rings, but it didn't work because the spell calls for blood and death. Getting someone of each Order is impractical—but then I remembered something I read about sympathetic magic, using one thing to represent other things, like using a feather for air. I wrote to Telleridge and he said he thought it might work. So all I needed was one of you."

He looked at Hennea and said spitefully, "I could have used you, but I thought you liked me. I didn't want to hurt you. I could have saved myself a lot of trouble, couldn't I?"

"You might have," Hennea agreed mildly.

He didn't know what to say to that, so he turned his attention back to Seraph. "I thought that it would be easier to use the youngest one. It wasn't hard to persuade Bandor that she was in danger and I could help her. You should be proud, Seraph; your daughter's death will return the Eagle to the world."

Sweat dripped from his forehead, though on the other side of his barrier, Seraph's breath fogged in the cold. Evidently the barrier blocked the effects of Jes's ire.

"*Solsenti* wizards," said Seraph, slowly shaking her head, "always making things much more complicated than they really are. The Stalker is already here at your request." She smiled at him. "You know I speak the truth."

His eyes widened for an instant as his stolen Owl ring, once she'd called her attention to it, told him she was right. Then he narrowed his eyes accusingly. "You just think you speak the truth, that's all it means. You are wrong."

"I can't give you proof of the Stalker," agreed Seraph mildly. "You'd have to be Hunter to see what you have done in your stupidity." He didn't like to hear the word *stupid,* especially as he knew that she meant it. But he wasn't going to lose his temper enough for her purposes; he was too buoyed up by his plans. She'd have to bring Jes into it.

"I can show you what Eagle is," she said.

The whole time they'd spent talking, Seraph had been sorting through the intricate work of the spell holding the barrier together. If he'd just used *solsenti* magic, she might not have been able to break it, but he'd woven Raven and *solsenti* magic together and the result was unstable.

"Jes," she said, "go get Rinnie and keep her safe. Lehr, when you can, take Bandor."

Volis frowned at her words. "Jes? Isn't that the name of your idiot son? He's not here." He shivered once.

"Yes," said Seraph, "he is. You just aren't looking. Jes, the priest wants to get a good look at you."

The Guardian was nothing if not dramatic, coalescing out of candle smoke into the oversized wolf he favored over other forms. He stood not two paces from Volis, frost shading his coat and moving from his paws to the hem of Volis's robes. Jes growled, a low rumbling sound. Seraph's pulse picked up until she could hear the sound of her heartbeat in her ears.

Volis, who had no warning or understanding of what Jes was, cried out in terror. That fear did for Volis's magic what anger had once done for Seraph's. His control of Raven magic failed, and Seraph ripped the barrier into pieces with a sweep of power.

"This is my eldest son, Jes," she said. "Who is Eagle and Guardian—and in no need of your summons."

She kicked aside the carefully placed candles, breaking the circles and removing any temptation he might have had to kill Rinnie.

As she walked she continued speaking, quoting from the book of Orders. " 'Thus is it said that when the Elder Wizards took upon themselves the need to fight the Shadow-Stalker, that they created them the Orders. Six Orders created they them, after the six who slept forever. First, Raven Mage, second, Cormorant Weather Witch to aid their travels, and third created was Healer who is Lark that they might survive to continue the fight. They rested and then made fourth, the Bard and Owl to ease their way among strangers, fifth, Falcon the Hunter to feed them at need, last created they Eagle who is Guardian for all to fear.' The Guardian, Volis, is an Order like any other, though, as you can see, more difficult to detect."

Jes took back his human form and gathered Rinnie into his arms. "The priest is *wrong*," he said, and the voice thundered in bass notes almost too deep to hear, as if he still held partway to the wolfshape.

"He's been shadowed," agreed Seraph.

But Seraph had given the priest too long. He threw a blast of raw magic at her and she was forced to counter it—more than counter it, because she had to protect those around her. She held the magic for a moment then returned it to him. Because it was his magic, it did not harm him, just allowed him to reabsorb it. Not an ideal solution, because he retrieved the energy he'd sent at her, but no one else got hurt.

While she'd been trying to decide what to do with it, he'd had time to gather more power and he flung it at her, forcing her back several steps. She caught it and flung it back again, but it was more of an effort. She couldn't keep doing it indefinitely because she continued to lose power and he didn't.

He also learned quickly. The third shot was no less powerful, but he broadened his target to include everyone in the room. She had no choice but to absorb the full force of his hit, or let something escape where it might hurt one of her children.

Tears of pain slipped down her face as she staggered and swayed, then someone touched her and the pain lessened.

For a dazed instant, the voice and strong hands that pressed into her shoulders were Tier's. Then, as the effects of the priest's attack faded, she realized it was Hennea behind her, offering her support and power.

She needed a shield like the one Volis had set to encase them when they had entered the room, but she didn't have time to throw a shield around everyone. Instead, she created a shield and set it around Volis. For a moment the whole area around Volis lit up, but then the shield fell apart, a victim of its hasty construction.

He laughed. "Try this," he said and sketched a sigil in the air.

She blocked most of it, but the straining of her magic past her reserves almost blinded her with pain, and the remnants of his sorcery sent both Seraph and Hennea tumbling to the ground.

She wouldn't be able to hold out against a second such blast.

"Hennea," she whispered. "When I tell you, jump away, then get the others out of here." If she could distract Volis long enough, maybe her children could escape.

"No," said Hennea.

A breeze blew a stray lock of hair into Seraph's eyes.

Wrath lighting his face, Volis drew back his hand in the manner of a man throwing a rock. Hennea took control of the remnants of Seraph's shields and refined them as Volis's hand released whatever it was he'd formed and the spell bounced off harmlessly.

Wind cooled the sweat on Seraph's forehead—she had just enough time to realize that there shouldn't be a wind when a sudden gust of it knocked her to her knees.

The wind picked up even more speed, turning Seraph's hair into a vicious whip that stung her eyes and cheeks as her left knee made painful contact with the floor. The table Volis had been working on skidded across the floor, hit the wall, then flung itself at the priest's head.

Temporarily occupied defending himself from his furnishings, Volis quit concentrating on Seraph; but any magic would draw his attention.

Seraph drew her knife and staggered to her feet, bracing herself against the wind.

"Hennea," she said, her voice low. "Is there a cure for the shadowing that you know and I do not?"

Seraph thought for a moment that Hennea had fallen too far away to hear her, but then Hennea said, "No. There is no cure but death."

Seraph crouched and used the motion of the wind and a feathering of magic to creep up behind Volis. When she was close enough she rushed forward, and stepped on the back of his knee, collapsing the joint so the wizard staggered backward, off balance. She threw her left arm around his chin to hold him steady and jerked her knife into his neck as Tier had once taught her. The sharp knife cut through Volis's throat, severing skin and artery.

Seraph stumbled back, fighting the wind for her balance. Victory came so quickly, brought to her by the sharp blade of her knife. Her first kill. She wondered if she'd used magic to kill him, if it would seem more real to her.

The young man's body fought for a while, but pain blocked his own magic and the extremity of his emotions kept Raven magic from coming to his aid—rings or no. Seraph watched because it seemed an act of cowardice to turn away from a death she had summoned.

When he was dead, Seraph turned away to survey the room. Lehr, bless him, had remembered what she told him. He had Bandor pinned face against the wall in some sort of wrestling hold. Hennea had gotten to her hands and knees and crawled against the wind toward Volis's body. Jes, looking exhausted, sat on the floor near—

Ah, Seraph thought ruefully, *that's where the wind came from.*

Rinnie's hair spread out in pale flames as she stood motionless, arms spread with palms out like some ancient statue, her skirts absolutely still though the wind still tore furiously through the room. Jes must have cut her loose because there were no ropes on her, though lines on either side of her mouth showed where they had been. Her eyes glowed with an eerie gold light that obscured her pupils.

Words of warning, long forgotten, came back to Seraph. To be a weather witch was always to long for the energies that coursed and strew themselves in tempestuous weather, always to be in danger of being so caught up that there was no way back.

"Rinnie," she said firmly. "We are safe, call back the winds and let them sleep."

Her daughter stared blankly at her with incandescent eyes and the winds swirled and played. An inkwell flipped out of nowhere and caught Seraph painfully on the elbow.

"Rinnie!" barked Seraph in the same tone she used to break up sibling squabbles. *"Enough."*

Rinnie blinked, and the wind died down to gentle gusts and then nothing. Small items dropped to the ground with clattering noises. Rinnie fell to her hands and knees, and Seraph hurried across the room and crouched beside her.

"How is it with you? Are you well?"

Rinnie nodded. "Sorry, Mother. I'm just a bit dizzy." Then

she gave a ghost of her usual grin to Jes. "That was better than changing into an animal."

"Mother," said Lehr, "What do you need to do with Uncle Bandor? I can't hold him here forever."

Bandor was shadowed. Her hand tightened on her knife— but before she could do more than rise back to her feet, Hennea said, "No, Seraph. I lied. The shadow can be cleansed."

Seraph stilled. "What?"

Hennea sat on the floor beside the dead priest, her cheeks painted with his blood. "I lied. I swore that this one would die. It is fitting that he should die in his sins. But I can cleanse the baker with your help."

"Seraph? Bandor?" Alinath's voice rang down the corridor.

If she and Hennea were going to help Bandor, Seraph didn't have time to be angry with her now.

"Jes? Can you keep Alinath at bay without hurting her or yourself?" asked Seraph. "If we are working more magic tonight, we can't have her interrupting us."

"Yes," said Jes, using the wall to get to his feet. He took a couple of half-drunken steps and came to the doorway. Alinath got there first, but stopped just short of Jes.

"We need to get this done," said Seraph. "I think I could just possibly light a magelight. Do you have the magic, and can you concentrate well enough to use it?"

Hennea rose painfully to her feet, using her good arm for leverage. "I think I'm too numb to hurt and I am not as spent as you are. It'll be all right."

She limped over to Lehr and Bandor and spoke a word. Glowing lines circled Bandor's wrists and ankles.

"Release him, please," she said, and Lehr stepped away from him.

With the silvery threads of magic, Hennea forced Bandor around so that he stood with his back flat against the wall.

He spat at her. "Shadowspawn Witch. You should burn in the fires of good rowan and oak."

Ignoring him, Hennea reached for his head and forced him to look at her. Seraph stood as near as she dared.

Hennea took a firm grip on Bandor's hair and then set another glowing line about his forehead to hold his head where she wanted it.

"You can't allow them to distract you," she explained to Seraph in Traveler's speech. "If you have to start again it's twice as hard to grasp it."

Once she had him unable to move she reached up to place a hand on his forehead. He struggled then, fighting the restraints like a madman—but Hennea had done a good job, and his head never moved.

"It's hard to find—the shadowing. It'll help if I'm more familiar with him. Tell me something of him—how the shadow caught him."

"His name is Bandor," said Seraph. "He is married to my husband's sister. He has always been a man of even temperament, a fair man if a bit greedy." But only a bit. The low price he'd given her for Jes's honey had been out of character, she realized. With family, he'd always been inclined to be generous. "His parents were not Rederni and he was never really accepted until he married Alinath, my husband's sister."

Hennea sent off questioning tendrils of magic, which passed through Bandor like a hot knife through butter, slipping and sliding.

"What does he want?" Hennea asked. "What drives him?"

That was harder. "I don't know," Seraph said finally. "Reducing a man to a handful of words is no gift of mine." She turned to her youngest, who knew him best.

"Rinnie," she said in Common tongue. "If Uncle Bandor could be, or have, anything in the world what would he want?"

"Children," said Rinnie promptly, though her voice shook. "He and Aunt Alinath want children more than anything. He also worries that Papa might decide to return to the bakery. Last year when the harvests weren't good, he was certain Papa would take the bakery. Nothing Papa said could reassure him."

Seraph remembered that now; it hadn't seemed important at the time.

One of the tendrils of Hennea's magic snagged and went taut, like a fisherman's net. Another slid to the same place and stuck fast as well. A third caught another place.

"More," said Hennea. "Tell me more about him, child."

"He loves Aunt Alinath," Rinnie said with more confidence.

"But he worries that she loves Papa better. He wants her to see him as a better man than Papa."

The rest of the tendrils snapped taut like the strings of a violin and emitted a sound as if an invisible musician plucked at the instrument.

"Envy," murmured Hennea in the Traveler tongue. "Small darknesses that allow the shadow to take hold and shake him a bit until the small darkness grows like a blot on his soul. You have to ferret them all out, Seraph, and not miss any. Could you have your Hunter see if I've missed anything?"

"Lehr," said Seraph. "Come here and look. Does the net she's woven encase the taint?"

Lehr examined his Uncle closely. "Missed something," he said.

"He wants," murmured Seraph. "He loves. He hates. He fears."

"He's afraid of you, Mother," said Rinnie at last. "He doesn't much care for Jes either." She gave her brother's back an apologetic look. "He doesn't like to be around people who are odd like Jes is."

Hennea, lines of strain appearing around her eyes and mouth, sent out more magic.

"Done," said Lehr.

"Mother," said Jes.

Seraph turned and saw that Alinath had company in the doorway. Karadoc was with her. He'd managed to take a few steps forward, so he stood several paces in front of the door. But when Jes looked at him, he stilled once more.

"We'll be done momentarily," said Hennea. "I wouldn't try this without one who can see the shadow. Otherwise it's too easy to fail—and you'll not know it until the shadowed one kills those nearest to him."

"Like the Nameless King, the Shadowed," said Seraph. "When he killed his sons first."

"He allowed no Travelers within his realm," said Hennea. "So now we go where we are needed, not where we are wanted."

"What next?" said Seraph.

Hennea smiled wearily. "The last part is more strength than finesse. I'll try to burn the shadow from him."

"Let me help," said Seraph. "I'm all but done up, but you may freely take what magic I have left." She followed her words with action, setting the blooded knife on the floor and placing her hands on Hennea's shoulders.

Hennea thanked her with a nod and then set about destroying the hold the Stalker had taken on Bandor's soul. It was, Seraph saw, much the same as burning wood with magic, just using a different fuel. If she had to do it herself, she'd know how.

"Done," said Hennea, but Seraph, feeling the last of the shadowing leave, had already stepped away.

Bandor had long since stopped his struggles, but now he hung limply in the bonds that held him to the wall, his face blank and his mouth drooping on either side. A drop of spittle dripped slowly off his chin.

"Lehr," she said. "Come help me with Bandor."

Lehr helped Seraph brace his uncle so that Hennea could release him. Once on his feet, Bandor seemed to recover a bit. At least he could stand on his own and his face started to lose the blankness and adopt some of Bandor's own personality, like a wineskin refilled with wine.

Lehr still braced him, but Seraph stepped away—remembering what Rinnie had said about his fear of her. She didn't want to cause him any more distress than she had to.

"All right, Jes," she said calmly, "You can let them in, now."

He stared at her a moment, then bowed his head shallowly. She hid her sigh of relief: the next few minutes were bound to be interesting enough without Jes running amok. Alinath slipped around them all without a look and stood in front of Bandor.

"Is it true," she said, "is he better now? Is he unharmed?"

Seraph raised an eyebrow and looked at Hennea, who had collapsed against the wall. She nodded.

"He'll be all right," Seraph said. "Give him a while to recover and he'll be all right."

Alinath's mouth trembled and she took one more step until she stood against her husband, looking small and frail. "Bandor," she said. "Bandor."

Karadoc, leaning heavily on his staff, looked closely at Jes.

"Ellevanal favors you, boy, though you never come to his temple; that told me there was more to you than it appeared. I didn't expect quite this much more. Some of your mother's magic in you, eh, that kept us from coming in?"

"Yes," agreed Seraph. "Jes is more than he appears."

"Traveler," Karadoc said sternly, as if reminded of his duty. "Traveler, what happened here?"

"Shadows and magic, priest," she said. "Volis and Bandor were shadow-touched. If I had known that the priest could be cured, I would have—" she remembered the satisfaction of stopping him with her knife and stopped, saying merely, "I was ill-informed."

"How did you know they were shadowed?" The old man, she thought, was playing the stern priest role to the hilt. It was a good sign. If he'd been frightened by all the magic, he wouldn't be taking the time to perform for his audience; he'd be getting the rest of the Council Elders.

"She found me tonight as Bandor left me," said Alinath, as she and Lehr helped Bandor sit on the floor. "Bruised and bound. I told her that there was something wrong with him, a bile of jealousy toward my brother after all these years." There was a pause, then she said, "I don't know what exactly he did, but he had a hand in my brother's death."

She sat beside her husband and raised her chin in a familiar gesture. "I have never approved of the choices my brother has made," she said. "I have no use for magic or Seraph. You know as much, Karadoc. I would never take her side against my Bandor. But I know that Bandor, if he were himself, would never hit me. He would never have made himself slave to another's will as he has enslaved himself to that false priest." She spat out the words. "If Seraph says that he was shadow-taken . . . well, I for one have to agree with her."

No one, thought Seraph with secret amusement, could miss how much it bothered Alinath to agree with Seraph.

Karadoc nodded formally. "Accepted." He grinned at Seraph, transforming in an instant from sour old man to mischievous gnome. "You should know that Alinath came to me several days ago—concerned with the oddities of her husband's behavior. I told her to keep watch, for as we all know,

those of us who live in the lee of Shadow's Fall have always to
be on guard against such."

He shook his head, "But of course we'll have to tell a different story to everyone else or Seraph won't be able to stay
here, and no one will really believe that he was cleansed."

Bandor was huddled against his wife, bowing his forehead
to touch the top of her shoulder. Seraph could hear his soft,
half-coherent apologies.

Karadoc leaned on his staff. "Let me tell you what happened tonight. Volis is an evil mage, not a real priest. He
needed a death to feed some dark magic and chose Rinnie, because he thought she was without protection. Her father is
dead—"

"Actually," said Lehr. "Probably not. That's what Mother
and I were doing when Rinnie was taken. We walked up to the
place where the huntsman thought he found Father's remains.
The bones weren't Father's. We think a group of human mages
surprised Papa and took him."

"Alive," said Alinath. "Tier is alive?"

"Alive?" asked Rinnie, grabbing Jes's hand in a tight grip.

"I think so," said Seraph.

"Ah," said Karadoc, "then Volis was one of a group of corrupt mages who helped him in his evil doings. He was responsible for a number of terrible happenings, Tier's
disappearance . . . oh, I'll think of a few more things. I'm
sure someone had a pet die in the last month or so. Volis has
been watching your farm with his magic—"

"Magic doesn't work like that," said Seraph. "Not even
solsenti magic."

"They won't know that," said Karadoc repressively. "When
he saw that you were away from home, he kidnapped Rinnie.
Alinath saw him take Rinnie by the bakery. She came to my
temple to get Bandor, who had come to talk to me about suspicions that he had about Volis. I am an old man. Bandor and
Alinath confronted Volis—he hurt Alinath, and Bandor killed
him."

"What about us?" asked Seraph.

"You, none of you were here. I don't know who you are,
young lady," he said to Hennea, "but I can see what you are,
and you'd be safer away from here."

"She can sleep at the farm tonight," said Seraph.

"How do you know that Tier is alive?" asked Alinath.

"Because they took him to use his magic," replied Hennea. "They can't use it with him dead—not this soon."

"Liar," said Alinath, rising to her feet. "My brother had no magic."

From his position on the floor, Bandor reached up and took his wife's hand. "Yes," he said. "Yes; he did."

Alinath froze, staring at the hand she held. At last she sank down again.

"Do you know where they took him?" asked Karadoc when it became apparent Alinath wasn't going to say anything further.

"To Taela," answered Hennea. "To the imperial palace at Taela."

"Before we leave here, Hennea and I will search the temple to make sure there's nothing left that could hurt anyone," said Seraph tiredly. They'd find all the Order stones, too. She glanced at Volis, but his hands were bare. Hennea must have already taken the rings Volis had worn.

"We'll go look for Papa tomorrow?" asked Lehr.

Seraph considered it. "The day after. We'll have to pack for the trip."

"If you leave, the Sept's steward will take away your land rights," observed Alinath.

"No," replied Karadoc. "He won't. He'd never get anyone else to farm that close to the mountains. I'll have a talk with him myself."

CHAPTER 11

Early the next morning, Alinath came to call. Seraph had already sent the boys and Rinnie out to the barn to sort through the tools and harness for things that they would need on their travel. Hennea was still asleep in the loft.

"I didn't know how soon you were going," said Alinath, in a sideways apology for the hour of her call. "I brought this." She set down a large basket of journey bread on the table. "We made it yesterday so it should last you a month or more if you need it." She hadn't met Seraph's eyes since she came in.

"How is Bandor?" asked Seraph.

"Almost himself again, though he doesn't remember much," said Alinath, at last looking up. "Thank you for giving him back to me."

"I'm glad you came," Seraph said after they'd both taken a seat on the kitchen bench, which was pulled away from its customary place at the table. "Otherwise I would have come to you. The trip to Taela is a long one, and getting Tier back might be dangerous. I hate to take Rinnie on a journey like that. Would you watch her for me?"

"Of course," Alinath said after a moment of shock. "Of course I will. There's plenty of space—she can have Tier's old room."

"Thank you," smiled Seraph. "I told her that Bandor would not be feeling well for a while and you needed her help. Give her something to do so she doesn't think I'm a liar."

"I'll do that," said Alinath. "Karadoc wanted me to tell you that the other Elders were happy with his story. All except Willon, who saw Bandor carrying Rinnie up to the temple. But Willon agreed to keep the real story quiet."

Alinath reached into a large pouch she carried and brought out several pieces of folded parchment. "Willon sent these. Maps, he said. And Seraph"—Alinath set a bag of coins on the table—"these are from the bakery's accounts. Use them as you need to—I'd like to have Tier back also."

Seraph took the coins. "Thank you. I won't deny that these will make the journey easier."

"I'll come tomorrow morning about this time," said Alinath, getting up briskly. "To get Rinnie, and to see you safely on your way."

"Thank you, Alinath," said Seraph.

Alinath stopped at the doorway and turned back. "No, Seraph. Thank you. I appreciate your trust, especially after . . ."

"He had no choice," said Seraph. "Remember that. Even shadowed, Bandor believed he was saving Rinnie."

The next morning was cold and the sun a pale line against the mountain as they adjusted the packs on Skew. Gura whined at Seraph from his self-appointed guard post by the packs still to be loaded.

"Fool dog," Seraph said, not unkindly. "You're coming, too."

"But not me," said Rinnie from the porch.

"I need you to take care of your aunt and uncle for me," said Seraph. "Aunt Alinath would like nothing better than to drop everything and come with us, but she needs to take care of Bandor and the bakery." She took a deep breath, "And I need you safe. Please."

Rinnie stared at her hard. "All right," she said. "I'll stay."

Seraph, Hennea, Jes, and Lehr set out for Taela before the sun was full up while Alinath and Rinnie watched from the porch.

A few miles to the south, the path from the farm joined to the main road. Though Willon's maps were useful, finding a road to Taela was no more difficult than finding a stream that would lead to the ocean.

"It's hard leaving Rinnie behind." Lehr patted Skew's neck. "I miss her already."

"I miss everything," said Jes happily.

Lehr lost his grim air and thumped Jes on his pack where it rested between his shoulders, "I see that you do."

"Do you know where your clan is?" Seraph ask Hennea, who walked beside her at the back of the small caravan.

"No," said Hennea. "But I can find them when I want to. I'll be of more use to you than I'll be to them."

"Hennea," said Seraph softly.

"Yes?"

"If you ever lie to me for your own ends again—as you did when I killed the priest for you—there will be a reckoning."

"I will bear that in mind," Hennea said.

"See that you do."

Seraph deliberately cut the first day's travel short. Hennea was looking pale and drawn; though her arm was healing nicely, it was still painful. The tent that they'd brought was the old one Seraph had used when she'd traveled with her brother. Seraph expected it would take a few days of practice before they could put it up in the dark.

After supper, she left the boys to clean up and took out Isolda the Silent's *memmora*.

"So you are the last survivor of your clan," said Hennea.

Seraph loosened the top of her bag so Hennea could see the assorted *mermori* she carried. "The last of any number of clans," she said.

"How many?" Hennea asked in a horrified whisper.

"Two hundred and twenty-four," replied Seraph.

Hennea frowned. "Why did they all come to you?"

"You mean as opposed to a clan leader who actually had a clan?" Seraph shrugged. "I don't know. I've given it a lot of thought over the years. The last eighty-three I found in one cache, presumably taken from one leader. That could mean that the *mermori* are being drawn by the other *mermori*. The more *mermori* someone has, the more likely it is that a lost clan's *mermori* will come to them. Or perhaps Shadow's Fall might have some influence on it."

"It's more than that," said Hennea slowly. "How did you find a *solsenti* who was Ordered? Why did the two of you have three Ordered children? It isn't like breeding horses; the Orders go where they will—though I really did think that the Order bearer had to at the least be of Traveler blood. I don't know many clans who can claim five Ordered people, nor have I heard of a family where every single person in the family was born to an Order."

"It frightens me," admitted Seraph, glancing at the boys, who were packing away the last of the dinnerware. "My father's favorite saying was, 'When you find a coin on the road and pick it up, it's certain that you'll need twice that ere you walk another mile.' He used to say that the Orders went where they were most necessary. I don't want to be in the middle of an event that needs a Raven, Owl, Eagle, Falcon, and Cormorant."

Hennea smiled a little. "Neither do I. Maybe I should go my own way."

She was joking, but Seraph nodded solemnly. "I would keep that in mind. Having you help us find Tier would be very helpful—but certainly dangerous. There is no need for you to risk your life for someone you've never even met."

Hennea laughed and shook her head. "That's the Raven's calling, you know that. Go out and risk your life for someone who'd just as soon that you burned as lived."

"Perverse," grinned Seraph. "It did always seem that the ones who most needed help were the ones who wanted it least. Anyway, I got the *mermora* out to call Isolda's house and see if someone in her time had managed something like the Ordered stones."

"They didn't have the Orders when Isolda's library was collected," said Hennea.

"No," agreed Seraph. "But they did a lot of evil in the search for knowledge. They might have come up with something that will help us. I don't want to destroy those stones without understanding what that will do to the Order trapped there."

Jes and Lehr, finished with their tasks, came to see what Seraph was doing. She pushed the *mermora* into the dirt and called Isolda's house into being.

"Come in," she said, "come and be welcome to the house of Isolda the Silent."

They settled into the patterns of journeying that Seraph remembered. Hennea and Jes in front, Seraph and Lehr bringing up the rear with Skew. Gura scouted about, taking anxious trips back to make certain they were all still walking as he'd left them. After a week's travel, Seraph felt as if she were slowly sloughing off the skin of the Redern farmer's wife she had been.

Every evening she took out Isolda's *mermora* and searched through her library to find out what to do with the Ordered stones.

"Why don't you use them?" asked Lehr, one evening. He was seated on the other side of the little table from Seraph, playing with the game pieces to a game no one knew how to play. "We almost lost all to Volis—and there will be more wizards with Papa. Wouldn't the extra power be useful?"

"Travelers don't like to deal with the dead," said Jes. He was curled up on the floor with as much of Gura on his lap as he could get, grooming the dog with a silver comb that Isolda had kept by her bed.

"It's not that exactly," said Hennea, looking up from a book. "But we understand that it can be dangerous to play with dark magics."

"Especially when doing so leaves you vulnerable to the Stalker," agreed Seraph. "Since we have seen that he is already concerned in these matters, we'd be foolish to allow him an invitation to one of us."

"I like walking," said Jes contentedly.

Hennea looked over at him. His eyes were half-shut and his face raised toward the sun. Seraph and Lehr had dropped behind them a while back; Jes's usual pace was faster than Skew liked. Seraph didn't want to push the old horse, so Hennea and Jes would walk ahead and then sit and wait for the others to catch up.

"What do you like about it?" she asked him.

"The Guardian is happy, because we're going to get Papa," he said. "And Rinnie is safe with Aunt Alinath. I don't like Aunt Alinath, but I know that Rinnie does. I know that Aunt Alinath will keep her safe. Mother and Lehr are safe, too, because they are with me and with Skew and Gura. I am outside and the sun is shining and making my face warm."

"I like walking, too," Hennea admitted.

"Why?" He bounced once on his heels and then turned his head to look at her with a bright smile that lit his eyes and summoned the deep dimple in his cheek.

She smiled back; she'd found that it was impossible not to respond to Jes when he was happy. "For the same reasons you have. Walking means that right this moment, nothing bad is happening. There are interesting things to look at. My feet like to feel the road under them."

"Yes," he said contentedly. "It's just like that."

After a minute he said, "Lehr is not happy."

"He doesn't like walking?" she asked.

He frowned, "I don't think that's it. I think he worries too much. He is like the Guardian, you know. He thinks that he needs to take care of everyone. He doesn't know about walking. He finds things that are bad and tries to solve them before they happen."

Hennea said, "You know your brother pretty well, don't you?"

Jes nodded. "He is my brother and I love him. He is not afraid of the Guardian; he loves the Guardian, too. I like that. Rinnie loves us, too. But she doesn't want to be a Guardian anymore because she can play with the wind."

"I like your family, Jes," Hennea said softly.

He smiled again. "I do too."

A week's travel from Korhadan, the first of the large cities that lay between them and Taela, they stopped to eat lunch a little distance from another, larger party that they'd been trailing for a few days.

"We could eat on the road, Mother," said Lehr to Seraph as

she sat down beside him. "We could make another mile in the time it takes for Jcs to finish eating."

She shook her head. "And lose more miles in a few days when Skew is too tired to go on. It's all right to push hard if your journey's end is in a day or two, but we have to strike a speed that we can hold on to for a month or more. How is that blister you had?"

"Fine."

"Traveler whore!"

Seraph was on her feet before the young man's bellow had finished; her eyes found Hennea standing by the side of the swift-running creek, her drinking cup loose in her hand while a chunk of wet mud slid from her cheek. Shock made her look young and vulnerable, but that wouldn't last.

Before Seraph could take more than a step or two, Jes, with Gura at his side, stood between Hennea and the small group of young men.

"Apologize," whispered Jes.

Seraph increased her speed.

The men backed away, most of them mumbling apologies. If they stared at the huge growling dog, or Jes, rather than looking at Hennea, it was understandable.

"Go," Jes said. "Leave us alone and we'll do the same."

"Hey, what goes on here! Are you vagabonds threatening my sons!"

"Jes, I'll deal with this," said Seraph in a low voice, moving until she was between Jes and the young men. When the older man, presumably their father, was close enough to hear her, she said, more calmly than she felt, "There were no problems until your sons made them."

The man strode past his sons and stopped not two paces from Seraph, clearly intending to intimidate her with his size. "*My* sons, Traveler?"

Anger was going to make her do something stupid, she knew it—and Jes would be no help at all. Where was Tier when a diplomatic word was needed? She could have left it to Hennea, but the younger woman had already been seen as weak: if she had to prove herself there would be blood shed here.

"One of your boys decided it was a good game to throw mud at a woman who was doing him no harm," said Seraph. She should have stopped there, but she couldn't abide bullies. "Obviously he was poorly raised; he has no manners."

"Poorly raised, Traveler bitch?" he snarled. "Who are you to say so?"

Jes, Seraph noticed gratefully, had taken her at her word and dampened the fear he generated. Fear fed anger, and might make the man do something more stupid than he otherwise would. Of course, she herself would have to control her tongue or risk pushing the man too far anyway. She knew, even before she spoke, what choice she had made, throwing away years of iron-willed control and prudence.

"Indeed." Seraph kept her tones polite, even though she knew that would inflame the man more than if she yelled. "It seems that they were not the only ones who were ill-taught." She paused for effect and then borrowed Jes's whispering technique. "Didn't your mother teach you that bad things happen to people who annoy *Travelers?*"

She didn't know if she wanted to scare him away, or force him to attack her. She'd assumed she'd long ago buried all this anger at the *solsenti* who hated and needed the Travelers. But all it took was a bit of mud to prove her wrong. The anger that flooded her felt good, even cleansing.

Whatever she'd wanted to gain by her threat, the people from his group who'd begun to gather around forced him to act rather than run. Perhaps if she had been a man he could have backed down and not lost face.

Perhaps if she didn't have a full bag of *mermori* to remind her how dangerous it was when *solsenti* began to lose their respect for Travelers she would have given him a graceful way out.

"Have a care, Seraph," said Hennea in Traveler.

The man took another step closer. He was a big man, but Seraph was used to looking up at people and a few inches more didn't make much difference to her. "Your man should have taught you respect for your betters, whore," he said on the tails of Hennea's words.

Seraph held her tongue. A raised eyebrow and a speaking

look at him did the job nicely: *You? My better? I don't think so.*

He raised a hand. Gura sank a bit, ready to defend her and she could hear the sheath of Tier's sword rattle as Lehr readied himself to draw it. She still might have let him hit her but for Jes breathing heavily beside her.

With a word and a breath of power, she froze his arm in place.

When she smiled at the crowd of *solsenti*, several of them backed up hastily. She had the feeling that her victim would have backed up, too, but he couldn't move his arm from where it was stuck.

"What's going on here?" said an authoritative voice—and a young man pushed his way through the crowd.

Ash-pale hair in a waist-length braid announced his Traveler bloodlines as well as a written sign. Soon he had a wide circle around him.

"Look by the road, Mother," whispered Jes.

Seraph looked, and sure enough, there was an entire Traveling clan waiting on alert.

Silence had fallen, mostly because the *solsenti* group hadn't yet noticed the Travelers beside the road and didn't know what to make of a man whose arm hung unmoving in the air.

"Well," he said again, "What goes on here?"

"I am Seraph," she said. "Raven of the Clan of Isolda the Silent. This one's half-grown sons offered insult to my young friend. We were discussing the issue."

The stranger tilted his head at the man's arm. "Interesting discussion?"

"No," said Seraph. "I was almost finished. If you'll excuse me a moment." She turned to the man. "I have no more patience with you. I *curse* you and your sons that if you ever hit a woman or child, you'll lose the use of that which men value most. Now go."

She released his arm and met the eyes of the few *solsenti* inclined to linger.

The stranger waited until they were gone before he started laughing. "I'm no Raven, but even so I could tell there was no magic to power that curse."

She smiled. "It doesn't need magic, does it?" If any of them ever hit a woman or child they'd remember her words and worry about it. Worry could achieve the effect she wanted more easily than magic.

"Who are you?" asked Jes, breaking into the shared moment.

"Ah, my apologies, sir. I am Benroln, Cormorant and Leader of the Clan of Rongier the Librarian." He bowed shallowly. "If we may join you in your eating we might exchange stories."

"Come and be welcome," agreed Seraph.

There was a fair bit of confusion as the Clan of Rongier organized a meal stop and the *solsenti* group packed hastily and left, most eating the remains of their meals in one hand while they started out.

The fear on their faces didn't bother Seraph nearly as much as the catcalls that came from the Librarian's clan. Her father would never have stood for such a thing, but Benroln was young, and perhaps he felt much the same as the young people who teased the *solsenti*. Still there were older heads about, and Seraph thought that someone should have said something.

A glance at the clan's wagons and clothing told her that having a young leader hadn't hurt the clan materially, even if their manners had suffered. Their clothing was without holes or mending and their wagons were all freshly painted.

Seraph's small family stayed close to her as the strange clansmen laid out food and attended to the chores of meal preparation. Doubtless the boys were intimidated by the foreign tongue and sheer volume of noise so many people set to a single task could make. Seraph finished the last of her meal as Benroln approached her with three other men.

"Seraph, this is my uncle, Isfain," he said, indicating the eldest of the men. "My cousin, Calahar" was a young man with unusual raven-black hair. "Kors" had reached middle age and middle height with slightly stooped shoulders.

"This," continued Benroln, "is Seraph, Raven of Isolda the Silent, and her family. This young man here is Eagle."

The older man Benroln had introduced as Isfain smiled. "Well blessed in the Order your family is. Will you introduce them?"

There was nothing in the words they spoke to raise Seraph's suspicions, but there was just a little extra stress in Benroln's voice when he named the Orders. That stress had been answered with a thread of smugness in Isfain's voice.

Seraph bowed her head. "This is my son, Jes, Eagle. My son Lehr, and my friend Hennea." No one had ever accused Seraph of being a trusting soul. She couldn't hide the Orders Benroln had noted, but there was no need to share information unnecessarily. Time enough to clear the matter up if necessary once Seraph knew more about the Clan of Rongier.

"May I inquire how it is that there are so few of you?" asked Kors diffidently. "I had heard that the Clan of Isolda the Silent fell to the sickness years ago."

Seraph nodded graciously. "Only my brother and I survived. When my brother died we were left without kin." Two decades of living with *solsenti* had not lowered her awareness of the disgrace of what she had done—so she lifted her chin, daring any of them to comment. "I married a *solsenti* man and we lived with him and his family until he died this spring. His relatives turned us out—but they did not know that he had investments in Taela. We are headed there to recover his monies."

The men considered what she told them. For a Traveler to marry or even lie with *solsenti* was expressly forbidden. It happened, but a very strict clan leader could punish the offender with banishment or death.

Only Kors looked taken aback, and Benroln tapped him on the shoulder before he could say anything.

Isfain merely said, in tones of apparent delight, "Ah, we take the same road. Our clan has business that lies along the road to Taela, and we have friends in the city who are willing to aid us. We'd be more than pleased to lend you escort until our roads part."

There was no way out of Isfain's generous offer without offense, so Seraph nodded. "Your escort would be most welcome."

Calahar glanced over at Skew and then moved toward him. "Nice horse," he said.

"My husband's warhorse," replied Seraph. "Careful. He's old now. But he was trained not to let strangers approach too closely."

"I've only seen a few horses with his coloration," he said. "Your husband get him as a war prize?"

"Yes."

"Too bad he's a gelding."

"Yes," replied Seraph. "But he serves us well as it is. Lehr, would you check to make sure we've gotten everything packed?"

Hennea waited until they were walking again and the fuss of adding new members had died down before approaching Seraph.

"You were less than forthcoming," Hennea said quietly. "And Skew's never objected to me."

"But they don't need to know that. I'd rather not have people ruffling through our packs. There's something off about this clan," Seraph replied. "Though it's been a long time since I walked with Travelers, so perhaps I'm misreading something."

"Perhaps you are right to be suspicious," agreed Hennea thoughtfully. "They certainly aren't going to be looking for Lehr and I to be Ordered, not when they know that two of us are Order-Bearers. Although if they have a Raven who looks at us, they'll know what you are up to."

"I've been *looking*," said Seraph. "The only Order-Bearer I've seen is Benroln himself."

"I suppose there will be no harm done," said Hennea.

"No harm to whom?" asked Benroln.

Seraph carefully maintained her smile. "To us. It's a relief to find a clan to journey with—but it bothers me that we might need your protection. This is a main road, there should be no danger for Travelers here—but I worry all the same."

"It's not just those hotheaded men either," said Benroln in grim tones. "There hasn't been a Gathering in a long time. The last one was disrupted by *solsenti* soldiers, and the clans felt that another Gathering might just be setting ourselves up for a *solsenti* sword. The illness that swept through our clans twenty years ago took out more than just your clan. If the *solsenti* have their way, in another twenty there will be no Travelers at all."

The clipped note in his voice when he said *"solsenti"* reminded her forcibly of the way some of the more frightened Rederni said "magic."

"Then it is their doom," said Hennea indifferently. "Travelers exist to keep the *solsenti* from paying the price of a failure that was not theirs."

"What failure?" said Benroln explosively, but Seraph saw calculation in his eyes. He was playing to his audience. "A story nattered at by the elderly? It is only a story—and it was old before the Shadow's Fall. It's a myth, and no more accurate than the twaddle the *solsenti* spout about the gods. There are no gods and there was no lost city. There is no evil Stalker. We have paid and paid for a crime committed in an Owl's tale. If we don't wise up we'll be nothing more than a *solsenti* minstrel's tale ourselves, something told to frighten small children."

"Wise up and do what?" asked Seraph.

"Survive," he said. "We need to keep food in our mouths and clothes on our backs. We need to teach the *solsenti* to leave us alone—as you did to that *solsenti* bastard who tried to injure Hennea." He paused, then said softly, "You taught that man and his sons to leave us be. If you had allowed your Eagle to teach them, the rest of the *solsenti* in that group would have taken the story to his village and they all would have trembled in fear."

"Maybe someone did," said Seraph coolly. "Maybe that's why, instead of welcoming us and looking to us to help them when my brother took us into the village years ago, the villagers feared us so much that they burned my brother."

"The *solsenti* already fear us, that is the problem," said Hennea. "Fear leads to violence. The villagers who killed Seraph's brother were very afraid and too ignorant to know that they had nothing to fear from a Traveler. Perhaps because, in the last few generations, we have taught them that they should fear us."

"Rot," said Benroln curtly before turning his attention back to Seraph. "You have lived among them for what?" He glanced at Jes and Lehr and came up with an accurate guess, "Twenty years or more? You are beginning to sound like one of them—or worse, one of the old ones who sit around the fire and say, 'We are supposed to protect them.' " The anger in his voice was honest now. "Let them protect themselves. They have wizards."

"Who are helpless against the evil we fight," said Seraph.

Benroln's lip curled. "When *solsenti* soldiers caught my father and our Hunter and Raven out alone, there was nothing we could do but bury them. Had my father not believed the old folktales, he could have taught that village what harming a Traveler might mean. When those villagers killed your brother—*you* could have saved him. Could have made them so afraid that the thought of harming one of us would never occur to them again. How many of us died because you didn't teach them what you taught that man today? How many more will die because you didn't loose the talons of your Eagle upon them instead of tricking them into thinking you'd set a spell on them?"

Part of Seraph agreed. Part of her *had* wanted to burn the village to the ground. She had spent most of that first night at Tier's side wondering how long it would take her to get back to the village and avenge her brother.

She could have killed them all.

"Your father was killed?" said Hennea softly, taking Benroln's arm in sympathy and distracting him from Seraph.

He nodded, his anger dissipating under Hennea's attention. "Our Clan Guide took us to the Sept of Arvill's keep. My father said that they'd never admit a whole clan, so he, who was Raven, took our other Raven—my cousin Kiris who was only fifteen—and our Hunter to see what was amiss. They didn't even make it to the gate of the keep before they were shot from ambush."

"Terrible," agreed Seraph. "When I think about that village where my brother was killed, I think of how helpless they would have been against my power. I think of the children who lived there, and the mothers and fathers. More death never solves a crime, no matter how regrettable." She tried to keep her tones conciliatory, but she could not agree with him.

Benroln met her gaze for a moment, then dropped his head in the respectful bow of a vanquished opponent. "And so I learn from your wisdom."

Lehr, who'd come upon them as Seraph had been giving her last speech, snorted and then grinned at Benroln. "*She* knows better than that. That's what *she* always said to Papa when she didn't want to agree with him but he was winning the argument."

Seraph smiled gently. "We can agree to disagree."

The Travelers were a highly organized people—just like a well-trained army, and for the same reasons. Every person had an assigned role.

Seraph hadn't realized, not really, how independent the life that they'd led in Redern had been. As long as the Sept's tithes made it to him, they were left largely alone to do as they wanted. If she'd been married to another Rederni man, that might have meant that she would have been at his mercy. But Tier was Tier. He'd sought her advice, and she'd worked shoulder to shoulder with him both in the fields and in the kitchen. She'd grown used to the freedom of making her own decisions.

When Isfain had pointed to a place and told her to make camp there, she'd nearly told him where to take his orders. If she hadn't caught Lehr watching her expectantly, Seraph would have done just that. Instead she'd just nodded and gotten to work.

At least they accorded Seraph some leeway for being Raven, and clan leader, if only just of her family plus Hennea. Lehr they treated like a green boy—Tier had never treated him so. She just hoped he was enough his father's son to hold his peace until she'd had time to learn more about this clan: they might be a great help in retrieving Tier.

Seraph pitched in to help prepare the evening meal. Some of the men tended horses and goats, some set out to fish, and a smaller group set out into the forest to see what game they could find. Jes and Lehr joined the latter group. She'd had time to talk with Lehr, and Seraph knew he wouldn't give himself away. He didn't care for Benroln much either.

"My Kors told me that you married a *solsenti*," said the woman on Seraph's left, while her clever fingers and sharp knife were making short work of deboning one of the rabbit carcasses that were the basis for tonight's meal.

There was such studied neutrality in the words that Seraph didn't reply, pretending that skinning her own rabbit took up all of her attention.

"What was it *like?*" said the woman on the other side of her with hushed interest. "I've heard that *solsenti* men—"

She was quickly hushed by several of the other women who were giggling as they chided her.

"Would you look at this!" exclaimed a woman in gravelly tones. Seraph turned and saw a tiny, ancient crone approaching the tables set up to prepare food. Her hair was pale yellow and thin; it hung in a braid from the crown of her head to her hips. Her shoulders were stooped and bent, and her hand as knobby as the staff she balanced herself with. "You'd think you'd never had a man before the way you act here! She is a guest. Ah, you embarrass the clan."

"Brewydd," said the woman who had begun the conversation. "What brings you here?"

"Brewydd?" said Seraph, setting down the naked rabbit carcass and wiping her hands on the apron someone had given her. "Are you the Healer?" Even twenty years ago, Brewydd the Healer had been ancient.

The old woman nodded. "That I be," she said. "I know you child—Isolda's Raven. The one who survived."

The woman on Seraph's right put aside the food she was working with and hurried over to tuck her hand under Brewydd's arm and lend support. "Come, grandmother. You need to get off your feet." Scolding gently and prodding, the woman took Brewydd away toward a wagon built up on all four sides and roofed like a small house on wheels—a *karis* it was called for the *kari,* the Elders, who were the only Travelers who rode in them.

"Raven," said the old woman, stopping for a moment to turn back and look at Seraph. "Not all shadows come from the evil one."

"People can be evil all on their own," agreed Seraph.

Satisfied with Seraph's reply, the old woman tottered back to her *karis*.

"She can still heal," said the woman on Seraph's left. "But she's a little touched. It's the years, you know. She won't tell anyone how old she is, but my Kors is her great-grandson."

Three days of travel with Rongier's clan taught Seraph a lot about them. Benroln and the old Healer were the only Ordered among them, though they had a few who could work magic in the *solsenti* fashion—with words and spell casting that hoped to gather enough stray magic to accomplish their task.

It was most remarkable, she thought, watching as a young man named Rilkin used a spell to light a damp log, that they got any results at all. Her father had been gifted that way, and they'd spent many a Traveling day exploring the differences between her magic and his. A *solsenti* spell cast out a blind net into the sea to haul in whatever stray magic might attach itself to the net; Ordered magic was more like putting a pail in a well.

She turned back to grooming Skew and to her current worries. Tier she could do nothing about until they reached Taela, so she tucked her fear for him away until it might be useful. Lehr and Jes were more immediate concerns. They were growing more and more unhappy with the continued association with the Traveling clan.

Skew stretched his neck out appreciatively when her brush rubbed a particularly good spot. Skew, at least, was having the time of his life with all the attention he was getting.

Lehr, however, chafed under the commands that all of the men and most of the women of the clan felt free to throw at him. Without hinting at what he was, he couldn't win their respect by his hunting skills so they treated him as they treated all the other young men.

No one gave Jes orders—they all knew what he was. Her daylight Jes was bewildered by the way they lowered their eyes around him and avoided him. Seraph didn't remember her clan treating her brother, the Guardian, that way. The Librarian's clan hurt Jes's feelings by their rejection, and that made the Guardian restless: Jes was one of the people he protected.

Hennea helped. She knitted in the evenings, and found things that required Jes's aid. He was calmer around her, too; perhaps it was the discipline of being Raven that made Hennea easier for Jes to bear. Some people, like Alinath, were hard for him to be in the same room with.

"Mother?" It was Lehr. "Have you seen Jes? He was with me at dinner, but someone decided they needed a dray mule and I was the nearest they could find. When I went back to the dining tables, Jes wasn't there. I checked the horses and he wasn't there either. Hennea was looking for him, too. He's not in the camp, Mother. I told Hennea I would check with you."

To see if she wanted him to search, even though someone might notice what he was doing.

"I don't—" Seraph stopped speaking abruptly.

Over Lehr's shoulder, Seraph saw Benroln, Kors, and Calahar approach with intent. Isfain, the fourth man, was nowhere to be seen. The air of grim triumph Benroln wore was as damning as the guilt on Kors's face.

She stepped around Lehr so she stood between him and the leadership of the Clan of Rongier.

"Is something wrong?" asked Benroln.

"I don't know," Seraph replied softly. "I think that's something you can tell me. Where is Jes, Benroln?"

Benroln held his arms out open-palm to show her he meant no harm. "He is safe, Seraph. I won't harm him unless there is no other way to save my clan."

Seraph waited.

"Jes is in one of the tents with Isfain at watch."

"What do you want?" she asked.

Benroln smiled as if to say, *See, I knew you'd do it my way.* Three days had obviously not taught him much about her— she hoped that her other secrets were as well-hidden.

"My uncle has been scouting for work for us, and he found some not five miles down the road."

"What kind of work?" asked Seraph.

"There is a merchant who buys grain and hauls it to Korhadan to sell. Last year one of the farmers with whom he had a contract delivered his grain himself and cost our merchant money and reputation when he wasn't able to deliver the grain he had promised his buyers. He went to the courts for redress, but they were unable to help him."

"I see," said Seraph neutrally.

"I want you to curse this farmer's fields."

"To teach him a lesson," she said.

"Right," he smiled engagingly. "Just like that man who assaulted Hennea."

"But this merchant will pay you money."

"Yes." He didn't even have the grace to look uncomfortable.

"And what will I get out of it?"

"Your family will have a home at last. A place where they fit in and no one taunts them for their Traveler blood. We will share with you all that is ours," said Calahar, as if he were offering her a gift instead of blackmailing her.

Benroln was smarter than that. "Safety," he said. "For you and your family."

Seraph stared at them for a minute.

"You can't hold Jes for long," said Lehr confidently. "He doesn't like strangers much—he'll know that there is something wrong."

He was right—or should have been. Seraph watched, but Benroln's confidence didn't falter.

"You have a *foundrael*," she said, suddenly certain it was true. There weren't many of them, but then there weren't many clans left either. They weren't such fools as to try to keep a Guardian prisoner without something to keep him under control.

"What is that?" asked Lehr.

"Guardians can be difficult to control," she explained without looking away from Benroln's face. "They are driven to protect their own at the expense of everything else. Sometimes their imperatives are inconvenient; guardians don't follow orders well at all." She wasn't going to tell them how common it was for an Eagle to lose his daytime persona and become completely violent, even toward the people he had previously protected. "A Raven a long time ago came up with a solution. She created ten *foundraels*—collars that keep the Guardian from emerging—before she realized what the end effect of repressing a Guardian is."

"What's wrong with it?" asked Lehr. "Is Jes in danger?"

Seraph fingered the knife at her hip. "Let's just say that if they thought they had problems with their Guardians when they decided to use the *foundrael,* they had real problems the first time they decided to take it off. The use of *foundraels* is forbidden except under the most dire conditions."

"My father will keep him calm—your Guardian will experience no difficulties unless you give him reason to think that there is danger," said Calahar, stung by the contempt in her voice.

"Seraph—I've looked all over . . ." Hennea's voice died out as she recognized the confrontation.

"These men have taken Jes," Seraph told Hennea. "So that I will aid them in cursing a man's field. They will receive gold for their efforts."

She saw Hennea's face as worry faded, leaving behind a facade as cold as ice—just such a face had Hennea worn as she knelt beside the dead priest in Redern.

"They take gold to curse people?"

Seraph spat on the ground in front of Benroln. "They have chosen to forget who we are. But they have me at a disadvantage." She shook her head in disgust and then looked at Lehr.

She needed someone to tend Jes, someone he trusted who would sit by him calmly until she could get Benroln to take the *foundrael* off—the collars could only be taken off by the person who put them on. But Lehr was too angry, she thought in near despair; Jes would know that there was something wrong.

"Where's Jes?" asked Hennea.

Seraph looked at the other woman's expressionless face thoughtfully. "Kors," she abruptly, "will take you to Jes. He's being held with a *foundrael*—Isfain is supposed to be keeping him calm. I would appreciate it if you would do your best to see that Jes is not discomforted while I go with Benroln."

"A *foundrael?*" If anything, Hennea's voice was colder than before. A blush rose on Kors's cheeks. Hennea's mouth was tight with anger, but she nodded her head at Seraph. "I'll take care of him—he's been helping me knit in the evenings since we met up with this clan. Sometimes simple tasks help."

"Thank you, Hennea," said Seraph, feeling vast relief at Hennea's confidence. She pointed to the tent entrance. "Gura. Stay. Guard." The last thing she wanted was for one of these fools to get their hands on the Ordered stones. Once the dog was sitting where she'd asked him to, she said, "Lehr, my dear, it looks like you might miss the Hunt today. You will come with me—I have no desire to lose anything more than I can help on this fool's errand."

CHAPTER 12

Hennea stalked behind Kors, the canvas bag that held her needles and woolen thread clutched tightly in one hand. Her anger was partly self-disgust. She knew better than to get involved; that always brought unnecessary pain. Poor Moselm . . . he'd been such a kind man, uncomplicated. They'd been lovers before they'd been taken, but it had been little more than a convenience to both. Moselm's wife had died several years before of one of the mysterious ailments that plagued the Traveling clans. They had come together for comfort.

But it was the Traveler's lot in life to confront things that no one else would face. If Moselm's death brought the light of destruction to the Path, he would have counted his life well-spent. But Jes . . .

There was no peace in dying among kinsfolk—and Hennea, like Seraph, knew that every minute that Jes spent collared by the *foundrael* brought him that much nearer to madness and a merciful death at the hands of those who loved him. She didn't want to do that ever again.

That *Travelers* would come to *this,* Travelers sworn and taught to aid the *solsenti.* For gold and hatred they betrayed their oaths, and put a good man at risk—perhaps they all deserved the fate that the *solsenti* intended to mete out.

Kors, subdued and somber with doubt, led Hennea toward one of the more distant campsites. The clansfolk they encountered on the way bowed their heads and refused to look her in the eye. They knew, she saw, and they were ashamed—but angry at the guilt they felt. Before long, she thought, they'd turn that guilt into righteous indignation.

See what the solsenti *have turned us into,* they would say to one another, so lacking in pride that they could not even accept the responsibility for their own downfall.

Kors stopped in front of a large tent and they both heard Isfain's harsh voice snap out. "Sit here and wait, boy, as I told you. Your mother has business with Benroln and then you may do as you wish."

Hennea's eyebrows climbed. "Supposed to be keeping him calm, is he?" she murmured to Kors, pleased when she saw that he was unhappy with what they'd just heard as well.

She swept open the tent with none of the usual courtesies. Isfain was standing in front of her and she shoved him ungently aside to see Jes perched unhappily on a tall stool in the middle of the tent. It was the only object in the tent—if Benroln had indeed given orders to keep Jes calm he had failed marvelously.

"Woman, watch what you do!" snapped Isfain.

Evidently, he didn't care for her entrance. She ignored him.

"Hennea," Jes said in soft-spoken relief. "I need to see Mother." One hand rubbed at the leather strap he wore around his neck, turning it about as if to find a buckle or lacing that wasn't there. To Hennea's eyes the leather was as smooth as if it had just grown around his neck.

"What are you doing here?" said Isfain. "Does Benroln know you are here?"

She ignored him again.

"It's all right, Jes," she said to the dark young man sitting restlessly on the battered old stool. "Benroln wants to force your mother to curse some poor farmer's land for money. They're holding you with an artifact that keeps your other spirit at bay—there's nothing wrong with you. Lehr went with your mother."

She didn't know how much he'd understand in his current state so she was gratified when Jes's swaying slowed down.

"They are safe?" he said.

"I don't think that Benroln will be able to do anything to Seraph that she doesn't want to happen. Lehr is with her."

He swallowed, "And you are safe here."

"Yes," she agreed. "I'm safe with you. Would you help me with my knitting until your mother's business is completed?"

She opened her bag and gave him a skein that she'd tangled just for this purpose. After a little hesitation he took it from her. He stared at it for a minute, but at last his long-fingered hands began to work patiently at untangling knots. The rough wool thread had a mind of its own, and it would take a while to unravel the mess she'd made.

She settled at his feet and began knitting with a ball he'd rolled for her yesterday. She leaned lightly against his leg, prepared to shift away if she made him uncomfortable. The long muscles of his thigh softened and relaxed, so she let him take a bit more of her weight.

She glanced into his eyes and saw the fury trapped impotently in the net of the *foundrael*. She shivered and looked back at the sweater she knitted. For a while he seemed calmer. Perhaps if the tent had not been so starkly furnished, or if that idiot Isfain had quit looking at Jes as if he expected him to explode, Jes would have been all right.

"I don't like this," said Jes, abruptly throwing his yarn on the ground. "I need . . . I need to be somewhere."

Hennea looked up at him and saw the despair in his eyes. Enough, she thought. "Wait a moment," she told him.

Kors was not a problem. He knew what was right when someone shoved it in his face, as much as he wished he didn't. Isfain, though, Isfain might be more difficult.

He was one of those gifted with magic, though not Ordered. Hennea knew that other Ravens had a tendency to look upon unordered mages as weak, but she was not so foolish. A good wizard used subtlety as well as power, and like a well-knit wool sweater, their spells could be difficult to unravel.

The trick with wizards was not to give them time to do anything.

"Isfain," she said simply. "Hush, be still."

It wouldn't have been worth doing to a Raven, because they needed neither word nor movement to call magic. A wizard could call magic that way, too—but it was a poor business they made of it. It would be a long time before Isfain worked his way free of her binding.

"What?" asked Kors incredulously, surprised at Hennea's rudeness.

She put her knitting away carefully, then she took the yarn Jes had thrown and set it in the top of her bag. Time enough later to unspell it so it could be organized more easily.

"He's too far," she said.

"What do you mean?" asked Kors, who still hadn't noticed that Isfain was now immobile because of her magic. He didn't know what she was.

"Have you ever seen a Guardian released from the *foundrael?*" she asked. "It's not bad if they haven't been upset—but your Isfain precluded that."

"Mother," said Jes sadly.

She nodded. "I know. Lehr will keep her from harm, but that is your job. To protect your family."

"Yes," he said.

She turned to Kors. "If I were you I'd leave this tent, so that you aren't the first thing he sees when he's free."

She'd given him warning enough. *If he didn't choose to follow . . .* she relaxed as she heard him leave. Really, Kors wasn't a bad sort.

"All right, Jes, I'm going to take this thing off."

She reached up, but he caught her hands. "Can't. Benroln said only him."

"Well," Hennea said. "I'm not as powerful as your mother, Jes, but I have spent a long time studying. I think I know how to take the blasted thing off. I'll not lie to you, there is some danger—but not as much as leaving it on."

"To me," he said, catching her hands before she could touch the *foundrael*. "Not you."

"Only to you," she lied, but she'd had a lot of practice lying and it came out like the truth.

He let her set her hands on the soft band around his neck. The leather was soft and new-looking, as if it had been tanned yesterday instead of centuries ago. That made it easier, because she knew which one it was.

"No," he said, pulling her hands away again.

"It's all right," she said.

"No," Jes said again. "The Guardian will kill the big man. That would be bad. He thinks that killing would be very bad for us. Killing is bad, but he would have no choice. He is very angry."

Hennea considered him. Everyone had a tendency, she thought, to ignore the daylight Jes in their fear of the Guardian. Oh, Seraph loved him in either guise, but she treated him with the same indulgence and discipline that she treated their dog and the others followed her example.

Jes, thought Hennea, was more than just a disguise where the Guardian resided. Impulsively she put her hand, still clasped loosely by his, on his cheek. He closed his eyes and leaned against it, moving so the light stubble, new-grown since his shaving this morning, prickled her fingers.

He was just a boy, she thought, uncomfortable with the instant response his innocently sensual gesture had called from her.

He might be right about killing. The Order of the Eagle came only to people who were empathic, a rare gift and usually weak. If Jes were a strong enough empath, killing might very well be enough to damage him.

"The Guardian won't calm until we take it off, Jes. He'll just feel worse and worse," she said, though she didn't move her hand from his face. "The longer we wait the more difficult it will be."

He nodded, but didn't open his eyes. "He's so angry," he said. Dark lashes brushed her fingertips, and she shivered.

He looked at her then, his eyes dark and hungry. "You could make him not angry," said Jes. "He likes you, too. Kiss me."

His suggestion startled her. She'd never heard of anyone trying something like this. Likely because only an idiot would think of kissing an angry Guardian.

Her lips were still canted in a smile when they touched his. It was an innocent kiss at first, because he called that from her—though not without arousal. His lips were a little chafed, and the rough surface scraped hers in butterfly-wing caresses.

She could feel him tense when her hands touched his neck again, so she opened her mouth to nip lightly at his lips, distracting him from what she did.

It distracted her, too—but not so much that she fumbled the Unlocking.

As soon as she finished, fear washed through the tent like a flash flood, taking her breath with its strength. She dug her fingers into Jes's shoulders, which had turned to iron. But he didn't fight her as she held him to her and touched his lips with her tongue.

Fear had driven away the embarrassment she felt at seducing him, but it hadn't erased the desire he called from her. When he took charge of the kiss, she softened for him and allowed him to vent his fury into passion.

It was the Guardian who gentled the kiss again and shifted his weight away from her. He rubbed his face against hers, like a cat marking his territory, and then pulled away despite the tension that shook his body.

"Benroln has Mother and Lehr?" he asked hoarsely.

She had to clear her throat before she could say anything. "Yes," she said.

She averted her face, knowing her cheeks were red, so she didn't have a chance to move away before he touched her again. He pulled her against him, and set his chin on top of her head.

"We'll go find them," he said. Then he must have noticed Isfain, because he stiffened.

"What have you done to that one?" he growled.

She used the excuse of looking at Isfain to step out of Jes's arms. "Not as much as I'd have liked to," she said. "Benroln was young when he stepped up to the leadership—if I understand the history that led to this stupidity. But you," she tapped Isfain's nose reprovingly, "you knew better. He was your sister's son and you taught him poorly."

"Release him," said the Guardian.

She cocked her head at him warily. "Why?"

When he growled at her, she found herself smiling despite the way the skin on her back flinched. "I think we'd better just leave him as he is until we find Lehr and your mother, don't you?"

"Soft-hearted," he said.

"Better than soft-headed," she replied. "Should we go after Lehr and Seraph?"

He stepped around her and held open the tent flap. "I'd rather eat someone," he said—she thought it was for Isfain's benefit, but she wasn't quite sure. "But we'll head out looking for Mother first. Is Gura here?"

"Seraph told him to guard the tent," she said.

As she ducked through the flap he put his lips near her ear and said, "Don't feel guilty."

She stopped so abruptly that the top of her head collided with his jaw hard enough that she heard his teeth click.

"Why should I feel guilty for kissing a handsome young *boy*?" she said sarcastically, without lowering her tone at all.

To her amazement he grinned at her. Guardians didn't grin. They smiled with pleasure while they choked the life out of some poor fool who crossed them. They bared their teeth. They didn't grin.

"I don't know. We both enjoyed it very much, Jes and I," his grin widened. "And we'd like to do it again as soon as possible."

"Here you are," said a young man in rich clothing who awaited them in a small clearing set in the side of a hill and overlooking a twenty-acre field with a tidy cottage at the far end. "I thought you might not make it."

Benroln smiled congenially. "I don't break contracts, sir."

"And besides," said the young man, "you knew there was more gold where you got the first, eh?"

He looked too young to have been a merchant for long, thought Seraph, then she reconsidered. There was a softness in his face that made him look exceedingly young, but his eyes were sharp and old.

I'll bet that he uses that young face of his, Seraph thought as she revised her estimate of his age upward by ten years.

"Of course, sir," said Benroln after he laughed politely at the merchant's comment. "This is the woman who will set the spell."

"And this is the farm right here," replied the merchant in a light, pleasant voice. "I want it cursed—you understand. Paid good money for a mage to curse it last year—but Asherstal still got a harvest out. I told that sorcerer I wanted nothing to grow on these fields, not even a weed. I want the other farmers to avoid Asherstal for fear whatever befell him will happen to them. I want him shamed. You'd better do the job or maybe some ill might befall you, eh? Like happened to that mage I hired last year."

Benroln looked taken aback, and Seraph wondered if he'd believed that sweet, innocent air the merchant exuded.

"Your mage's curse is still here," she murmured. "Perhaps you had him killed too soon. I'll have to take it off before I can work."

"I don't tell a tanner how to do his job," said the merchant. "I just pay him for good work." He made an odd motion with his hand that might have been accidental—but Tier had taught the boys the signs soldiers used. It had the look of one of those.

Lehr had caught it, too, she thought. He faded back silently into the night. Neither the merchant nor Benroln seemed to notice—she doubted the merchant had ever seen him to begin with.

"I'll have to go down to the edge of the field," Seraph said.

"Fine, fine," he agreed. "It's dark enough that they won't see you. We can wait in the trees that border the field."

He led the way down. If Benroln was worried by anything, Seraph couldn't tell—but she thought not. If he'd been properly worried about the merchant, he wouldn't have left Isfain and Kors to tend Jes and Hennea. More fool he, to trust a man who'd curse another man's living.

She suspected that the hidden men were to come out when she finished to make certain neither Benroln nor she told anyone that he'd paid to have this poor farmer's fields cursed.

Lehr wondered if his mother had caught the signal the merchant had sent. There were men out here somewhere, men waiting to kill Benroln and his mother when the merchant decided he was finished with them. Personally, Lehr wasn't worried about Benroln one way or the other, but his mother was another matter entirely.

Lehr backtracked the merchant until he found a place where the man had waited with four others. Enough men to account for a couple of Travelers as long as they took them by surprise. Each had taken a different path.

They left no tracks that he could see, because the forest was inky-dark; not even the starlight illuminated the ground under the trees. But he knew they had been there because he could smell them.

He shuddered. What was he that he could scent a man like a dog? He drew his knife and picked a trail to follow.

When they came to the edge of the woods, the merchant motioned Seraph on. He and Benroln settled in to wait under the cover of the trees while she worked her magic.

She sat down on the ground at the edge of the field, just outside of the area of planting. She could see the weaving of magic through the soil. The mage this merchant had hired had done well; it was going to take her a long time to clean the field. Time for Lehr to find the merchant's men. Time for Jes to be lost to the effects of the *foundrael*.

She began plucking the threads of the dead mage's spell without further ado. As she did so, the familiarity of what she was doing settled around her with a feeling of rightness: this is what she had been born to do.

After a while the merchant became impatient. "I don't see anything. I don't pay good money for nothing—and I don't put up with people who try to steal from me."

"Tell him I can't work unless he's quiet," said Seraph serenely, knowing that the calmer she was the worse the merchant would take it. His sort always liked to see people cringe in fear of him. She could have given him a light show, but the people her magic told her were sleeping in the cottage might be awakened. She didn't want them coming out to investigate with the merchant's armsmen lurking about—the wrong people might be killed.

"Come away," Benroln said to the merchant with an air of determinedly cheerful deplomacy. "This will take a while.

I brought a pair of dice with me. We can pass the time while Seraph works."

Just as well he'd intervened before she'd pushed the merchant too far, she thought and turned her attention back to the field. Lehr needed all the time she could buy him.

Now why didn't you work? she asked as she pulled the cursing magic away from stalks of wheat only half the size they should be this time of year. Nonetheless, with the strength of the spell she was unravelling, this field shouldn't have grown anything more than a sprig of cheatgrass.

Night fell, but she didn't pay any attention—what she was looking at didn't require light for her to see. Finally, she detached the last of the spelling and, unanchored, the weave fell apart and lost its form.

The magic the wizard had imbued in his casting drifted off when the spell lost its power. It didn't go far before it was caught firmly, and pulled back into the earth to enrich the soil. That was when Seraph realized how it was that the farmer had managed to grow wheat in this field.

There were other creatures that used magic besides the shadow beasts who lived in the Ragged Mountains. Most of them had died fighting at Shadow's Fall. But some of them escaped.

This one hadn't been strong enough to remove the spell, but it had done a great deal to mitigate the effects. Likely whatever it was, it had felt her meddling and was watching from nearby.

"Mmm," she murmured, smiling in pleasure as she leaned forward and pressed her hands onto the field, sinking her hands into the soft ground where the magic held in the grains of dirt made her fingers tingle.

Seraph sent out a drift of Seeking magic again, this time looking for a creature not human. She found something almost immediately, but it was different than she expected: darkness but not shadow, somehow more natural, more elemental than the woods around her, something frightening. It could only be Jes.

The time had come whether Lehr was finished or not. She set the mystery of the farm's protector aside and began her show.

She stood up and held both arms out theatrically, calling out in the Old Tongue. They weren't words of power—she didn't need them for this. She didn't know many words of the Old Tongue, but she was willing to bet that Benroln knew even less.

Theatrics, her father would have scolded her, but her grandfather would have understood. Some people wouldn't believe in magic until it came with light and sounds.

The merchant himself had given her the idea for this, and the magic embedded in the soil gave her the power. She called light filaments to sparkle and grow like cobwebs on the wheat, dancing from stalk to stalk until the whole field glittered in light that shifted rapidly through the shades of the rainbow in waves. It was a pretty effect, she thought, though it was merely light.

But there wouldn't be a *solsenti* alive who would turn their heads from the field to look behind them when Seraph's children approached. Benroln and the merchant stepped out of the trees, but a flicker of magic held them where they were.

Now to leave the merchant in no doubt of what his gold had purchased for him. This was more difficult and she would never have even attempted it if it hadn't been for that dark, tingling soil that ached to aid the growth of the plants rooted in it.

Slowly she raised her arms together as she pushed her magic into plants. *Grow,* she urged them, *grow and be strong.*

Stalks thickened slowly and stretched up . . .

A defter hand than hers touched them and straightened and strengthened; balancing root, stalk, and bearding head in a way that Seraph would not have, though she knew, from the *rightness* of the path of magic, that this was how plants ought to grow.

Since her magic was not needed, she glanced toward the source of the magework and saw it, sitting near a fencepost. It wasn't much bigger than a cat, a small, mossy creature with rounded, droopy ears and large eyes that gleamed with power. Its coloring matched the earth and wood so closely that she doubted that she would have seen it if the field hadn't been thrumming with its power.

"Earthkit," she said softly to herself. "This farmer must keep to the old ways."

"When he had naught but old bread and milk for his own children he didn't forget me," agreed a voice she felt as much as heard. "Such acts are to be rewarded."

"Indeed," agreed Seraph. Since she wasn't doing anything else, she added a crackle to the lights so that the merchant and Benroln wouldn't hear her talking to the creature. "I would not have been able to heal this so well without you."

"Nor could I break that other spelling," said the earthkit in its rusty voice. "But I am done now." The magic ceased abruptly and it left in a scuttling run that her eyes could not quite follow.

The wheat swayed under Seraph's lights, ready to harvest now—at least two months early. She lowered her arms and allowed the glitter and noise to die away slowly.

"I won't do the work of petty criminals," she said clearly.

"Raven," spat Benroln. "Fine. See what happens to your children now. And as for this," he waved a hand at the field, "You may be Raven, but I am Cormorant."

Electricity began gathering in the air.

Stupid, stupid, arrogant Raven, Seraph thought, bitterly ashamed. A storm with the heavy wheat heads atop slender, drying stalks would be disastrous.

If she'd just left the field alone once she'd broken the curse, the earthkit would have seen to it that the wheat grew normally. She knew what Benroln was, and being a farmer's wife she should have remembered what disasters the weather can bring.

"Benroln," she said harshly, "you are a fool. This man has assassins in the woods—do you think they lurk there to watch the magic?"

"I don't know what you're talking about," said the merchant.

Benroln stopped his casting and looked at the other man.

"Why do you think that a man like this would come here without guards?" said Seraph. "There has always been a problem doing the work of *solsenti* who are willing to hire Travelers to make evil upon others of their kind."

"What do you suggest?" Benroln said bitterly. "My people will starve. I tried it your way. We were driven from one place to another, sometimes by people who feared what we might do and sometimes by people because we wouldn't do as they asked. I've had four—*four*—*mermori* come to me. Four more clans dead and gone."

"Do not air our quarrels before *solsenti*," she said sharply.

Benroln glanced at the merchant and bit his lip.

"Lehr took care of three of the men who were watching," said Hennea, coming out of the woods with Gura at her side. "Jes has the other one immobilized."

"So what do we do with him?" Benroln asked.

Jes appeared and grabbed the merchant's hand.

"You don't want to draw that knife," Jes said quietly. "My brother's over there with one of your men's bows. No use anyone else dying tonight."

The merchant all but collapsed at Jes's touch, and Seraph's oldest son relieved him of several throwing knives.

"Asherstal," said Seraph, snapping her fingers. "The owner of this field. He has managed to survive this long; I suspect he can handle this one if we deliver him. Hennea, Jes, could you escort him there?" She turned to Benroln and said, "I need you to call a meeting of your people tonight. I'd like to tell you some things that you need to know."

If she could persuade the entire clan to follow her to Taela, she'd have the clan's healer for her husband when she found him. She just wished she were as good at persuading people as Tier was.

Benroln didn't wait for her, but stomped off, angry at her, at the merchant, and at a responsibility he didn't know how to fulfill.

When Benroln was gone, Jes said, "He bears no open wounds, Mother, but Lehr is hurt."

Seraph nodded. "Take this one to the farmhouse and don't get anyone hurt in the process, and I'll do my best for Lehr."

She waited until Jes and Hennea were halfway to the cabin, but before she called out, Lehr came. It was too dark to see him well, but she could smell the blood on him.

"Thank you," she said. "If you had not been here tonight, Benroln and I would doubtless have been dead."

"There are three men dead instead," he said. "Jes tied the fourth one up before I got to him."

"They were men who were willing to kill for no cause but

gold," said Seraph. Words were not her strength, but for Lehr she searched for the right ones. "They have doubtless killed others on the merchant's orders. Now they will not kill anyone again."

"When I killed them," whispered Lehr, coming toward her, "it was so easy. Easier than hunting deer. What am I, Mother?"

"This is what it means to be an Order-Bearer," she told him. "None of the Orders are easy. You are Hunter, and among the tasks of the Hunter is the bringing of death."

She opened her arms, and, when he dropped to his knees in front of her, she pulled him close. He buried his face in the crook of her neck.

"I don't like it," he said.

"Shh," she held him and rocked lightly back and forth, as she had when he'd been a child. "Shh."

"Someone's waiting in front of our tent," said Jes just as Gura gave a happy bark and ran forward with his tail wagging.

"So," said Brewydd from a bench someone must have carried over for her. "You stopped Benroln from his folly. That's more than I've managed to do." Gura sat beside her and put his big black muzzle on her knee and heaved a contented sigh.

"Hardly," said Seraph. "I just pointed out that the merchant he chose to do business with was a thief and a killer—and that any other *solsenti* he'd find to pay for the same sort of favor will probably be equally bad."

The old woman cackled, "I never thought of that."

"It won't stop him," said Seraph. "He's obviously done similar things before; he'll do them again."

"Most of them weren't this bad," said Brewydd. "Though making certain that a village was dry a month or more in high summer, then forcing them to pay him to bring the rain is no noble deed."

"No," agreed Hennea dryly.

"Talk to him at this meeting tonight," Brewydd told Seraph. "Make him understand what he does is folly."

"What good will talking do?" asked Lehr. "Haven't you told him what he's been doing is wrong? Why would he listen to Mother when he won't listen to you?"

"Hah!" exclaimed Brewydd. "A man would rather listen to a beautiful woman than a wrinkled old crone. You, boy," she said pointing at Lehr. "You can help an old woman to her home."

Lehr took a deep breath, tightened his jaw, and nodded his head. When he took her arm, Brewydd patted his biceps lightly before using him to lever herself up. "Your mother teaches you well, boy. It is good when a youngling is kind to old women." She winked at Seraph and continued to mutter at Lehr as he led her back to her wagon.

"Right," said Seraph, hoping Brewydd could do better for Lehr than she'd managed. "Let's go find Benroln."

"Seraph," said Hennea, "if you go and start attacking Benroln for what he's done, you'll make Lehr happy and we'll all go our separate ways tomorrow. Benroln will still take gold from the next *solsenti* who wants to pay to have his neighbor's fields destroyed, and you'll have the satisfaction of telling them what you think of them."

"You have another suggestion?" said Seraph.

"The Secret Path is very powerful," said Hennea. "They claim that they run the Empire, and that might very well be true. Having more people to call on for help could be very useful."

"I've thought of that," said Seraph. "But—Hennea, I am not a Bard. Yelling I can do, but persuasion is another matter entirely. Would you try?"

She shook her head. "To Benroln and his people, you are our leader. To have me speak to them would be an insult. You can do this. Just remember that Benroln is frustrated because there's nothing he can do to keep his people safe. Give him something to do other than rob the *solsenti* of their gold, some way to strike back, and he'll forget about the games."

Isfain was angry with Hennea, Seraph observed as she sipped her hot tea. But Hennea had told her the state she'd found Jes in, and Seraph didn't mind seeing him grit his teeth when Hennea got too close. What chance had given Hennea the knowledge of loosing the *foundrael,* Seraph didn't know, but she was grateful for it all the same.

Hennea had certainly impressed a few people with her freeing of Jes. The whole Rongier clan, at least those present at the small gathering in front of Benroln's tent, were treating Hennea as if she'd grown a third head.

Or maybe Hennea was just sitting too close to Jes.

Jes had no intention of forgiving anyone for imprisoning him. He lurked in a wolfish form only half-revealed by the flickering light of the bonfire. It might have been easier if he'd chosen to be wolf in whole, but the wolf's muzzle and eyes in an otherwise human body was particularly disturbing. Low growls told everyone that he was unhappy with them all. Seraph rather thought the shape was an illusion, but it was difficult to tell.

Brewydd had brought Lehr with her. He looked tired, but the sickness had faded from his eyes. When the old woman griped at him and ordered him to move her camp chair three times before she sat in it, he actually grinned.

Benroln came out of his tent at last, and looked around to see that everyone was there. He sat down directly opposite Seraph and nodded his head at her: so the meeting would begin with her comments.

Unhappy people, all, she thought, glancing around at the faces of the clan.

"We could spend the night throwing accusations and debating ancient history," said Seraph. "If you were not honest with what you wanted of us, well then, we were not entirely honest either."

"I'd like to rage at you, and tell you how wrong what you've been doing is, but you already know what I think." She took a deep breath. "So I'm going to tell you the things that we didn't tell you when you invited us to journey with you to Taela. It will take a while, and I am no Bard. I ask for your patience just the same."

"I am Seraph, Raven of Isolda the Silent and wife to Tieragan of Redern, Owl in his own right, though he has not a drop of Traveler blood . . ."

By the time she brought them into the present she was hoarse. Benroln refilled her cup and urged it upon her solicitously— as if they had not just fought a battle over a farmer's field.

As clan leader, it was his place to respond, so everyone sat silently while he considered her story.

"This Path," he said, "they have been taking our people for years and stealing their Orders?"

Seraph nodded.

"You have some of the stones?" asked Brewydd.

Seraph had thought the old Healer was asleep.

"Yes."

"I'd like to see them," Brewydd murmured. "Bring them here when we are done and we'll sit in the Librarian's home, you and I, Hennea and Benroln, and see just what evil the *solsenti* have wrought."

"All right," Seraph said and then changed the subject. "Tomorrow, my family and I will continue on to Taela where my husband is being kept."

"You say your husband is Ordered," said Isfain. "But he is a *solsenti?*"

"That's right."

"Could this Secret Path you told us about be the reason that the *solsenti* laws have become so stringent against us?" asked Kors.

Seraph thought that they could look to themselves and to other clans who had gone after gold rather than fighting evil for the cause of the antipathy *solsenti* had toward Travelers, but she wasn't such a fool as to say so.

Benroln, unaware of Seraph's thoughts, nodded intently. "It could be. If what we have heard tonight is true, this Path could be very powerful." He nodded his head once more. "Then this is what we will do. Isfain, send out messages to the other clans we know of and warn them of this Path and their methods. See to it that they in turn pass the message on." He waited until Isfain nodded. "Tomorrow we also strike out at speed for Taela."

He turned to Seraph. "There are things that we can do to help. We have friends in Taela."

Seraph looked at his eager face. "I would be very grateful for any help you can give," she said.

Seraph was exhausted, but she found herself as unable to say no to the old Healer as everyone else was. Besides, she wanted to know what the Healer could tell her about the rings. So it was that she found herself inside the house of Rongier the Librarian with Hennea, Benroln, and Brewydd.

Rongier's home had been larger and more prosperous than Isolda's. His library had a table large enough to seat eight or ten people.

Seraph took the seat next to Brewydd and dumped the bag of rings on the table.

Brewydd hesitated and lightly fingered each ring before settling on an old ring set with a stone of rose quartz.

"Well," she murmured, "how did they do that then? You told me that they took the Orders and bound them to a ring."

"Right," said Seraph. "That's what Hennea said, and that's what seems to have happened."

"Indeed." Brewydd put the ring down and pushed it away from her. Her hand was shaking a little. "So that's one of the reasons," she murmured.

"Reasons for what, Brewydd?" asked Benroln. He'd made no move to look closer at the rings.

"There were only ever so many Orders," she said. "I don't know the numbers, I'm not certain where to find an exact count of most of them—but there were only ever ten healers. One would die and another would be born. But now there are only six." She pointed at the ring she'd been handling. "That one is one of the missing."

"Do you mean to say that the Orders are . . . like a . . ." Seraph searched for a proper comparison.

"Like a suit of armor," said Brewydd. "One that is fitted at birth and stays with you, grows to be a part of you until it is like your skin. When you die, the skin sloughs off and cleanses itself of everything that was yours—your scent, your shape, the sound of your voice. Then, once more only a suit of armor, it goes off and seeks the next person to fit itself to."

She folded her hands and rested her chin on them. "The Orders don't go to just anyone." She nodded her head toward Seraph. "You would have been a mage even if you hadn't been Raven. Your husband would still have sung. Benroln would have been one of those people who always seems to know when a bad storm is coming in. The Orders go where they will be welcomed."

"So when they made these stones," said Benroln somberly, "each ring was another Traveler born without an Order."

Brewydd nodded her head. She looked at Hennea. "You

said that the wizards of the Path, these Masters, find that they cannot use some of these. I believe that they took the Order too soon, that there are bits of personality still clinging to the stones. The only time I've ever seen something similar is when I had to deal with a Raven's Memory."

"A Raven's Memory?" asked Benroln.

"A Raven's Memory," said Brewydd, "happens only when a Raven is murdered. A Raven can take the power that always comes with death and a part of himself to the Order and bind the result to a false life until it carries out vengeance against his murderer."

"But it's not only the Raven stones that . . ." Seraph's voice trailed off because she wasn't certain how to explain it.

"No." Brewydd sorted out a half dozen rings. "Here is the Lark, a couple of Ravens, a Hunter and Bard, these all contain part of their last Order-Bearer. They're bound, tied to the stones so they can't act like Raven Memories—but I bet the wizards who tried to wear them got a rude surprise."

"Do you know what to do with them?" asked Hennea.

"Not yet," said Brewydd. "Do you mind if I keep these?" She indicated the jewelry.

"No," said Seraph. "If you can figure out what to do with them, how to free the Orders, it is more than Hennea and I have managed."

Brewydd nodded and collected the rings into Seraph's bag. "Tell that boy of yours to come to my wagon tomorrow when we stop to camp," she said.

"Lehr?" asked Seraph cautiously.

Brewydd nodded. "I know a few odd things about Hunters he might be interested in." She got to her feet. "I know a lot more than I let on," she said. "But I only share with those I like. Your boy was exhausted and heartsick, not to mention tired of taking orders and angry with the whole of my clan— yet he still was courteous and gentle. I like him." She glared at Benroln.

He got up off the chair with a crack of laughter. "I love you, old woman." He leaned over and kissed her cheek. "I'm going to get some sleep before I fall over. You'll want to keep the *mermora* until you've solved this puzzle with the rings, and you are welcome to it, Brewydd. Good night."

Brewydd turned to Seraph. "I'm an honest woman, so I'll tell you that I'm not used to learning wisdom from those younger than I. I thought that I had to convince him that what he was doing to earn gold was wrong. I never considered trying to find something else for him to do instead. Thank you."

Seraph shook her head. "I'm afraid you have Hennea to thank for that."

Hennea smiled and got up. "You're welcome to any bits of wisdom I pick up. Now, I'm with Benroln; it's time to sleep. Can I escort you to your wagon?"

Brewydd laughed and winked at Seraph. "I'll say yes, only because that handsome young Guardian who's been waiting outside will come, too."

Seraph laughed, yawned, and left for their tent.

"Seraph, wake up," Hennea's voice was soft and disappeared into the dream.

"Mother," murmured Jes.

At the sound, Seraph sat up and opened her eyes almost in the same motion. "Jes, are you all right?"

He smiled his sweet smile. "Fine, Mother, but you're going to wake the camp."

Seraph yawned and tried to find the reason they'd woken her up in what Jes had just said. It was still dark out and everyone except her was lying down. Hennea had a gentle grip on Seraph's arm.

"You were having nightmares," said Lehr, rolling on his side so he could see her more easily.

When he said it, she remembered. Tier had been sitting on a throne of oak, ash, and rowan while a spell was worked around him. He'd been playing one of the songs he played often at the tavern, though she couldn't remember which one it was. She'd run to him, knelt at his feet, and set her head in her lap as she had sometimes when the nightmares had been so bad after her brother had died. But there had been something wrong. He'd kept playing, ignoring her entirely. Finally she'd reached up to touch the skin of his arm and screamed. His flesh had been warm, she could feel blood pulse under her fingertips, but she knew that he was dead.

Nervously she ran her fingers in her hair. "Thank you for waking me," she said, lying down again.

"What did you dream of?" asked Hennea.

"I don't remember," Seraph lied. She had no talent for foreseeing, she reminded herself firmly. It had only been a dream.

She lay back and stared at the top of the tent. She knew that Jes and Lehr assumed they'd find Tier hale and whole and the only problem would be getting him out, but Seraph had too much experience to believe in happy endings.

He might be dead.

She'd never told Tier that she loved him. Never once.

She had done her best to turn herself into a good wife, tried to become the person he needed as helpmeet. She knew he'd assume that she'd never told him that she loved him because she didn't.

He was wrong.

Tier felt guilty for so much: that she'd been forced to marry him, that she'd been so young. Their marriage had freed him from the burden of taking over the family bakery and he felt guilty about that, too. He'd gained his freedom and she'd lost hers, lost her chance to rejoin her people. If she'd ever told him that she loved him, he'd have told her that he loved her, too.

He'd have lied for her.

Tier was the most truthful person she knew. He'd have lied to her out of guilt, and she couldn't abide that, so she'd never told him.

Dry-eyed, she stared at the tent ceiling and hoped that she'd get the chance to hear him lie to her.

CHAPTER 13

Phoran nervously caressed the stack of parchment on his bed. He had already carefully organized it, placing the one that would make his first bid for power fifteenth down. Far enough down that many of the Septs would have relaxed their guard, but not so far that they would have quit listening entirely.

A light tap at his door made him take three quick steps away from the bed. Then he realized that the bed was an odd place for formal documents, so he ran back, snatched them up, and placed them on his writing desk. He wouldn't want anyone to think that he'd spent all day and most of the night going through them. Most of the Septs would think that he was merely tormenting Douver, the council secretary: everyone knew that Phoran couldn't stand the worm.

The quiet tap sounded again. "Your Highness?" said the guard who stood his watch at the door to the Emperor's bedchamber. "My lord, Avar, Sept of Leheigh, begs entrance."

"Avar?" Phoran said distractedly. Now that he thought of it, the writing desk was an odd choice as well. He couldn't remember ever actually sitting at it—something Avar would have noticed.

"Yes, Your Highness."

"Yes, yes, let him in." It was too late to change anything anyway.

The door opened and Avar made his entrance. "Phoran," he said as soon as the door was closed behind him. "I've been looking for you since yesterday afternoon. Did you really take all the proposed laws and run off with them?"

Surprisingly, Phoran didn't have a prepared reply. He hadn't even thought about what Avar would say. Not that he didn't care—but it didn't seem as important anymore.

Avar misread his hesitation.

"Not that you didn't have every right to—but you might have warned someone you intended to take a closer look. It wasn't necessary to give poor Douver an anxiety attack."

Phoran found himself smiling. "Wasn't it? You'll have to forgive me if I've forgotten that I could have just called the things into my review. I suspect everyone else has forgotten as well."

A frown chased itself across Avar's perfect brow. "What are you up to, my friend?"

"Do you know anything about the Secret Path?" It was an impulsive question born of years of trust, blind trust he was no longer certain he felt. But even after the question left his lips, Phoran didn't regret it.

"The secret, *secret* club that everyone knows about?" asked Avar with a grin. "Where a bunch of young hotheads go to pretend they are villainous Travelers? My brother, Toarsen, and his tagalong, muscle-bound friend, Kissel, belong to it."

Phoran walked back to his bed and perched on the end, offering a nearby padded bench to Avar with his hand. "Tell me everything you know."

"Does this have something to do with taking the proposals?" asked Avar as he availed himself of the offered seat and leaned back against the wall.

"I don't know," said Phoran truthfully.

"Well then." Avar put his head back and relaxed. "They choose young men of noble blood when they're fifteen or sixteen and induct them in some sort of secret ceremony. They don't pick a lot of boys—no more than five or ten a year. I don't know what they do at the ceremony—but my brother carried bruises from it for a week or more. The people they

choose are usually the ones who are . . . well, problems for
their families."

He looked at Phoran a moment, then sighed. "I know they
had something to do with that mess last year when some young
thugs destroyed the weavers' market. I saw Toarsen coming
home in the wee hours of the morning, dead drunk with a
hatchet in his hand. I should have said something, but"—he
shrugged ruefully—"he's my brother."

"Do you know any of the older members?" asked Phoran.
"The Raptors?"

"Some," answered Avar with a quick grin. "The ones my
brother gripes the most about. The council leader—the Sept
of Gorrish is one of them and Telleridge is another. My father
was—I think that's how my brother was selected."

Phoran closed his eyes and thought. "Didn't the Weavers'
Guild file a complaint against Gorrish just before the market
was destroyed? They dropped it because he was instrumental
in getting funds to help them rebuild it."

"You're right," said Avar in an arrested voice. "I never
thought to look for a deeper motive. I've always thought of the
Secret Path as a game for boys who are at loose ends."

"I have heard that you cannot be an heir to a Sept and belong to the Path," said Phoran.

"Gorrish's father and three older brothers died in the
plague that hit the Empire about twenty years ago," said Avar.
"He's not the only younger son who has inherited." He
smiled. "My own father was a second son."

Phoran had a terrible thought. Maybe it was because he'd
just spent the night talking to a bard that he'd thought of the
old story of the Shadowed. How the first magic the Shadowed
had loosed was plague. Maybe it was all the talk of magic—or
maybe it was his current affliction of Memory. "How many of
those second and third sons, or cousins who inherited a Sept
were members of the Path?" he asked.

"I don't know exactly—I was about four at the time,
Phoran. The younger sons who inherited unexpectedly . . . oh,
Seal Hold, Telleridge, Jenne, and a few others. You aren't going to tell me that the Secret Path is responsible for the plague,
are you?" Avar shook his head. "A lot of people died, Phoran,

Most of them weren't Septs with heirs who happened to be members of the Secret Club."

"Doubtless, you're right." Phoran smiled and changed the subject. "I am calling a Council Seating for tomorrow," he said.

"*You* are?" asked Avar, surprised into insult.

Phoran smiled at him grimly. "It may have become usual, since my uncle died, for Gorrish to call the Seat, but it is the imperial prerogative he uses. I am calling it, and I'd like you to deliver the messages. See if you can convince them that it's just a silly whim of mine—that I said something about being bored."

Avar stared at him for a long time, then nodded his head. "I'll do that. Tell me what time you'd like to meet."

The Memory came again that night. Phoran waited impatiently for it to finish. At last the cold tongue licked the puncture wounds clean and the Memory gave him the usual offer.

"Were you a Traveler held by the Secret Path?" Phoran asked.

"Yes," it said and was gone with its usual abruptness.

Pale and a little dizzy, the Emperor went to his closet and pulled on a robe. With only a little caution—because the Path's rooms were in an obscure corner of the palace—Phoran made it back to the bard's cell with little trouble. He found Tier's door unlocked, but when he went in, Tier lay unmoving on his bed and nothing Phoran could do would awaken him.

Phoran took up a seat on the end of the bed and stared at Tier's face—but other than being a little pale, he seemed healthy enough. At last Phoran arose unhappily and returned to his suite.

When Tier awoke, he knew they'd come for him again, though his last memory was of settling in to play a bit of music after leaving the party in the Eyrie. He moved and the lute tucked beside him dug into his ribs.

He sat up with sudden anxiety and inspected it for any damage it might have taken. He found something that could have been a new scratch on the finish, but nothing that would impair its use. He settled back against the wall with a sigh of relief. His head throbbed, his body ached, and his mouth was uncomfortably dry—but the lute could not heal itself.

He hugged the lute against his body.

What was it that they did to him?

Someone knocked on the door. Tier gathered himself together and stood up.

"It's dinnertime, sir," Myrceria explained after he'd opened the door to her. "I can have food brought to you, or you can eat in the Eyrie with the Passerines." She hesitated, then said, "You might have noticed that your movements have been restricted unless you have an escort. I was told to inform you that you now can move freely around most of the rooms used by the Passerines. If you'd like to wait and go alone, you may do that also. Food will be provided at any time upon your request."

He stood up slowly, but the movement seemed to help some of his aches and pains. "By all means," he said with as much charm as he could muster over his fading headache. "Let us go to the Eyrie."

The room was almost full to bursting. When Tier stepped inside, the dull roar quieted as the young men all watched him. Like a duck who had the ill luck to drop to earth in the midst of a pack of wolves, Tier thought with amusement.

Food of every description was spread out on the bar for the taking. Tier, following Myrceria's example, took a wooden platter and began filling it. When she led the way to an unoccupied table he followed her.

He ate without seeming to look up, but his peripheral vision was very good. He saw the boys' cautious approach.

The first to arrive and sit at Tier's table was a tall boy, too thin for his height. Before he opened his mouth, Tier knew a few things about him. The first was that he was a loner. The Passerines, he noticed, tended to travel in packs, and there was no one moving with this boy. The pads of his fingers were calloused from instrument strings and in one of those calloused hands was a large case.

He sat down beside Myrceria and put the case on their table in the place of the food dishes that an efficient servant had just whisked away.

"You said last night that a Bard could play any instrument," he said. "Try this one."

"What's your name?" asked Tier. He ignored the shuffle as a number of young men pulled up stools and benches to listen in on their conversation; instead, he kept his eyes on the case as he undid the various hooks that kept it closed.

"Collarn," said the boy. "I am an assistant at the Imperial College of Music. What do you think?"

The challenge in Collarn's voice was such that Tier wasn't surprised to discover that the case held an instrument he'd never seen before. He coaxed the thing out of its close-fitting case and scooted his stool back so that he could rest it on his lap for a closer look.

It looked somewhat like a lute, he decided, but it was squarer and deeper-bodied. There were tuning pegs, but the strings were hidden inside the body. Below the pegs it had two rows of buttons on the side.

On the side was a—"A handle?" Tier said, and turned it. At once an odd, penetrating, grinding sound issued from the bowels of the instrument. He grinned in delight.

Tier tilted his head and closed his eyes, turning the handle again. "It's like a violin," he said. "Or pipes. What do you call it, Collarn of the College of Music?"

"It's a symphonia. There's a wheel-bow inside that turns with the handle."

Collarn had obviously come to flummox the Bard— probably for usurping his place as the Passerine's musical entertainment, but he shared Tier's love of music too deeply not to fall into a discussion with someone willing to explore the possibilities of his obscure instrument.

Tier hid his smile—he liked Collarn, and the boy obviously took himself too seriously to enjoy a laugh at his own expense. After trying several positions, Tier shifted the symphonia until he could turn the handle with his right hand and touch the buttons on the side with his left.

After a moment he managed a simple melody—but he heard the possibilities of much greater things. The instrument was louder than his lute, making it a good choice for performing outdoors or before a large audience. A pair of strings played the same note continuously like a bagpipe's drones, lending a sonorously eerie accompaniment to the rest of the notes that changed at the touch of his fingers on the buttons.

Tier stood up and handed the instrument to Collarn. "Would you play something for me?" he asked. "I'd like to hear it played by someone who knows what it can do."

The boy was talented—though his grandfather's old friend Ciro could have taught him something about softening the straight rhythm Collarn held to when the song wanted to fly.

Finished, the boy looked up, his face a little bright. "That's the only song I know on it. We have no music written directly for it. The masters at the college don't think much of the instrument—it's an odd thing someone brought to the college a dozen years ago."

"May I try it again?" asked Tier, and the boy handed the symphonia over.

"The piece you played"—Tier played a bit, deliberately more hesitant than Collarn had played so that he didn't rob the boy of his performance—"is something written for violin. It's a good choice, and plays to the instrument's strengths."

"I can do it better on a violin," said Collarn. "There's no dynamic range to the symphonia." He grinned and the sweetness of the unexpected expression reminded Tier of Jes. "It just doesn't do quiet."

"Bagpipes are like that," said Tier. "You might try piping music."

He fell silent and searched the instrument for range and effect. When he turned the handle at just the right speed and the instrument added a buzz to its already odd sound, Tier stopped and laughed outright.

"I can see why your college masters have a problem. It's just a bit brash, eh? A little boldness isn't necessarily a bad thing." He hummed a little tune under his breath. "Let me try this . . ."

He knew he had it right when the toes of the boys nearest him started moving. When Collarn took a small silver pennywhistle out of his pocket and added a few runs, it made Tier think of playing with the old men in the afternoons at the tavern in Redern. He played through the song twice—the second time his fingers found their own way as he looked around the room at all the young faces.

He'd come here this afternoon to gather information, and instead he'd gained a friend. Speculatively, Tier's eyes fell on a promising young man who was using the haft of his knife to tap out a rhythm on a tabletop.

Tier knew about recruiting young men.

Phoran was deliberately late going to the Council chambers. He wanted them to gossip, to fret. If Avar had done as he asked, they would be more annoyed than worried.

The Emperor stopped before the door, took a deep breath, and nodded to the chamberlain to announce him.

"Rise for the Emperor Phoran, may his reign never cease!"

If it doesn't ever begin, thought Phoran, *can it ever cease?*

Silence fell in the room and Phoran strode leisurely through the doorway, followed by the young page he'd chosen for his small size to make the stack of parchment the page carried look even larger than it was.

Phoran himself was in his most glittering, gaudy clothes—clothes that had caused his valet to mutter about street whores. Phoran had started out to wear a more conservative outfit—but he'd decided that would send the wrong message. He didn't want to announce, *Look! I've changed for you.* He wanted to force them to acknowledge him emperor on his own terms.

His hair was curled, and his face was powdered paler than any court dandy. A small blue star painted beside his eye matched the glittering blue and silver stars embroidered on purple velvet portions of his costume.

He didn't hurry, forcing himself to keep his appearance languid while the impatience of the Septs grew almost palpable. At last he reached the place reserved for the Emperor. A thin coat of dust covered the inlayed surface of his podium, where he gestured for the boy to set the parchment before waving him off in the general direction of Douver, the council secretary.

The page relayed the message he'd been given and the secretary looked up at Phoran incredulously. Phoran stared back, doing his best to look neither nervous nor smug as his page rejoined him.

Douver cleared his throat. "Septs of the Empire. I call a

general roll so that His Glory the Emperor shall know who
attends this meeting. Each Sept will call out as I read his
name." He took up a paper and Phoran made a show of removing the top sheet of parchment, which was a copy of the
clerk's.

In the end, twenty-four Septs were absent. Phoran was
careful to mark each of their names with a stylus while the
council watched. Everyone in the room knew that at least
eighteen of those named were in the palace.

"Thank you," said Phoran graciously, and without a speech
or any further delay, he picked up the first of the proposed
laws. "The matter of the trade agreement between the Septs of
Isslaw and Blackwater is declared to be Imperial Law."

He set the first parchment to one side and picked up the
next. By the tenth parchment the Septs began shifting uncomfortably in their seats—except for Avar, who sat in his chair
with arms folded across his chest, and stared at Phoran
thoughtfully as Phoran continued his show.

Phoran took the fifteenth parchment and read, "For his services to the Empire, the Sept of Jenne is to be awarded the
land from Iscar Rock to the eastern field of Kersay Holm in a
path no more than ten miles wide."

He looked up and found the Sept of Jenne in his usual
place in the council. "So, what service did you perform for the
Empire, Jenne?"

The man he'd addressed stood up. A contemporary of
Phoran's father, he was in his late middle years, with iron-grey
hair and a short beard. He bowed. "If it please Your Imperial
Majesty, it was in the matter of the trouble the Weavers' Guild
had last year. I found myself in the position of being able to
perform some little service in the matter of raising funds for
the displaced merchants."

"Ah," said Phoran. "We had wondered. In any case, this
proposal is denied. You may reseat yourself, Jenne." He set it
to his left, away from the neat stack of signed documents.

He'd picked up the next proposal when the paralysis wore
off and the Sept of Gorrish jumped to his feet followed by a
fair number of his followers.

"I protest!" he said, and that was the last thing that anyone heard clearly for several minutes as the Council of Septs roared its displeasure with the Emperor.

Phoran set the parchment he'd picked up back where he'd gotten it and waited for the uproar to die down with as cool a manner as he could force over his pounding heart. His instincts told him that if he were not able to take control of the Septs at this meeting, he never would.

He watched the flushed faces of the men who protested, seeing the hidden satisfaction on Telleridge's countenance at the strength of the Septs' outrage, though Telleridge said nothing. Avar caught Phoran's gaze and raised an eyebrow, then he made a subtle gesture toward himself as if to ask, "May I?"

Avar thought he could do something about this? Phoran raised his own eyebrows (he had never learned the trick of raising only one) and nodded his head.

Avar stood up, jumped the waist-high barrier and landed on the council floor, six feet or so below the seating area. His action caught the attention of the Septs, buying him a momentary lull in the noise.

"Gentlemen," he bellowed. "Any man who is still standing and talking after a count of five, I shall personally challenge to armed deadly combat. Even if I have to fight each of you. His Imperial Majesty will then have a much more pleasant time with your heirs. One. Two. Three."

Avar could do it, too; Phoran knew. Could defeat each and every one of the Septs. That they agreed with Phoran's assessment was demonstrated by the fact that they were seated and silent before Avar reached "four."

Avar scanned the seats to make certain they were occupied, then with that easy athleticism that Phoran envied so, he jumped up, caught the bottom railing and scaled the barrier to resume his own seat.

"We give thanks to the Sept of Leheigh for his service to the Empire," said Phoran with more aplomb than he felt. Avar's audacious and effective ploy to silence the Septs had left Phoran the opportunity for a bit of cleverness—or stupidity depending upon how it turned out.

Phoran turned his head to the council leader. "So, Ombre, Sept of Gorrish—you object to my rejection of this proposed law?" He picked up the offending document and appeared to look at it more closely.

"Permission to speak, please?" Gorrish ground out between clenched teeth.

"Oh, of course," said Phoran in surprised tones. "We are always glad to hear your concerns, Gorrish."

The council leader dropped his eyes and took a deep breath. "This is a matter that was already put forth and approved by the council."

"For me to consider putting into law," agreed Phoran lightly. "I decided that it was ill-considered." He reached for the next parchment again.

"Please, Your Majesty, hear me out," said Gorrish. "The particulars of the case were made known to the council at the time the lands were granted. There were no objections at all."

Phoran raised his eyebrows again in surprise. "What, none?" He looked around the room. "Avar?"

"Yes, Imperial Majesty?" Avar stood.

"Did you not just put your life at risk in Our Service?" questioned Phoran.

To Phoran's delight, Avar looked at the Septs around him and shook his head slightly. "I suppose someone might have gotten in a lucky blow, Your Majesty, but I did not feel imperiled."

"Nonetheless," said Phoran, "there was risk and you did not hesitate to serve me. Is this not a greater deed than raising funds to help a few merchants? A matter, I understand, of some two hundred and thirty-five gold pieces?"

The air went still as the more observant Septs began to realize that Phoran knew more about the affair than he'd appeared to at first.

"Perhaps, Your Majesty," agreed Avar with seeming reluctance.

"Avar, Sept of Leheigh, please enlighten those here with the amount that you spent on that magnificent mare you purchased yesterday."

Avar cleared his throat. "Ah, two hundred and forty gold pieces, Your Majesty."

"We believe that the life of a Sept is of more value than a horse," said Phoran firmly. "Therefore Avar, Sept of Leheigh, I put it before the council that I intend to gift you with a piece of land from Tisl to Riesling of a width not more than three miles—"

"But—" Servish, the hotheaded young Sept of Allyn, surged to his feet. Servish, though, was loyal to a fault and he caught his tongue and began to sink down.

"But what, Allyn?" invited Phoran gently. He had picked Servish especially for this role.

Servish swallowed and straightened up. "I am, always, your loyal servant, Majesty."

Phoran nodded. "Please," he said. "What was it you were going to say?"

Servish flushed and took a deep breath. "The land you spoke of is within my Sept, Majesty."

Phoran smiled at him and then looked at Avar, who had remained standing. "Avar, I am afraid that I cannot grant you lands that belong to a loyal Sept. It would not be right."

"No," agreed Avar.

"What say you, my lords?" Phoran looked to the Septs. "Those who would grant me or any other such powers, stand and say, 'Aye' now." The room was silent.

"Nor, Gorrish, can I take lands away from any loyal Sept just to grant them to someone who performed some small service to the Empire. The Sept of Gerant has never shown me anything but loyalty. It would be a poor emperor who took lands away from Septs who have committed no offense. You may all take your seats."

He could feel it happen, Phoran thought. He could feel the reins of the Empire slip into his hands. He kept his face clear of triumph and picked up another piece of parchment.

"In the matter of the border dispute . . ." And the Septs all sat silently in their seats as Phoran read through every last one of the documents.

"What is your purpose?" Phoran asked, his hands only a little shaky as he pulled down his sleeve. The triumph of this afternoon was such that even the Memory's bite wasn't enough to sour his mood. If he could control the Septs, then surely he could rid himself of this curse.

"To destroy the Masters of the Secret Path," it said.

"Ah," said Phoran.

He'd known the answer, but he hadn't thought of a better question. He had to steady himself when he stood up. "I'm going to see if our friend in the Path's dungeons is any better. You may join me if you'd like."

Truthfully, he was tempted just to go to bed. He had been tired before the Memory showed up, and losing more blood hadn't helped any. But the memory of Tier's unnaturally deep sleep had been with him all day. The Memory, for whatever reason, followed him to Tier's cell.

There was music coming from the Bard's cell, but the door was too thick to hear more than that. Drawing his short sword, Phoran tapped lightly on the door.

"Come in." Impossible to mistake that voice: it was Tier.

Phoran sheathed his sword and opened the door. The Bard was sitting on his bed with a lute in his hands. He was pale and looked nearly as tired as Phoran felt, but when Tier saw that it was Phoran, he set the instrument aside and got quickly to his feet. "My emperor."

"Just Phoran," Phoran advised him and shuffled over to plop down on the end of the bed. He scooted back until his back was braced against the wall and motioned for Tier to do likewise. "I'm glad to see you in a better state than last night."

"You came last night as well?" Tier sat down and pulled the lute back into his lap as if it were a baby. He glanced over at the Memory, which had taken up the same place it had on the first night.

"I couldn't wake you," Phoran yawned. He'd forgotten that he hadn't gotten much sleep the night before. At least he had a better excuse for being tired. "I waited for a few hours, but decided that I'd give you a night to recover from—?"

"Something the wizards have cooked up," said Tier unhappily. "I'm not certain what." He shook his head and gave Phoran a small smile. "Nothing anyone can do about it right now. I do have some information for you. You asked about Avar, the Sept of Leheigh. I heard his name mentioned, mostly because his brother, Toarsen, is a Passerine, but if he's a member, the Passerines don't know about it."

Phoran heaved a sigh of relief. He'd been almost certain after the council incident, but it was good to be sure.

"There are a number of Septs who are Raptors," said Tier and rattled off a list of thirty or forty.

Phoran would have been more impressed if the list hadn't frightened him so badly. "Could you go through them again, please?" he said tightly.

Tier complied, listing the same people in the same order.

"Did you hear any other names?" asked Phoran, almost afraid to ask. "Not of the Passerines, but the wizards."

"The Masters, the wizards, except for Telleridge, keep their identities hidden," said Tier. "I do have the names of more Raptors."

Phoran listened to a recital that consisted of people ranging from Douver, the council secretary, to the captain of the palace guard, including any number of influential tradesmen and scholars.

"You have a remarkable memory," said Phoran neutrally. "You heard all of those in the past two days?"

"Mostly today," agreed Tier. He gave Phoran a small smile. "Bards have to have a good memory, and the Passerines weren't at all unhappy to discuss the glories of membership in the Secret Path."

Phoran believed him, and wished unhappily that he did not. "What if," he said slowly, "what if I told you that the Path recruits the restless younger sons and cousins among the nobles of the Empire at the age of fifteen—the kinds of boys who are an embarrassment to their families. Remember, the one rule the Path has when the young men join is that they cannot be direct heirs of any Sept."

"I have noticed that there are a lot of Septs among the Raptors," agreed Tier, clearly seeing what was bothering Phoran. "But since I haven't heard of a wave of assassinations of Septs and their heirs, I assumed there was an explanation—the last war or that plague."

"You told the Memory the story of the Shadowed," said Phoran.

Tier wasn't stupid; he understood where Phoran was going. "You think that one of the Masters of the Path created that plague?" he asked. Unlike Avar, Tier had no incredulity in his voice; he was considering Phoran's theory.

Thus encouraged, Phoran continued. "The plague twenty

years ago was very convenient for a number of Raptors. To-morrow I'll bring paper and ink so you can write down the list of Septs for me again. Then I'll do a little research, but I know that Telleridge, Gorrish, Jenne, the old Sept of Leheigh, and a dozen others you named inherited then. Some of them were six or seven people away from inheritance."

Phoran glanced at Tier.

"Go on," the Bard said.

"My father died in the plague. His brother, my uncle, was named regent. When I was twelve he was poisoned by his mistress, and the council, under Gorrish, took over an informal regency. The Sept of Leheigh's son, Avar, took me under his wing." Phoran smiled without humor. "He's mellowed out a lot in the past few years, but when I met him he was a lot less respectable than his reputation would have shown him."

Phoran had done a lot of thinking since his conversation with Avar before the council meeting. "He was a boy, and his own father had encouraged him to be wild. It wouldn't have struck him odd that the old Sept would encourage him to take a twelve-year-old places that were at best unsavory and at worst outright dangerous—I don't think that he'd have sought out my company without his father forcing him to do so." It hurt to admit that, but he knew it was true.

"You have gained a reputation of being volatile and unreliable," said Tier slowly. "Even we in the hinterlands of Redern have heard so much."

"Not to say that I wasn't a willing participant," Phoran said staunchly, though he wanted Tier to like him and it was difficult to admit responsibility. "But if my uncle had lived I would never have been allowed the excesses I have visited."

"And you would have come to power by now," said Tier. "You are what, twenty-four? The Septs would have been under you directly for five years."

"Am I seeing shadows that don't exist?" Phoran asked.

"I don't know," said Tier. "But if you are, then so am I. I've been looking upon them as my problem, or even a Traveler problem. But so many Septs would make any group powerful, and powerful groups seek more power. I don't know that wizards can create convenient plagues, but it is odd that so many of the Path survived to inherit."

"I sent a letter to your wife," said Phoran hesitantly.

Tier's head jerked up, but Phoran couldn't read his expression.

"I told her that you were here in the palace," Phoran continued quickly. "I told her you were alive, but that it would be dangerous to come. I told her that she could send word to me or you through the messenger—he was one of my uncle's men, retired this past decade. My uncle was a canny man; I doubt that any of his would be suborned to the Path."

Tier laughed abruptly. "Told her it was dangerous, did you?"

Phoran nodded. "I thought it best."

"We can plan on her showing up a week after she receives the letter, then," he said. "And we'll be the better for it. I'm not a Traveler—but my wife is, and, if you gave her enough information, she'll bring the whole of the Travelers with her when she comes." He laughed again. "Thank you."

"I wrote to Gerant as well," Phoran said. "Directly after the council meeting. I thought he ought to know what the council had almost done." He hesitated. "It was a long letter. I told him of the situation I've made for myself, then asked him to come here and help clear out the Path. I told him that I had it on good authority that he was an honest man."

Tier laughed. "He'll want to thank me for that—but he'll come, right enough. He's almost too old for fighting—fifty or thereabouts by now—but he had several sons, good men all." He began to play a quiet melody as he talked. "If the Path is as bad as we think, then it will be good to have Gerant at your back. The wizards won't scare him off either; one of his daughters-in-law is a wizard, and he employed a few more when I knew him. I take it that you saved his land?"

Phoran launched into the story of his triumph. Tier was a good listener. He laughed in the right places—grinned, when Phoran told him about the way Avar had silenced the court.

"I can see why you like him, Phoran," said Tier, "would you take some advice from an old soldier?"

"Try me," Phoran replied.

"There are a lot of the Passerines here who might turn out to be good men if they had some goal, some task to work at. No one is more loyal than someone who feels good about himself and his accomplishments—someone who has a stake in the stability of your throne. Find them jobs to do."

Phoran laughed. "If anyone should have hope that reformation is possible, it should be me. Get me a list of names and I'll come up with something."

"Military would work for most of them," said Tier. "Bloodless dueling seems to be a pastime around here—and there are a number of fine swordsmen in the bunch."

Phoran shook his head. "I don't know where I'd put them. The city guards are political appointments through the merchant guilds. The palace guards are mostly inherited positions—and one of the Raptors is the captain of the guards. Neither troop is one a nobleman would willingly join."

"You're a Sept yourself, aren't you?" asked Tier.

"Yes, Sept of Taela and of Hawkshold—but Hawkshold is a meaningless title. It's been part of Taela for several hundred years. My lands are cared for by the palace guard, the city guard, and, if those won't do, I can call upon the Septs to create an imperial army."

"If the council leader were to countermand one of your orders to the palace guard, who would they obey?" asked Tier.

Phoran didn't answer, because the answer was obvious.

"Gerant's men will obey him, and he'll obey you," said Tier, his question answered by Phoran's silence. "But his Sept is in a border area. He cannot stay in Taela for long without risking disaster to his own lands."

"You're saying that if I make up a troop of the Passerines they will obey me rather than the Raptors?"

Tier smiled a little grimly. "The Raptors provide the Passerines with drink, sex, and a place to lurk about and pretend to be dangerous. They are sent out periodically to destroy a tavern or rape and pillage or maim. There are sixty of them and I've seen five or six already that I wouldn't want at my back—but there are some good men. If you make them feel like men, not boys, they will follow you to hell and back."

Phoran was flattered, but he knew what he was. "They won't follow me, Tier. A drunkard and a stupid fop."

"You may be right," agreed Tier readily. "But that's not who you are, Phoran. It is what you once allowed yourself to become. But you do not smell of alcohol tonight, and there's not a stupid man alive who ever got the best of the Council of Septs. Be honest with them, Phoran; they know what you have done. Lead and they will follow, my emperor. Just as Gerant and I follow."

Phoran swallowed hard. "Get me a list of the men you think could work."

"I'll do that," agreed Tier. "Let me have some more time with them first, maybe a couple of weeks. Then I'll have a better idea who is suitable and who is not." He hummed a haunting descant to go with the song he played, and then suddenly he smiled. "I have one for you already. There's a young man named Collarn. Do you know him?"

Phoran shook his head.

"He is a musician, but one with more technical ability than talent. What he is good with are instruments and their care. And the stranger the instrument, the better he likes it." Tier silenced his strings. "Am I mistaken in assuming that this labyrinth of yours might have a musical instrument or two?"

Phoran laughed and held up a hand. "I'll find out."

After a moment, Tier said, "If the Raptors are playing games with the merchant guilds as you think, you might go to them if you need more support. It seems to me that a group who's being blackmailed, like the Weavers' Guild is, wouldn't be unhappy at removing their blackmailer's ability to hurt them."

Phoran smiled back, "Likely not."

He closed his eyes and listened to the music, wondering when he'd ever been this content before. This was the feeling he'd been looking for since his uncle died. He had a larger purpose, if he could hold on to the gains he'd made today. But there was more, too: for the first time in his life he felt like an adult. He smiled to himself—Tier was right, it was a powerful feeling.

CHAPTER 14

Tier staked out a table on the edge of the Eyrie where he could observe the Passerines. Myrceria sat with him as she usually did, never giving the appearance of being bored. He wondered at her attentions, though he said nothing to her. She was in charge of the running of the Eyrie: the servants, whores, and cooks all looked to her for guidance. From little things the Passerines let drop, she was a great favorite of several of the Raptors and a few of the older Passerines. Even so, none of them approached her while she was with him, and, if he was out of his cell, she was with him.

She was not the only one who attended him, though. Wherever he went there were always a few Passerines who came to gossip and quiz him about his life as a Traveler. Since Tier had never so much as seen a Traveler clan, he told them stories of being a soldier instead—which they seemed perfectly happy with.

All the while he watched them. Sorting the salvageable from the worthless in a process the Sept of Gerant had called "sieving the ferrets." The Sept would gather all of the new recruits together and start them training with two or three veterans. Then he'd send in a man just to observe—usually Gerant himself, though Tier had done that duty more than once.

At the end of several weeks, the observer would pick out the troublemakers, the cowards, and the men just not physically cut out for warfare and send them on their way with a bit of silver for their trouble.

Tier found that sorting the boys of the Silent Path was a bit more difficult because the Path encouraged just the kind of behavior he was looking to weed out. He'd found five or six that he'd not have in any of his fighting troops, and ten more that he'd have been able to whip into shape eventually—but he was going to turn these boys over to Phoran, not an experienced military leader.

Phoran had good instincts, but he also had some things that would make commanding a group like the one Tier proposed difficult. First of all, he was young. But worse was his reputation. It would make leading the Passerines in anything but drunken debauchery difficult.

Tier had decided that he'd have to do a little training first. He took a judicious sip of his ale. He'd just wait until the next fight broke out—which, if the night ran to form, would be in the next hour or so.

"Came and knocked on our suite this morning," Collarn was saying with palpable excitement. "My father thought they'd come to arrest me for something stupid I'd done. I thought he'd die of shock when they told him that the Emperor had decided that the Keeper of Music needed help and that the masters at the School of Music had recommended me for the position."

Tier smiled at him. "So are you going to take the job?"

Collarn grinned back. "And have to slave around after an old man for years, cleaning, tuning, and refinishing instruments? Absolutely. Do you know the kinds of things that are rabbited away in these rooms?" He gave a vague wave around to indicate the palace. "Neither do I. But I've already gotten to play instruments that are worth more than all my family's holdings combined."

Tier talked with him a bit more, and gradually turned the conversation over to Myrceria. When she had Collarn's attention fully engaged, Tier excused himself and began meandering through the auditorium because the unmistakable sounds of another fight were starting to rumble from somewhere near the stage.

He spoke casually to a few boys as he passed. By the time he made it to the fight, a crowd had gathered around to call encouragement to the combatants. They parted for Tier willingly enough. Once he had a clear view of the action, Tier folded his arms and watched.

The first boy was Toarsen, who was a hotheaded, bitter young man and, like most of his fellows, spoiled by too much money and nothing to do. But he was smart, which Tier liked, and he wasn't a coward.

His opponent was a little bit of a surprise, one of the twenty-year-olds who Tier had pegged as the worst kind of troublemaker, the ones who sat by and let other people do their dirty work. Nehret was not one of the boys who usually found themselves in duels.

Watching them closely, Tier could see signs that both of them had been trained to sword since birth, as many noblemen were, but they were trained as duelists, not as soldiers.

When he'd seen enough, Tier turned to the boy on his right, "May I borrow your sword?"

The boy flushed and fumbled, but handed the weapon over. When Tier asked the boy on his left for his sword also, that young man laughed, drew with a flourish and presented it to Tier on one knee. With a short sword in either hand, Tier walked into the makeshift combat floor.

He watched closely for a moment, staying out of both opponents' immediate line of sight as he tested the swords he held for balance. They were lighter than the one he'd left in Redern and of a slightly different design—made for letting blood rather than killing, he thought.

Finished with his preparations, he darted forward and attacked. Toarsen lost his sword altogether. Nehret kept his blade, but only at the cost of form and balance. He landed ignominiously on his rump.

"If you're going to fight," said Tier. "At least do it right. Nehret, you lose power because your shoulders are stiff—you're making your arms do all the work." Tier turned his back to Nehret, knowing from the past few days of observation just how well the boy would take being criticized and what he would do about it.

"Toarsen," Tier said. "You need to worry less about trying to scratch your opponent, and more about defending yourself. In a real fight you'd have been dead a half dozen times." He turned and caught the blade Nehret had aimed at his back.

"Watch this and see what I mean," continued Tier as if he weren't fending off the angry boy's blows. It wasn't as easy as he made it look. "Nehret is extending too much—ah, see? That attack is what I was talking about earlier. If you'd had your body behind it instead of just your arm it might have accomplished something. Look, he wants to really hurt me, but he's been so trained to go for touches rather than hits that he doesn't stand a chance of hurting me beyond a scratch or two. That's the problem with too much dueling, you don't know what to do in a real fight."

Tier put his left hand behind his back to get that blade out of his way. Then he turned the blade in his right so that when he hit Nehret he didn't take off his arm, just numbed it so the boy lost his sword.

Tier tapped him on the cheek. "By the way," he said, "never go after an opponent when his back is turned unless there is more at stake than your pride." Then he turned his back to Nehret again, knowing that he'd gone a fair way to reducing the amount of influence the boy had upon the other Passerines in the last few minutes. "Toarsen, why don't you try a round against me?"

After the council meeting, Phoran found that he was quite popular. People followed him wherever he went—to his bedchamber if he didn't get the door shut fast enough. Tradition would keep all the Septs at the palace until just before harvest; if they kept this up until then, he'd have the whole lot of them thrown out. Finally, having had enough of the fawning, resentful Septs, Phoran sent for Avar to go riding with him.

He'd been avoiding Avar, since he'd put words to the fears he'd always had. It was poor payment for the Sept's swift support during the council meeting, and Phoran had to do something to change it.

In the stable, he mounted without aid, but he had other

things on his mind and took little note of it. For hours he
dragged Avar from one merchant guild master to the next. It
was not out of the ordinary for the Emperor to visit a guild
master's shop—an emperor would hardly buy goods from a
lesser man. If anyone was watching Phoran—and he thought
there was at least one man following them—they would see
that Phoran purchased something at every shop.

Phoran knew all the guild masters of course, but this was
the first time he'd set himself to be pleasant to them. After
they left the Weavers' Guild, Avar gave in to the curiosity
Phoran had seen building all morning.

"You don't need a bed hanging," said Avar. "You could
care less about silver candy dishes and tables with fluted legs.
Just what are you doing?"

Phoran had come to believe Avar innocent of anything
other than being assigned to keep the Emperor company and
told to keep him occupied. Even so, he didn't quite trust his
own evaluation. He should not have had Avar come with him.

Blade tossed his head, and Phoran let his reins slide
through his fingers then gradually shortened them again to
keep a light hold on the stallion. "After my uncle died, who
told you to befriend me?"

Avar stilled.

"It's all right," said Phoran, though he watched the
crowded streets rather than Avar. "I just would like to know
who it was."

"My father," said Avar. "But it wasn't—"

"I suspect it was," said Phoran ruefully. "I was, what,
twelve? And you seventeen. It would have been an unhappy
chore—and I thank you for it."

He took a deep breath and chose to trust. "I'm trying to
build some kind of a power base. The Septs will require a lot
of work on my part before I know who will back me and why.
But the city is as important to the stability of the Empire as the
Septs. I thought it would be good to find backing here, where
the Septs are too proud to look."

"I do like you," said Avar quietly. "I always have."

"Ah," said Phoran, for lack of anything better to say. How
could Avar have liked him when everyone, including Phoran
himself, had despised him? What had there been to like? But

Avar had done his best to forward Phoran's plans, and for that, and for so many years of duty, Phoran owed him the chance to keep his white lies.

They rode in silence to the shop of the master importer, who brought goods from all over the Empire and beyond.

"Is Guild Master Emtarig in?" asked Phoran of the boy who manned the shop.

"Not now, sir. May I help you?"

He was new, this boy, and Phoran doubted that he knew even who it was who entered the shop. Phoran was dressed in riding clothes without imperial symbols—there was nothing to say who he was except his face.

"Boy," said Avar, gently enough, "tell your master that the Emperor awaits him in his shop."

The boy's eyes darted between Phoran and Avar, trying to decide who was the Emperor. At last he bowed low to Avar and scuttled through a curtained passage and, from the sound of his feet, up the stairs to the master's private lodgings.

Phoran began sorting among the items on the laden shelves and hid his smile. Avar couldn't help that he looked more like an emperor than Phoran did.

By careful negotiations with the other guilds, the importer's guild members could sell items that were not made in the city. There were beautifully tanned skins of animals Phoran had never seen—and likely never would. Valuable blown-glass goblets stood on a high shelf where no one was likely to knock them off accidently. Phoran was fingering a handful of brightly colored beads that caught his attention when he heard the boy leap back down the stairs.

He didn't turn until the guild master said, "Most Gracious Emperor, you honor my shop."

"Master Willon?" Phoran said with honest delight. He had to turn back to put the beads away. "I thought that you had retired to some gods' forsaken province, never to return to Taela?"

"Careful, Phoran," said Avar, who was grinning. "He went to Redern, which is part of my Sept."

"And Leheigh is truly a gods' forsaken place," agreed Phoran. "What business brings you back? I hope that there is nothing wrong with Master Emtarig."

"My son is well," said Willon. "But I have not seen my grandchildren in too long. I thought it was time to visit. My son is out to the market to speak with the Music Guild about a drum I brought back with me. Also, I had some people to see here."

"Good," said Phoran. He thought of asking Willon what he knew of a man named Tier—but when he spoke, all he said was, "What would you take for three of these hangings?" He would ask Tier about Willon instead.

They bargained briskly until they reached a price both thought fair. Phoran let it drag on for longer than he might have, hoping to catch Emtarig. Willon was an old friend of his uncle's, but Emtarig was the master guildsman now, the man Phoran needed to impress. But Emtarig did not return, so Phoran paid for the hangings and asked Willon to send the goods to the palace at his leisure.

They went to three more guild masters and bought a cobalt blue glass jar, four copper birds that sang in the wind, and an eating knife inlaid with shell before Phoran headed back to his rooms for a private evening meal with Avar. They talked, but not about anything serious.

Soon, thought Phoran, he'd tell Avar all that he'd found out about the Path—but not yet. Avar wouldn't believe him as easily as Tier had; he wasn't used to Phoran being anything except a jaded drunkard. Though to do him justice, Avar didn't have the motivation to believe in evil that Tier had.

Tier returned to his room tired, bruised, and ultimately satisfied—a usual state these days. His daily sword lessons had become more of a favorite activity than the dueling had ever been.

The Passerines blossomed under his attention and some, especially Toarsen, had come around and grown more than he'd thought possible. He'd always had a knack for turning boys into fighting men, which was why Gerant offered him a job in his personal guard when there were other men, born in the Sept, who were as good or better with weapons.

There were a few that weren't worth saving. Nehret was one, and there was one of the youngest batch who was, if Tier wasn't mistaken, one of those very few who seemed to be born without any morals or courage at all. He'd toady to those more powerful and hurt anyone he saw as weaker. In a few years, if he wasn't already, he'd be a rapist and murderer, and never lose a night's sleep over it. Tier had set Toarsen and his large friend Kissel to watch over that one and protect the younger Passerines.

The door to his room was open. Some of the boys would stop in at night, so nothing struck him as odd until he saw who it was.

"Myrceria?"

Sitting on his bed, her legs folded neatly underneath her, she smiled at him brightly. "I hope that you don't mind that I came here this evening."

"Not at all," he said.

She looked away. "Play something for me, please," she said. "Something to make me laugh."

He closed the door and sat on the foot of his bed, taking the lute off the hooks he'd had installed in the wall. He played a bit of melody on the lute, tuning automatically until it was acceptable.

"How do you do it?" she asked. "Collarn doesn't like anyone—and they generally return his feeling with interest. The only thing he loves is music. He works so hard at it, and he is never good enough. He hated the thought that because of your magic you would play better than he, no matter what he did or how much he practiced. I saw you take his hatred and turn it to hero worship in less than an hour. Telleridge said that you can't use your magic on us."

"It's not magic," Tier said. "Collarn loves music, and that is more important to him than all the hurts the world has dealt him. I just showed him that I loved music, too."

"What about the rest?" she asked. "The Passerines follow you around like lost puppies."

"I like people," said Tier with a shrug. "I don't think most of these boys are used to dealing with someone who likes them."

Unexpectedly she laughed, but it wasn't a happy sound. "The Masters are very concerned with what you have done to their control of the Passerines. Be careful."

She turned her head and he saw that there was a bruise on her jaw.

"Who hit you?" he asked.

She picked up a pillow and began straightening the fringe. "One of the Masters told Kissel that they were worried because Collarn was spending so much time away from the Eyrie. They told Kissel that he was to remind Collarn where his loyalties should lie—and Kissel refused them. He said that you would not approve of him picking on someone weaker than himself."

Tier stilled his strings. "I don't suppose it even crossed his mind to agree and then either fake it—or tell me about it. Ellevanal save me from honest fools. Why couldn't they have gone to Toarsen?"

Myrceria stared at him, her hands stilled. "You've done it on purpose, haven't you? You're taking control from the Masters on purpose. A month ago Kissel would have been happy to please the Masters, to win the fear of the other Passerines. How did you do it?"

Tier played a few notes of a dirge Collarn had played for him on a violin—it sounded odd on a lute.

"They are trying to ruin those boys," he said at last, "to turn them into something much less than they could be."

He'd been certain that she was a spy for Telleridge, and that might still be true—but his instincts told him that it wouldn't take a lot to turn her against the Masters of the Path. He would just have to find the right words.

He played a few more measures. "What happens to the ones who don't play their little game, Myrceria? Boys like Collarn who would never agree to the kinds of real damage the Path metes out? Or ones like Kissel, who is discovering that protecting someone weaker than he is makes him feel better about himself than tormenting them ever did?"

She didn't say anything.

"There aren't as many Raptors as there should be," he said gently. "Not for the numbers of Passerines they have."

"That's how they progress in the Path," she whispered. "The boys who would be Raptors are given the other boys' names—the ones like Collarn. They have to bring back proof that they have killed the bearer of the name they were give before they are Raptors."

She set the pillow aside. "How do you do that?" she said.

"If they knew what I told you, they would kill me."

"You know it is wrong," he told her. "You know they must be stopped."

"By whom?" she said, her incredulousness fueled by anger. "You? Me? You are a prisoner in their power, Tier of Redern. You will die as they all do at the end of their year. And I am as much a prisoner as you."

"Evil must always be fought," Tier said. "If you don't fight—then you are a part of it."

She rose to her feet and walked without haste to the door. "You know nothing of what you face, or you would not be so arrogant, Bard."

She shut the door tightly behind her.

Well, thought Tier, *that was unexpected.* Whores learn early that survival means that they have to look out for themselves. Myrceria had been a whore for a long time, but she wasn't talking like a whore who cared for no one else.

She cared about those boys. She wasn't happy about it, but she cared.

Tier slapped one of the scrawny first-year Passerines on the shoulder after the boy finally executed the move Toarsen had been struggling to teach him for days.

"Drills," Tier called. There were groans and half-hearted protests, but they formed up in three ragged lines, lines that straightened at his silent frown.

"Begin," he called, and worked with them. Drills were the heart of swordplay. If a man had to think about his body and how to move his sword, he'd be too slow to save himself. Drills taught the body to respond to information from eyes and ears, leaving the mind to plan larger strategy than just how to meet the next thrust.

The sword he held wasn't the equal of the one he'd taken from some nobleman on the battlefield, but it was balanced. Myrceria had brought it to him when he requested it.

Tier'd continued to work with his sword over the years, but the past weeks had sharpened him until he'd almost reached the speed and strength he'd held while he was a soldier. His left shoulder was always a bit stiff until he worked it out, but otherwise he hadn't lost much flexibility to age.

He drilled with the boys until sweat made his shirt cling uncomfortably to his shoulders, then he brought his sword around in a flashy stroke that ended with it in its sheath.

"Pools!" shouted the boys in one voice, and they dashed, swords in hands, to the washroom to play in the cold pool.

Tier laughed and shook his head when Collarn stopped to invite him to the waterfight. "I've no wish to drown before my time," he avowed. "I'll wash up in my rooms."

Loyalty, he thought, watching the last of them disappear into the hall, was won by sweating with them.

"They've improved," said Telleridge.

Tier hadn't noticed the Master, but he'd been concentrating on the boys. He took a glass of water from a servant.

"They have," he said, after taking a long drink. "Some of them had further to go than others."

"I knew that you were a soldier, but you were more than that—I've been looking into it," Telleridge said. "Remarkable that a peasant boy, no offense, could be set to command soldiers. Are you one of the old Sept of Leheigh's by-blows?"

"Do you know where I'm from?" asked Tier with a lazy smile as he handed the empty glass off to one of the silent waiters.

"The Sept of Leheigh," replied Telleridge.

Tier shook his head. "I'm from Redern, the first settlement the Army of Man created after the Fall of the Shadowed, named for the Hero of the Fall, Red Ernave. We are farmers, tanners, bakers . . ." He shrugged. "But scratch a Rederni very deeply and you'll find the blood of warriors. If you'll excuse me, I need to wash up and change clothes."

When Tier reached his cell, he closed his door and washed quickly with water from the basin left there for that purpose. Once he'd changed into clean clothes he lay down on his bed.

The last time Phoran had visited, a few days ago, Gerant had sent word that he was on his way. It couldn't be too soon for Tier's comfort: the Masters weren't going to wait forever while Tier wrested control of the Passerines from them.

He woke for lunch and spent the rest of the day in his usual manner, talking and socializing in the Eyrie. In the evening he played for them, mostly raunchy army songs—but he feathered in others, songs of glory in battle and the sweetness of home.

Looking over the faces of the men who listened to his music he knew triumph because, given a chance, most of them would grow into fine men. Men who would serve their emperor, a boy who was showing signs of being the kind of ruler a man could take pride in serving: shrewd and clever with a streak of kindness he tried hard to hide.

When he returned to his room for the night, Myrceria tucked her arm flirtatiously in his and accompanied him.

When they were inside his room, she dropped her flirtation and his arm and settled on his bed. Stroking the coverlet absently she said, "I swore I was done talking to you. I have survived here a long time—and I did it by keeping my mouth shut. How dare you demand more of me?" She said it without heat. "I have no power to affect the men who rule here. I am just a whore."

Tier leaned against the wall opposite the bed, crossed his feet at the ankles and did his best to look neutral.

"I haven't seen the sun since I was fifteen," she murmured, almost to herself. "Sometimes I wonder if it still rises and sets."

"It does," said Tier. "It does."

"Telleridge is planning a Disciplining." She flattened her hand and stared at it as though she'd never seen it before.

"What is a Disciplining?" asked Tier, not liking the sound of it at all.

"When a Passerine disobeys a Raptor, they hold a meeting to decide what his punishment will be. Then they are punished in the Eyrie with all the Passerines in attendance. They usually do one every year, just as a reminder."

"Who is being disciplined?" asked Tier. They wouldn't pick him, he thought; they were too smart for that. They didn't need a martyr, they needed an example.

"I don't know," she said.

"Collarn," he said. "Or maybe Kissel or Toarsen. But Collarn if they're smart. If they hurt Toarsen, Kissel won't stand for it. If they hurt Kissel, Toarsen will go to his brother—and Avar has enough friends, including the Emperor, to hurt the Path. Collarn has no close friends except for me, and he's the kind of person that people expect bad things to happen to.

When it does, it won't disturb the Passerines much."

"That's what I thought," said Myrceria softly. "I like Collarn. He has a vicious tongue when he wants to, but he's always polite to the people who can't defend themselves."

Tier heard the grief in her voice. "This is more than a caning or a beating," he said.

"All of the boys are forced to participate in the Disciplining in some way—and the punishment can be anything," she said. "Telleridge is very creative. Whipping is the most common, but some of the others are worse. One boy they forced to drink water . . . he passed out, and I think he died. They poured water on his face while he choked and gagged. And when he stopped, they just kept pouring."

"Can you make sure I know about it before it happens?" he asked.

She kept her eyes averted, but nodded quickly. "If I know in advance. I don't always."

"Can you get word to Collarn?" If they could warn him . . .

"Tomorrow," she said after a moment. "I have to do it myself—I can't trust any of the girls with a message like that. And I can't leave the Path's rooms anymore than you can. Tomorrow should be soon enough." She spoke those words quickly, as if she could make it true just by saying so. "It should take a day or two for them to arrange to get word to everyone anyway."

"Right," he said. "Tell him to find a reason to leave town for a week."

She nodded, started to get up to leave, but then settled back, wrapping her arms around her middle. "Would you play something for me? Something cheerful so I can sleep?"

He was tired, but she was tired, too, and no more than she could he have slept—not with the knowledge that the Masters had decreed that one of his boys was going to suffer for what Tier had done.

"I'm not going to sleep anytime soon either," he said. "Music would be nice."

He sat on the other end of his bed and started to tune his lute again. He'd just finished bringing the second course of strings in accord with the rest, when the door opened unexpectedly.

Tier'd grown used to the respectful knocks of his captors—even Phoran knocked. It was too early for a visit from Phoran. Tier opened his mouth for a reproval but stopped, shocked dumb when Lehr entered the room wearing Tier's own sword.

Joy lit Lehr's face, then dimmed a bit when he looked past Tier and saw Myrceria. He made a move to block the door—perhaps Tier thought with a touch of amusement that threaded past his astonishment, to allow Tier to assume a less compromising position. Did Lehr actually think that his father would take a leman?

But the door popped open wider before Lehr could reach it, and Jes took two full strides into the room. The comfortable temperature of the room plummeted until Tier could see his own breath, and Myrceria let out an abortive squeak.

Tier got to his feet slowly, because it was never smart to move too quickly around Jes in this mode, and opened his arms. Jes's glance swept the room comprehensively. But he apparently didn't see anything too threatening in Myrceria because he took two steps forward and wrapped his arms around Tier.

"Papa," he breathed as the room warmed. "Oh, Papa, we thought we'd never find you."

"Of course you did." A woman's voice, deep, rich, and beloved filled the room like the sound of a cello. Tier looked over Jes's shoulder to see his wife enter. "Ever since Hennea told us that he'd been taken alive. Are you well?"

Seraph looked so much like the empress-child he'd first met that it made him smile. An ice princess, his sister had called her with contempt. Being a straightforward person herself, Alinath had never seen that the cool facade could hide all manner of emotions that Seraph chose not to share.

"I'm fine," Tier said, and seeing that she was not going to run into his arms immediately, he continued speaking, "and much happier than I was a few minutes ago. Lehr, come here."

Lehr had grown in the months since he'd seen him last, Tier thought, hugging him tightly. So had Jes for that matter; his oldest son was a little taller than Tier now.

"We missed you," said Lehr, returning his hug.

"I missed you, too." He held him for a moment more.

"Lehr killed some people," said Jes. "He saved Mother."

   Lehr stiffened in his arms, but Tier merely hugged him
tighter. "I'm sorry, son," he said. "Killing another man is not
something that should rest easily on your shoulders."
   When he stepped back at last, he looked at Seraph, who'd
stayed by the open door. "Is Rinnie out there, too?"
   As was her habit with him, she answered the real question
he asked. "She's safe with your sister. Frost, it seems, was the
only family casualty of this mess—though we were quite worried about you until just now."
   "They killed Frost?"
   She nodded, "To make it look as if the both of you had
walked into one of the Blighted Places. We might have believed it if a cousin of mine hadn't straightened us out."
   She hadn't looked at Myrceria, but he knew that she didn't
have any cousins. She must have met another Traveler.
   "It's not safe for your cousins here," he warned.
   She smiled like a wolf scenting prey. "Oh they know that,"
she said. "I just hope these *solsenti* of the Secret Path choose
to try their tricks again." Her tongue lingered on "Secret
Path," making it sound childish and stupid, which, of course,
it was.
   "You know about the Secret Path?" he said.
   "We know about the Secret Path," said Lehr. "They're
killing Travelers and stealing their Orders."
   "What?" said Tier, looking at Seraph.
   She nodded. "They take them from the dying Traveler and
place them in a stone that they wear on jewelry so that they
can use them."
   "How did you find out so much?" he asked.
   "Hennea told us," said Jes helpfully.
   "My cousin," agreed Seraph.
   "They have someone in Redern who has been watching our
whole family," said Tier.
   "Not anymore," said his wife coolly.
   "Mother killed him." Jes had found a perch on top of a
small table and was playing with the vase that had occupied
the table first.
   Tier glanced back at Myrceria. "I told you they'd be sorry
if they ever ran afoul of my wife. Myrceria, I'd like you to
meet my family. My wife, Seraph; my eldest son, Jes; and my

youngest son, Lehr. Seraph, Jes, Lehr, this is Myrceria, who has helped make my captivity bearable."

Jes nodded with the shy manner that characterized him in front of strangers, Lehr made a stiff bow, and Seraph turned on her heel and walked out the door.

Lehr's smile died, so Tier took a moment to explain to him. "She knows me too well to think I've taken a mistress after all these years—as you should. Myrceria is an ally, so be polite. I need to take a moment with your mother."

He followed Seraph and closed the door behind him softly. Seraph was studying the stone wall of the hall as if she'd never seen stone laid upon stone before. They were safe enough, he thought. Anyone who walked down this hall was coming to see him—and at this hour that meant one of the Passerines. There was time, so he waited for her to show him what she needed from him.

"There is death magic in these stones," she said. She didn't sound as if it bothered her.

"They've been killing people for a long time," he said. "There's a message awaiting you in Redern telling you that I'm still alive. It should have gotten there by now."

"Hopefully someone will direct the messenger to Alinath," said Seraph, without looking away from the wall. She set a palm against it and said, "Once we convinced her you were alive when you left, she was most eager to hear if you'd stayed that way."

She pushed away from the wall abruptly. When she turned toward him he thought she'd look at him at last, but her eyes caught on the floor and stayed there.

"We need to get you out of here," she said in a low voice. "This place is a labyrinth, but Lehr found you, which was the difficult part. He'll be able to backtrack on the way out."

"I can't leave, Seraph," he said.

Her face came up at that.

"There's a boy about Jes's age who's going to be hurt because of me if I can't put a stop to it—and they've put some sort of hex on me anyway so I can't wander around at will."

She reached out to touch him for the first time since she'd appeared at his door. Gripping his hands lightly, she turned his hands over to look at his wrists.

"I can break this," she said positively after a moment. "But it will take time—and will do us no good, since as long as this boy of yours is in danger you won't leave anyway."

He twisted his hands until he could grip hers. "Seraph," he said. "It's all right, now."

Her hands shook in his but he could only see the top of her head. "I thought you were dead," she said.

She looked up, and the empress was gone, lost in a face wild with emotion. Unexpectedly he felt the lick of her magic caress his palms.

"I can't *do* that again," she told him. "I can't lose anyone I love again."

"You love me?" He moved his hands to her shoulders and pulled her close. She leaned against him like a tired infant.

It was the first time she'd said that to him, though he knew that she loved him with the same fierceness that she loved her children. She had been trained to maintain control, and he knew that she was uncomfortable with the strength of the emotions she felt. Because he understood her, he'd never pushed her to tell him something that he'd known full well.

He knew it would make her angry but he had to tease her. "I had to get myself kidnapped by a bunch of stupid wizards and dragged halfway across the Empire to hear that? If I'd known that's what it would take, I'd have gotten myself kidnapped twenty years ago."

"It's not funny," she said, stomping on his foot in her effort to get away from him.

"No, it's not," he said, pulling her tighter. The ferocious joy of holding her when he'd been half-certain he'd never see her again kept him teasing her beyond prudence. "So why didn't you tell me you loved me before? Twenty years didn't give you enough time? Or did you only figure it out when you thought I was dead?"

"Oh, aye, if I'd have told you—you'd just have said the same back," she said.

Her answer made no sense to him—except that she really didn't find anything amusing in the situation. He didn't want to hurt her feelings, so he tucked the laughter of her presence inside his heart and tried to understand what had upset her.

"If you had told me that you loved me," he said carefully, "I'd have told you the same."

"You wouldn't have meant it," she said firmly. "Haven't you spent the last twenty years trying to make up for marrying me by being the perfect husband and father?"

Her words stung, so his were a little sharp in return. "I'd have meant it."

"You married a woman you thought a child, married her so that you would not have to take over the bakery from Alinath and Bandor. You felt guilty."

"Of course I did," he agreed. "I told them we were married. I did it knowing that you were too young for marriage and that you would have to give up your magic and your people. I knew that you were frightened of rejoining the Travelers and having to take responsibility for so many lives again—but I knew that was where you felt you belonged and I kept you with me."

"You did it to save yourself from being forced into the bakery," Seraph said. "And that made you feel guilty. If I'd told you then that I loved you—you'd have said you loved me, too, because you wouldn't hurt my feelings."

Abruptly Tier understood. He pulled her back to him and laughed. He started to speak, but he had to laugh again first. "Seraph," he said. "Seraph, I was never going to be a baker— even Alinath knew that. I wanted you. And I was extremely glad that circumstances forced you to turn to me. I don't know that I loved you then—I just knew that I couldn't let you get away from me." He stepped back so he could look into her face. "I love you, Seraph."

He watched, delighted, as tears filled her eyes and spilled over, then he kissed her.

"I was so afraid," she said when she could talk. "I was so afraid that we'd be too late." She sniffed. "Plague it, Tier, my nose is running. I don't suppose you have something I can wipe it on?"

He pulled back and stripped off his overshirt and handed it to her.

"Tier," she said, scandalized, "that is silk."

"And we didn't pay for it. Here, blow."

She did. He wadded up the shirt and wiped her eyes with a

clean spot. Then, the expression in his eyes holding her motionless, he tossed the shirt on the floor. He put a hand on either side of her face and kissed her, open-mouthed and hungry.

"I love you," she whispered when he pulled his head away, breathing heavily.

He kissed the top of her head and hugged her close. "I know that," he said. "I've always known that. Did you think that you could hide it by not saying the words? I love you, too—do you believe it now?"

Seraph started to answer him, but then remembered that he'd know if she lied. Did she really believe him when he said that he loved her?

Whatever he believed now, she knew she was right about the reasons he'd married her in the first place—he needed a reason to leave the bakery that would allow him to stay near enough so that he didn't feel that he was running away from his family again. But that didn't mean that he wasn't attracted to her. It didn't mean he couldn't have grown to love her.

Yes, she believed him. She started to say so, but she'd waited too long.

"You know, for an intelligent woman," he said, exasperated, "you can be remarkably stupid." He threw up his hands and paced away from her. "All right, all right. Maybe if I married a woman and felt I'd taken advantage of her, if she asked me, I might tell her that I loved her. Maybe I wouldn't want to hurt her feelings. You could be right about that. But why do you persist in believing that I couldn't love you even if I felt guilty about marrying you so young? Is it impossible that I've lusted after you since you stood on the steps of that inn and defied the whole lot of grown men who'd just gotten finished killing your brother?"

She tried to hide her smile, but he saw it, and it only made him angrier.

So he did what he always did when she'd pushed past that air of pleasant affability he showed the world. He dragged her back against him and kissed her again. Hot and fierce he moved his lips on hers, forcing his tongue through before she could welcome him. The stone was cold on her shoulders as his hips settled heavily against her midriff and demonstrated quite admirably that, if nothing else, his lust was quite real.

"All right," she said mildly, if a bit breathlessly, when he freed her mouth at last. "I believe you love me. Likely our sons and that poor woman you left with them believe you love me, too. Shall we go see?"

He laughed. "I missed you, Seraph."

CHAPTER 15

Inside Tier's cell (for that's what it was, even decked out in luxuries befitting royalty) Seraph saw that she had been exactly right about what everyone had been doing. Lehr looked uncomfortable, Jes, inscrutable, and the woman, Myrceria, looked vaguely panicked.

"I am sorry," said Seraph sincerely to Myrceria. "I meant no insult to you, Myrceria, but crying in front of strangers is not something I do willingly. We had all but given Tier up for dead these months past and I could hardly believe that he is here safe."

Myrceria looked distinctly relieved at Seraph's calm manner. She got to her feet. "Of course I understand; I'll leave you, Tier, to your reunion."

"Thank you," said Tier. "Let me know about the Disciplining."

She paused by the door. "I won't tell them that your family is here," she said.

"I didn't think you would," said Tier. "Sleep well."

"I think I will," she said and closed the door behind her.

Tier sat down on the bed, pulling Seraph down next to him and tucking her under his arm. Lehr sat on the other side of him, not quite touching, but close.

"So," said Tier. "Tell me about your adventures. Not you, Seraph, I want more than the bare bones. Lehr, what happened? You thought I was dead?"

Seraph was happy to let Lehr do most of the talking. Tier seemed to think that they were all safe here for now, and she was content with his assessment. She closed her eyes and breathed in Tier's scent, felt his warmth against her side.

At the end of the story, Tier shook his head. "My love," he said, and she saw the laughter in his eyes. "You have changed: you brought a whole Traveler clan out to Taela to rescue me. When did you learn how to be so persuasive?"

She scowled at him. "When I discovered it was more useful to have pawns to do what I wanted them to than it was to kill them all and do it myself." Triumph flooded her when she saw that Tier wasn't absolutely certain she was joking until Lehr laughed.

Tier rolled his eyes. "Leave for a season and see what happens. The women and children don't remember the respect they owe you. What are you planning on doing with a whole clan?"

"We'd have never found a way into the palace without them," said Seraph.

Lehr laughed. "Turns out that one of the emperors hired Travelers to work some magic for him a few generations back. He didn't want to be seen consorting with them, so he brought them in by a secret way."

"We went under the ground," said Jes, his voice dreamy. "Fungus hung from the sides of the tunnel like strings of melted cheese."

"Jes found a girlfriend," said Lehr.

Tier looked at Seraph, but it was the first she'd heard of it. Jes smiled sweetly, and said nothing.

The girls of Rongier's clan wouldn't come within a dozen yards of Jes if they could help it. "Hennea?" she said.

Lehr grinned. "I think that's how she feels about it, too—sort of shocked and dismayed, but Jes is smug."

"Hennea is the Raven you found, right?" asked Tier.

She nodded.

"Don't worry so, Mother," said Jes.

Tier smiled and kissed the top of her head. "Trust Jes," he

said. "He'll be all right." He looked over at Lehr. "How do you like being a Hunter?"

"He's always been a Hunter," said Seraph acerbically. She wasn't certain that she wanted to hear Lehr's answer to that question. She didn't want her son to be unhappy. "He just didn't know about it."

"The Lark of Rongier's clan has been teaching me some things that are pretty interesting," said Lehr.

Tier reached out and patted Lehr's knee sympathetically.

"Rinnie wanted to be a Guardian," Jes said, his gentle eyes gliding over Lehr. "She wanted to turn into a panther, like me."

"I'll just bet she did," said Tier. "I've missed you all."

"We should go, Papa," said Jes abruptly.

"We can't," answered Seraph. "One of Tier's friends is in danger, *and* the wizards here have bespelled Tier so he can't leave the Path's domain." She saw the Guardian rising through her son's eyes and said, "It's nothing I can't fix, but I'll need a little time to study it. In any case he won't go until his friend is out of danger. Tier, Lehr's told you our story, tell us what happened to you."

They weren't as polite an audience as he had been, interrupting him frequently. Seraph pestered him for details about what little he recalled from the times the Path's wizards had taken him. Lehr teased him about the women who'd bathed him and braided his hair and fretted when Tier told them how he was imprisoned by magic. Jes was quiet until Tier told them about his royal visitor.

"The Emperor?" said Jes. "The Emperor visited you in your cell?"

"How did he know you were here?" asked Lehr suspiciously.

"I'm sworn to secrecy so I need to get his permission before I tell you," said Tier. "But that's another story entirely."

Both of the boys enjoyed Tier's explanation of how he'd begun winning over the Passerines.

Seraph shook her head. "They didn't know what they were doing, kidnapping you."

"Well," said Tier. "I may have outsmarted myself. Seems

Telleridge tried to set one of my boys out on a bullying mission, something that boy had done a number of times. Kissel refused and, being a straightforward sort of fellow, he told Telleridge that the reason he'd refused was because I wouldn't like it."

"Is he the one that you were worried about?" asked Seraph.

"Myrceria told me tonight that the Masters, the Path's wizards, are organizing something they call the Disciplining." He told them what he knew of it. "I don't think that they'll actually go after Kissel; he's got friends in high places. I think they'll take the boy that they tried to send Kissel after."

He leaned his head back against the wall. "Seraph, you said that Bandor and the Master in Redern were shadowed."

"Yes. Lehr and Jes both could see it."

He inhaled. "When Phoran and I combined all the information that we had about the Path we came to some disturbing conclusions. That plague that swept through the Traveling clans twenty years ago also visited the noble houses of the Empire and when it was finished, the Emperor was dead, leaving only an infant on the throne. Also a high percentage of the followers of the Path found themselves Septs, though they might have been as many as eight or ten people away from the inheritance when the plague hit."

"You think that there might be another one," she said, cold chills tightening her spine. "Not just shadowed, but willingly shadowed like the Unnamed King. You think it might be this Telleridge?"

He nodded. "Phoran's sent for my old commander, the Sept of Gerant. He's on his way, now. With his military and tactical advice, Phoran hopes that he can break the Path. If we take them by surprise and Phoran is ruthless enough, he'll be right."

"But Gerant won't be here in time to save your boy," said Seraph softly.

"Probably not."

"These Passerines of yours," said Seraph thoughtfully. "They won't willingly participate in hurting another boy."

"I don't think so," said Tier. "Some of them, maybe, but most of them won't."

Seraph smiled. "Then the Masters will be straining to enforce their will upon them with their stolen Bardic Orders. Tell me, Tier, if all of the Path were in the same room together, how many would there be?"

"There are about sixty Passerines," he said. "I don't know exactly how many Raptors—I have the names of about a hundred. Perhaps double that."

"And the wizards," said Seraph. "You said there were five."

"Five," he agreed. "And a handful of apprentice and hedge-witch types."

"We have an Owl, a Falcon, an Eagle, and two Ravens," said Seraph. "I don't know how many ordinary wizards the clan has, but they'll come along. There are probably fifty Travelers who would love nothing more than an excuse to attack a bunch of *solsenti* who've been preying upon Travelers."

"You are short one Owl," said Tier. "They've done something so that my magic doesn't work on them, remember?"

Seraph frowned. She didn't like the mysterious magic that these Masters had been working on Tier. "That kind of thing works better on wizards than it does on Order-Bearers." She tapped her fingers against her lips as she worked it out. "You said that it just keeps your magic from working on them, right?"

He nodded.

"That would be a very difficult and odd thing to do on purpose," Seraph said. "They'd have to have something personal from everyone who is a follower to do that—blood or hair. It would be an incredibly complex spell and the power it would require . . ." She stopped when a better idea occurred to her. "I'll ask Hennea to be certain, but it sounds to me that it is more likely that their spell is imperfect and erratic. Hennea told me that they don't really know as much about the Orders as they think. Blocking the powers of an ordinary wizard would be simple if they had enough power. But in order to block the powers of an Order-Bearer they'd have to be very specific about everything they want to stop. I'll bet that some of the odder magics still come to you without a problem. Because they didn't get it right, their spell will be unraveling slowly." She nodded because the explanation fit what she knew of magic and Tier's experience here. "Your magic didn't work on them, because they and you know it won't work. But even that effect will fade with time."

She smiled at him. "But even if it doesn't fade, you have already made your contributions in the number of Passerines who will take your side. If we attack them during the Disciplining, we'll have the Travelers, both warriors and wizards; our Order-Bearers; and most of the Passerines. You said that the Disciplining is mandatory for the Passerines, but not the Raptors."

"That doesn't mean that they won't be there," he said. "But I see where you're going. They'll all be there, the Masters who are the real danger. Once they are gone, Phoran can take his time to eliminate the rest. We'll have to talk to Phoran, though. I'll not bring a clan of Travelers into his palace without his permission if I can help it."

A light knock sounded at the door, sending Tier to his feet, "A moment, a moment," he said, glancing around the room, though he knew there weren't any hiding places.

"Peace," whispered Seraph. "He won't see Jes, and—" She turned to Lehr, but couldn't see him either. "I'm going to have a talk with Brewydd about what she's teaching Lehr," she murmured. "Go ahead and open the door, Tier. He won't see me either, not unless he's one of your wizards." With a whisper of magic she ensured that she'd not attract any notice. Tier's visitor would see her, but he would just ignore her presence unless something called her to his attention.

Tier's eyebrows climbed and his mouth quirked with amusement—at himself, she thought. It was one thing to know everyone in your family could work magic; it was quite another to have them do it.

"Toarsen," he said when he'd opened the door. "Come in."

"I came as soon as I heard," said Toarsen. "The rumor's being passed all over the Eyrie. There's going to be a Disciplining."

"I heard," said Tier. Seraph could see her husband weighing some decision.

"Toarsen," he said, "if you needed to get in to see the emperor, could you? At this time of night?"

"I—I suppose I could," Toarsen said, "but not without my brother Avar's help." He hesitated and thrust his chin up. "But

I won't do anything that will imperil my emperor—even if he's a stupid sot more interested in the newest wine from Carek than in running his Empire."

"Agreed," said Tier. "What I'd like you to do is persuade your brother to get you in to see the Emperor—tell him it's urgent that you do so. Then—" Tier paused and shook his head. "Then tell Phoran you have a message for him that you can't give him in front of anyone except for Avar. The Emperor knows too much about you, my lad, to trust himself to you, but he trusts Avar. When the three of you are alone, you tell Phoran that his Bard would like an urgent word. Tell him that you and Avar will accompany him, if he doesn't mind. Tell Phoran that I have a plan, but time is of the essence."

Toarsen stared at him. "Phoran knows about you?"

The Bard grinned wickedly. "Don't go dismissing your emperor out of hand, lad. I have a feeling that a lot of people have underestimated him, and they're about to get a rude awakening."

Toarsen nodded slowly. "All right. I'll do it. If I can't get in, I'll come back alone."

"Good, lad," said Tier, patting his shoulder and shooing him out the door. He waited until the sound of Toarsen's footsteps grew faint.

"That was Toarsen, the Sept of Leheigh's younger brother," he said, sitting back down beside Seraph. "He'll find Phoran for us."

"You know," muttered Seraph, who'd been working through Tier's story while he talked with the boy, "I knew that we were in trouble when all of our children were born Ordered. I should have resigned myself to fighting against another shadowed with the Emperor at my side years ago."

Jes looked back at her impassively, but Lehr smiled. "Maybe the gods are making you make up for those wells and blights you didn't fix for all these years in one fell swoop."

Seraph stole Tier's eye roll—she could do it when she chose. "Cheeky. Carry them for nine months, feed them, clothe them, and what do I get? Impertinence."

"Seraph," Tier asked, "if they want my Order—why didn't they just take it? Why wait for a year?"

"I'm not certain," said Seraph, "but magic works better on

something you know well. I could cast a spell better on you than I could on a stranger. Their magic isn't foolproof; a lot of their stones don't work right. The year wait might be time for one of their wizards to get close to you so that their spells will succeed."

Tier rubbed his face. "I can't tell a *solsenti* wizard from anyone else unless he's gathering magic, can you?"

Seraph shook her head. "I can see the Orders, if I look. But simple wizards, no."

Tier yawned. Seraph frowned at him.

"How many nights do you sit up plotting?" she asked briskly, but didn't wait for an answer. "Boys, can you settle yourselves to being quiet? Tier, you won't do anyone any good if you fall over asleep. You lie down here, and the boys and I will keep watch until the Emperor comes."

He started to protest, and it was a mark of how tired he was that he stopped himself. "My love, if you make yourself comfortable, I'll lay my head upon your lap and dream sweetly for a year."

"See," said Lehr in a stage whisper, "that's how you get women to do things for you. You ought to try it, Jes. Think Hennea will let you rest your weary brow upon her lap?"

"Lehr," said Jes, "shut up and let Papa sleep."

Seraph didn't sleep, though truthfully she was tired as well, but sitting peacefully on the soft bed with her husband's head in her lap was as effective as a week's worth of sleep. While she waited she worked on loosening the magic net the *solsenti* wizards had bound around Tier. She didn't fight them but just encouraged the unraveling that time would have brought.

When she had done what she could, she half-opened one eye and saw that Lehr was sleeping sitting up. Jes was alert and watchful—he nodded his head at her so that she would know that he'd seen her looking. The very peace that had settled in her heart told her it was really Jes who watched and not the Guardian. She thought that it was a good sign that the Guardian would trust in Jes.

She closed her eye and let herself enjoy the quiet.

"Someone's coming," said Jes softly.

Tier rolled to his feet and stretched. "Thank you, love.

Would you all please stand so that you aren't directly in line with the door—but no disguises, eh? If this isn't Phoran, I'd rather keep your presence quiet, but if it is Phoran, I don't want him thinking that we're trying to ambush him."

"There's three of them," said Lehr as he obediently shifted over without getting up. "One of them is Toarsen, one of them is wearing a lot of metal, and the third is in soft-soled shoes."

Tier looked at Lehr in surprise. Well, thought Seraph, she'd told him that the children had been growing into their powers.

"How do you know it's Toarsen?" Tier asked.

Lehr grimaced, "I know. It bothers me, too. Mother says I'll get used to it. But I liked it better when I just thought I was a good tracker—bringing magic into it robs me of the satisfaction of having a skill. Toarsen's wearing leather-soled boots and there's a nail sticking out of one heel. Gives him a stomp-click, stomp-click kind of walk."

There was a soft knock on the door, and Jes's soundless response made Seraph shiver with the cold.

"Who is it?" asked Tier, deliberately sounding groggy and irritable.

"Phoran," replied a firm tenor not a whit less irritable. "Here at your command."

Tier grinned and opened the door. "Thank you for coming, Your Greatness. Come in."

"I really hate that one," said a young man who could be none other than the Emperor. His bright eyes slid over Seraph and Jes, paused on Lehr, and returned to Tier. "It's bad enough to be Your Mightinessed and Your Highnessed by people who consider you a fool. But to be insulted for my extra weight"—he patted his waist, which was plump—"is beyond the pale. I hope you didn't wake me up to meet your family—although your wife is certainly lovely enough to be worth any effort on my part. I'm afraid that Avar is miffed with his brother for having the audaciousness to force him to get me up—and twice as miffed that I hadn't told him that I was meeting a prisoner in the bowels of the palace."

Tier grinned at him. "How did you know they're my family?"

Phoran snorted. "A lovely Traveler lady and two boys— one who looks like her and the other like you? Please, I'm supposed to be a drunkard but I am not a complete idiot. I know that you told me she'd come, but isn't she a little early?"

He turned gracefully and indicated the big man who'd closed the door behind them—the one Lehr said was wearing metal. "Avar, I'd like to introduce you to Tier of Redern— from your own Sept. Tier this is Avar, Sept of Leheigh, and my friend."

"My Sept," Tier said, bowing his head briskly.

"Who are you that you call the Emperor to attend you?" said Avar, ignoring Tier's greeting.

Jealous? thought Seraph.

"I am his humble servant," said Tier smoothly.

"He's helping me," said Phoran. "The Path is more danger- ous than you think. It is thanks to Tier that I realized how dan- gerous. He's been helping to find out who the Raptors are and at the same time subverting the Passerines."

"That's why you started the sword drills," said Toarsen, sounding disillusioned.

Seraph, being a mother, heard the unspoken—*you didn't really care about us.*

"He told me," said Phoran, not looking at Toarsen, "that there were a number of young men who wanted but a little di- rection to be the best chance I had of controlling my empire."

"You thought *we* could aid the Emperor?" said Toarsen, sounding almost shocked.

As if, thought Seraph with exasperation for the male half of the species, being used by the Emperor were a great thing.

"I know you can," said Tier. "Where else is he likely to get a bunch of hotheads who can fight and aren't sworn men of some Sept or other?"

"Collarn's job," said Toarsen. "You arranged Collarn's job."

"Actually," said the Emperor, clearing his throat. "That was me."

Toarsen's face was bewildered when he turned to Tier. "The Emperor is a drunken sot," he said, as if the Emperor weren't standing next to him. "He follows Avar around like a lost puppy and does whatever Avar tells him to. You, Tier, are a bored soldier who has found a hobby to help make a year in captivity pass more quickly. You find the Raptors annoying and the Masters even more so. So you decided to see what you could do to tweak their tails and gain the admiration of the Passerines. When you started, you found that you actually liked a few of us."

"I was never allowed to be anything but a drunken sot," said Phoran coolly, but without anger. "And everyone follows Avar around like lost puppies."

"I saw a bunch of rowdy boys being led into hell by a pack of carrion-eaters," said Tier. "As I rather liked some of you and despise men who play games with other people's lives— I decided to see what I could do about the situation."

"It works because he does care," added Lehr. "If he'd just been trying to use you, you'd have seen through him."

Avar, leaning against the door, rubbed his face. "Would someone care to tell us why we're here now? Certainly there are better times for theatrics than the wee hours of the morning."

"The Path is preparing a move to preempt me from taking control of the young men from them," said Tier. "Myrceria told me that they are intending to have a Disciplining—a particularly brutal method they employ to keep their secrets. One of the boys is singled out and punished by everyone. I gather that the boy who is punished sometimes doesn't survive. I think that they'll choose Collarn—but they might take Toarsen or Kissel as they are the three who are my closest associates."

Phoran humpfed, then said, "I can warn Collarn on my way back to bed without anyone being the wiser. But we ought to finish the introductions before we attend to business further. Do be a credit to your parents' instructions in manners and introduce us to your family, Tier."

Tier bowed and grinned sheepishly. "This is my wife Seraph, Raven of the Clan of Isolda the Silent. My son Jesaphi, whom we call Jes, Guardian. My younger son Lehr, Hunter. Seraph, Jes, Lehr, may I introduce you to Phoran the Twenty-Seventh."

Over the polite murmurs and shuffles, Toarsen said, "Twenty-Sixth."

Phoran grinned. "Only if you don't count the first one. I always do, since without him there wouldn't have been an Empire, whatever his son Phoran the First or Second said."

Toarsen smiled reluctantly. No wonder her husband liked this boy who happened to be emperor, thought Seraph. They were very much alike.

"I had intended to warn Collarn," said Tier, returning to the matter at hand. "But my wife pointed out that this Disciplining is the best chance we'll have of clearing the whole lot. Everyone is supposed to attend them. They'll be expecting some resistance from the Passerines—too many of them have begun to look at the things the Path wants of them—but they won't be expecting an outside attack."

"When will it be?" asked Phoran.

"Sometime in the next few days," replied Tier.

Phoran shook his head. "There are two hundred of them—and five wizards, and the Sept of Gerant and his men aren't here yet. I have—"

"I have twenty men here," said Avar, "who are my men, not my father's."

"And my wife tells me that she can bring another fifty or so—light foot, armed mostly with knives with a few swords," said Tier. "Travelers."

Suspiciously, Avar asked, "Why would you Travelers be interested in this?"

"Because our people are dying out," Seraph said. "For as long as I remember the Septs have been trying to destroy them. If my friends help you, Phoran—would you be willing to return the favor?"

Phoran nodded his head slowly. "I'll do what I can. I don't have the power that an emperor should, and championing the Travelers is not going to help. But I'll do what I can."

"Will that be good enough?" asked Avar.

Seraph smiled. "The Path have been killing Travelers for centuries. We just didn't know about them until now—if Phoran would not invite us in to help him, we would go after them on our own. But it's much safer to invade the palace under imperial command."

"Myrceria will try and find out when this Disciplining will take place," continued Tier.

"I'll know sooner," said Toarsen. "Myrceria will have to wait until someone tells her about it—me they have to send for. With your permission"—he glanced from Tier to Phoran as if he didn't really know whose permission he needed—"I'll let Kissel know, too, in case it's me they've decided to use as an example."

"How much lead time do you need to bring in the Travelers?" asked Phoran, and they all began planning.

Seraph settled back and gave them information as they asked for it. Clearly the Emperor, Avar, and Tier were having the time of their lives, and the younger men were almost as bad—except for Jes, who seemed content to stay in the background.

It amused Seraph to see that the Emperor, the Sept of Leheigh, and his younger brother all ceded the leadership to Tier, though they all outranked him—and he had them hanging on his every word.

CHAPTER 16

*The next morning Tier was bone-tired, but more peace-*ful than he'd been for a long time. Seraph was here. Well, not *here*. She'd gone off to play diplomat among the Travelers, which was pretty strange—the only person that he knew less suited to diplomacy was Alinath.

"Keep your guard centered," he told one of his Passerines. "Remember this isn't about first blood, it's about who lives and who dies. Make sure you're one of the former and not the latter."

He paced behind his troops, watching foot positions, when a servant caught hold of his sleeve.

"Telleridge requests a moment of your time."

"Toarsen," called Tier. "Kissèl. Run the drills for me. If I'm not back, break when every man's shirt is wet through."

Toarsen stepped out of the line and made a quick mocking salute as he did. He didn't look nearly as tired as Tier felt, and he'd had no more sleep. It made Tier feel old.

The servant took Tier to one of the smaller rooms that served as the Raptors' meeting halls and opened the door for Tier's entrance. The room had been partially screened off with a delicately carved wooden panel. Four black-robed figures sat in gold upholstered chairs ringed in front of a cheerful fire, two empty chairs in the center. Telleridge, also in his robes, stood in front of the fire.

Telleridge looked up when Tier entered, though the others kept their eyes on the fireplace.

"Ah, thank you for attending me. Baskins, you may leave."

The servant shut the door, leaving Tier alone with the Path's wizards.

"Come have a seat, Bard," Telleridge said in an unreadable tone.

Warily, Tier sat on the edge of one of the empty chairs as the Master took the other. He had the odd impression that Telleridge's calm was just a thin film spread over turbulent waters.

"You have cost us much, my friend," Telleridge said. "Whatever possessed you to try and take the Passerines from us? Did you think that we would allow it?"

"You aren't doing anything with them," replied Tier. "There are a number of fine young men amongst the Passerines—and a few who are a waste of shoe leather."

"They are useful to us." said Telleridge, sounding distantly amused. Tier took note of the effect, planning to save it for some time when he wanted to be obnoxiously patronizing. "Just as they were. We've called a Disciplining, which will return control to us, but I fear that very few of these Passerines will make it to Raptor now. I was particularly upset when you took the Sept of Leheigh's young brother. I had great hopes for him. And it's too bad about the young musician, Collarn— we shall miss having music in these halls when you both are gone."

"I see," said Tier, deciding to let the Master direct the conversation into the gently ironic tones he seemed to prefer. "I take it that my demise will happen a little sooner than you planned?"

There was a noise from behind the screen, but it was too faint for Tier to identify.

"I'm not any happier about it than you are," the Master said. Apparently the others had all been told to sit and be silent, because none of them had done anything more exciting than breathe since Tier entered the room. "Owls are few and far between, and this haste will destroy our plans. That makes two failures in as many years. We've never had this much trouble controlling a Bard—I assume it's a Bardic talent you are using to win over the Passerines?"

Tier frowned at him. "How could it be? You've told me that you have my Order under control." He'd used the methods Gerant had taught him instead, because he'd never relied on his Order for much—unlike a Traveler-raised Bard.

"I wonder that none of our other Bards have done such a thing," said the Master.

Because a Traveler Bard was hardly likely to worry about the lives of a bunch of *solsenti* thugs-in-the-making, thought Tier, but he didn't say anything.

The Master waited politely, but when Tier didn't respond he shrugged. "At any rate, I, personally, am most distressed at a few other things you've cost us," he got to his feet and strolled to the screen, "Come, Bard. And maybe you will be sorry as well."

For want of a better thing to do while surrounded by five mages, Tier got slowly to his feet and followed the Master's beckoning. The others got up silently and followed.

A woman was tied naked to a chair, and someone had obviously been testing, in the time-honored fashion, how well flesh fared against knives and other things. Her face was so battered that it was unrecognizable—but Tier knew the hair.

"Myrceria," he said.

She stiffened when he spoke, and he realized that her eyes were so swollen that she must not be able to see at all.

"Myrceria has been telling us things," said Telleridge. "Haven't you, my dear?" He patted the top of her head, then took out a dagger and cut off the gag.

"I'm sorry," she said, her face turned blindly toward Tier. "I'msorrysorry."

"Shh," said Tier, putting some force behind the words. "It doesn't matter. Shh."

She kept shaking, but she quit apologizing. Either his words worked, or Seraph was right about the unraveling of the Master's spells and she'd felt the magic push he'd given them.

"I was angry about the Passerines," said Telleridge. "Angrier still when I questioned Myrceria this morning and realized that instead of keeping an eye on you as she was supposed to—you had taken her from us, too. She has been a valuable tool for years, and you've ruined her."

His movement was so quick, so unexpected that before Tier realized what the Master had done, Myrceria's blood showered him from chest to knee.

Telleridge pulled up her head and held it through the throes of death. "She's been so useful over the years. Where am I going to find another wizard who is so good at getting close to our Traveler guests? I have no more daughters." He dropped her head and wiped his hands on his robes. Black robes hid the blood much better than Tier's light-colored clothing.

It wasn't, thought Tier, that he hadn't believed they were evil. He had just forgotten how sudden death could be, and how final. He'd liked Myrceria.

Tier still had his sword from practice, but this was too well-orchestrated. If his sword would have done him any good, they'd never have let him keep it.

Had Myrceria betrayed their plans? She hadn't known it all—but she'd known enough.

"But you know the thing that bothers me the most?" asked Telleridge, intruding on Tier's grief and anger. "How did you get to the Emperor? Do you know how long it took us to come by a harmless ruler? How many people gave their lives so that I could mold the proper emperor? Then suddenly, he is making an effective grasp for power. It wasn't until I spoke with you the other day that I drew a parallel between what you've done to the Passerines and what happened to the Emperor."

Telleridge shook his head. "And what have you left us to rule in his place? Avar is next for the throne; but although he is an idiot, he is a well-meaning idiot. You've ruined Toarsen." He heaved a theatrical sigh. "Not that it will matter to you how much trouble you've caused, but I thought you might enjoy sharing the stage tonight. I'll leave you for last so you can watch your little projects die."

Tier stared silently at Myrceria's corpse.

"Ah, no words for me, Bard?" taunted the Master.

Yes, thought Tier, it was time to see just how much control they had over his Order.

"Only cowards torture women," he said, not bothering to dodge the staff that took him across the cheekbone.

* * *

Toarsen rubbed his hair dry with a towel as he walked down the secret ways that would lead him back to the rest of the palace. Alone, he allowed himself to smile with remembered satisfaction at Avar's face when Toarsen had burst into his rooms ánd demanded to be taken to the Emperor.

Firmly convinced that it was some stupid wager, Avar had almost refused him. But he hadn't.

Toarsen was surprised about that. His brother had seldom paid any attention to him at all, except to order him about.

When he'd sworn on his honor that he carried an urgent message to the Emperor, Avar had heaved a martyred sigh, rolled out of bed, dressed, and done as Toarsen asked. On the way back to their rooms after they'd spent the night in councils of war, Avar had patted him on the back, an affectionate, respectful gesture he'd never given Toarsen before.

The passage Toarsen had taken opened not far from his rooms in an obscure storage room. He glanced cautiously out of the room, but there was no one in the hall to see him as he slipped out of the storage room and into his own.

He'd changed into the uncomfortable clothes of court and was halfway to the door before he realized that there was a vellum envelope on the cherrywood table near his bed.

His pulse picked up as he slit it opened and read the invitation.

"Now?" he said.

Seraph curled up, enfolded in the bedding that smelled of Tier. She'd left him while the sun was only a faint hint in the sky. It had been even easier than she expected to talk Benroln and his clan into serving as the Emperor's foot soldiers. She'd left Lehr and Jes sleeping and left the sheep farm just outside of Taela where they'd been staying to come back here.

Tier hadn't been here when she'd returned to tell him of her success, but she'd known that he would have to continue his normal habits or risk alerting someone. So she'd climbed into his bed and reminded herself that he was alive. If someone came in, they'd not see her unless she wanted them to.

Someone knocked at the door.

"Tier? It's Toarsen. Are you back?"

Reluctantly, she got out of the bed and pulled the covers flat. She opened the door and motioned the young man in.

"He's not here," she said.

"I can't find him anywhere," Toarsen said, sounding a little frantic. "The Disciplining is set for early this evening, and I can't find Tier."

"It's all right," said Seraph, his anxiety lending her calm. "He'll want to know, but it's Phoran, your brother, and my people who really need to know right now. Go to your brother and tell him to get word to Phoran and to get his men and meet my people in the passages we discussed. I'll get the Travelers, and after you've told Avar, you go about your day as if nothing were wrong. Avar can get word to Phoran. Just make sure you are armed when you go to the Disciplining."

He nodded and left the room. Seraph set out at a dead run through the labyrinth of passages—there was no time to waste. She needed to get Benroln. Tier had survived a long time here without her to watch over him. She had to believe he'd be all right.

Avar and his men waited for them as he'd promised, in a long, dark corridor large enough to have held twice as many people. Relief crossed his face when he saw Seraph and the Librarian's clan.

"I don't like this," he said without waiting for introductions. "Toarsen said he couldn't find Tier anywhere. He looked for Myrceria to give her a message for him, but he couldn't find her either, and none of the other whores knew where she was. He said that he'd last seen Tier at sword practice, but that one of the Masters called him to a meeting. Then I couldn't find Phoran in any of his usual haunts, though his horse is still in the stable."

Seraph pushed her anxiety aside and forced herself to think clearly. The Path were upset with Tier for taking control of the Passerines . . . so they took him and . . . Her thoughts stuck there. Would they simply have killed him?

"I don't see anything to do except follow the plans we laid out last night," she said at last.

Beside her Benroln nodded his head. "If what Seraph told us about this group is true, this is the best chance to destroy them. It would be better for us if the Emperor is there to bear witness for us—but the Path needs to be destroyed here and now."

"Neither Tier nor Phoran are essential to the destruction of the Path now," said Seraph with painful honesty. "Without Tier, though, we might have to fight the Passerines, too. And if Phoran is not there, Benroln, your men will have to try and get out as soon as this is finished and take all of our fallen, too. Maybe Telleridge has taken them for part of the performance tonight. If the Masters have hurt Tier, they'll have a hard time controlling the Passerines."

"You don't know the Passerines," said Avar.

"I know my husband," she said.

She didn't miss the uneasy way Avar's people surveyed the exotic lot of armed Travelers or the puzzled looks aimed at Brewydd. Old women were not usually part of a battle force—but Healers could look after themselves on a battlefield.

"We need to take them tonight," Seraph said again.

Avar nodded slowly, then turned to the troops around him. In short, punctuated sentences he described what they were doing and why.

The white robes she'd taken from an unwary Raptor were woolen and itchy, but Seraph stood quietly next to Brewydd, who was carrying on a conversation with the white-robed Raptor beside her, talking, of all things, about growing tomatoes.

Hennea had laid spells on all of them: look-away spells to keep them from being noticed and minor illusions to hide things—like Seraph's lack of height and her sex—that would otherwise attract attention. When Hennea had told them all to avoid being noticed, Seraph didn't think that exchanging gardening tips with the first Raptor they happened upon was what she'd had in mind.

Seraph looked out over the room. Jes was somewhere, too, though he hadn't bothered with the white robes. No one would see him until he wanted them to. Lehr was with the rest of their little army.

The Passerines were gathered already; she'd counted them.

Assuming Tier's protégé was the boy they intended to pro-
duce, all of the Passerines were there. Though they didn't
have hoods on their robes, Seraph found that the robes obscured enough differences that she had a hard time picking out
Toarsen, the only Passerine she knew, from the rest. There
were chairs in rows in front of the stage, and the Passerines
were all directed to those; even as she watched, the last of
them took his seat.

There were more Raptors than she'd hoped, nearly three
times the number of Passerines. Well, enough, she told herself, it would be even less likely that anyone should spot the
cuckoos in the mix.

"Followers of the Secret Path."

Seraph stiffened at the whiff of magic that accompanied
the words so that they rang out and appeared louder than they
really were.

The room quieted. Brewydd softened her voice to a mur-
mur, but continued comparing the benefits of growing tomatoes in various soils.

It had been Raven magic that gave power to the words the
black-robed man standing in front of the curtained stage had
said. Why hadn't he used the Bardic Order? A Bard would
have done more than just overpower the talking of the crowd:
he could have caught the attention of everyone, even tomato
zealots like Brewydd's conversation partner, and held it.

Perhaps they didn't know that, or maybe they just preferred
to work with more familiar powers. A *solsenti* mage, she
thought, would be used to having magic work a certain way—
like Raven or even Cormorant. They wanted the Orders for
power, but even Volis had had no use for subtlety.

"When you come to our Eyrie you take vows," said the
wizard. "First, never reveal to anyone what we do here. Second, to attend the Eyrie at least three evenings a week. Third,
to obey the Raptors and the Masters over and above all other
oaths. One of you has broken the last two of these rules. We
are here today to discipline him—not in hope of reformation,
because he will never again be welcome to our Eyrie."

"Telleridge sure knows how to capture his audience,
doesn't he," marveled the Raptor talking to Brewydd, his
voice shaking with age, but he returned to his favorite subject

with more ado. "I find that the tomatoes I grow in the orangery—"

"But that is not all we are here for." The Master's voice dipped into sorrow, but Seraph thought he overdid it a bit. "In recent weeks it has come to our attention that our Passerines have been led astray by the magic of our Traveler guest. The magic that keeps his at bay, here in our halls, is dependent upon your resistance. If you want to be his follower, his servant, there is nothing our magic can do to protect you. So we have to take more stringent measures with him."

They had Tier. Was he alive?

"There is a third problem that has held our attention these past few years. Our Empire, founded by heroes, built by men of vision, men of intelligence is, even now, presided over by a drunken sot. Bored with the available women and wealth, he has decided to interfere with the men who try to preserve the Empire. Who is to save us when our frivolous Emperor chooses to change the ancient boundaries of the Septs? Who? We shall save ourselves."

He raised both hands and the great curtains behind him creaked and squealed as they slowly opened to the Master's magic.

On the stage was a frightened young man, naked and chained by his wrists to a ring in the floor of the stage. In the center position was the Emperor. They hadn't stripped him— too worried about arousing the wrong emotion in the crowd, judged Seraph—but he was wearing the same robes he'd been in last night, and they looked the worse for wear. But it was the third man, Tier, her eyes found and locked on.

He was alive, she thought with a rush of relief; she could see his ribs move as he breathed. Like the Passerine he'd been so worried about, he'd been stripped naked and chained, but he lay curled up and still, his skin red and black from beating.

Rage rose up in Seraph like a red tide. She stared at the Master who orchestrated this mess and took what her magic could tell her. He was a *solsenti* wizard of moderate power, aided by two Raven rings—one of them very old.

"We deal first with the greatest offense. Phoran the Twenty-Sixth, we, the Followers of the Secret Path, judge you unfit to rule our Empire!" The Master turned to the audience and gave the signal for a response of some kind. A roar of approval perhaps?

But it never came, because Phoran spoke.

"Actually," he said with dignity that caught at the heart of every person in the room, "it's Phoran the Twenty-Seventh. I've always felt that since the old farmer started the Empire, he ought to get credit for it."

Even Brewydd's new friend quit speaking.

Seraph felt a relieved grin tug at her lips. Tier was doing better than he appeared if he could give Phoran's mundane words that much power.

Phoran looked a little taken aback by the response his quip had drawn. *Go, Tier,* thought Seraph fiercely. She glanced at Telleridge, but even with the partial immunity the Raven rings he wore gave him, he was too close to Phoran to do anything except listen.

Phoran was not at a loss for more than a breath. "Some of what Telleridge has said is correct. I have not been the best of emperors, but I didn't realize that anyone needed me to be that. Like you, I thought that the Council of Septs—ruled by people like Telleridge here—were far more capable than I ever could be. That should have been true."

He was taking too long, thought Seraph, watching Telleridge struggle against the Bardic touch. Tier couldn't possibly maintain his hold on the whole room for very long, not in the condition he was in.

She stepped away from the wall and began making her way down toward the auditorium. If she could get to him, she could help.

"They are intelligent men, and well-trained to their office. If they chose to rule justly, they could surely do so. But they rule instead for personal gain. Some of you were encouraged to work a little mischief in the street of the weavers last year. Did you know that the council leader's riches increased by half after that incident because the weavers now pay him for the right to sell their goods in their own craft stalls? Gorrish is one of the Raptors who sent you out to attack the weavers— did any of you gain from that?"

Phoran took a deep breath, and Seraph felt the crowd stir as the Bardic touch faded momentarily and then strengthened again. With the shifting of the crowd, her only path to the stage closed up.

"Those Raptors among you will know that almost half the Passerines who are here will die mysteriously shortly after they graduate to being Raptors. Some of you know that it is not so mysterious, because you aided in those men's deaths. Why kill so many? Because some of you are already outgrowing the trappings of childhood. Some of you realize that it is not necessary to prove who you are by how much destruction you can cause—you are the first ones they will kill. Like this young man beside me who was targeted only because he loves old instruments more than he loves tormenting the younger Passerines."

"I haven't been much of an emperor," Phoran said. "I've disappointed people who cared about me all of my life—just as you have. Mostly, my failures have been passive failures—things not done rather than great and terrible acts. Just as yours have been, until today. If you harm men whose only crime is to fall afoul of a power-mad politician, then you take a step that cannot be undone."

Tier crooked his neck and peered out of his one good eye to see how Phoran was holding up. Something, he thought, something had walked close to the Emperor. It leaned nearer as if it were whispering something in Phoran's ear, then faded from Tier's view.

Jes, he thought. Anxiously, Tier looked at the audience, but they didn't seem to have seen that nebulous shape.

Phoran took a breath. "You have a choice tonight. You can hold to the oaths you made to the Masters of the Path. Realize that they have not given you an oath in return—as I did when I became emperor. I owe you fair hearing in disputes, I owe you a place in our society, and I owe you an emperor worth serving in return. You must choose now." He looked up, scanning the crowd. When he saw what he sought he nodded once. Then he began speaking rapidly. "Choose who you fight carefully, because this is a battle for the soul of the Empire."

He swung one of his chained wrists to indicate the wall of the Eyrie and, as if he'd wielded the magic himself, the wall disintegrated into so much plaster dust and splintered wood.

The noise and magical backwash distracted Tier, and he lost his tenuous hold on his own magic.

The failure of his control hit Tier like a blow to the head. It awakened every inch of the screaming flesh the Masters had abused. He cried out, and his vision blackened. The sounds of battle erupted around him, and half-dazed as he was, he couldn't remember where he was or what he was doing here without a sword.

The destruction of the wall caught Seraph by surprise. She had been supposed to help bring it down, but, unable to see over the crowd, she must have missed the signal—or Hennea had used an opportune moment in the Emperor's speech.

Irritably, Seraph poked the tall, bulky Raptor who stood in front of her. Since she'd used a touch of magic, he jumped aside with a yelp, pushing several other men over and briefly clearing a visual path for Seraph just as Avar's men and the Travelers began pouring into the room with a war-cry that was even more effective in a room designed as a theater than it would have been on an open battlefield.

The astonishment of such strangeness held the Followers of the Path oddly still until the first of Avar's men gutted the nearest Raptor.

A man near Seraph drew his sword, but he was looking toward the far side of the room for his enemy, so he never even noticed Seraph until her knife intersected his belly. A young blue-robed boy drew his sword and finished the job—but gave her white robes a wary look.

"I'm Tier's wife," she said, tossing back her hood.

"Pleased to meet *you*," he said, grunting the last as he used his sword to catch the blade of a Raptor who was a bit quicker than most to realize that the Passerines were as much a threat as the fighting men who'd come through the wall. "I'm Kissel."

She had to get to Tier. Discarding the robes both because they got in her way and because they might get her killed by one of Tier's Passerines, she aimed for the most direct path to Tier, whom she still couldn't see.

The fighting was widespread by now, and the heaviest

fighting lay between her and the stage. Seraph called her magic to her.

Blindly, instinctively, Tier tried to rise to his feet, since a down man on a battlefield was a dead man, but something held his wrists and he couldn't call any strength to his muscles.

"It's all right, sir," said Toarsen's familiar voice. "I'll keep you safe."

"The Emperor," managed Tier, falling back to his damaged knees and biting back a moan. Screams were for people who weren't as weary as he was.

There was a series of clanking sounds, battle sounds that ended in a grunt and a thunk. Toarsen, panting a bit, said, "Kissel's with him, and someone cut him loose and gave him a sword. I never knew that Phoran knew how to fight. Never thought"—another thunk and gasp—"someone as fat as he is could move that fast."

"The Masters?" asked Tier. Seated and calmer, he found that his vision was coming back a bit, but not well enough to sort through the chaos of battle. He wiped his good eye with the back of his hand. His hand came away wet, but he could see again.

"I don't see 'em," Toarsen said. "I was watching Avar and his men boil into the room. When I looked back, this place was covered in fighters and I thought I might come up here and bear you company a bit. We've a nice view of the fighting up here—those two boys of yours can surely fight."

Someone in white blundered into the small area of stage that Toarsen was guarding, and he sent the Raptor on his way with a kick that impaled him on a sword held by a man with moon-pale hair.

"*Gessa,*" said the man.

"Anytime," said Toarsen.

"Collarn?" asked Tier, his returning vision allowing him to see that the boy's place was empty.

"Naked as a newborn," said Toarsen cheerfully. "You're not able to get high enough to enjoy the sight, but I can see him from here. Remember all those times you told him that he carries his guard too high?"

"Yes?"

"You should have made him fight naked."

Tier laughed, one short bark, then held his breath and his ribs. "No joking right now," he managed.

Lehr rolled onto the stage and then bounced up and ran over. "Good to see that you're alive, Papa. But I think I speak for us all when I tell you that I'd rather not worry about you again for a while. Parents are supposed to worry about their children, not vice versa. Let me get a look at those chains."

He held the manacles in his hands and closed his eyes. After a moment, the locks clicked open. Lehr grinned at his father's expression.

"I don't know how opening locks ties in with being a Hunter either, though Brewydd explained it to me a dozen times." He sounded pleased with himself. He looked at Toarsen.

"Go ahead," said Toarsen. "I'll stay here."

"Thanks," said Lehr, and he leaped off the edge of the stage.

Having completed the task Hennea had given him, the Guardian took a quick glance around the room. Lehr was fighting at Avar's side and accounting for himself quite well. Just as his gaze found Seraph, she raised her hands and tossed a half dozen men into the air. Obviously she was in no need of immediate protection.

He turned to go to his father, but the Sept of Leheigh's brother was standing over Papa's crumpled form and seemed to be having no trouble fending off attackers. The wizards, who posed more of a threat, had other things on their minds than hurting his father. A double handful of Passerines were doing their best to get onto the stage and attack the Masters— too many of them to allow the wizards' magic to be an effective weapon. The Guardian knew—*remembered from other battles fought long ago, before Jes's father's father had been born*—that keeping the Passerines away would soon weaken the *solsenti* wizards too much for them to be a danger to Tier.

Satisfied that they were all safe for the moment, the

Guardian jumped off the stage to return to Hennea's side, slipping between fighters who mostly moved out of his way without ever looking at him directly.

The noise of swords clashing and men screaming excited him almost as much as the smell of blood.

A man bumped his arm and the Guardian turned on him with a snarl and a flash of fangs. If the man hadn't retreated, falling backwards over a body on the floor, even Jes could not have held the Guardian back.

Hennea stood alone near the fallen wall. He couldn't tell if her spells to avoid being seen were working on everyone else, or if they were just smart enough to stay away. Mother had told him that spells usually didn't work right on him.

There were two men attacking a boy who was stepping back rapidly to avoid being overrun. The Guardian could see that the boy wouldn't stay away from their blades for much longer. He glanced at Hennea, but she was all right. The Guardian dropped the sword he held and reached for the form of the great cat—he wanted to taste blood, not feel flesh part against steel.

He picked the nearest Raptor and leaped onto his shoulders, driving him down to the floor. As his claws sank deep into meat, the man's pain and fear washed through Jes. The Guardian reveled in the searing sensations, which only raised his bloodlust further.

The other antagonist paused to stare, but the Passerine recovered a little faster and killed his opponent before beating a rapid retreat. Death and the boy's fear fed the battle rage and Jes turned his attention to the man who lay beneath him.

"Jes!"

The great cat halted, his mouth already opened to still the struggles of his prey.

"Jes, come back. I need you!" Hennea sounded frantic.

Her hand touched his tense back. "Jes," she said.

Trembling, fighting, Jes forced the Guardian to step away from the downed man even as the beast roared its thwarted rage.

"What?" he managed, the emotions and pain of the battle raging around him raw without the Guardian's protection.

Hennea smoothed her hands over him and the worst of the clamor faded until it was manageable. The Guardian would have been better, but Jes couldn't let him loose until he had a moment to calm down.

"Look on the stage," Hennea whispered. "What do you see?"

There had been wizards on the stage when he'd carried Hennea's message to the Emperor. Five stood in plain view, but the other held to the shadows. When his father had lost control of them, they, like Hennea, had stood back from the battle and aided their people as they could.

Now four wizards lay crumpled on the ground, and something—something that caused the Guardian to take control again—fed on the fifth.

"What is that?" asked the Guardian.

"A Raven's Memory," she said. "A vengeful ghost— though I've never seen one so substantial. It's almost alive."

The sixth wizard, anonymous in his robes, slipped off the stage and toward the destroyed wall. No one looked at him, though he passed a few men quite closely.

"One of the wizards is getting away," the Guardian observed to Hennea, calm again.

"Where?" she asked, but when he pointed, she didn't see him.

"I'll follow him," he decided and Jes, anxious to get away from the battle, agreed with the Guardian's decision. Neither of them listened to Hennea's protest as the great cat leaped over a heap of rubble to follow the escaping man.

Seraph blew her hair out of her eyes wearily and kept moving forward. The large young man who had been so helpful in dispatching that first Raptor had stayed by her side as she used whatever means necessary to push through the battle.

There was a limit to her magic, and after the first blast won her only a few yards before the fighting spread into the cleared area she'd made, she decided that she was going to have to use more subtlety and less power. With a sword she scavenged from the floor, she used magic to lend force to her blows until the blade slid through bone as if it were water. She'd taken the time to add her own *see-me-not* spell to Hennea's efforts. Blood covered her from the elbows down, weighting down her clothes with more than physical burden—but she wasn't here to fight fair. She needed to get to Tier.

"You know it's true what he said," panted her young friend Kissel.

"What's that?" she managed, dropping another Raptor who was raising his sword to attack a blue-robed man from behind.

"A man would be smarter to face an enraged boar than to cross my wife." The boy managed to imitate Tier's style.

"Huh," she grunted, kicking an unsuspecting man behind his knee and dropping him onto his opponent's blade. "How flattering."

The boy grinned wearily. "He doesn't seem to mind."

"Can you see him yet?"

"No," he said. "But I can see Toarsen on the stage—he'll do his best to keep him from harm."

Tier knew that he should get to his feet and claim a sword, but he just couldn't manage it.

As if he read his mind, Toarsen said, "It's all right, sir. Just having Avar in here fighting for the Emperor took most of the heart out of the Raptors. All the Passerines called out his name as soon as they saw who it was—even that squid you've had Kissel and me watching was attacking the Raptors. Remind me never to let him behind me with something sharp. All that's left now is just a few of the Raptors and mercenaries who didn't leave fast enough. Avar will call quarter in a minute, as soon as he thinks that his men have had enough of killing."

Sure enough, through the sounds of battle—all the louder for being inside the cavernous chamber—came a bass rumble still distinguishable as the words: "Quarter give quarter! Surrender or die!" picking up in volume as more voices took up the cry.

"Waste of time," murmured Tier, just before he passed out. "They're all guilty of treason—Phoran will have to hang 'em all."

* * *

He wasn't actually out all that long because there were still clashes, as a few desperate men continued to fight, when he woke up.

He opened his eyes just as an old, quavering voice said, "Woo-eyah. I see that those giggling twits were right about *solsenti* men."

Tier stared at the oldest woman he'd ever seen, then grinned. "You must be Brewydd," he said, "the Healer."

"And it's a good thing for you, young man," she agreed. "You must be the Bard that woman's been so upset about. Now let me see what this old biddy can do about making you want to stay with the living."

She clicked her tongue against her teeth when she saw what they'd done to his knees. "Good thing you did this with a Lark nearby," she said. "If you'd done it somewhere else you wouldn't be walking on these again."

"I'd give you a kiss," said Tier, then he had to stop and grit his teeth as her touch brought burning pain that was worse than the original blows had been. "Except that my wife would finish what the Path began."

"It is good that a man knows his place," said Seraph comfortably from somewhere behind him.

He hurt too much to turn so he could see her, so he gave her a vague wave.

She crouched down on her heels beside him. "So," she said, "I know where there is a white robe you can have—but that might make you a target. On the other hand, parading around in nothing at all might make you a different sort of target."

He laughed, then moaned. "Why is it that the first thing someone does when you've cracked your ribs is make a joke?"

"You don't have cracked ribs," said the Healer, looking up from his battered knees. "You have broken ones. And hold off on that robe, girl, until I see to them as well. He doesn't have anything that I haven't seen better."

"Hello," said a Traveler, crouching down on Tier's other side. "You must be the Bard."

"Tier," said Seraph, "this is Kors. Kors, my husband, Tier. Kors, what do you want?"

Ah, thought Tier contentedly, all that in under a breath, my Seraph at her charismatic best.

"We were wondering if you'd seen the Guardian? We know he was here, but none of us can locate him."

"Most all of what I've seen is a bunch of people from the knees down," quipped Tier. Then he added, "Actually I saw him—or at least something that was probably him, whispering to Phoran. I suppose he was telling Phoran that Avar was waiting as planned because it was just after that that Phoran signaled the Ravens to bring down the wall."

"I didn't see it," said Seraph sourly. "I was trying to get down to you and I got caught in the crowd. Hennea brought down the wall by herself—I didn't even get to singe that bloody wizard to ash. By the time I got in the clear, all of the Masters were down and dead—or at least not moving."

"Well," said Kors, clearing his throat a little, "that's kind of why Benroln sent me over to see if you could find your son. A lot of us saw something kill the Masters, one after the other, but we couldn't quite see it. We'd all appreciate it if you could find Jes and make certain he doesn't mistake anyone else for the enemy."

"Jes isn't that stupid," said Tier. But he worried about what all the violence had done to the Guardian, too. "He's probably gone off to find someplace quiet."

"Wait until I've gotten the ribs stabilized, young man," chided the Healer, moving creakily from his knee to his side—pushing Kors out of the way. "And then you can go looking for your boy."

It took more than a few minutes, but finally with Lehr under one shoulder and Toarsen under the other, Tier gained his feet, Seraph's robe stopping a few inches below his knees. The joints in question still felt like they'd been hit with a club—which they had—but at least he was able to shuffle over to take a look at the victims.

His first clue was the rather sick look Phoran sent him before he turned back to talking with Avar.

They'd piled all the Masters' bodies together. When Tier arrived, Kors and Kissel hauled one of the bodies out and pulled back the cowl. The dark veil that lined it, making the

robes a more effective disguise, had been ripped so that the
face could be revealed.

Tier had the boys help lower him until he was sitting on the
ground. The sight he had out of his good eye was getting
worse, and he supposed it would be swollen all the way shut
by tomorrow, but he wanted to see them, to know that they
were dead.

Tier's first reaction was a dull sort of surprise. He'd never
actually seen any of the Master's faces except for Telleridge's,
but somehow he felt as if he ought to recognize them anyway.
He didn't even know which one it was. His second was a real-
ization that the dried, sunken look was due to more than age.
Almost hidden on the man's neck were two fading puncture
wounds.

"The Travelers tell us that your son is capable of this," said
Avar as he and Phoran approached. "And that he has magic
that can make him hard to see—much like what they saw kill
these men."

Tier opened his mouth, then saw Phoran's pale face behind
Avar and realized what had killed the wizards. "Must have
been him, then," he said, trying to hide the rush of relief. Jes
hadn't been running amok—the Memory had.

Lehr stiffened, and Seraph put a hand on Tier's shoulder.
He patted her hand, then Lehr's leg. "Do the rest of them look
the same?"

"Yes," said Phoran. "Just the same. As if they'd been
drained."

"Work of the Guardian," said the Healer briskly. Tier
hadn't realized she'd followed them. "Work of the Guardian
to protect his own. Get that man up off the floor and don't put
him down until he's somewhere he can rest comfortably. Do
you have a chamber where we can store him overnight?" She
asked the last question of Phoran.

He bowed. "I suspect that the one that he's been occupying
will be the easiest for him. He's welcome to take as long as
necessary—and as soon as he's up to it, I'd be happy to find
him better accommodations."

Brewydd looked at Seraph. "You wanted to burn him to
ash, girl, do it now. It's not a good thing to leave wizard's bodies intact," she said.

Lehr and Toarsen managed to lever Tier up once more. Seraph waved a hand and the bodies of the Masters burst into a dark blue-white flame that consumed them utterly in a moment. She gave Tier a look that told him that he'd better have a good reason to put Jes in a position that would make it even more difficult for others to accept him.

"Let's get him back to his cell," she said. "Then Lehr can hunt Jes down and bring him to us there."

The trip down that short hallway was miserable. Halfway there, Lehr exchanged a look with Toarsen, and with his help, shifted Tier until Lehr could pick him up and carry him the rest of the way.

Seraph sent Toarsen off to help Avar with a kiss on his cheek, ignoring Tier's indignant "Hey."

When Toarsen was gone, she said to Lehr, "Doubtless your father will explain why he blamed Jes for that nasty business. So just find your brother and bring him back here so Tier can explain it to Jes, too, before he gets hurt by the reception he gets."

The Healer had accompanied them, and she checked Tier over thoroughly to make sure the mending she'd done on him would hold. When she was through she patted him on the shoulder.

"Hardest thing that a Healer learns is when to stop healing," she said. "There's always a price to pay. You're going to be very tired in a short period of time, and you'll spend the next few days more asleep than awake. So you'd better tell me quickly why you're blaming that poor lad for the work of a Memory."

Seraph drew in her breath. "A Memory?"

"Can't," said Tier. "Promised."

"Promised what?" asked Phoran, slipping into the room and shutting the door behind him.

"Not to explain why he'd want his son to bear the blame for deaths caused by a Raven's Memory," said the old Healer sourly. She took another look at Phoran. "You have the signs of being afflicted by a Memory, boy."

Seraph raised an eyebrow, but cleared her throat. "Emperor," she reminded Brewydd.

"When you're as old as I am," said Brewydd. "You can call anyone anything."

Phoran smiled. "It's my Memory," he said. "It's all right, Tier. Go to sleep, I'll tell them."

The Emperor patted the end of the bed and found a safe place to sit. He spoke quietly and told them how the Memory came to be bound to him. At some point in the story, Tier drifted off.

"They were guarded," said Brewydd, after Phoran finished his story. "It couldn't take them. In the normal course of things, unable to feed, it would have just drifted away. But you were there." She nodded her head. "I've heard of something like that happening. The Memory attaching itself to the wrong person. As long as it gave something back, its victim will continue to live. What did it give you?"

"Answers to my questions," said Phoran. "That's how I found Tier."

"Why was it able to kill the Masters now?" asked Seraph. She was touched by the way that Phoran kept patting Tier's feet.

"They were draining themselves trying to control the Passerines and fight our wizards," explained Brewydd. "I expect that weakened the protections that kept the Memory from killing them before."

"It will leave Phoran in peace, then?" asked Seraph.

"If it has accomplished its task it should," said the old woman. "I suppose your son will understand that the life of an emperor who just might be what this Empire needs is worth a little discomfort. Tell your man to try not to make anyone mad enough to hit him in those knees again and he'll be right as rain in a month or so. I'd better go back and see if my services are needed elsewhere."

Phoran got up reluctantly. "I suppose I'd better go as well—before some idiot thinks I'm lost."

"I'll be fine," Tier said faintly. "Go reassure the idiots."

Phoran was laughing as he left. Seraph shut the door and took Phoran's place on the end of the bed.

"Is there anyway I can lay down beside you that won't make it worse?" she asked.

"No," he sighed without opening his eyes. "Come here anyway."

When she was tucked against him, he buried his face in her hair.

"Telleridge killed Myrceria in front of me," he said. "He'd had her tortured, but she didn't tell him anything. Telleridge didn't know about you."

"There was nothing you could have done," Seraph said, hurting for him and for the woman she'd met only briefly.

"How do you know that?" he whispered, because he needed to believe she was right.

"Because if you could have done anything, you would have. It's all right, Tier."

"He was her father, and he tortured her and killed her," said Tier. "And he enjoyed doing it. Was he shadowed?"

"Can't people be evil on their own?" she asked with a sigh. "You'll have to ask your sons; Ravens can't see shadowing— but I think so. Shh," she said. "I love you. She did, too."

She let him hold her while he cried quietly into her hair until the tiredness of being healed overwhelmed him. Then, between one breath and the next he slept.

Seraph awoke from a doze to a light knock on the door. Carefully, she extracted herself so Tier slept on undisturbed.

Lehr and Jes waited out in the hall. Seraph motioned them out, went out herself, and shut the door so they wouldn't disturb Tier.

"I told him what Papa said," said Lehr. "Jes said he didn't kill anyone."

Seraph looked up and down the hall and quietly explained.

"It's fine, Mother," said the Guardian. "No one will be much more afraid of me than they already are."

"Mother," said Lehr, "You need to hear why Jes left the Eyrie."

"I was following a black-robed wizard," said the Guardian. "Father was right, all the wizards were tainted. But there was one . . . did you see him, Lehr?"

"No," Lehr said. "I only saw the five wizards the Memory killed."

"There was one who left when the wall disintegrated. He wasn't just tainted, Mother, he was the taint itself."

"Like the Unnamed King?"

The Guardian nodded. "I didn't see the taint at first, Mother. I followed the wizard out of the room and into the halls on the other side of the wall. Before I could get close, the Memory was there. It touched the wizard." The Guardian flinched. "I don't know what the Memory did, but it felt as if a veil had been pulled away and revealed the wizard for what he really was." He took a shaky breath. "Jes is very brave, Mother, even I don't scare him—but what hid beneath the wizard's illusionary veil was evil. The wizard hit the Memory with some kind of magic, and the Memory was just gone. The wizard didn't see us. When it left, we didn't follow."

"Good," said Seraph, reassuringly. "You did the right thing."

"When I caught up with him," said Lehr, "he showed me where the man had gone—and I couldn't find his trail. Mother, I could see where rats had been running down the hall, but I couldn't pick up his tracks."

Seraph touched Lehr's shoulder. "It's all right," she said and hoped it was true.

CHAPTER 17

If it hadn't been for Skew, Tier would have had to wait another week before setting out for Redern, but the old horse's soft gaits were easy on Tier's ribs. He seemed to understand that Tier was hurt: not even Gura's anxious weaving in and out around his legs caused Skew to alter his smooth stride.

If he remembered to breathe shallowly, it didn't even hurt too much—but he didn't like to do that, because it only increased the number of Seraph's anxious glances. She had wanted to wait, but he needed to get home to Redern—needed to have all of his children together where he could protect them.

There was another Shadowed who walked the land.

There were other explanations for all that had passed. He wasn't certain if even Seraph really believed it in the light of day—but the Healer knew. She hadn't said anything, but he could see in her eyes that she believed.

Tier glanced over at the brightly colored cart that Brewydd rode in. It was her voice, he thought, that had made Benroln insist on accompanying them back. Benroln had said that Phoran would do better without Traveler aid now that the Sept of Gerant was there.

Doubtless Benroln was right about that. The Sept of Gerant

had said as much when he'd come to see Tier off in lieu of the
Emperor. The political situation was unstable and Phoran
clung to the throne primarily because there were so few of imperial blood around to fight him for the Empire. Phoran had
wished him good travels in secret the night before they'd left.

"I like your Gerant," said Seraph. "He reminds me of Ciro,
a little. Quiet and unassuming until his skill is called upon."

Tier smiled down at his wife who walked at his stirrup as if
she were afraid he'd fall out of the saddle. "He liked you as
well. Told me that I'd made a good exchange when I chose to
follow you instead of the sword."

"He laughed when you told him you were a farmer," she
said.

Tier glanced at her sharply, but her face was tilted down,
watching the ground.

"Not this year," he said. "But with the money Phoran sent
us back with we'll be able to survive this year and buy another
horse to replace Frost for next planting season."

"You don't think we'll be planting next season either," she
said softly, her hand coming up to grip his calf.

He shook his head, then realized that she wasn't watching
him. "No," he said.

She took a step closer to Skew, until her shoulder pressed
against his leg. "I don't know what awaits us, but I don't think
the Stalker is through with us yet."

Jes laughed, and Tier glanced up to see the Traveler Raven
Hennea stalk away from his son. He'd thought at first that she
was younger than Seraph until he'd gotten a good look at her
eyes. When he'd asked Seraph, she'd told him she didn't know
how old Hennea was either. Ravens seldom lived as long as
Larks, but it could be very difficult to tell how old they were.

He'd worried until he'd seen how she watched Jes when
she thought no one was watching. He knew what love looked
like.

"Today," Tier told Seraph, "the sun is warm on my face.
Let's save tomorrow's troubles for tomorrow."

ABOUT THE AUTHOR

Patricia Briggs lived a fairly normal life until she learned to read. After that she spent lazy afternoons flying dragonback and looking for magic swords when she wasn't horseback riding in the Rocky Mountains.

Once she graduated from Montana State University with degrees in history and German, she spent her time substitute teaching and writing. She and her family live in the Pacific Northwest, where she is hard at work on her newest project.

Visit her on the web at www.hurog.com.

From national bestselling author

Patricia Briggs

DRAGON BONES
0-441-00916-6

Ward of Hurog has tried all his life to convince
people he is just a simple, harmless fool...And it's
worked. But now, to regain his kingdom, he must
ride into war—and convince them otherwise.

DRAGON BLOOD
0-441-01008-3

Ward, ruler of Hurog, joins the rebels against
the tyrannical High King Jakoven. But Jakoven
has a secret weapon. One that requires
dragon's blood—the very blood that courses
through Ward's veins.

Available wherever books are sold or
to order call 1-800-788-6262

From "a natural born storyteller"*

PATRICIA BRIGGS

The Hob's Bargain

0-441-00813-5

Hated and feared, magic was banished from the land.
But now, freed from spells of the wicked bloodmages,
magic—both good and evil—returns.
And Aren of Fallbrook feels her own power of sight
strengthen and grow.

Overcome by visions of mayhem and murder, Aren vows to save
her village from the ruthless raiders who have descended upon
it—and killed her family. She strikes a bargain with the Hob, a
magical, humanlike creature who will exact a heavy price to
defend the village—a price Aren herself must pay.

Available wherever books are sold or
to order call 1-800-788-6262

Coming September 2004 from Ace

Loamhedge
by Brian Jacques
0-441-01190-X

Martha Braebuck, a young hare-maid, wheelchair bound since infancy, wonders about a mysterious old poem relating to the ancient abbey of Loamhedge—and whether it might hold the key to her cure.

Starhawk: Storm Over Saturn
by Mack Maloney
0-441-01191-8

In 7205 AD, Hawk Hunter's most perilous mission ever is to find the one man who can stop the Solar Guards from from seizing the source of all power in the Milky Way.

Also new in paperback this month:
F.T.L.
by Kevin D. Randle
0-441-01192-6

Heroics for Beginners
by John Moore
0-441-01193-4

The Omega Cage
by Steve Perry and Michael Reaves
0-441-62382-4

Available wherever books are sold or
to order call 1-800-788-6262